# BROTHERS IN ARMS

By Marcus Wynne from Tom Doherty Associates

*Brothers in Arms*
*No Other Option*
*Warrior in the Shadows*

# BROTHERS IN ARMS

## MARCUS WYNNE

A TOM DOHERTY ASSOCIATES BOOK
New York

BROTHERS IN ARMS

A Forge Book
Published by Tom Doherty Associates, LLC
175 Fifth Avenue
New York, NY 10010

www.tor.com

Forge® is a registered trademark of Tom Doherty Associates, LLC.

Library of Congress Cataloging-in-Publication Data

Wynne, Marcus.
     Brothers in arms / Marcus Wynne.—1st ed.
         p. cm.
     "A Tom Doherty Associates book."
     ISBN 0-765-30782-0 (acid-free paper)
     1. Special operations (Military science)—Fiction. 2. Torture
victims—Rehabilitation—Fiction. 3. Terrorism—Prevention—Fiction. 4.
Minneapolis (Minn.)—Fiction. 5. Washington (D.C.)—Fiction. 6. Assassins—
Fiction. 7. Twins—Fiction. I. Title.

PS3623.Y66B76 2003
813'.6—dc22

                                                                    2003061217

This book is dedicated to the men and women of the
US special operations community, especially those who lost their
lives in Afghanistan and Iraq.

# ACKNOWLEDGMENTS

I'd like to thank, as always, my literary agent, Ethan Ellenberg, my foreign-rights agent, Danny Baror, and my film agents, Kevin Cleary and Josh Morris. Special thanks to my great publicist, Elena Stokes, her assistant, Jennifer "Buttercup" Hunt, and to Jennifer Marcus, Brian Callaghan, Tom Doherty, Linda Quinton, and Kathy Fogarty.

As this is written, we are still at war in Iraq. While the outcome is not in doubt, many of the particulars I've mentioned about Iraq may have changed by the time this book sees print. I've made revisions to reflect the most likely course of events. There's a military acronym: OBE, overtaken by events. That's what happened in the writing of this book.

Godspeed to our military, and good hunting.

**PART 1**

LINDEN HILLS NEIGHBORHOOD,
MINNEAPOLIS, MINNESOTA

When the bodyguard team pulled up across the street, Dale Miller
thought of a ballerina he once dated. She didn't care that he couldn't
tell her what he did for a living; she enjoyed the intrigue and the edge
it gave to their sex. Dale taught her to shoot and to street fight and she
taught him how a ballet was built to a single vision and how each element of the dance reflected that vision. Later in his career, when he
was introduced to the discipline of VIP protection, he found, to his
surprise, that his girlfriend's lessons had prepared him for the intri-
cate moves a bodyguard team makes to protect the principal.

So on this fine Minneapolis summer morning, comfortable in
the tree-shadowed outdoor courtyard of his favorite coffeehouse,
Dale was able to appreciate the complex moves of the bodyguard
team moving into place across the street. He watched a tan four-door
Ford sedan pull up in front of the Linden Hills Art Store and dis-
gorge four large men in business suits, their jackets unbuttoned. One
went immediately into the art store. The other three took up posi-
tions in the street, ignoring the cars that slowed to watch them, while
the driver pulled the sedan forward. Seconds later, a black BMW
sedan pulled up between the three men. The man on the street side
blocked the rear driver's side window with his body, while the two

men on the curbside blocked the rear passenger door and the back window.

The right front door of the BMW opened and a lean grey-hound of a man in an expensive black suit got out. He went to the rear passenger door and stood there, his hand on the door handle, while he scanned the street thoroughly, first close, then far, left, then right, and let his hard eyes roam over the windows of the buildings that overlooked the store. Then he looked over his shoulder at the art store, where the first bodyguard stood in the open door, his right hand extended with the thumb up. Only then did the lean body-guard open the BMW's rear door.

A short plump man, dark skinned, his suit carelessly folded around him and wearing a dusting of dandruff that was clearly visi-ble from across the street, got out of the car, catching his toe in the door well and nearly falling. The lean man, the bodyguard team leader, caught his client and eased him out onto the sidewalk, where the plump man stood hesitantly while the other bodyguards closed in around him, forming a tight protective cordon that blocked him from any interference—or gunshot. The plump man looked down, as though embarrassed by the display, then at the ring of men, and then at the team leader. Only when the team leader nodded did the plump man move, the mobile barrier of big men surrounding him as he went into the art store. When they entered the store, two men peeled off the formation and remained on guard at the door.

At the table next to Dale's, a dark-haired woman in a T-shirt and Calvin Klein shorts said, "What's going on over there?"

Dale lied with the ease of long practice. "I don't know. Looks like somebody important just went into the art store."

"Two cars of bodyguards?" she said. "Someone should tell him that that many is tacky."

Dale laughed. "It is conspicuous consumption."

He sipped his latte while he studied the protection detail. They were well practiced and sure in their movements, but they weren't policemen. Cops had a way of standing that set them apart. Even in plainclothes they looked as though they were in uniform and wearing bulky pistol belts. This was either a high-level private crew or the feds. But who would go to an art store with a full bodyguard detail? There were plenty of wealthy people in the Twin Cities who could afford what it took to field a team like this, but Dale had done many threat assessments here and there was little to justify such a high level of protection. It could be a visiting diplomat or foreign businessman used to that much protection.

Dale set his tall coffee cup down and shifted cautiously in the metal chair, careful not to bump the pistol he wore concealed beneath a baggy Hawaiian-pattern shirt against it.

A small crowd of onlookers formed on the sidewalk outside the courtyard, blocking Dale's view. He slid his chair first one way, then another, then settled back, content for the moment with brief glimpses of the stone-faced men standing across the street.

A college-aged man, tanned in a tank top and shorts, said to his friend, "Why don't you go over there and see who's in the store?"

"Look at those guys," his friend said. "You go look."

"Not me," the other said. Both men laughed.

The crowd scattered suddenly as two young women on a moped pulled up on the sidewalk. They were both blond and wore short summer dresses they kept decent by tucking the front hems tightly beneath their legs. They each had a Patagonia courier bag slung across their back.

"What's going on?" the driver said. She had brilliant blue eyes and a pixie haircut framing a squarish face. Her passenger had green eyes that shimmered in a long, aquiline face; her hair was pulled back in a braided ponytail.

The young man in the tank top nudged his friend and said, "Somebody important's in the art store. Those are his bodyguards."

"Who is it?" the moped driver said.

"We don't know," the hopeful young man said. "Why don't you go ask those guys?"

"What, are you afraid?" the moped driver said. She had a faint accent. "It doesn't hurt to ask. Maybe we can get an autograph."

Her ponytailed companion laughed, a deep and throaty laugh

that made her seem older than she looked, and said, "Let's go over there and see who it is!"

The two college boys looked at each other and grinned. They followed as the moped riders swung their bike in a wide U-turn, crossing the street. The other onlookers followed. Their departure left Dale with a clear view of the protection detail parked in the street. He had to stifle a laugh at the look on the faces of the two bodyguards outside the store as they watched the herd of curious pedestrians, led by the two blondes on the moped, come across the street at them. The two drivers, sitting in the idling cars, scanned their side and rear mirrors constantly, trying to keep an eye on the crowd.

Small groups of onlookers had formed across the street as well. One of them was a tall blond man with a heavily lined face, dressed casually in a denim work shirt with the tails out over faded Levis. He stood with a coffee cup in his hand and watched the crowd grow around the art store. Something about him drew Dale's eye. Maybe it was how the man had positioned himself to see the bodyguards; he watched them the way a coach might watch his players. Dale's vigilance was rewarded a moment later, when the man shifted his stance and the material of his shirt bunched unnaturally a few inches behind his hip.

The man was armed with a pistol concealed beneath his shirt—just as Dale was.

Dale set his coffee cup down, pushed it to the center of the table, then eased his chair back a few inches. His view of the man across the street was obscured momentarily by passersby, then he saw him again. There was tension about the man, but it seemed more like close attention to the events unfolding in front of the art store than a preparation for violence. Dale had long experience in looking for those cues. This man didn't look like an off-duty cop, either.

So who was he and what was he doing here?

• • •

There was a Unitarian church just up the block from the art store, at the top of the hill where Forty-fourth Street and Upton Avenue intersected. A van with the logo of AAA PLUMBING SERVICE on its side, eased slowly into a short-term parking space in front of the church. From that position one could easily see all the activity in front of the art store, as well as down the length of the block. That was why the driver had waited till the spot was free. In the back of the van, sophisticated electronic surveillance equipment crammed the tight quarters, forcing the two men there to sit thigh to thigh beside each other. They faced a small bank of video screens ringing one larger one where the circus in front of the art store played out.

"This is a mess," the first man said. He was in his early thirties, heavily muscled beneath the coveralls with the logo of AAA PLUMBING on the back.

The other man was older, with short cropped gray hair and the lean build of a distance runner. "Good lesson here. These guys should have deployed low profile . . . look at the commotion they've caused."

"Truth," said the first man. His name was Robert Sanders, and he and his partner Marcus Williams were surveillance specialists for a clandestine government operation called DOMINANCE RAIN. "They'd have been better off in one car."

"Heavy threat, though," Williams said.

"Harder to spot and follow."

"There's that," Williams conceded. "These guys aren't bad at working the man. They've got good moves."

"Good moves don't count if you create a circus everywhere you go."

Williams shrugged his thin shoulders. "Maybe they didn't have a choice. The man likes having all his bully boys around."

"You see the legs on the moped beauties?"

The older man grinned slyly. "I don't pay attention to things like that when I'm working. What girls on a moped are you referring to?"

"Like you'd miss that," Sanders said. "Let me refresh your ancient brain."

Sanders turned a control knob while working a toggle stick with the other hand and zoomed the telescopic lens hidden in the ventilator hood onto the two girls. They were still perched on their moped, watching the door of the art store with the rest of the curious.

"Some lookers, huh?" Sanders said.

"Not bad. Probably kill a young guy like you, though. They need the proven stamina of an older man."

Sanders snorted and wiped sweat from his forehead with the back of his hand. He pulled the focus back to expand the point of view to include the whole crowd again.

"People will be talking about this for a week," he said.

Williams nodded. "You got any possibles in the crowd?"

"No . . . you?"

"That one guy, with the work shirt untucked? Over there, same side of the street as the little blondies."

"I make him. What about him?"

"Everybody else is either coming forward or staying where they started . . . he came just far enough to get a good look."

"You make him for a shooter?"

"Zoom his face, we'll run him through the database. Just to be sure. He's got the look."

"Roger that." The younger man zoomed in on the lined face of the man in the work shirt and touched a button. The picture froze for a moment, then continued with the live feed. "Want me to run it now?"

"No, stay on the crowd. Put the image over on my screen, I'll run it myself."

Sanders pushed buttons and the face of the man appeared on a small screen directly in front of Williams. Williams used a touch pad to move the cursor to a pull-down menu on the screen, then watched a progress bar beneath the man's picture tick off percentages. The computer program he ran matched the face of anyone they imaged against a huge database of known terrorists, criminals, and other people of interest to the US intelligence community. If they were in the database, the program would match the face to a file and bring up the pertinent data. After a few seconds, the percentage bar disappeared and a message box saying POSSIBLE MATCH came up.

"Well, well, what do we have here?" Williams said. He clicked on his touch pad and a small window opened beneath the man's picture, with another full-face photo, an official-looking one, and a text file that he began to scroll through.

"We've got one Charles Payne, former staffer in CIA's Special Operations Division, operator with the Special Activities Staff . . . a shooter. It's a small world. What the hell is he doing here?"

"Is he operational?" Sanders said.

"Nope," Williams said. "Says here he resigned, no contact with the outfit since then. Working as a contract photographer for the local PD."

"Think he's packing?"

"Doubt it. Why would a contract photographer be carrying a gun?"

"Guy with history with SAS, why wouldn't he be packing a gun?"

"Hmm," Williams said. "Only if he had need, and he doesn't have any need."

"I'll keep an eye on him."

"That would be a good idea," Williams said. "Let's do just that."

• • •

Charley Payne felt conspicuous. He reminded himself that he was just an onlooker like the rest. His professional curiosity had gotten the better of him when he saw the protection detail pull up, and he'd moved with the certainty of long experience to the best vantage spot to watch them. While he'd been through the Secret Service protection course and the CIA's own intensive training course, close protection was one special operation he had limited experience in. It was interesting to watch how this team was working. They were certainly attracting a lot of attention.

As he was.

He saw the athletic man with big sunglasses hiding half his face in the shaded courtyard of the Sebastian Joe's coffee shop across the street. That guy was tuned in to everything going on around him, and while everyone else was watching the bodyguards, that guy was watching Charley. Another operator for the team? Planting a few plainclothes people in the crowd to monitor things would be one way of ensuring additional security. That didn't seem likely, though. If they were going to do that, they could have run the whole operation in a more low-key fashion.

Charley smiled at how his imagination got away with him. The man across the street had the look, but he was probably an off-duty cop or some other kind of security professional. He felt as though he had to second-guess himself these days; his operational days were behind him. The only reason he maintained a civilian concealed carry permit was, well, he didn't really know why except that he'd carried a gun for a living for most of his adult life and it just seemed natural to be armed. He touched his elbow to the butt of the pistol concealed beneath his baggy work shirt.

He admired the two leggy blondes on the moped. They were laughing and having a good time, urging on the curious gawkers, beeping the moped horn and trying to talk to the two bodyguards outside the art store.

"Who is in the store?" the one with the short hair said. "C'mon, give us a clue!"

"Hey handsome," the ponytailed blonde said. "I'll show you something pretty if you tell us."

Grins flickered across the faces of the two men.

"Ooooh, he wants us to show him something pretty," the short-haired one said. "Hey, here they come now!"

The two outside guards straightened up as the door opened and a bodyguard came out, holding a framed and wrapped painting in both hands. He was followed closely by the pudgy principal and the other bodyguards, who attempted to herd the principal quickly across the sidewalk. The pudgy man hesitated, one hand to his wrinkled lapel, and looked at the people gathered to watch him.

"Who is that?" someone called out.

Charley watched as though in slow motion as the two blond women, their legs holding the moped firmly in place, dipped into their matching courier bags and came up holding machine pistols. He recognized them as Czech Skorpions, with the suppressor attachment and the wire stock unfolded. The twin blondes tucked the thin stocks into their shoulders with the familiarity that only long practice can achieve and they rolled the triggers expertly, putting a short burst each into the two outside guards, tracing a three-round burst across the bridge of their target's nose and directly into the brain, dropping the men cross-legged where they stood.

Then they smoothly tracked onto their next target, each woman taking her time and full advantage of the sudden shock that stopped everyone, even the bodyguards, for the brief seconds necessary for them to put the next two bodyguards down with neat bursts to the head, avoiding the body armor that bulked them up beneath their business suits.

Four down, two to go and then the drivers, who couldn't hear any gunshots and had their view of the scenario blocked by the crowd, got out of the cars, aware only that something was going horribly wrong. The team leader was the toughest of all. He sprang and grabbed the principal while pulling out his own pistol and actually got off shots as the point man dropped the painting and went for his gun and died with a diagonal burst across his face at nearly point-blank range from the pixie-cut blonde, who blinked as blood splashed across her face. Her ponytailed partner didn't flinch as bullets from the team leader's High Power whipped by her face. She kept tracking and worked a burst first into the team leader's pelvis, below his vest, dropping him down to be finally anchored with a burst to the head.

Then it was time for the drivers, who waved their pistols ineffectually, trying to aim through the panicked crowd, their leader's gunshots a signal that all had gone wrong, and the two women had no compunction about shooting into the crowd, dropping a young woman in a Spandex top and shorts, suddenly bloody, and the two drivers were down. The pudgy man stood amid the bodies of his protectors, naked and alone and sadly resigned as he sought out the eyes of the two assassins.

One of them fired to his head, the other to his pelvis, and he dropped to the ground. They speed-loaded their machine pistols with fresh magazines and fired short bursts into his head until his brains and his teeth scattered across the sidewalk.

Then there was a sudden stillness, one of the lulls that come in combat, when the guns fall silent and everyone involved takes in how the picture has suddenly changed.

Charley dropped his cup of coffee, shattering the porcelain mug on the sidewalk, and drew his Glock .45 from beneath his shirt.

• • •

Across the street, Dale Miller kicked his table out of the way and came up out of his seat, drawing his Browning High Power as he came.

• • •

In the surveillance van at the top of the hill, Sanders shouted, "Marcus! They're all down!"

"Stay put!" Williams said. "We don't engage, we don't engage."

"They'll get away!"

"Make sure we're getting good feed, make sure we've got the tape. That's our job, keep your mind on it."

Williams's hands sped over the camera controls, zooming the lens in on the two women.

• • •

The pixie-cut blonde dropped her smoking machine pistol into her open courier bag and put both hands on the handlebars of the moped, pushing forward with her feet as she gave the moped gas. Her partner held her weapon in one hand and pushed with her legs as well. Charley sprinted forward, both hands on his pistol extended out in front of him, and cut through the crowd like a football player on a broken field. For an instant he had a clear shot and he took it, a fast snapping shot at the back of the ponytailed blonde.

She hunched suddenly and looked back over her shoulder,

extended the Skorpion in one hand and fired a burst single-handed at him, forcing him to duck to one side, then between a building as the silenced rounds whipped around him.

• • •

Dale leaped across the low flower planters that separated the court-yard from the sidewalk and crouched behind a car parked directly in front of the coffee shop. From here he had good cover and a stable brace for his pistol. He saw the man he'd been watching come up and snap a shot at the two blond assassins, then duck behind the cover of a building with all the sure moves of a pro.

He didn't know who he was, but he was on the side of the angels today. Dale braced himself and took a quick shot at the moving moped before fleeing passersby blocked him. He moved quickly along the back of the car, hoping for another shot, but the moped was off and away before he could get set again. Across the street, the man he'd been watching eased out from around the corner of the building and leveled his weapon at the fleeing women.

• • •

Charley had the ponytailed blonde in his sights for just a second before an innocent passed in front of him, obscuring his vision. It was no good. The blondes were gone around the corner, and he could hear the moped accelerating away. Pros—and there was no doubt after watching their performance that they were pros—would have a separate vehicle standing off to pick them up. They'd be gone in moments, and the sirens of responding police vehicles hadn't even started yet. He reholstered his pistol and took out his cell phone to call in. He looked across the street and saw the man in the big sunglasses rehol-ster his pistol and come toward him.

Charley watched him come while he spoke briefly to the dispatcher. There had already been plenty of calls already, the dis-patcher said, and Charley could now hear the sound of sirens. Too late for everybody involved.

The man from across the street was of average height but thick through the shoulders and thin-waisted, with the build of someone who trained for strength and not for show. He stood in front of Charley, balanced as though ready to spring in any direction.

"You on the job?" the man said.

"Yeah," Charley said. "I already called it in."

"Guess we'll have some questions to answer."

"No doubt."

The man held his hand out. "I'm Dale Miller," he said.

Charley reached out and took the offered hand. It was hard and strong, and he noticed on the web of the hand the scarring that came from catching the slide of an automatic pistol.

"Hey, Dale Miller," he said. "I'm Charley Payne. I'm not a cop, but I'm working with Minneapolis."

"That makes two of us," Dale said. "What do you do for them?"

"Forensic photographer. You?"

"Special reserve, work with the training unit and the ERU."

"Running and gunning, eh?"

"Yeah. You?"

"I'm too old to play with those guys. I can't keep up anymore."

"Did you get a make on those two?"

"Not much. Real pros, though . . . I wonder who the hell they were?"

• • •

In the surveillance van, videotape hissed as the two operators recorded the conversation between the two men. Williams zoomed the camera in on them.

"Jesus, Mary, and Joseph," Sanders said. "You know who that is?"

"I used to work with him," Williams said. "He was one of us."

"They'll be going bugfuck over this back at base," Sanders said.

"No kidding," Williams said. "What are the odds? Dale Miller and Charley Payne on the same street on the same day as a major hit. There's more to this than meets the eye."

"They weren't shooting at the BGs . . ."

"No, they weren't, were they? Check the computer for any other faces in the crowd."

A cell phone trilled in the back of the van. Williams picked it up and said, "Hello?"

After a moment he said, "Yes, sir. Yes, sir, I recognized him once we got a clear picture of him. We got it all on tape and we'll send it via satellite feed. We're out of here now."

He set the phone back into its charging cradle and said to Sanders, "Let's break it down and get out of here before the cops get set up."

"Is that it, then?"

Williams said, "No, young Jedi. That's not it. This is just the beginning."

• • •

Four blocks away, the blondes drove their moped right up the ramp of a small parcel delivery truck. As they rode in, the driver shoved the ramp up behind them and pulled the door down and shut it. He got into the front, started the vehicle, and pulled away even as the two women laid the moped down on its side. They stepped clear, then kicked off their shoes and pulled the dresses off over their heads. They stepped into matching overalls set out for them, pulled them up and zipped them closed. Then they checked the Skorpions, charging the weapons with fresh magazines. One went to sit by the backdoor, the weapon in her lap, the other one crouched in the well behind the driver.

The driver had a portable police scanner set on the floor beside his seat. The van's occupants could hear all the instructions, directions, and call information coming across the police secure net.

"We'll head south on France Avenue," the woman crouching behind the driver said.

"Right," said the driver.

"Marie?" the crouching woman with the ponytail said. "Would you like some water?"

"Please, Isabelle. I need to rinse my face. Some of that last one's on me," the pixie-cut blonde said.

Isabelle reached into a bag behind the seat and pulled out a bottle of drinking water and tossed it underhand to her partner, who caught it one-handed, then opened it.

"Do you have a napkin?" she called to Marie.

"On the other seat," the driver said. Isabelle reached onto the seat and took several napkins from the small stack there, then scuttled into the rear of the moving van and handed them to Marie, who poured some water on them and dabbed at the blood spray on her face.

"Did I get it all?" she asked.

Isabelle took the damp napkin from her, and touched a few spots beside her nose.

"There," she said with satisfaction. "Good as new." She leaned forward and brushed her lips against Marie's. "How are you feeling?"

Marie smiled and pushed her away gently. "We're still working. Go on, get back up front."

Isabelle pouted, then went back to the front, her Skorpion handy. "Who were those two, you think? The two shooters who came at us?"

"I don't know," Marie said. "I'm glad we got free of them. Perhaps off-duty police."

"They were professionals," Isabelle said. "I don't think most policeman would have been that fast."

"I don't know," Marie said. "But no worry. They're behind us and we're away. We won't see them again."

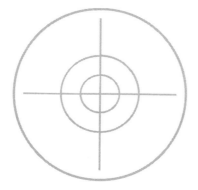

## TORTURE REHABILITATION CENTER, UNIVERSITY OF MINNESOTA CAMPUS, MINNEAPOLIS, MINNESOTA

The Torture Rehabilitation Center is a large Victorian house surrounded by a few outbuildings in a green and out-of-the-way corner of the University of Minnesota campus. Within its quiet, pastel-painted rooms, some of the best medical and psychological practitioners in the country went about their business, which was the rebuilding of human beings. To this quiet place came people whose screams had beaten on walls in Guatemala, Iraq, Iran, Rwanda, China, and other places. Either thrown out of the country, or bought out by relatives, the broken ones found their way to the Center, which worked on only the worst cases, those in the profoundly broken psychological state that only the worst forms of torture could manifest.

Dr. Rowan Green was a slight woman in her late forties, with a perpetually frizzled hairdo untidily pulled back from her face. She wore her glasses round her neck with a chain for the practical reason that she would otherwise forget them in her rounds of the patients' quarters and therapy rooms. Today she walked briskly down a polished hallway, her low sensible heels clacking a quick cadence, and as she walked she twisted her eyeglass chain around her finger again and again.

She came to a patient room and stood outside the door for a

moment, listening, then opened the door gently and went in. Inside, a man in an expensive sweat suit and running shoes sat in the armchair beside the powered bed. The man was dark complected, with shaggy black hair, and he was thin in the way of someone who had once been bigger. His shoulders, seemingly too wide for him, were hunched forward as though he were a ball player protecting the ball clutched tight to his chest. He stared at the small television mounted in the wall which was set to a local news station.

"Mr. Uday?" Dr. Green said. "Mr. Uday? What are we watching?"

The man smiled and looked at her, then his eyes rolled to show the white.

"Some days, they are very close," he said.

"Who is very close, Mr. Uday?"

"I never know."

"What are we watching?" Dr. Green looked at the screen. The sound was muted, but the videotape showed ambulances and bodies being carried away. She recognized the area immediately; she spent a fair amount of time in the Linden Hills area, and her children enjoyed going to the ice cream parlor that figured so prominently on the screen. She took the remote control from the unresisting fingers of Mr. Uday and turned on the sound.

"... the shooting of a business executive in West Minneapolis today has police ..."

She turned the sound off again and looked at Mr. Uday.

"They think they are close, but they are not so far," Mr. Uday said.

"Are they close?"

"Ask the one they found."

"Who did they find?"

Uday looked at the television set with dark, dead eyes. "They found who they think they found."

"It's time for us to talk, Mr. Uday. Would you like to come with me now?"

"They want the talking for themselves. They want to have a sad holiday. They don't want you."

"Come," Dr. Green said. She turned the television off, set the remote down, then took Uday gently by his arm. His muscles were flabby and hung on the bone like overdone meat. "Let's go to my office, shall we?"

The man rose. He limped as he came forward.

"Yes," he said. "Let's go."

## DOMINANCE RAIN HEADQUARTERS, FAIRFAX, VIRGINIA

Ray Dalton was a tall, aquiline man who dressed in expensive custom-tailored business suits when he came to his offices in Fairfax, Virginia. His offices were in a building owned and run by the CIA, and anyone entering the building had to run a gauntlet of security measures, some overt, like the big capable armed guards at the front reception area, others covert, like the hidden cameras and biometric sensors outside the doors to his suite. The security was there for a reason, as Ray Dalton ran one of the most secretive units in the US government, a special project called DOMINANCE RAIN. DOMINANCE RAIN was a black operation run completely off the shelf and reserved for only the most critical and strategic of special operations, which was why he had his pick of the best from Delta Force, the SEAL teams, Marine Force Recon, and the Agency paramilitary program.

He sat behind his sprawling desk and watched with intense interest the videotape of the Linden Hills hit, and quashed the feelings that rose in him when he saw Dale Miller and Charley Payne talking together. He knew of both men. Charley Payne he knew from the records; Payne was a former operator with the CIA's Special Activities Staff, an elite paramilitary unit that had much in common with his own. The two units had worked together in the past on missions.

But it was Dale Miller who he kept coming back to. Dale Miller had been one of Ray's best, a hand-picked DOMINANCE RAIN operator. Ray had sent him out after an escaped convict named Jonny Maxwell, who had worked for Ray till he went bad and went to prison. He'd also been Dale Miller's best friend.

And Dale, as ordered, found and killed him.

And then Dale orchestrated his own retirement and put himself on the outside by choice. Though DOMINANCE RAIN kept track of their own, their attempts at contact had been rebuffed by the bitter ex-operator. Dale had moved in with a woman, a female detective he'd met during the operation to find Jonny Maxwell, and found part-time employment as a firearms and tactics instructor for the Minneapolis Police Department. He kept a low profile and had no known contact with any current operators. He'd burned his bridges and seemed glad about it.

It was sheer coincidence that he was there when the Linden Hills hit went down. But the fact that he was there gave Ray Dalton an insight into how to solve the problem he had before him now. He sat back in his executive chair and riffled through his Rolodex. He found the name and the number he was looking for. The number he dialed was of an elite international security company headquartered in the Washington Beltway, its offices not far from his. He told the secretary who answered the phone his name and that he wished to speak to Michael Callan. After a moment the man came on the line.

"Hello?"

"Mike, it's Ray Dalton."

"That's what my girl said. I looked out the window, but I don't see any pigs flying. That's how long it's been since we talked. What are you up to, Ray?"

"Same thing as when you worked for me," Dalton said. "Got a job over there for me?"

"I couldn't hire you, you'd have my job in a week. But if you're serious . . ."

Ray chuckled. "I'm not quite ready for the life of the corporate security pro, Mike. It's tempting, but I've still got a few good years over here."

"You don't know what you're missing. It's not just the money . . . we do things right. There's some politics, but nothing you couldn't handle."

"I could use some peace from that. But that's not why I called."

"I didn't think so. What do you need that the G can't get for you?"

Ray laughed again. It was a pleasure not to have to talk around a subject. "I need you, Mike. I need you to come have lunch with me and talk with me about having a talk with someone else. There's somebody I need brought in on a job and he won't talk to me. But he worked with you and would listen to what you have to say."

"Worked with me but won't talk to you? Is this a civilian we're talking about?"

"He is now."

Callan paused for a long moment, and then his voice grew hard. "That's a short list we're talking about. And if it's who I think it might be, I'll remind you he's my friend. I didn't think much about how that whole thing went down."

Ray's voice was soothing. "That's why we need to have lunch and a talk. I've got some tape to show you. Then we can discuss what we're going to do and I think you'll find it to be okay."

"What are you going to ask me to ask him?"

"I'm going to offer him a job."

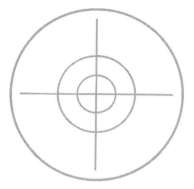

LINDEN HILLS NEIGHBORHOOD,
MINNEAPOLIS, MINNESOTA

In the chaos of the crime scene in Linden Hills, Dale Miller and
Charley Payne surrendered their personal weapons to a female forensics
technician in a blue jacket emblazoned with POLICE across the back.

"I'll take care of these for you guys," she said. "We'll see about
getting them back to you as quick as we can."

"Thanks, Francine," Charley said. "I hate feeling naked in such
a violent world."

"That your only shooter?" Dale said.

The two men studied each other. Payne was tall and thin, but
hard muscled beneath his baggy work shirt. His face was long and
lined with grooves that started at his hairline and ran to his chin.

"Yeah," Charley said. "You?"

"There's always a spare if you're a firearms instructor."

"Lucky you. Want to lend me one?"

Dale looked Charley up first, then down. "I'd have to know you
better. Maybe you should buy me a cup of coffee."

"That would be an interesting conversation."

One of the detectives standing nearby looked up from his notebook. "I'd've thought you two secret squirrels would have run into
each other by now."

"Is that right, Rocco?" Dale said. "We're secret squirrels?"

"You were," Rocco said. "Charley too, I hear."

Charley pursed his lips before he answered. "Something like that. We'll catch that coffee sometime, Miller. I've got to go."

"All right," Dale said. He pointed at the Sebastian Joe's outdoor patio. "I'm over here every morning, just like clockwork. And you're over there at the Linden Hills Diner, just like clockwork. Cross the street sometime, take a walk on the wild side. I'll buy you coffee and a roll."

"I'm that obvious, huh?"

"Not too many top-flight shooters working this block, big boy."

"I'll do that," Charley said. "Maybe tomorrow. I've got to go."

Dale watched Charley walk down the street and through the doorway that led to the apartments above the Linden Hills Diner.

"You know that guy, Rocco?" Dale said.

Rocco nodded. "In a way. He works for the department, forensics photographer. That's how he knows everybody. He was friends with Bobby Martaine, that cop that got whacked in that Cannibal Killer case a year back."

"What's his history? You know?"

"Some kind of contract guy for CIA supposedly. Quit them and came out here to work as a photographer. Don't know much else. He's a pretty good guy, gets along, and the guys in the bag like him. Good sense of humor and he takes good pictures. Did a wedding for one of the guys not long ago."

"What do you have on the guy that got whacked?"

"Which one? You may have noticed we have a few."

"The one they were protecting."

Rocco brushed back the long black hair that fell across his forehead and flipped through his notebook. "He had a Honduran passport on him, name of Rhaman Uday. His team was from United Security, expensive local outfit. The team leader, we knew him, he was an ex-cop from Minneapolis, sergeant on the ERU named Heritage. One of the other dead bodyguards was a cop, too."

"Anything on the shooters?" Dale said.

"The women? They were stone pros. Disappeared without a trace. We're canvassing the neighborhood and putting out the word on the TV that we want to talk to anybody that saw them or the moped. Nothing yet, and I'm not too hopeful. If we haven't heard anything yet, I don't think we're going to."

Dale rubbed his hands together, then stuck them in the rear pockets of his Levis and looked over the street, blocked with police cars and yellow tape. "I'm going home and get another gun. This neighborhood is getting too damn dangerous for me."

• • •

Charley Payne returned to his small apartment above the Linden Hills Diner. He stood and looked out at the street from his window, and absently touched his elbow to the empty holster at his side that should have held his Glock .45. Unarmed and shooters on the loose. He didn't care for that. The police cars and other emergency vehicles still blocked the street below, and their lights, even in the bright of day, flickered up and through his window and across the photographs he covered his otherwise plain walls with. The other shooter, Dale Miller, was still talking with the detective. Charley felt strange watching Miller talk; he was sure they were still talking about him. Even after all this time he clung to the remnants of a way of life that demanded secrecy in all things.

He didn't like people who actually knew something about him to talk.

And Miller might be one of the very few who would know something about Charley Payne and the elite shooters of the Central Intelligence Agency's Special Activities Staff, would know his history and what it meant in the small community of special operators. Charley had run and gunned with the SAS all over the world, conducting the "special activities" that ran the gamut from assassinations to complex bugging operations to striking down terrorists in their own backyards. They were legends in the community, and Charley had been one of the best.

Charley dragged his small armchair close to the window and

sat down, kicked his feet up on the windowsill and made himself relax. He was still working off the adrenaline rush of the shooting. The big muscles of his legs and shoulders trembled. He rolled his head slowly to ease the kinks out and thought about having a drink, but decided to wait.

He'd done okay today. Not bad for being out of practice. The time on the range he spent keeping tuned up had paid off. He'd often questioned his need for carrying a gun and keeping in practice; he was a photographer now and that was what put bread on the table. But he'd spent a lifetime carrying a gun, and he felt incomplete without one. Lucky for him today he'd had one.

Miller was damn good. Some kind of spec ops shooter before, the detective had said. Charley wondered. It would be good to talk to somebody with the same history. Maybe he should take Miller up on that cup of coffee. The younger man's cockiness and self-assuredness put him off a little bit. Maybe he was feeling his age, and the younger man prickled his vanity, which he had to admit was considerable.

Charley laughed and ran his fingers through his thinning hair, flecked with gray. Hell, he should buy Dale Miller a cup of coffee or a beer—after all, the young shooter had covered this old gray dog's ass today, and done it well.

And maybe he'd loan him a pistol.

## MEDICAL EXAMINER'S OFFICE, MINNEAPOLIS, MINNESOTA

Patrice Nordby had been a medical examiner in Minneapolis for ten years. In the hundreds of autopsies she'd performed, she'd seen the entire range of abuse that human beings could mete out on one another. But this was her first mass killing. She looked over the long row of bodies, stiff and cold on their gurneys, waiting for her attention in the City Morgue. She snapped the cuffs of her surgical gloves and got ready to work.

"I'll start with the boss," she told her assistant. "Bring him on in."

The small chubby man, his face distorted from bullet wounds, his dental work shattered, was wheeled in and transferred to the autopsy table. Patrice reached up and adjusted the microphone above the table and began her initial examination. She measured the man and found him to be five feet, eight inches tall. He weighed one hundred ninety pounds. Something nagged at her when she had the height and weight.

She called to her assistant. "Jerry? This one had the passport on him?"

"Yeah."

"Did we get a copy of it?"

"Right here."

Her assistant handed her a Xerox copy of the inside front page of the passport. The man in the picture looked like the man on the table, as battered as his face was. But the passport said the man was six feet, one inch tall, and weighed two hundred ten pounds. Something was wrong here.

"Jerry? Get me the lead detective, will you?"

• • •

Patrice went over her autopsy notes with the lead detective, Rocco Rococelli.

"This isn't the guy in the passport," she said. "The passport says six feet one inch, this guy is five feet eight. The passport says two hundred ten pounds, this guy is one hundred ninety. He might have lost the weight, but you don't lose five inches in height. The face looks the same, mangled as it is, but this is the kicker—he's had plastic surgery."

"Plastic surgery?" Rocco said.

"Yep," Patrice said. "On his face. Expensive, too. Altered his looks and I'm betting it's to make him look like the guy in the passport. If there is a Rhaman Uday, which is a funny name for a Honduran, it's not this guy."

Rocco sighed. "Bad enough I got a mass shooting, I got to have a John Doe mystery, too. You sure on all this, Patrice?"

"You know me. I'd go to court with what I've got."

"All right. Thanks."

Rocco slapped the covers of his notebook together and stuffed it back into the inside pocket of his wrinkled sport coat.

"Damn it," he said. "So just who do I have here?"

TORTURE REHABILITATION CENTER, UNIVERSITY OF
MINNESOTA CAMPUS, MINNEAPOLIS, MINNESOTA

Dr. Rowan Green looked out the window at the rolling green lawn,
and the trees that hid a direct view of the river. She felt a tug to be outside in the summer warmth, but turned her attention back to her
patient. Rhaman Uday sat across from her, his tall frame bent into an
overstuffed chair beside a long couch. He plucked over and over again
at a loose thread on the zipper of his exercise-suit top.

"How are we feeling today, Mr. Uday?" she said.

He kept his attention on the loose thread. "Lost. Always lost."

"Can you remember what it was like to be found?"

The man's face darkened. "To be found is to be hurt. To be lost
is to be safe."

"You're safe here. Are you lost here?"

He nodded. "Yes. Safe. Lost."

Dr. Green jotted a note to herself on the progress worksheet.
At least now she could engage him in some dialogue. When he'd first
come to her, weeks ago, she'd been unable to get anything out of him.
He'd been pushed to the top of the Center's waiting list after his initial examination and, fortunately for him, an opening came quickly.

"How long have you been lost?" she said.

Uday pulled at his lip and stared over her shoulder at the wall and her diplomas there. "Not as long as I was found."

"How long were you found?"

He dropped both hands into his lap. The fingers knotted together, writhing like snakes.

"Many weeks," he said. "Many, many weeks."

"Yes," she said. "I know. Do you know who I am?"

"You're not the One. My wife told me."

"The One?"

"No more screaming. No more . . . with the wires. No more. You're not the One. I know the One. For me was the screaming, many times when he brought us to work, he brought screaming for us."

"Who brought screaming for you?"

"Saddam brought it for us. We were lost and then we were found. Then we were the screaming while others watched." He fell silent and studied his hands in his lap.

Dr. Green measured him with eyes used to calculating the human toll of disclosure. Saddam. She'd dealt with the handiwork of the Saddam regime before. She quietly flipped through the notes section of Uday's folder. According to his wife, who'd brought him to the center, he'd been a government bureaucrat high in the favor of Saddam Hussein. He'd been close to Saddam's son-in-law. After the son-in-law defected and then returned, there was a purging of all those close to him. Uday had been one of those tortured to madness. He'd languished in a prison cell till his wife had been able to bribe his jailers and buy him out. They'd escaped to the west, to America, to the Center where his mind and body could be repaired.

So he was safe here, as safe as he could be.

"Saddam," the broken man said. He closed his eyes and began to hum tonelessly as he rocked back and forth in his seat. "Saddam."

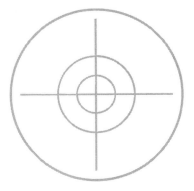

## DOMINANCE RAIN HEADQUARTERS, FAIRFAX, VIRGINIA

Michael Callan, a senior consultant with Kroner-O'Hanrahan, one of the country's most prestigious international security firms, sat on Ray Dalton's office sofa and forked Caesar salad out of a Styrofoam to-go box. Ray sat across the low coffee table from him in an armchair and munched on a roast beef and Swiss sandwich. Their favorite place for lunch was too crowded for a quiet talk, so they'd opted for a takeout meal in the privacy of Ray's office.

Callan wiped his mouth on a napkin and said, "Who were the hitters?"

"The Twins," Ray said. He set his sandwich down on the table and picked up the remote control for the VCR and television unit mounted in his wall. He rewound the tape of the hit in Minneapolis to a close-up of the two beautiful women on the moped.

"Top-shelf," Callan said. "They still in Amsterdam?"

"That's where they are. Marie Garvais and Isabelle Andouille, the only all-woman crew working in the business of taking out heavily protected targets, with a stellar record of success for a wide variety of clients. Everybody from the narco cartels to a sampling of European government agencies. Even, once or twice, for us."

"That's very much off the record, I suppose."

"You probably have it somewhere in those expensive computers you maintain in Tyson's Corner."

Callan grinned, a smear of salad dressing on his upper lip. "You got that right. We get the same take from the same people."

"Which goes back to my original statement. We're all working on the same side of the street."

"You want me to approach Dale and see if he'd take a contract? Doing what?"

"This Uday that got killed . . . he's one of a small group of Iraqi exiles we've been watching. They're related, either by blood or by the time they spend together in Saddam's prisons. For some reason, why we don't know, what's left of Saddam's apparat is looking for these people. They got close enough to put the Twins to work on taking them out. One down, and there's only a woman and one other man left. The woman is married to one of them, she's not a player. But the man may be."

"Where's the other man and the woman?"

"Still in Minneapolis. The woman is in a private-sector safe house with a crew around her; the man is a psychiatric patient at a specialty clinic at the University of Minnesota. The Torture Rehabilitation Center. They're used to getting patients on somebody's hit list, so they maintain low profiles for their patients and practice decent security. Problem is, they're not prepared to deal with the Twins. So that's where we come in. We want to take over protection of this man and move the woman to a secure location. We want Dale Miller to be a team leader of the protection team on the man."

Callan pushed his Styrofoam plate to the middle of the coffee table, then cracked his knuckles one by one. "Not to blow my own horn, but I've got top-shelf executive protection teams I can rent you, Ray. Ex-Delta, SEALs, Secret Service . . . I've got shooters as well as technical support. Why run a contract with a loner when you can get a top flight team?"

Ray bobbed his head in quick agreement. "Dale was one of us. As far as I'm concerned, he's still one of us. We want to keep things compartmented, but you're right, you've got the resources. We want

Dale and a contract crew for deniability, with you as a fallback."

"Little conflict of interest here, Ray. If I succeed with your favor, I'm doing myself and the company out of a tasty bit of business."

"There's a substantial consultation fee to soften the blow. And favors in the favor bank."

"There's that," Callan conceded. "Me and Dale go back to Delta. So if I can help him, I will. What are you not telling me?"

"Full disclosure," Ray said. "I'd like to bring Dale in myself, but there's that ugly bit of history between us."

Callan stood up, wiping his hands with a napkin, then balled it up and dropped it into his plate. He went to Ray's big window and looked out. "Jonny Maxwell drove a wedge into everybody. He needed to die sooner than he did." He paused for a moment, then said, "I'm sick of this traffic. It takes forever to get anyplace. You know it took me forty minutes to get here?"

Ray leaned back in his chair, stretching his legs out and crossing them at the ankles. "Will you do this for me, Mike?"

"Minneapolis is a pretty city. I'd like to see Dale again, and it'd be nice to get out of here for a day."

Ray got up and went to the window and stood beside Callan. "Thanks, Mike."

"I'm doing your dirty work again, Ray. Big favors in the favor bank."

"Done."

AMSTERDAM, THE NETHERLANDS

Youssef bin Hassan stood outside the Central Train Station in Amsterdam, part of the milling crowd composed mainly of young people on holiday from all over the world. He was a thin, stoop-shouldered young man with a perpetually narrowed look on his face, dressed casually in baggy denim pants, light boots, and a white collared shirt open at the neck. He had a courier bag slung over his shoulder, weighty with his laptop computer, the latest I-Book from Apple.

It was a beautiful day in Amsterdam, clear and warm, and the sunlight glittered from the windows of the hotels that looked over the canals. He stood by the arched stone bridge that crossed over to Dam Street, and watched the canal water buses go by. When he judged he'd killed enough time, he looked at his wristwatch, an inexpensive Casio, then went to a public phone outside the tourist information center beside the bridge. He swiped a locally purchased phone card in the slot, waited for the tone, and punched in the local telephone number he'd been given. The phone was answered on the third ring.

"Yes?" a woman's voice said. The voice sounded tinny and crackled with static as a cellular phone would.

"This is Joe from the States," Youssef said in good English. "I'm looking for Marta from Minnesota."

"This is Marta, Joe," the woman said. "Do you have it?"

"Yes," Youssef said. "I can do it for you anywhere, from your location if you like."

He listened intently. The woman said nothing for a moment, but there were noises in the background and the babbling of a small child.

"It's not necessary," she said. "Do it and let us know. We have our own means to verify it."

"But there are other matters to discuss," Youssef said as he'd been directed to.

"Are there?"

"Yes. There's your payment, and then the final disposition of the project in Minnesota."

"One moment, Joe."

The background sounds were lost in more static as though she held her hand over the mouthpiece. He heard the blurred sounds of a short conversation, then she came back on the phone.

"I'll come to you," the woman said. "Where are you?"

"At the VVV, the tourist information booth, at the Central Train Station."

"How will I know you?"

Youssef thought for a moment. "I'll be standing beside the phone booths. I have on a white shirt and blue pants, and I have a navy blue courier bag on my shoulder."

"I'll be along shortly."

"How will I . . ."

She hung up the phone and he heard nothing else. He shrugged, and hung the phone back in its cradle. He looked at the crowd under the bright sun, and decided he had time to go into the train station and get a cup of espresso. After he bought his coffee, he took it in a paper cup and brought it back outside, where he stood beside the phone booth in the warmth of the sun.

• • •

Marie Garvais stood on the city side of the canal that separated the Central Train Station from the Old Center, beside the railed bridge, and watched Youssef bin Hassan. She'd taken her time coming to the meeting, riding her bicycle from the canal where the houseboat she and Isabelle lived in was moored, and paused beside the bridge as though she were merely taking a break or enjoying the summer day. But what she was looking for were the signs of surveillance. A top flight team with time to prepare would be nearly invisible, even to her seasoned eyes, but she had sufficient confidence in her ability to determine that it was a reasonable risk to meet the cutout in public. All of her dealings with the people the young man represented had been professional; while this meeting was less so, there was a great deal of money involved, which made it necessary. When she was satisfied, she mounted her plain black bicycle and eased into the steady stream of cyclists crossing the bridge, and rode till she was almost upon the young man. She stopped her bicycle, still astraddle of it, right beside him.

"Joe?" she said, as though delighted in meeting a friend. "Fancy seeing you here!"

The Arab smiled nervously. She got off her bicycle, put down the kickstand, and hugged him in greeting. Her hands moved surely over him, checking for weapons.

"Hello, Marta," he said. "How nice to see you again."

"Nice to see you, Joe!" Marie said. She plucked the courier bag from his shoulder, opened it and looked inside. "You have a gift for me?"

"Only what's in my computer," he said.

"Then let's go where we can have a look," Marie said. She slung the courier bag over her thin but muscular shoulders and pushed her bike along, leading the young man back across the bridge toward the Old Center. "There's a cyber café nearby that has laptop portals."

They walked along in silence for a time, Marie cutting through the crowd, using her bicycle to carve them a path. They came to a cyber café and went in after Marie locked her bike to the rack in front. She got them two cups of coffee while Youssef paid for a card that allowed him to dock his laptop in a portal and access the Internet. He powered up his computer while Marie watched. Once his machine was up, he accessed the communications program and logged onto the Internet. After a few minutes of working the keyboard, he showed her the screen, which contained financial information and the routing address of a bank in Oranjestad, Aruba, in the Dutch Caribbean.

"Does it look all right?" he said.

Marie looked over the substantial figures and said, "Yes. It's fine."

"Would you like to . . ."

"Yes," she said, smiling girlishly. She pushed the RETURN key and watched the progress bar appear and count off the percentage of the money transfer taking place between two secured accounts. It took only a few brief moments for the transaction to be completed, and now Marie and her partner enjoyed a substantial increase in the funds available in one of their many numbered accounts protected by Dutch privacy laws.

"That concludes that part of our business," Youssef said. "But we have some other . . . what about the other man and the woman?"

Marie shrugged. "The only obstacle is payment."

"Money is not a problem . . . when could you do it?"

"Do you have the same quality of intelligence on those two?"

"Yes."

"We'd need a reasonable amount of time to work it up."

"Then I'm told to tell you to consider it a tasking."

Marie nodded sharply and said, "Wire the initial amount, then. Same as the last. Do it now, if you're in a hurry."

Youssef nodded and said, "As you wish."

It took only a few keystrokes to transfer more money.

Marie stood and said, "I'll be in touch the usual way. Check your e-mail often. Do you intend to stay here in Amsterdam?"

"For a few days. I'll need to pass on to you what we have, when I get it."

"Enjoy your stay. This is a civilized city."

"Yes," said the young terrorist. "It is."

• • •

Marie locked her bicycle against the rails that separated the sidewalk from the canal, then stepped gingerly down the stairs that led to the

deck of their houseboat. She ducked through the low door entranceway and almost stumbled over the small blond girl playing with
blocks beside the doorway.

She knelt by the child and said in a scolding tone, "Come, Ilse.
Not so close to the door. Isabelle, you must keep her away from the
door."

Isabelle came into the front room from the kitchen. She was
dressed in a black unitard that clung to her muscled arms and legs,
with a blue denim smock worn over it.

"Give her to me," Isabelle said. She took the smiling child from
Marie and said, "Come here, you naughty girl. What have I told you
about playing so close to the door?"

The little girl laughed and buried her face in Isabelle's shoulder,
and wrapped her arms and legs around the tall woman.

"Oh, you think you can get away with it by playing one against
the other?" Marie said, smiling. "No, you don't."

"So?" Isabelle said, stroking their daughter's hair.

"The money went fine," Marie said, chucking Ilse under the
chin and then going into the kitchen. She poured herself a cup of
coffee and leaned in the doorway between the kitchen and the front
room. "They want us to go back and do the other two."

"I thought he was the important one."

"They want to be thorough. They paid the initial fee in
advance and they promise the same quality of intelligence."

"I want to take Ilse to Bruges next week," Isabelle said. "To see
the swans . . ."

"I don't think so," Marie said. "We'll be traveling. We can take
her later, we have the whole summer."

"She's growing so fast, Marie. We need to think of that, too."

"We need to make a living, and this goes a long way . . ."

Isabelle hugged her child and set her down. Ilse sank cross-
legged to the floor and began to sort through her blocks. Isabelle
watched her, a fond faint smile on her face, then said, "You're right,
of course. I just hate leaving her. Each time it seems as though she's
grown so."

"They do," Marie said softly. She sipped her coffee and smiled at her lover. "I wonder what she'll be when she grows up."

"Que sera, sera, whatever will be, will be . . ." sang Isabelle.

Ilse looked up in delight and clapped her hands.

•  •  •

Youssef wandered aimlessly through the cobblestone streets of the Old Center of Amsterdam. He stopped often for coffee, always drinking it alone, and watching as though from a great distance the activities of the young people his own age all around him. He felt lonely, but fought it down with the patience of long practice. He forced himself to think through and recall the tenets of his advanced training as he studied the flow of people in the public places and the residential districts. The concentrations were on the trams and street-cars, the streets busy with bicyclists and pedestrians. His instructors had drilled into him that concentrations made excellent targets, especially those indoor places where air flow could be controlled. He paused beside a wall where a flyer for a concert, the Irish band U2, was plastered. There would be a huge audience.

An indoor audience.

But it wasn't time for target selection. This was an exercise to keep his mind from other things. He made his way back to the inexpensive youth hostel where he kept the rest of his meager gear: a backpack, a sleeping bag, some clothes, a small locked Pelican hard case. A few extra euros had bought him a room to himself, and he went to his room and sat down at the tiny table and set up his laptop. He busied himself composing an e-mail to his handler that he would send from a cyber café later, then set the computer aside and lay back on the thin mattress of the bed and stared at the ceiling.

He was very lonely.

Youssef wondered about the blond woman he'd met and wondered if that was her child he'd heard playing in the background. He liked children. It was doubtful that he would ever have any. There were times that the life he'd chosen for himself seemed very hard.

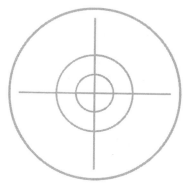

TORTURE REHABILITATION CENTER, UNIVERSITY OF
MINNESOTA CAMPUS, MINNEAPOLIS, MINNESOTA

Rhaman Uday stood in his private room before a window that looked out over a flourishing garden tended by patients. Uday liked to look at the flowers. He didn't care much for the thriving vegetable garden, preferring to spend his attention on the flowers. His room gave him a good view, and the staff often found him standing here in front of his window.

A nurse's aide opened the door while knocking. "Mr. Uday? Would you like to walk outside?"

He paused for a moment to consider, then said, "Yes. Walking would be good."

He followed, like a large, well-mannered child, in the wake of the small nurse's aide who steered him through the hallways and out to the garden.

"See?" she said brightly. "How lovely the flowers are."

"Yes," he said. "See how lovely the flowers are."

He stood, his hands limp at his side, looking at the different roses, the impatiens, the marigolds and the daisies, the neat rows of violets and daffodils and other flowers. His shoulders settled, unlocked for a moment from their rigid set, softened by the aroma and the sight of the flowers.

"The blooming," he said. "Blooming starts earlier. A longer period followed by the blooming. There is no sad holiday without the blooming. That makes us sad."

"Why are you sad, Mr. Uday?" the nurse's aide said. "It's a beautiful day. It's not a sad holiday here."

"No," Uday said. "It will be a sad holiday. Even here."

LINDEN HILLS NEIGHBORHOOD,
MINNEAPOLIS, MINNESOTA

The outdoor seating area in the patio of the Sebastian Joe's coffee shop is shaded by trees on three sides. The last side faces the sidewalk and the busy street there. Mike Callan and Dale Miller sat in the patio facing the street and people-watched. There was no shortage of things to see: bicyclists fresh from a ride around Lake Harriet, only a few hundred yards away; suntanned couples strolling hand in hand, licking at the ice cream cones Sebastian Joe's was famous for; and others, like Miller and Callan, just sitting and watching the summertime flow of people.

"You're like a shark among the penguins here," Callan said.

"Same old Mike," Dale said.

"So what do you think about my proposition?"

Dale touched his finger to the bridge of his Ray-Bans. "I don't know. I need to think it over, talk with Nina about it."

"You that serious?"

"She's a factor in everything I do."

"I envy you. Margie was my last and final attempt at domesticity. She left me light in the moneybags."

"We're not like that."

Callan nodded, and watched a short, trim blond woman jog by.

"You'd have full license . . . use who you like. You'd be responsible only to me. I'd sign the checks, and you'd report directly to me."

"Like I said, I'll think about it."

"What's to think about? Is training SWAT cops so exciting? It's not like you couldn't use the money. I had a look at your finances . . ."

Dale laughed.

Callan said, "Hey, two K a day is nothing to sneer at."

Dale took up his tall glass of iced tea and swirled the melting ice around in it. "You're right, it's not. But it's been a long time since I worked a protection detail. I'd need to put together a team. Why don't you just use one of your off-the-shelf teams instead? Don't tell me that Kroner-O'Hanrahan doesn't have VIP protection teams."

"You know that we do. But we want you. You're right here and you've already got the best police liaison."

"I don't know if I want to wrap my mind around that kind of problem again."

Callan crossed his arms on his chest. "You've gotten too used to the easy life, brother. You're not fooling anybody. You need some edge to be happy."

"I like what I'm doing just fine."

"Maybe so. Look, will you take a ride with me to look at the principal? The guy is in bad shape, he needs top-shelf people to look after him."

Dale watched a bird perch on a branch, then flit away. "How long would we be talking? I couldn't take an open-ended commitment."

Callan turned and leaned toward Dale. "Just a couple of weeks. Till the powers that be decide to keep him here or move him to a secure facility and bring the doctors to him. They'd have moved him by now, but the Center has the best people, and they won't work off-site. They want control of their environment, and who can blame them? They're the best in the world at what they do. So you're looking at just a few weeks."

"I could use whoever I wanted?"

"I've got a short list of experienced freelance operators if you need it. But you can use who you like. Maybe you've got some local people. Up to you."

Dale slouched in his chair and uncrossed his ankles, stretching his legs out. He sipped from his iced tea, and brushed at his shirt where a few drops of condensation dripped from his glass. "Look around you, Mike. This is life. People out enjoying themselves, raising their children, going to work. You ever feel like you're missing something?"

"I like what I do," Callan said.

"So do I," Dale said. "All of it."

• • •

Nina Capushek was thirty-four years old, a brunette athlete with a model's face, and a respected detective in the Sex Crimes section of the Minneapolis Police Department's Special Investigations Unit. She and Dale lived together in her lakeside condominium overlooking Lake Harriet, a short two blocks away from the ice-cream parlor Dale used as his hangout. The two of them sat in her front room with its big windows that looked out on the lake and the tree-shaded pedestrian paths there.

"What do you think I should do?" Dale said.

"That's not for me to answer," she said. "That's your call. We don't need the money, but I don't think you want to do this for just the money anyway. You need engagement, and I don't think you're getting what you need from training and riding along on entries. I think you miss having a mission of some kind. You don't need my permission to do this."

"I'm not suggesting that I need your permission," he said, heat in his voice. "I'm looking for your input."

"In that case, I think you've already decided to do it. You're just seeing if you can talk yourself out of it or not. You'd be in charge and you can run it your way and it's short term, right? Couple of weeks? Why not? We can use the money for a vacation."

"You make it sound so easy."

"You make it difficult when you get in your own way. Why not do it?"

"I don't know if I want to get involved with the G again. Even if they're hands-off and keeping their distance."

"I don't blame you for that. But it's short term, you've got a trusted friend running it, and it's a contract—you can walk when you want to."

"You're right."

"Of course I am," she said. She touched his thigh. "Want to go for a run and then get laid, or get laid and then go for a run?"

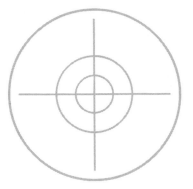

## LAKE HARRIET, MINNEAPOLIS, MINNESOTA

Kroner-O'Hanrahan was a world leader in security, and the management insisted that the corporate staff carry only the latest of state-of-the-art communications equipment. So Mike Callan was able to have a secure cell phone conversation with Ray Dalton, even while Callan was comfortably seated on a sunbathed bench looking over Lake Harriet, admiring the tanned and athletic women passing by.

"Uday was much more important than we thought," Callan said. "I've been running back and forth between the Minneapolis PD and the security outfit that had the protection contract. The guy that got whacked was carrying Uday's identification. He'd also had plastic surgery to make him look like Uday."

"A double?" Ray said.

"You got it. Saddam arranged for only his highest confidants and most important people to have doubles—they had to be critical to his operations, and under the threat of assassination. The guy that got whacked was Uday's private secretary in Iraq."

"So the Twins thought they were taking Uday out?" Ray said. "He was the principal target?"

"Yep."

"Curiouser and curiouser. What else do you have?"

"Not much more than what we started with. He was a senior

Iraqi official and personally acquainted with Saddam. Caught up in the purge Saddam oversaw after the defection of Hussein Kamel. Broken in the prisons, until his wife and secretary managed to bribe his way out after the war. Then here to the States."

"Nothing on what he did for Saddam?"

"We can only speculate," Callan said. "The guy is a wreck. Totally psychotic and out of touch with reality. One of the worst cases the Torture Center has ever seen, and they've seen the worst you can imagine."

"We need to find out more about Rahman Uday," Ray said. "Have Dale monitor his sessions with the doctors, see what comes out of it."

"You got to give Dale some time," Callan said, irritated. "He's not even on the job yet and you're already tasking him with additional duties."

"You're right," Ray said. There was no contrition in his voice. "But once he is, put him on to it."

LINDEN HILLS NEIGHBORHOOD/TORTURE REHABILITATION
CENTER, UNIVERSITY OF MINNESOTA CAMPUS,
MINNEAPOLIS, MINNESOTA

Charley sat at a table outside the Linden Hills Diner and basked like
a big cat in the sunlight. But, like a cat, he kept one eye open and he
saw Dale Miller across the street at Sebastian Joe's in his normal spot.
The younger man got up and walked down the sidewalk till he was
directly across from where Charley sat. Then he waited for a break
in the traffic and jogged across the street.

"Mind if I join you?" Dale said.

Charley pushed one seat out with his foot. "Sit down. I'd be
glad for the company."

Dale sat down and plucked the menu from the spring clip that
held it in the middle of the table. "Anything good?"

"It's all good here. You like coffee?"

"Yeah."

"Try their house blend. It's great."

A waitress came out of the diner and hovered over Charley's
shoulder. "Got a friend today?" she said.

"My one and only friend, Jan. Bring him a cup of that good
coffee you make."

"You got it, Charley," Jan said, smiling brightly. "Charley's friend, do you want anything else?"

"The coffee will do it," Dale said. "Thank you."

The two men sat in silence and studied each other. Jan brought out a cup of coffee in a big mug and set it down in front of Dale, then went back inside.

Dale blew on his coffee, smelled it, and let the smell grow in his nose.

"Good," he said.

"You decide to loan me a gun?" Charley said.

"Might could happen," Dale said. "Guy with your history, I'm surprised you don't have a few extra stashed."

"My history. Been checking up on me?"

"A little bit. You?"

"Not a bit. Figured you'd come over here and fill me in one of these days."

"Charley Payne," Dale said. "A few years back, a shooter with the Special Activities Staff. Before that, a Charley Company door kicker on Okinawa. Your first sergeant was a Filipino named Evan Coronas; he went to Delta. That's where I met him."

"You spent some time there, huh?"

"A little bit. Seventh Group originally, then over to Delta. Then DOMINANCE RAIN."

"You just impressed me."

Dale shrugged and sipped his coffee. "You just impressed me, too. Not too many people know about the RAIN."

"Our guys ran with you all on occasion, when the bosses weren't trying to cut up the same piece of turf."

"Not during my time."

Charley nodded, and stroked one finger down the bridge of his nose. "You were in on that Green Beret rapist thing a few years back."

He watched how Dale's lips tightened and pursed, as though the coffee had soured in his mouth.

"That's right," Dale said.

"Ugly business."

"Not for the weak, any of it. If you don't mind me asking, why'd you get out?"

"Got sick of bureaucrats trying to run field operators. Got tired of good people being wasted in every sense of the word over misguided bullshit from desk jockeys."

Dale nodded and narrowed his eyes.

"There's a lot of that going around in government," he said.

"You, too?"

"The same."

Charley drummed his fingers on the tabletop. Dale sipped again at his coffee, then set the cup down and leaned back in his chair and laced his fingers across his flat stomach.

"How do you like your photographer's gig?" Dale said.

"What brought you to Minneapolis?"

"The thing you mentioned. I stayed because I didn't want to go back. I have a woman here."

"Ah," Charley said. "Women. They will move us war dogs from time to time, now won't they?"

"You?"

"A friend. He got me the gig with the PD. I was a photographer before."

"Surveillance?"

"No, I was a shooter. But I got into it on the side. Sold a few pics after the Shield and the Storm, and got into it then. When I was ready to hang up the one, I had the other to pick up. I enjoy it."

"It's a good thing to be into. And you make a living at it?"

Charley laughed.

"Such as it is, friend. Such as it is. I'm not getting rich, I'll tell you that much."

"Ever consider taking on a part-time gig?"

Charley slouched a little more in his chair, then straightened up. "What do you have in mind?"

Dale shook his head from side to side and grinned.

"I guess I'm out of practice at this," he said.

"Always best to cut to the chase with guys like us."

"There it is," Dale said. "Would you be interested in working a high-threat VIP protection detail for a couple of weeks?"

"Now there's something I hadn't anticipated," Charley said.

"The guy that got whacked here," Dale said. "He wasn't the real target. His boss was."

"Wait a minute. You got something to do with all that?"

"I do now."

"That's serious business."

"It's serious business. You'd be the number two, fifteen hundred bucks a day plus all expenses."

"I like the numbers. I'd have to know more about the gig."

"It's only for a few weeks. It's something you know how to do, and you won't have to travel, it's right here in town."

"There's that," Charley said. "How current are you?"

"I'm rusty, but I still remember how. I've got a couple of other guys coming in to work for us, they're up to speed."

"I haven't decided yet."

"Sure you have," Dale said. "You sit out here every day, drink your coffee, and eat your rolls. You take pictures, sometimes for the PD but mostly for yourself. A couple of weeks of this gig, short-term, get in and get out, and you can buy yourself a lot of worry-free time to do just what you like to do. And the truth is, Charley, I think you'd like the job. I know I had to think about it, but it's good to have a mission again. You got a mission, Charley?"

Charley took his sunglasses off and rubbed his eyes, then his furrowed brow. He looked at Dale, his face carefully blank.

"You got a pretty good handle on me," Charley said.

"It's not like that," Dale said.

"Just want your friendly neighborhood gunfighter along for the ride?"

"Anybody in the business long enough to get gray hair is somebody I'd like to work with."

Charley laughed loud, his head thrown back. He looked at the younger man.

"It's just like riding a bicycle, isn't it?" he said. He leaned forward in his seat. "Sure. Why not. I can use the money."

• • •

The other two members of the team were a matched set: Harrison and Ford. They were both ex-Special Forces NCOs who'd gone into VIP protection after their military service. Callan counted them among his most reliable and favored operators. Harrison was short and squat and massively muscled, while his partner Ford was whippet thin, a marathoner with lots of nervous energy. They were both current in VIP protection, having just stood down from a longish stint in Ohio a week before.

The handover was quick and easy. Teams of federal agents descended on the offices of the private security company handling Uday. The CEO was more than happy to hand over his files and be rid of the client after he'd been apprised of the national security interest and the new level of threat. A team of US marshals took Mrs. Uday into their care and she disappeared into the machine called Witness Protection, there to wait for her husband. Dale got the working files, a detailed briefing from Mike Callan, and an introduction to Dr. Rowan Green while Harrison, Ford, and Charley Payne walked the landscaped grounds of the Torture Center.

"Have there been any security incidents?" Dale asked.

"Nothing," Dr. Green said. "We weren't aware of his connection to the Linden Hills incident. I think you've seen we have good security here. But our best protection is not letting people know who or where our patients are."

"How is Mr. Uday?"

"How much do you know about psychology?"

"Next to nothing," Dale said.

"Torture does terrible things to the mind. Mr. Uday is psychotic. He hears voices without his medication, and even with that he has under the best of conditions a tenuous grasp on reality. He has times when he is almost normal and can carry on a coherent conversation. But most often he has little understanding of what is going on around him. He hardly even recognizes his wife when she comes to visit him."

"Can I see him?"

"Of course. We'll cooperate with you as much as possible."

Dale followed the doctor out of her office and down the hallway. Dr. Green paused outside a door with a small window in it. Dale looked inside and saw a tall, dark-complected man, stooped and thin, dressed in a blue and gold track suit staring out the window. Dr. Green opened the door and let the two of them inside.

"Mr. Uday?" she said. "You have a visitor."

Uday continued to stare out the window, then turned slowly to face them. He studied Dale for a long moment, then said, "He is not the One. He is new, but he is not the One."

"Who is not the One?" Dr. Green said.

"This one is not the One," Uday said. "He is of the same kind, but not."

"What's he talking about?" Dale said in a low voice.

"It's part of his delusion . . . he's constructed an interior reality that helped him get through the worst of his torture. The One is a figure of some importance to him. If you listen to him long enough, you'll hear about the One and some other recurring themes. Apparently he knew Saddam Hussein personally."

The Iraqi man looked at Dale with dark, blank eyes. "You'll have a sad holiday. We'll all have a sad holiday. Even the One. That's what you want to know."

Dale felt embarrassed for some reason. The man's intense look unsettled him.

"What will he do under pressure?" Dale said. "If I had to grab him and run, what could I expect him to do?"

"He'd more than likely shut down, curl up in a protective position. In the face of any violence, he'd resist any attempt to take him out of that protective position."

"There is no protective position," Uday said. His voice was surprisingly deep. "We talk but there is none. Nowhere to go except with the One and he is on a sad holiday."

"What's the sad holiday?" Dale said.

"We don't know," Dr. Green said. "He makes constant references to the One and to the sad holiday, but we haven't been able to piece it together. I can go over some notes with you, but I'm afraid it won't make much sense."

"It might give me some insight into why people are trying to kill him," Dale said. "Has he ever spoken about what he did in Iraq? Do you have any idea what he did?"

"No. Only that he was a high-level intimate of Saddam Hussein and his son-in-law."

Dale found himself sneaking a look at the broken man, who returned his gaze with a guileless stare like that of a child.

"I expected him to look differently," Dale said.

"Why so?" Dr. Green said.

"I suppose I had a picture in my mind of what a torture victim is supposed to look like."

"For the most part they look quite normal, Mr. Miller. The one thing they have in common is that they're all broken. You can see it in their body language when you know what to look for. It's in his posture—you see how his shoulders turn in, how he seems stooped all the time? Exaggerate that posture and you have the fetal position, the position we fall into when we're overwhelmed by events, the basis of the protective position when you're being beaten."

"Do you know anything else about his background? Schooling, education, whether he had any military experience?"

"Only what his wife told us. He had no military experience, but apparently he was afforded certain military privileges because of his high position. He was educated in Iraq and England. His advanced degree was in biochemistry."

"Biochemistry?"

"That's what his wife told us."

Dale turned and looked once again at the tortured man.

A biochemist.

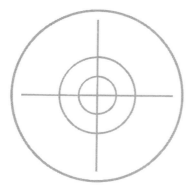

## TORTURE REHABILITATION CENTER, UNIVERSITY OF MINNESOTA CAMPUS, MINNEAPOLIS, MINNESOTA

To protect someone, you must think like an attacker. To protect someone from a terrorist attack, you must think like a terrorist. It's the ability to anticipate the moves of the attacker that's essential to a protector, and that ability was shared by Dale Miller, Charley Payne, and their two teammates. When they surveyed the Torture Center, they walked the grounds as an attacker would, analyzing avenues of approach, cover and concealment, alarmed points of entry, location of the lights, and the places of deepest shadow at night. Inside the old Victorian they identified all possible entry points, studied the locks, doors, and windows, and every possible way to approach the room where their principal slept at night. They brainstormed scenarios ranging from a stealthy entry to a full-scale armed assault and built contingency plans to counter each. The team was light with only four men, but their skill and experience made them formidable. They all knew the strength of a protection team is not the ability to fight, but the ability to avoid a fight and flee with the principal if necessary. While they could fight and fight well, each man knew the basic tenet of bodyguard protection: if they were drawing their weapons, they'd failed in their preplanning and situational awareness. And, more than likely, they were already dead and just hadn't realized it yet.

While both Dale and Charley had worked as protection operators before, they quickly came to rely on the recent field experience
of Harrison and Ford. The stocky Harrison was especially good at
survey work and preplanning, and Dale liked the way his mind
worked. The bodybuilding ex-Special Forces NCO had a cunning
and devious mind and cooked up all kinds of possible attack scenarios, which they then gamed to a defense. His greyhound-thin partner
Ford was the team diplomat, popular with the center's staff, and
became the secondary liaison, after Dale. The team worked a routine
twelve hours on, twelve hours off, with the off shift staying on-site in
a bedroom converted to their use.

Dale came down the hallway from the bedroom they used as
their operations center and tapped lightly on Uday's door, then went
in. He found Uday dressed and standing by his window, looking out
at the flowers as he liked to.

"Good morning, Mr. Uday," Dale said.

"It is morning," Uday said. "The morning after the night. The
night was quiet."

"I'm glad," Dale said.

He gently took Uday's arm and guided him to the door. Uday
stiffened when Dale touched him, then relaxed. Dale took him down
the hallway to the commons room, where Uday took his breakfast
with the other patients and staff. Dale sat him at a table and a white-
clad staff member brought a tray with his breakfast. Dale took some
coffee, and nodded to Dr. Green where she sat at a nearby table with
some of the staff. She waved him to the table.

"Excuse me, Mr. Uday," Dale said as he stood. Uday didn't
answer, concentrating instead on spooning oatmeal into his mouth.
Dale brought his coffee to Dr. Green's table and sat in the open chair.

"How was your night, Mr. Miller?" Dr. Green asked.

"Uneventful. Just the way I like them. And you?"

"Good. How is Mr. Uday this morning?"

"He seems to enjoy our company."

"I have him for therapy this morning."

"I have it on the schedule. Would you mind if I sat in?"

"Is it necessary?"

"No. Would it be a problem?"

"I think not," Dr. Green said. "Do you have specific concerns?"

"I'm curious about some of the threads that come up, like his insistence on a sad holiday. Any ideas about that?"

"It may not mean anything. At this point I don't have any specific idea what he means by that. It's a recurring theme, but his delusions are still very much internal, and we only have these small bits that rise to the surface, like his sad holiday and the One, to work with."

"Have you been able to determine why he was tortured? Or was it just luck of the draw and a byproduct of his relationship with Saddam?"

"We don't know," Dr. Green said.

"Sad holiday," Dale said. "I wonder what that means."

• • •

Charley Payne was enjoying his job. He walked outside on the manicured lawns and carefully maintained flower beds that bordered the Victorian house, and drank in the summer air. He lingered for a little bit on a wide piece of grassy space that was bathed in sun, and he closed his eyes for a moment and let the heat of the sun warm him.

Life was good.

He was banking $1,500 a day plus his minimal expenses and working with a fine crew. He enjoyed his conversations with the younger Dale, who was a good team leader—seasoned and confident enough to clearly state what he wanted and then get out of the way of his people while they did their work. He enjoyed being partnered with Dale. The younger operator had a hell of a resume, bits and pieces of which came out in their frequent conversations. Charley relished the interplay between him and the other members of the team, and it reminded him, painfully, of his best days as an operator. He knew his best days were behind him, but Dale was just into his prime, and Charley wondered what his team leader would do once this operation got handed over. Charley had his photography, but Dale didn't have a mission. The suppressed mentor in Charley wanted to take Dale under his wing, urge him to find something he could lose himself in, but he wisely bit his tongue and let the young man run.

That was the beginning of wisdom, to know when you didn't really have anything to say anymore.

Charley let his arm down and pressed slightly against the Glock holstered beneath his shirt. He was dressed in Levis and a short-sleeved denim shirt worn with the tails out. A small walkie-talkie was tucked into the shirt pocket of his shirt, with an earpiece running from the pocket to his ear. The team was small enough to maintain an open single frequency.

"One-Zero, this is One-Two," Charley said.

"One-Zero, go ahead," Dale's voice was tinny in the earpiece.

"All clear at the quarter hour," Charley said.

"Roger all clear," Dale said. "One-Zero out."

Charley continued his stroll around the grounds, and walked up the slope of a small hill that bordered the center. The access road came in from the parkway road there, wound around the hill, and then made a horseshoe loop in the driveway in front of the center. A bicycle and jogging path followed the road along the parkway, and from where Charley stood he could see people jogging as well as a solo bicyclist slowly peddling along.

It was a beautiful day, and there was no sign of a threat in sight.

• • •

Marika Tormay peddled her bicycle as slowly as she could without stopping. She saw the lone man standing atop the slight hill that hid the Torture Center from the main road. She had come this way several times a day for the last few days, looking for signs of security. There was the uniformed presence of the university campus police, who patrolled the grounds of the center and other properties here on the edge of the campus area, but in recent days she'd seen men in plainclothes lingering on the grounds of the center—not staffers, but not patients either. Their attention to who and what was in the immediate area marked them out as security.

She'd ridden her bicycle down the access road and made a loop around the driveway. While no one had challenged her, she was aware of the scrutiny of a man in the garden, who'd been joined by another man. Both muscular, dressed in casual clothes, with their shirttails out, no doubt to hide their weapons. They had the look. She had plenty of experience with armed men, first in the West Bank, then in Beirut, and her training in the camps in the Bekaa Valley of Lebanon had refined her eye even more. As an intelligence gathering operative for the Al-Bashir network, she had been idle, a sleeper agent on a student visa in the cosmopolitan—and very large— student population in Minneapolis and St. Paul. She'd been activated to surveil a small group of Iraqi exiles, and had for the first time met another sleeper agent in the Twin Cities area. The two of them worked up a profile of one of the men—who ended up dead in a spectacular hit. The woman and the other man had been harder. They hadn't been able to finger the man's location, and the woman stayed in for the most part, hidden behind formidable security. Now the woman had disappeared, but before she had gone, a small convoy of cars had driven her here to the Torture Center, where Marika had walked in on the grounds and was rewarded with a glimpse of the woman talking to a tall man in a track suit accompanied by a doctor.

They'd found the third man.

Since that time, the surveillance cell had worked up a target folder focusing on the center. Marika had dressed in business clothes and paid a visit to the offices of the remodeling company that had renovated the Victorian house that housed the center; she'd left with a complete set of floor plans and photographs. Her partner, a silent and serious Palestinian, had carefully, over a series of days, taken digital video of the house and the surrounding avenues of approach, and on his I-Mac computer carefully edited the raw footage into a detailed and comprehensive documentary on the center and the surrounding grounds. They had reached a point where more was not possible with the standoff approach; someone would have to get inside the building and see if they could identify where the target was located to take their work to the next level.

While she was not a shooter, she recognized, from her training in the camps, the demands of a shooting team: which way did the doors open, what sort of locks did they have, what was the distance from the little hill to the house, what was the response time of the campus police to the center, how many men and did they appear to have long guns—these were the questions that trained assault personnel needed answered.

She knew there'd be a shooting soon.

AMSTERDAM, THE NETHERLANDS

Youssef bin Hassan sat alone in the Golden Herb coffeehouse, surrounded by dozens of young people whose chatter washed over him like water over a stone. He slowly nursed one of the many coffees he drank throughout the day, and wondered why no one spoke to him. So many young people, from so many countries, all of them looking for friends in this friendliest of cities, let their gaze pass over him quickly. Not that there hadn't been a few attempts, but Youssef had rebuffed them without really knowing why. He told himself it was for operational reasons, but his loneliness nagged at him and was plain to see in his face, which made him all the more confusing to the few who dared to cross the wall of silence he surrounded himself with.

Youssef was new to the Al-Bashir network. He was only recently out of the Sudanese training camps. He smiled to himself and touched his coffee cup with one finger as he remembered the camaraderie of the camps and the fun he'd had in training with other operators. The training course had been rigorous, with challenges presented to them in hand-to-hand combat, shooting, tactics and planning, and many long speeches from the imams on the nature of the armed struggle against Israel and the United States. The shared experiences had fostered a tight bond with his training group, a bond that Youssef, a rare single child in an Arab family, had thrived on.

All the lectures on preparation for operating in hostile territory hadn't prepared him for the loneliness of the singleton operator. He had permission to shave his beard, miss prayer, even to drink alcohol if it was necessary to preserve his cover, but there was an iron-clad prohibition about unburdening himself to a sympathetic ear other than his controllers. Those meetings were few and far between, and most of his communication took place through e-mail. He was starved for human contact. As an only child, he hadn't learned how to easily make idle conversation, to strike up dialogues with the people around him. So he made the rounds of the coffee shops, and eavesdropped on other people his own age, planning their excursions and laughing with one another.

It made him angry.

There was a seed of bitterness in him that the Al-Bashir recruiters had seen, a deep loneliness that had been assuaged by his membership in the terrorist organization. It was like belonging to a large company. There were picnics with the families of other operators, parties where the senior organizers and leaders socialized with rank and file soldiers, regular infusions of money for living expenses, and tasks to accomplish. But he had none of that now, and comparing his past experiences to the present just made him more bitter.

Today would be a good day to spend in rehearsal. His final operation wouldn't take place here, but it was good training ground. He'd been taught, and taught well, how to conduct reconnaissance and prepare the ground for his actions. Taking action now would be good, and give him a satisfaction that his action would someday show the world that he wasn't small and insignificant; no, he was someone of hidden importance and that was something these young people shunning him would someday see.

He finished his coffee and left a few small coins on the table when he left. He shouldered his courier bag, weighty with his laptop computer and a few belongings, and strolled toward the Central Train Station with its gray towers and gabled walls. At the bridge that crossed the canal in front of the station, he paused for a while and let the crowd move and swirl around him, watching the station and the people coming and going. Then he entered the station and wandered in the crowd, one hand curled in his pocket around the atomizer he carried there. He took out his hand, the atomizer concealed in his closed fist, his thumb resting on the spray head, and let his hand swing naturally with his body motion.

The first target was an old woman dressed neatly in a black dress and stockings; she got a spray on her back. A young man about Youssef's age was chatting up a group of girls; he took a spray on his sleeve as Youssef brushed by him, eyes straight ahead as though nothing were taking place. Two girls ran by to catch a train; they got a spray directed at their head scarves. None of them noticed the faint mist from behind or the side; Youssef was doing well, the natural motion of his hand hiding the atomizer that sent a mist on each victim. Today it was just water.

Soon it would be something else.

## TORTURE REHABILITATION CENTER, UNIVERSITY OF MINNESOTA CAMPUS, MINNEAPOLIS, MINNESOTA

"Hi, Darla," Ford said to the cook as he squeezed through the narrow kitchen toward the back door of the center. He was dressed in running shorts and singlet, and had his radio and handgun concealed in a blue fanny pack strapped around his waist.

"Hi, Greg," the young black woman said. "Going for your run?"

"Yeah, thought I'd get a quickie in."

"Quickie sounds good."

Ford grinned and said, "I wouldn't want to hurt you, girl-friend."

"You're so bad!" Darla said. She snapped a dish towel at his lean flanks. "Go on, get out of here!"

Ford laughed as he shouldered open the back door. He paused, from long force of habit, and looked far and then near, wide and then close, before he set off in an easy shamble that ate up the miles. He went over the little hill that adjoined the center and down to the bicycle and jogging trail that paralleled River Road and followed the banks of the Minnesota River as it meandered south. The path was pleasant: level with gentle curves and plenty of hills, tree-lined, with a good view of the river. His basic course took him five miles out and back. Normally he wouldn't take such a long run on a job, but the boss had said to go ahead and get his run in. He liked Dale Miller. He'd never worked with him before, though they had been in Special Forces at the same time, but they knew some of the same people in Delta and in Seventh Group where they'd both done their A-Team time.

Ford's runs were his favorite time of day. He liked being alone with the rhythm of his body and he relished the challenge of the hills and the occasional encounter with a runner in his class. He saw a woman on the path ahead of him, running, not jogging, with the easy, relaxed upper body and smooth pace of a coached runner. He kept his pace strong and hard and drew up even with the woman with the long blond ponytail.

"Hi," he said, between breaths.

She looked over at him and smiled. "Hi, yourself. Great day for a run, isn't it?"

She had a faint accent.

"Sure is," Ford said. "How far you going?"

"Not far . . . I'm coming back from an injury. You?"

"Just five out and back."

"Don't let me hold you up," the tall blonde said.

"See you!" Ford said, picking up his pace. He felt the woman's gaze on his back and that warmed him.

Isabelle Andouille stretched out her pace, enjoying the easy run ahead of her and the feeling of being uncramped after her long transatlantic flight. Men were so easy, she thought, not for the first time in her career. They never consider women a serious threat.

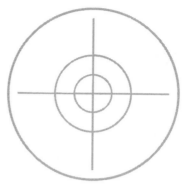

DOMINANCE RAIN HEADQUARTERS,
FAIRFAX, VIRGINIA

"So what kind of take are you getting?" Ray Dalton asked Mike
Callan.

"Just interesting tidbits," Callan said. "The detail is going well.
I hooked Dale up with a good crew. He talked Charley Payne into
being second in command."

"How is Payne doing?"

"Good. It's an easy detail. They haven't spotted any surveillance, they keep Uday buttoned up tight on the grounds, they've got
assistance from the campus police . . . they're in good shape. Payne
seems to thrive on it."

"How is Dale?"

"He wouldn't be happy to know that you're signing his check.
He's still carrying baggage over the whole Jonny Maxwell job, but
then so is most anybody who was involved in that operation. He's
doing a good job."

"What else?"

"Dale's been sitting in on Uday's psychiatrist sessions. Uday
keeps making reference to someone called "the One" and something
about having a sad holiday. Dale thinks this is important and linked
to why he was tortured. It seems that Saddam may actually have

witnessed or even taken part in the torture of Uday, which means he was pretty damn high up in the pecking order."

"Should we take him over?"

"I don't know if the Agency shrinks could do a better job. The people at the center are the best in the world at what they do, and I don't think that scooping up Uday at this point is going to help his recovery. I don't think you'll get anything more than what they're getting. I'd wait, and see what develops. What have you got on Uday in the computer?"

"Not much. Uday is an Iraqi, high in Saddam's social circles, and doing some kind of secret work. A close associate of Saddam's son-in-law Hussein Kamel, who defects in 1995 long enough for us to debrief, and then goes back to Iraq, where he's tortured and executed. Uday, because of his association with Hussein Kamel, is scooped up by Iraqi intelligence and internal security, and tortured till his mind breaks, and for no other reason we can discern except that he was close with Hussein Kamel. We know that Uday has to be a big muckety muck because he's got a double, at least one, in his personal secretary. After the war, Uday's family money buys him out of prison and gets him, his wife, and personal secretary out of the country and into the United States, where he comes up on our radar. Seeking asylum, with immigration paperwork pending, they come to Minneapolis where Uday is accepted into the Torture Center's rehab program. Uday's secretary takes Uday's name and makes himself seen with heavy bodyguard protection, all of which serves to be useless on the day the Twins settle their sights on him."

"So the Twins thought they were taking Uday out?"

"Yeah. And they probably intended to take the wife and secretary out, too, as a matter of housekeeping. But I think Uday is number one on their hit parade. So what makes him so important that Saddam himself supervised his torture, and when he escapes out of Iraq, someone hires the most expensive and talented team of hitters you can find to take him out?"

"Dale reported that Uday had been trained as a biochemist. What about that?"

"That adds up to a bad scenario. Hussein Kamel was in charge of the biological and chemical warfare program."

"And Uday was a biochemist and a close associate of Hussein Kamel."

"Which takes us to something about their biowarfare or chemical warfare programs."

Ray Dalton leaned back in his leather chair and steepled his fingers. "I can have our people run cross-checks and see if Rahman Uday comes up in connection with the biological and chemical warfare program."

Mike Callan shook his head from side to side. "Maybe you do have enough to swoop up Uday and hide him away till he gets well enough to spill his guts about what he was up to."

"Like you said, we don't know if we'd get any more from him that way. It might hamper getting what we need out of him. Better that Dale continue doing what he can to see what comes up in Uday's therapy sessions."

Ray stood up and went to the window.

"This has the feeling of something spinning out of control. We just can't see it yet," he said over his shoulder.

"I don't know about that," Callan said. "You've got good people on the ground . . . let it play out a little."

"We've got a lot of information on the biological and chemical program from Hussein Kamel's debriefing. It's been an administration priority . . ."

"You've got a little more, now. See what comes up."

"Right," Ray Dalton said. "We'll see what comes up."

## TORTURE REHABILITATION CENTER, UNIVERSITY OF MINNESOTA CAMPUS, MINNEAPOLIS, MINNESOTA

The best time for a raid is in the darkest hours of the night, in those hours right before daylight, when the body's rhythm is at its slowest, and the brain struggles in the landscape between dream and waking. It's an old military axiom that you want to strike when the enemy is at his weakest, and it's at night that the defender is weakest.

Jimmy Harrison kept that in mind as he walked the perimeter around the center at 3 A.M. He struggled to keep his mind focused and alert as he patrolled. He and Greg Ford—who was inside, sitting outside the door of Rahman Uday's bedroom—were working the 6 P.M. to 6 A.M. shift. Dale Miller and Charley Payne were both sleeping in the spare patient bedroom the detail had turned into a security ready room.

Harrison stretched both hands over his head as he walked and shook them down to keep the blood flowing. Earlier in the evening he'd gone through his own workout between patrolling the perimeter: working with a rubber resistance unit, countless push-ups and chair dips and sit-ups and crunches to keep himself toned and tuned up, ready for what might come their way. It also fought the boredom of the protection lifestyle. He smiled wearily as he thought of all the starry-eyed rookies who came in on the VIP protection circuit, expecting to be taking on terrorists in between fine dinners at the best hotels. It didn't take long for reality to sink in, and many, in fact most, grew disenchanted with standing outside hotel rooms and pissing in potted plants because the principal was too cheap to hire enough protection. But for those who had the right stuff, and stuck it out and worked their way up the ladder, there were the gigs the rookies dreamed about, and a man could make a decent living with his earnings and still have a good time on the boss's dime.

This was a pretty good gig. A real world threat, which helped to keep everything in focus and get a bit of the old adrenaline flowing. The pay was very good. Harrison and Ford were pulling down one thousand dollars a day each plus their minimal expenses, and Miller was a good team leader. Harrison and Ford, in their private conversations, had given him a thumbs-up and another for the second in command, Charley Payne. They thought that there should be more BGs on the detail, but agreed that whoever was footing the bill had hired the very best, and having four of the best beat having eight of the second team.

He paused to look up at the little hill. All in all, it was a good gig.

• • •

Marie Garvais studied the man walking the perimeter. She wore night-vision goggles that dropped down over her eyes and rendered everything she saw in shades of green. The ambient light from the stars and the nearby streetlights was sufficient to illuminate her target brightly. The MP-5 submachine gun she carried had three illumination sources mounted beneath the barrel: a high-powered flashlight, a laser designator, and an infrared light. She could choose which one she wanted by sliding the fingers of her support hand along the forearm stock of the MP-5 and pushing one of three pressure switches.

Marie noted that the man wasn't wearing night vision or carrying a long gun. She'd have been surprised if he had, as he was a civilian providing protection, or so her intelligence briefing had told her. She looked over at the rest of her team. Isabelle lay flat on the grass with her partner, a Frenchman named Andre, and Marie's partner, a Belgian named Dougard, lay beside her within arm's reach. Marie was the planner, and she figured four operators with submachine guns, striking at night, were sufficient. So far they had only seen two bodyguards working, and the surveillance team had confirmed that they had only seen two bodyguards as well. A ratio of two-to-one was close; she would have preferred three-to-one, but chose to rely on speed and violence of action, like any good special operator.

And of course, surprise.

Marie watched the man stroll along the grounds and go around the back of the Victorian house. She waited till she saw the flare of light as he opened the back door to go back in, then signaled silently to her team. The assassins drew up on line, shoulder to shoulder with five meters between them, and began their stealthy approach to the house. They approached from the side of the house, skirting the little hill that provided them some cover from observation, and moved carefully from shadow to shadow, submachine guns at the ready, fingers hovering over their infrared illumination switches. They moved like deadly shadows, figures of the night stalking carefully forward, the muzzles of their weapons tracking each possible location for an opponent.

The team came on line at the side of the house, where the shadows came together from the lights on the front and rear of the house.

They were ready.

• • •

Harrison took a bottle of water out of the kitchen refrigerator and walked down the hallway to where Ford sat outside Uday's room.

"Here you go, bro," he said, handing his partner the bottle of water. "You got to take a leak?"

"Yeah," Ford said. "Thanks."

Ford took the bottle of water and set it down beside the chair, stood and stretched the kinks out, then walked down the hallway to the handicap-accessible bathroom. He went in and turned on the light.

• • •

The light from the bathroom window washed over Isabelle and Andre; the sudden brightness caused a flare in their night-vision optics, causing Andre to stumble for a moment and catch himself with one hand against the wall of the house.

• • •

Ford felt rather than heard the contact outside the bathroom. He zipped up his fly and turned off the light, then slipped back into the hallway.

"There's someone outside," he hissed to Harrison. "Right outside the bathroom window."

Harrison drew his pistol, then opened the door and looked in at Uday—who slept soundly—then stood outside the door, his pistol held in a low ready. Ford drew his own pistol and went swiftly down the hallway and opened the door into the converted bedroom. He shook Dale's foot and said, "Dale? We've got company."

Dale sat bolt upright, blinking off his sleep. His transition from sleep to alertness was instantaneous. He slid his feet into his semi-laced boots and stood up. Charley was right with him, opening his eyes first and taking it all in, then sliding his own shoes on. The two of them were already dressed in loose-fitting street clothes under their light blankets.

Dale opened the closet and took out two civilian AR-15s with short barrels and a flashlight mounted beneath each barrel. He handed one to Ford and one to Charley. The two operators took the carbines and charged the weapons, pulling the handles back and letting them go forward with sharp clacks.

"Those are stoked with hollow points," Dale said. "They'll break up in the walls, so remember that if you have to shoot through anything."

"Roger that," Ford said. He ducked back out into the hallway. Harrison saw him coming and nodded.

Charley and Dale came out into the hallway, weapons at the ready. They moved quietly and quickly to vantage points in the hallway, then crouched down with their weapons covering the back door and the front entranceway.

They were ready.

• • •

Outside, Marie cursed silently. Andre covered the lit bathroom window, which went out quickly. Marie took stock of the team, all in position, and weighed her options. There was no sign of an alarm or any indication that someone had heard Andre fall against the building. She briefly considered calling it off to be safe and coming back another night, but dismissed the thought. She waved the team forward and they moved in a cautious line behind her as she went around the side of the house to the rear kitchen door. She paused, then carefully, setting each foot down delicately, mounted the stairs to the back door. She tried the handle. Locked. The doorjamb was reinforced, as she had expected. She covered the door with her submachine gun and waved Dougard forward and pointed at the lock.

Dougard came forward and let his submachine gun dangle from its straps. He reached into the canvas courier bag he wore tightly across his back and shoulders and took out a small explosive charge, a lock cutter. He set it on the door between the doorknob and the jamb, then turned a switch and stepped back. Marie raised her hand and counted with her fingers the five seconds.

The charge detonated with a loud bang that rang through the dark and Marie threw open the door and led her assault team into the darkened house.

• • •

Even though they were ready for an attack, the sudden explosion and flash of the detonation jarred Dale and his crew; but now they knew there was an attack and which direction it was coming from. Harrison ducked into Uday's room, threw the big man to the floor, and covered him. Ford covered his arc, which provided security back toward the front entrance, leaving Charley and Dale to cover the assault coming from the rear of the house. Dale extended his firing hand, his Browning High Power in his fist, and reached with his other hand for the light switch that controlled the hallway lights. He hit the lights and then put both hands on his weapon and began to acquire targets.

• • •

The sudden flash of light drove fear like a spike into Marie's stomach; the sudden lights flared and blurred her vision in the night optics she and her team wore. Worst of all was the realization that the element of surprise was lost and she was running into a prepared group of gunfighters.

Through the optics she saw the dim shape of men crouched in the hallway; she brought her submachine gun up and fired a three-round burst at the first of them.

• • •

Charley saw the submachine guns and pressed his AR-15 into his shoulder and rolled the trigger. One shot, one squeeze, but he had to attain fire superiority right away, and he pulled the trigger quickly, *crack crack crack* as fast as he could across the front of the approaching gunmen.

Dale took his time and put his front sight on the chest of the lead assaulter and double-tapped the leader, then tracked his sights onto the next one even as they fired at him.

• • •

Marie felt Dougard press up beside her and the two of them opened up full-auto down the hall despite their hampered vision. Surprise was lost and violence of action was their only hope at this stage. That meant superiority of firepower. They were the only two inside and they faced a wall of rifle fire from the AR-15s. Marie stumbled as two bullets slammed into her chest; the heavy body armor she wore absorbed and dissipated the blow, but it still felt as though someone had stabbed an iron pool cue into her chest at close range. She felt Isabelle behind her steady her with one hand even as she opened up full-auto with her MP-5.

"Fall back!" Marie cried. "Fall back!"

• • •

Charley saw one of the assaulters, the point man, stumble, and then shout, "Fall back!"

It sounded like a woman.

• • •

Marie and Dougard retreated out the door, emptying their magazines on full-auto as they went. Doors and woodwork splintered down the hallway, and one light went out. The two of them, reloading on the run, ran past Andre and Isabelle, who covered them as they came.

"Back!" Marie shouted. She led the way, running and stumbling a bit from the pain in her chest, to the rally point she'd designated on the far side of the little hill beside the center.

• • •

Charley and Dale stood shoulder to shoulder, covering the back door.

"Secure the principal!" Dale shouted.

"Roger that," Ford shouted back. He moved till his back was directly against the door to Uday's room.

"I've got him!" shouted Harrison.

There was shouting and screaming from the other rooms and the upstairs.

Harrison and Ford stayed poised to defend Uday's room, while Charley and Dale moved forward, each covering the other, till they were at the back door. A string of bullets cut through the door, forcing them back into the relative safety of the hallway.

• • •

"Immediate evacuation!" Marie said into the handset of her portable radio. Just outside the grounds of the center, Marika Tormay and her partner started the two minivans they waited in. Moments later, scrambling through the bush, the assault team, all four members, came into the clearing where the vehicles waited. They went, two by two into each vehicle, and then drove slowly away, heading away from where the responding police units from the campus police would come.

• • •

"Are they gone?" Charley said.

"They're outside and moving away," Dale said. "Ford! Call the campus police!"

"Roger that!" Ford called back. He took his cell phone out of his pocket, and rested the rifle against the wall while he dialed direct the dispatch center for the campus police.

"Campus police, what is your emergency?"

"This is a private security detail at the Torture Rehabilitation Center at Sixteen-fifteen River Road," Ford said. "There's been an attempted home invasion by several armed attackers and shots have been fired."

"Do you need an ambulance?"

"Not at this time, just police."

"Please stay on the line."

Ford relayed directions to the dispatcher, who guided the responding units in to where Dale stood, his pistol holstered, waving them in. It took less than five minutes for the police to arrive in full force. As the ranking officer came to meet him, Dale said to Charley, "This is going to take a while."

• • •

Several miles away, Marie Garvais listened to the responding units on a portable police scanner. Satisfied that there was no description of their vehicles, she sat back on the seat to ease the pain in her rib cage where two bullets had hit. She opened the vest and dug out the two slugs: pistol bullets, nine millimeter it looked like. The rifle bullets would have penetrated her vest, but the rifleman had been firing high down the hallway and her team had taken no direct hits. She had been struck in the chest by someone firing a pistol, Dougard had a round graze his hand, and Isabelle and Andre were untouched.

The minivans crossed a bridge over the river into a suburb of St. Paul, and drove to a house with a two-car garage. The automatic garage doors opened as the vans pulled into the garage, and then the doors closed. The assault team dismounted. Isabelle came to Marie and said, "Are you all right? Are you injured?"

"I'll be bruised," Marie said. She touched Isabelle lightly on her face. "I'll be fine, really."

"Is everyone else all right?" Isabelle said.

Dougard held up his hand and said, "Only a graze, not bad. If you would dress it . . . ?"

Marika Torkay came forward with a first-aid kit. "I'll do it," she said.

Marie massaged her chest, then took off the vest and examined the widening bruise beneath her black T-shirt. Isabelle touched the bruise, lightly, with one finger.

"Are you sure you didn't break a rib?" she asked.

"I'm all right. It was pistol fire. We weren't expecting that rifle."

"They were professionals," Isabelle said. "They were ready very quickly and they handled it well. They didn't follow us outside; they stayed put and called the police."

"Yes," Marie said. "We'll have to find out more. They'll move him now to some place harder. Marika, can you find out more about the team?"

"I don't know," Marika said, finishing the dressing of Dougard's hand. "It's not as though we can get employment there, it's a very small and handpicked staff. I don't think it's possible."

"Do you have someone watching now?"

"There's one of our people with a video camera in the woods; they've probably pulled out so that they won't get caught up in the police sweep. They'll be checking the ground for clues."

"Have them do what they can," Marie said.

85

"Of course," Marika said. "But there won't be much to do now that the police are there."

Marie muttered under her breath and went into the kitchen. She took an ice-cube tray out of the freezer and emptied it into a plastic garbage bag, then wadded it up and stuck it beneath her black T-shirt against her spreading bruise.

Isabelle followed her in.

"Mistakes happen," Isabelle said. "Andre couldn't help it. And the intelligence we had didn't say there were more bodyguards with rifles. We were expecting a handful of sleeping men with pistols. This is a very professional operation."

"It doesn't make me feel any better. This is a hard target that has just gotten much harder. I'm not giving up on this."

"We have to back off until they get better intelligence for us, Marie. We can't just go running a gauntlet of fire each time hoping to get him."

"You're right, but it doesn't make me feel better. We'll have to consider something beside close-quarters assault."

"You sound so dangerous . . . 'close quarters assault,' indeed."

Marie laughed, and reached out and draped an arm around her lover's neck.

"Come here," she said. "Massage these ribs for me."

TORTURE REHABILITATION CENTER, UNIVERSITY OF
MINNESOTA CAMPUS, MINNEAPOLIS, MINNESOTA

As soon as she was notified by a call that woke her, Dr. Rowan Green rushed to the center. Her identification got her through the first perimeter and into the confusion of police vehicles parked outside the center. She saw Dale Miller, dressed in rumpled clothes, talking with several police officers. After she parked her car, she hurried to him.

"Is Mr. Uday all right?" she said.

Dale nodded. "He's all right. No injuries." He said to the police officers, "Anything else?"

"No," a sergeant said. "You can go back inside. If we have anything else, we can find you in there."

Dale followed Dr. Green into the center. She walked around the back and lingered for a moment, looking at the blackened back door, riddled with bullet holes and blackened from the explosive charge that had shattered the lock. Then she hurried down the hall to Uday's room, where Rahman Uday sat in his armchair, curiously formal. Harrison stood behind him, while Ford stood guard outside the door.

"Are you all right, Rahman?" Dr. Green said.

Uday nodded slowly, once. "They want the One."

Dale eased into the room behind Dr. Green and studied the quiet psychotic. "Are you the One?"

"I am not the One," Uday said. "The One is the One. But I have seen the One."

"Who is the One?" Dale said.

"He will bring the sad holiday," Uday said. "Men with guns are with him. Like tonight."

"The sad holiday, it's men with guns?" Dale said.

"No," Uday said. "It's a sad holiday. When the blooming comes."

"When the blooming comes," Dale said. "What does that mean?"

PART 2

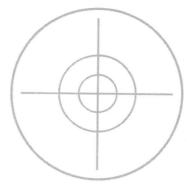

## RAY DALTON'S RESIDENCE, FAIRFAX, VIRGINIA

A lifetime of phones ringing in the night had conditioned Ray to come wide awake from deep sleep at the first ring. He opened his eyes and reached for the phone, but not before looking over at the empty space in the bed beside him.

"Dalton," he said.

Mike Callan's voice was tinny over the phone. "I take it you haven't had your coffee yet."

"What's happened?"

Callan gave him a short, succinct briefing on the attempt at the Torture Center.

"So they made the hit," Dalton said. "They had some good intel."

"Not good enough," Callan said. "They weren't expecting our crew. Our boys did a good job. There were at least four shooters with buzz guns and night vision. Our guys got into one of them. None of ours got touched."

"No injuries?"

"Not a one. The center is shot up, and the staff is shaken. It's time to get Uday out of there."

"What does his doctor say?"

"She doesn't think anyone is going to get any more out of him right now. The attack didn't even faze him, that's how out of touch he is. She thinks he can be moved to a facility where he has medication management and therapeutic support and he'd be no worse off than he is there. She thinks that he poses a danger to the other patients as long as he's there. They want him out."

"Do you have a safe house there?"

"Dale planned for that contingency. He's got a buddy, a retired master sergeant out of SF, with a farm down in Decatur, Illinois. It's about ten to twelve hours south of the Twin Cities. His pal has run some training courses for Agency people down there. It's near a good-sized town but out in the country, no close neighbors, got his barns and outbuildings set up for garages and dormitories, even got a shooting range. His neighbors mind their business and they leave him alone. Dale says we can put Uday down there and bring in our own medicos to work on him. Then the detail can go to a much harder posture without anybody seeing it."

"Do it. What do you need from me?"

"Just keep signing the checks. We're going to bring in more shooters and that will get expensive."

"Whatever they need, they'll get." Ray paused. His room began to lighten with early-morning sun. "Do you think Dale would talk to me at this point?"

"No need to get him riled up right now," Callan said. "I don't see the point. That's what cutouts are for." He paused. "Right?"

Ray was quiet for a moment, then said, "You're right. Let me know how it develops."

"Just keep signing the checks, Ray. I'll take care of the rest."

AMSTERDAM, THE NETHERLANDS

Youssef bin Hassan killed time wandering the cobblestone streets of Amsterdam. It was a bright and warm summer day, and the sun felt good against his bare arms. He wandered the twisting streets of the Jordaan District, pausing to peer through dirty windows into bars brown with nicotine stains, looking up at the gabled row houses leaning up against each other, following the sinuous winding of the canals and watching the tourist boats go by. He stopped at a cyber café and checked his e-mail, but there was nothing for him. After some time, he stopped outside of a plain-fronted building with a sign that said HOMELESS SHELTER. There was a small group of unwashed men lingering in front, who looked Youssef up and down. He ignored them, as he'd learned to ignore the many homeless in Amsterdam. The liberal Dutch welfare policies ensured that all the homeless could have a roof over their head, something to eat, and a blanket to cover themselves. This was such a place.

Youssef went in. A short plump woman, her blond hair braided in cornrows, stood behind the front counter. She looked up and smiled at Youssef.

"Can I help you?" she said.

"I was wondering if you ever needed volunteer help," Youssef said.

"We can always use help," the woman said. "Do you want to sign up?"

"Could you show me around?" Youssef said. "Give me an idea of what is needed?"

"I can give you the tour," she said. She placed a sign on the counter that said BACK IN TEN MINUTES, then came out around the counter. She stood only as high as Youssef's shoulder. "Come on then."

She showed him the commons room, where two televisions blared news commentary and rock videos, and old sofas and folding chairs provided seating. Then she took him into a dormitory-style sleeping area, with double bunk beds, battered dressers, and a small green locker for each bed. Beside the sleeping area there was a supply room, where blankets were neatly stacked beside a half door.

"They get fresh linen every night?" Youssef said.

"No," the woman said. "They get a blanket when they check in, and we change the sheets twice a week."

Youssef lingered behind when the woman went out, then brought out his atomizer and sprayed a fine mist across the stack of blankets and sheets. It took only a heartbeat. Then he followed her out.

"What about during the winter?" he said. "Do you give them coats?"

"Yes," the woman said. "In here." She pointed at another door, paused, and then opened it to show him the racks of donated coats inside the room. "If they don't have a coat, we'll give them one."

Youssef walked down the aisle formed by several racks of coats, running his hand along it. He touched the atomizer briefly each time as he walked, his body obscuring the actions of his hand from the woman behind him. He turned and walked back and said, "You are very generous in this country."

"Where are you from?" she asked.

"My family is from Saudi Arabia."

"We have some Muslims on the staff."

Youssef raised his eyebrows. "Really?"

"One man is Palestinian. We also have a family that comes in and works together when they donate time; they are from Jordan. The husband is a doctor here."

They returned to the front counter.

"Well," the woman said. "Are you interested?"

"Yes," Youssef said. "Let me think about it for a while."

"We'll be here," she said, going back behind the counter and taking down the sign. "We could use your help . . . and you'd meet some people."

"That would be good."

"If you don't mind me saying so, you seem lonely," she said. "My name is Britta. Come by anytime you like."

"Britta," he said, rolling the consonants over his tongue. "I'm pleased to meet you, Britta. My name is . . . Youssef. Youssef bin Hassan."

"Youssef bin Hassan . . . Youssef is Arabic for Joseph, isn't it?"

"Yes, that would be my name in English," he said. "Joseph."

"Joseph, the father of Jesus, who brought a miracle into the world. Maybe you'll bring a miracle into the world?" Britta said. She smiled. "Helping someone, maybe?"

Youssef flushed as though slapped.

"I have to go now," he said, stammering.

"Come back anytime," Britta said. "You're welcome for coffee or tea."

"Yes," Youssef said. "I'll be back."

He hurried out the door, leaving Britta looking puzzled. He stood outside for a moment in the bright light, a breeze blowing slightly, the sun warm on his upturned face. He felt water at the corner of his eyes and blinked them rapidly as he walked away and put distance between himself and the homeless shelter. What was wrong with him that other people saw his loneliness so easily? He'd been trained better than that. The woman was harmless and had meant nothing, but her simple gestures of kindness had struck deep in him.

He wandered aimlessly, steering away from the cafés thick with the smell of hashish and marijuana where clusters of people his own age gathered to smoke and to laugh. He thought of how good it would be to have his five daily prayers with someone else, instead of always being alone in his room. It felt so far away for him, the time-less time of his childhood, the prayers with his family and friends. He had not suffered as so many in the Sudanese training camps had, not like the Palestinians or some of the mujaheddin who had fought the Soviets in Afghanistan. His had been an easy youth, growing up with the wealth of his family protecting him from the troubles of the world outside their villa walls. He'd grown to feel guilty about his wealth and that protection as he'd gotten older, gone to school and gone abroad, and seen for himself how the rest of the world lived. That made him an easy target for the Al-Bashir recruiters, who thought an English-educated Saudi with a trust fund was an impor-tant acquisition. First he'd donated money, then the recruiters at the mosque he'd attended urged him to study with them privately, and then came the offer of the training.

He'd gone, excited with the prospect of doing something, and naively thinking that he would be just another soldier in the cause. But the imams and the leadership cadre had other plans for him.

He was, after all, the One.

## ENROUTE TO DOUBLE O FARM, DECATUR, ILLINOIS

The inside of the chartered turboprop felt cramped and small to Charley Payne; he was used to civilian jetliners and military aircraft. The roar of the engines was too loud, and the one lone flight attendant had to hunker down when she came through the narrow aisle to offer them peanuts and coffee. Two seats in front of him, Dale Miller was sleeping soundly, twisted sideways in his seat. Directly across the aisle was a male private nurse hired to accompany Rhaman Uday, who sat next to the window and stared out, as he had done since they had departed Minneapolis. Behind him, the rest of the twenty-one seats were empty.

Time in aircraft always passed too slowly. Charley had come to loathe air travel, having spent too many hours in too many aircraft. He would have preferred to have driven with Ford and Harrison and the new members of their augmented team. Dale had chosen to keep Uday under wraps while the team deployed into Central Illinois, and only then move him quickly via chartered aircraft into his new safe house.

Charley had never been in this part of the country before. They had left the rolling hills and lakes of Minnesota behind, and they were now well into the true prairie of the heartland. Long flat fields, remarkably square and uniform from the air, with giant sprinklers in the center of each square, marched in neat unison off to the horizon. Corn and soybeans were what Dale said they grew out here. Thousands of acres of corn and soybeans, and every so often small towns dedicated to the processing and shipping of them. The turboprop flew low enough so he could see cars on the narrow two-lane roads below.

He leaned his head out into the aisle and caught the eye of the flight attendant. He held up his empty soda can and gestured for another. She smiled and brought him another full can of cola and said, "Can I get you anything else?"

"A bigger seat and a faster flight, if you've got any of those up there," Charley said, favoring her with a smile.

She laughed and said, "Tall as you are, it's no wonder you're uncomfortable. It won't be long now. We're almost there."

"Make this route often?"

"I grew up out here. In Kankakee, which you'll be going over in a few minutes. I had a girlfriend in college, she was from Decatur."

"What's the town like?"

"It's a good size, about one hundred thousand people. Mostly blue-collar, food-processing and they used to have one of the big Firestone plants there. Not much to do there."

"The nightlife is lacking, then?"

She laughed and flipped her short black hair with one hand. "Yes, the nightlife is lacking."

"Will you be staying over?"

"No, sorry," she said. "We deplane you all, and then we're right back to our base."

"You do a lot of these?"

"Lots of medical transport," she said. "Most of the time we're going to Rochester, Minnesota to the Mayo Clinic there, but I've been on some trips out to Johns Hopkins in Baltimore and other places. It's easy work, not like hustling to keep a full cabin happy."

"I was hoping we'd have a drink," Charley said.

"Not this time, cowboy," the flight attendant said. The aircraft bumped in the air slightly, and she caught herself with one hand. "I've got to get to work."

She went back to the front of the cabin and tapped twice on the cockpit door, then entered the cockpit. Charley shifted his legs again uncomfortably. There just wasn't enough room in the seat for him. He looked up at Dale with envy; the younger man had the operator's knack for sleeping whenever possible against those long intervals they might have to go without sleep. Charley had that knack, too, but being so much taller made it harder to get comfortable.

"We are very high," Uday said suddenly from across the aisle.

"Yes we are," the male nurse said. He was short and thin with pinched features and coal-black lank hair that gave him a cadaverous look.

"It is not high enough," Uday said.

"We're high enough. We're just fine," said the nurse.

Charley studied Uday with interest. The Iraqi was animated, looking out the window with interest, and mumbling to himself.

"Is it high enough for the One, Rhaman?" Charley said.

"It is too high for the One," Uday said. He looked around the cabin and fixed his lugubrious gaze on Charley. "The One would be inside. Not outside. The dissipation would not be sufficient."

"What dissipation?" Charley said.

"Particulate formation depends on the amount of moisture," Uday said in a matter-of-fact tone. "That was the problem in the sad holiday. Many, many products and not enough consumers. The testing was long."

Charley looked up the aisle to where Dale still slept.

"What is he talking about?" the nurse asked.

"Shh," Charley said to the nurse. "What testing, Rhaman? Testing during the sad holiday?"

"Saddam wanted a sad holiday," Uday said. "We all wanted a sad holiday then. We celebrated after the testing. It was a nice party. Very clean. Everyone wanted a bath after the testing."

"What were they trying to wash off, Rhaman? What was the testing?"

Uday turned and looked out the window. "Testing. There were many tears during the testing. We had a sad party, inside. Inside it was very clean. We wore hats and masks, and pretended to be doctors. Doctors heal. We did not. Some of them tried, but they were lost. I became lost, too."

Charley leaned across the aisle and said softly, "What were the doctors doing, Rhaman? What were the doctors testing?"

"Smallpox," Uday said. "But the vesicles are not so small anymore. Not for the One."

• • •

The handoff at the Decatur airport was handled with military efficiency. As the turboprop taxied toward the general aviation terminal, two Chevy Suburbans with blacked-out windows wheeled across the tarmac and paced the aircraft to its parking spot. The doors on both vehicles opened and men spilled out, creating a rough perimeter around the front exit of the aircraft. As soon as the flight attendant let down the stairway, two men came up inside the cabin. Dale stood to meet them.

Greg Ford was the first in the door. "Hey Dale," he said. "Ready to move?"

Dale took down his single carry-on bag and said, "Let's roll."

Dale, Charley, Uday, and his nurse came down the stairwell. Two steps down and they were ringed with big men, who split the nurse off and put him in the rear vehicle. Uday, Charley, and Dale got into the lead Suburban along with two gunfighters, big silent men who wore photographer's vests to hide their handguns. Their vehicle led off the tarmac; the other vehicle, crammed with gunfighters and the cadaverous nurse, followed closely behind. The vehicles turned out onto the highway that paralleled the runway of the Decatur airport, and they moved briskly on their way.

Rows of corn and soybeans fell away on both sides of the highway as they went out into the country. Charley looked out the window and thought he'd never been in a place quite so flat, where the horizon fell away with nothing to break the eye except the occasional silo or house. He remained silent, as did the others, during the half-hour drive that took them well away from the city and out into the flat country. Eventually they turned onto a gravel county road that bisected a huge cornfield, and drove along in a cloud of dust for a mile or more before they came to a roadway that turned at a right angle from the road and went toward a farmhouse and a collection of outbuildings.

As they drove closer, Charley saw other things. A berm had been bulldozed up to provide a backstop for a shooting range right where the front lawn of the house should have been. There was a twenty-five-yard range with a variety of handgun targets set up, and there were rifle benches set up on a hundred-yard range.

"Nice thing about country living," Charley said. "You can go right out in your front yard and bust some caps."

Greg Ford and his partner laughed. Dale grinned.

"Oh, yeah," Charley said.

They rolled slowly by the outbuildings and then stopped in a cloud of dust in front of the house. A screened-in porch ringed the house. Standing on the front porch in bib overalls, an olive-drab T-shirt, and combat boots was a big man, stocky and built like an oversized fireplug.

"That's the man?" Charley said.

"That's him," Dale said. He opened the door and got out and called to the man, "Hey Rhino! What say?"

The big man grinned and came forward, his hand extended.

"How the hell are you, Dale?" he said.

Dale turned to Charley who followed him to the stairs. "Charley Payne, meet John Onofrey, best known as Rhino to his friends and enemies alike."

Charley shook the big man's hand; his hand was lost in the shovel-like mitts of the other man.

"Good to meet you, Rhino," he said.

"Likewise, Charley," the big man said. "Welcome to the Double O Farm."

"Seems like you've got all the comforts of home: gun range, plenty of privacy . . ." Charley said. "Where do you keep the bikini-clad beauties and the booze?"

Rhino laughed. "I'm a bachelor farmer," he said. "There're some girls in town, but I don't think you guys will have much time for that."

"I can only dream," Charley said.

"Let's get you settled," Rhino said.

After showing Charley and Dale their room—right beside a fully equipped operations room complete with radios and television monitors that covered the approaches to the house—the range, and the outbuildings that served as dormitories for the rest of the team, Rhino introduced them to the new members of the team. There were twelve gunfighters including the drivers and Charley and Dale. Rhino didn't count himself in the number as his job was, as he said, to oversee the overseers.

"You do a lot of this?" Charley asked.

"I've put some people up before," Rhino affirmed. "And some of the folks I've had out here for training had special security needs. Those gigs pay for the equipment . . . I've got my pension and these gigs, and I don't eat much, so most of what I make goes back into the facility. I had that range built last year, told the contractor I wanted a place to shoot my guns. Illinois is not the most gun-friendly state, but  out here is the sheriff's country, and I know that old boy and we leave each other alone . . . the old ways still apply out here."

"People are good out here, then?" Charley said.

"Yep," Rhino said. "This is the last bastion of civility in an uncivil world. Folks around here mind their own business, help out when you need it, and leave you alone unless you feel like company."

"I envy you," Charley said. "You got good living out here."

"Well," Rhino said, "I'll leave you two alone and make sure our guest Uday is all set up. Do you want to keep the nurse? Two of these young shooters are SF medics and they can do anything that nurse can."

"He's used to the nurse, and the nurse to him," Dale said. "We'll let them be, Rhino."

"Right-o, then," Rhino said. "I'll be out on the porch later. If you'd like, the early evening is good whiskey-sipping time."

Dale and Charley watched the big man go inside and shut the door behind him. They pulled two chairs together and sat out on the porch and watched one of the team walking along the range and then around to the side of the house.

"Are you going to put patrols out?" Charley said.

"We've got the video coverage," Dale said. "I've got a ready team standing by. We'll put light patrol coverage out at night and enhance the video coverage with the infrared equipment Ford and Harrison brought."

"State of the art," Charley murmured. "So what do you think about what Uday said on the plane?"

"Smallpox? That's a scary thought. Uday was an associate of Hussein Kamel, Saddam's son-in-law. He was in charge of the biological warfare program and we know that Iraq got smallpox samples from the old Soviet Union's Biopreparat organization."

"I thought smallpox was wiped out."

"In the world at large, it has been. It was the first disease the World Health Organization considered eliminated by aggressive vaccination and surveillance. Supposedly the only two samples left in the world were in the Soviet Union Biopreparat and our Center for Disease Control. But that's what makes smallpox such a danger . . . there's no pool of immune people since we haven't vaccinated against it since the seventies. It's highly contagious . . . you only have to get within six to ten feet of an infected patient to pick up airborne pathogens, and there's over a thirty percent fatality rate in the standard bug. That doesn't take into account any improvements that the genetic engineers might want to make."

"I hate the thought of that."

"You and me both. I'll pass that on to Callan; I'm sure he'll want to look at that angle. I wish we could make more sense out of Uday when he has these clear spells. Keep on it, and see if you can get anything else out of him."

"Of course, dude. I'll do what I can, take my meals with him and all that."

"That would be good, Charley."

Charley nodded and propped his feet up on the railing, the soles of his SWAT boots resting against the fine-mesh screen that did nothing to hide the view of the sprawling cornfields.

"What do you want to do about the Twins?" he said.

"I've been thinking about that very thing," Dale said. "I'm wondering if you're thinking the same thing I'm thinking."

"Those two have had two fair whacks at us. One for them, one for us. They're too damn good for us to sit around and wait for them to come back."

"This isn't the same situation as the Torture Center," Dale said. "We've got information security buttoned up tight here. There're no leaks and no exposure to the public like there was at the center. There's no way they could have tracked us here. And even if they did, we could fight off a reinforced company with these guys. This is a real good crew."

"It goes against my nature to let them get away with just a little bruising," Charley said.

"So what are you thinking?" Dale said.

"I'm thinking you got a world-class crew in a hardened facility . . . I think Uday will be just fine here. I think you should have Callan bring in his medicos and have them on-site, buttoned up just like the shooters, and have him wring what he can out of Uday. The kid-gloves treatment is fine and humane and all that, but I've come to believe that Uday is sitting on something else . . . something operational. And I think you and I should go pay the Twins a visit and put them off."

"Take them out?"

"That's a bit personal," Charley said. "Though it wouldn't cost me any sleep. I'm thinking more of bracing them in their home territory, let them know they're vulnerable, too, and warn them off. They're pros, they know they've missed their chance."

"Why bother to warn them off?"

"Well, if Callan's people have such deep pockets, maybe we could just pay the Twins to find out just who is putting up such big bucks to have Uday whacked."

"I doubt they'd go for that . . . they work all over the board as it is and they wouldn't want it out that they turned over a client to the US for money."

"Why not? It's done all the time. That could be part of the package, our silence on the matter."

Dale nodded in thought. There was merit to the idea, and he too chafed at the passive role called for in close protection. He didn't want to sit around in the cornfields and wait for trouble to come his way. He wanted to take the fight to his opponents. He knew who they were, and they were formidable women. But they were women with a base in a city that was known to the special operations community, and they were professionals.

Therein might be the key.

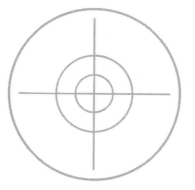

## FAIRFAX, VIRGINIA

Ray Dalton held a secure cellular phone to his ear while he rested in his golf cart on the Sunnyside Golf Club course. Mike Callan's voice was slightly distorted by the encryption equipment that ensured that their conversation remained private.

"So what do you think, Ray?" Callan said. "A little direct action? Is that what you were herding Dale toward?"

Ray was quiet for a moment. Then he laughed softly. He looked out over the golf course at his next lie. "I'll say this . . . I wouldn't be disappointed if the Twins were taught a lesson, even taken off the books."

"So what's it going to be, paymaster?" Callan said. "Time to cry havoc and let slip the leash on the dogs of war?"

"Yes," Dalton said. "I think it's time."

"I think you've been playing me, Ray. I don't like that."

"I haven't been playing you."

"This is a different game now, you give Dale his hunting license. That's putting him out there as a deniable operator. That's not running a protection detail."

"Dale can handle it."

"It'll be him and Payne."

"Payne was a good operator."

"You're going to have to let your cover slip, Ray. They'll need assistance that doesn't come easily from any security company—even us."

"You have all the necessary information, equipment, and resources to make this happen . . . after all, we've made sure of that, haven't we?"

Callan was silent. There was only the hum of the phone in Ray's ear.

"Yeah," Callan said finally. "I guess we have made sure of that."

"Then let's get it done," Dalton said.

ATHENS, GREECE

At night, the proud pillars and colonnades of the Acropolis are lit like a beacon atop the hill it stands on in Athens. Picking out the lights of the ancient temple from the sea of lights that lap around it is a pleasant way to spend a few moments. The air on this night was, for once, clear enough to lend sharpness to the battered old pillars gleaming from the powerful lamps that illuminated them. In a high hotel room near the Plaka, a man stood and looked out his window and thought of the old English poem about Ozymandias, and the line, "How mighty are the fallen."

That line would soon apply to the Americans.

His face was long and saturnine, dominated by a hooked nose that gave him the look of a regal bird, a raptor of some kind. He stood at his window, his hands clasped behind his back, and looked out at the myriad points of light. It reminded him of his first trip to the United States, to New York City. He had gone with trepidation, as though he were going into the belly of a great beast. But there was much to admire in America, though the excess of western culture found its apex there. He was especially taken with the public libraries with their wealth of books on every possible subject; it was possible to be entirely self-educated if one could read and had a New York City Public Library card.

Athens had once been like that, a bright and shining beacon in a sea of darkness and ignorance. But its time had passed, and now it was the polluted capital of a third-rate state that made its living hawking the tarnished remains of its former glory. The government of Greece, while not entirely sympathetic to the cause of the handsome man, looked the other way at his coming and going. As long as no operations were conducted against Greek citizens or on Greek soil, the state security apparatus was content to keep a casual eye on the terrorist organizations that came and went. That made Athens a good place for the man, whose name was Ahmad bin Faisal, to do his business.

His business was terror.

Ahmad bin Faisal was the equivalent of a corporate vice-president in the Al-Bashir terrorist organization. He had only one specific tasking, a single job given him by the clerics that made up the board of directors of his organization, and he was here to meet with the single operative who comprised his tasking. After his flight from his home in Damascus, and after checking into his favorite Athens hotel, he'd enjoyed a walk around the Plaka before he returned to his room, where he waited for his guest.

There was a knock at the door, and he turned away from the window and went to greet his visitor.

"Hello, Youssef," bin Faisal said. He embraced the younger man, who stood stiffly, then returned the embrace. "You are well?"

"Yes, I am well, thank you," Youssef said.

Bin Faisal closed the door and ushered Youssef to a seat at the small table set up before the big window.

"Sit, my friend," bin Faisal said. "Have you eaten today?"

"Yes, thank you," Youssef said. "Would you have juice?"

"Of course," Faisal said. He took a small bottle from the minibar, opened it, and poured it into a glass. "Here you are."

"Thank you."

Bin Faisal stood and studied the young man sipping his orange juice. Youssef avoided his gaze, looking instead around the room and finally out the window at the lights of Athens.

"What is on your mind, Youssef?" Faisal said. "You seem troubled."

109

The younger man shrugged. "It is difficult to be alone."

"Yes. It is difficult to be alone. Only the best could do such a thing as you are doing."

"Surely there must be others," Youssef said. There was a hint of something like hope in his voice.

"No, my friend. There is only you. You are the One."

• • •

Later, Ahmad bin Faisal worried about his lone operative Youssef bin Hassan. Youssef was young and inexperienced, but his background and his demonstrated ability in the camp had marked him out as the one to be chosen for this most difficult of missions. The loneliness of work far from home and the dangers of that was dealt with in the training camps; most deep-cover operatives that went to America found ways to relieve their loneliness, often getting married as that was a way of establishing legal residency. But that was not an option in this case.

Bin Faisal hurried through security at the Athens airport, his long-practiced eye watching the guards for any undue interest in him. But there was nothing there, and he passed the soldiers with their submachine guns without another glance. He caught a direct flight to Damascus and in his comfortable first-class seat, he glanced over a few cryptic notes he'd taken during the debriefing of his field agent.

It was a risk to use the One as a cutout for the elimination of Uday, to be a go-between for communication with the hired assassins and bin Faisal, but it was easy work and allowed Youssef to stretch his wings in a foreign venue and practice the tasks he would perform in America. He'd done well, thinking of new ways to spread the genetically altered smallpox virus. Using the blankets of the homeless was a brilliant stroke; the long incubation period of the altered virus coupled with the conditions of the homeless in the United States would guarantee a widespread contagion occurring simultaneously in several locations.

Soon it would be time to provide the real virus to Youssef.

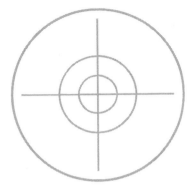

AMSTERDAM, THE NETHERLANDS

On a pathway that followed the sinuous curve of a canal, with row houses on either side, the windows gleaming brightly in the sun, Marie Garvais and Isabelle Andouille walked with their daughter. Ilse toddled between them, each mother holding a tiny hand. The little girl was dressed up for the day in a blue skirt and white blouse, a black beret on her head, and shiny black patent shoes with white socks. After passing a tobacco shop and a small appliance repair store, they came to an Italian gelato shop, a favorite stop for the family.

"Shall we have an ice?" Isabelle said.

"That would be good right now," Marie said.

They took their time selecting their flavors, the old man behind the counter smiling indulgently as he scooped a small peach cone for Ilse, who managed it with both hands, chocolate for Marie, and peach for Isabelle. They took their treats to the canal side and sat at a bench that looked over the waterway, a heavy chain linked between posts in front of them, and watched the passersby on the other side of the canal.

"Be careful, Ilse," Isabelle chided, taking a napkin from her pocket and brushing at a smear of gelato on Ilse's chin. "We don't want you to dirty your pretty dress."

"Have you thought more about what we should do with that contract?" Marie said.

Isabelle brushed the child's hair away from her face and tucked the loose ends under the beret.

"There we go," she said. "Now your hair won't get in the way." Isabelle brushed her own hair back and dipped her tongue delicately into her cone. "No. I haven't thought about it."

"There is no new intelligence," Marie said. "The target has disappeared . . . he was moved from the center, and our people were unable to determine when and how or where he was moved. The trail is cold, and we still have an open agreement with the Saudi."

"We earned our fee," Isabelle said. "They can keep the completion installment."

"They want us to go after him."

"I know that, Marie," Isabelle said. She licked at her cone. "I'm sorry."

"I told the cutout we couldn't do anything without better intelligence, and that we weren't going to spend our money doing the work-up . . . that wasn't the agreement and they know that. Money doesn't seem to be an object."

"I don't have a good feeling about this," Isabelle said. "We have made two high-profile operations, and whoever is providing protection for them is very good. Good enough to make me think that it's American intelligence who is protecting them, and we don't want to go up against them. They have long memories and deep pockets."

"The money could help us . . . we took some bad losses in our investment portfolio."

"I know the money could help us, Marie," Isabelle said. "But all the money we've made will be of no use if we're not there to spend it. And Ilse needs us. When is enough enough?"

"We're not there yet," Marie said. She crossed her legs at the ankles, then uncrossed them and brushed at her pants. "We need to do some more work."

"Then we should look at something close to home. I don't think we need to work this contract anymore. There is something larger at play here and we don't have enough of a picture . . . we've been exposed here and the problem is open-ended. We don't have enough information to mount another operation against that target."

"I told the cutout that. He's going to speak to his controller and see what information they can gather for us . . . and if they get enough, they want to know if we'll take it on, complete the contract."

Isabelle reached out and stroked the back of their child and was silent for a long time. Then she spoke.

"I'll do whatever we have to do, but I don't think we should try to complete this contract. We have upheld our end of the bargain and done the best we could do. Their intelligence was incomplete and contributed to the failure in Minneapolis. I don't understand their insistence on us completing the contract; we took only the first half of the contract payment and that they got full value for, considering their intelligence failure. There's something we don't know about, and I am afraid . . . afraid that they are setting us up to take the fall for them. I know I don't trust at the best of times, but this, this is something we must be careful for."

"Yes, we have to be careful," Marie said. "I'm sorry to be the one who must say it, but we need the work. There's nothing else on right now."

"Then perhaps we need to find something new."

"If there's work, there's work," Marie said. "If there isn't, there isn't. That's all there is to that."

"Yes," Isabelle said. She wrapped her arms around herself as though suddenly cold, even though she sat in full sunlight. "Let's put this aside, shall we? We'll discuss it more later. We're neglecting Ilse."

"Is that right, Ilse?" Marie said, stroking the child's face. Ilse laughed and smiled, her lips gleaming with peach gelato. "She hardly looks neglected."

Isabelle stood, took a napkin, and wiped Ilse's face. She plucked the soggy remnants of the cone from her daughter's fingers and wiped the sticky fingers with a Handiwipe she took from her purse.

"Let's go," Isabelle said. She took Ilse by the hand and began to walk away, leaving Marie on the bench.

"Isabelle? Isabelle?" Marie called. "Don't be like this."

"Come along, Marie," Isabelle said over her shoulder. "We are wasting a beautiful day."

Marie got to her feet and slowly followed her lover and her daughter.

## DOUBLE O FARM, DECATUR, ILLINOIS

Charley and Dale sat inside the screened-in porch of the big farm-house and watched the sun drop low in the west, casting long shadows across the packed dirt of the gun range.

"You know you can hear corn grow?" Dale said. "It cracks at night when it's growing."

"You grew up around here, didn't you?" Charley said.

"Right here in Decatur," Dale said. "Until I went into the army."

"Just a regular country boy, huh?"

Dale laughed. "Thank god for that."

"I'm a city boy myself."

"Where?"

"San Francisco mostly, then San Jose."

"Nice out there."

"Yeah, the city is sweet. I miss it sometimes, but I get back there to visit my family pretty often. Too damn expensive to live there anymore."

"I've heard that."

Charley nodded, then sipped at the small glass of whiskey, well iced, he held in his hand. "So what does Callan say about the Twins?"

"We're getting our hunting license," Dale said.

"Really?" Charley said. "Hunt as in find or hunt as in kill?"

"Don't know yet. What do you think?"

"They're pros, Dale. They knew the risks going in, but they've got powerful friends, lots of low people in high places. I think just warning them off is enough, now that they've blown their last shot at getting Uday. They didn't know who was protecting Uday, and they don't know that they're messing with the best. A good warning should be enough."

"What kind of message does that send? That you can take a whack at us and walk away from it?"

"You're certainly bloodthirsty," Charley said. "They obviously didn't know who they were going up against or they would have come heavier. They thought they had a superior grade of rent-a-cop. They've backed off and I don't think we'll see them again."

"The fact that they were operating on our soil is a factor to me."

"We're not operating for the G," Charley said. "We're protecting the client with his own funds, albeit through Callan."

"We're working for the G and you know it," Dale said. "We have been all along. Callan's a black company exec and always has been."

"Well," Charley said, sitting back in his chair and rolling his eyes in mock astonishment. "You think so?"

"There's something to Uday," Dale said. "This smallpox thing . . . Callan didn't say anything about passing that on to the right people . . . not that he would anyway to us."

"You're sticking your nose where you shouldn't, Dale," Charley said. "We get our checks from Callan and that's all we need to know. Need to know, remember that? As for teaching the Twins a lesson, I'm all for a visit to the fleshpots of Amsterdam. But they won't be easy to whack on their home turf and I don't like killing women anyway. Put my vote down for a stern warning."

Dale shifted in his seat. "Just warn them off?"

"That's what I'm saying. Anything else and we get into more trouble. That's direct action. That's not what we're getting paid for."

Dale stood and stretched his back, raising his arms above his head and stretching his palms toward the roof.

"I talk to Callan tonight," he said. "But I think we'll be taking a trip to Amsterdam. Just you and me, I think. That's enough for a warning."

"Wow," Charley said. "Does that mean you're going to listen to me?"

"Yeah," Dale said. "That's exactly what it means."

"You're finally learning," Charley said. "Old age and wisdom will beat out youthful enthusiasm every time."

"Fuck you," Dale said. He grinned and slapped Charley on the shoulder. "Get your old tired ass up and let's check on the troops."

Charley took a stick of gum out of his shirt pocket and unwrapped it carefully, saving the foil in his pocket. He popped the gum in his mouth after he hastily swallowed the last of his whiskey.

"Alcohol abuse," he said. "Let's go, fearless leader."

• • •

After a walking patrol of the perimeter and checking on the operators manning the camera monitors in the operations center, Dale and Charley went back out onto the porch. John Onofrey opened the front door and said, "We'll be eating pretty soon."

"Sounds good, Rhino," Dale said.

"All this and he cooks, too?" Charley said.

"You bet," the big man said. "Got a big pot of venison stew going and some fresh dinner rolls. We'll have us a feast. You want some more whiskey?"

"Maybe later," Dale said.

"Yeah, later," Charley said reluctantly.

Rhino laughed. "You don't sound so sure, Charley."

"No, that's fine," Charley said. "After dinner would be good."

Rhino went back into the house, letting the screen door slam behind him.

"That's a good man," Charley said.

"The best," Dale said.

"Do you ever miss the life?" Charley said.

"What do you mean?"

"The life," Charley said, waving his hand and taking everything in around him with the gesture. "This. Running and gunning."

Dale shrugged, then looked out at the lingering twilight. In the clear air, far from the lights of the city, a few stars could be seen.

"I mean, you've been out of the game for a while. Just like me. Are you glad to be back in it?" Charley said.

Dale pushed his chair back and kicked his feet up onto the railing beneath the screened portion of the porch. "I've got a woman back in Minneapolis. She's a detective with the PD, a real operator. She said something to me, when this gig came up, she said I needed engagement."

Charley laughed. "Maybe she was talking about the marrying kind."

"No. She said I needed a mission to give me something that I wasn't getting from training the cops. Something with teeth in it."

"So do you?"

"Yeah," Dale said. "I guess I've missed that part. I was so fed up with the way things were done, I just didn't want to have anything to do with the Outfit anymore. And that colored everything for me. I didn't even carry a gun for a while."

"That's serious."

"What about you? The life of a photographer give you everything you want? I guess not, since you're here."

Charley pursed his lips. Long lines, deep wrinkles, cut from his mouth to his cheeks. "We're a lot alike, bro. I got fed up with the Outfit, too, threw my hat in and moved on. But I had photography to fill that gap. There's always something missing when you leave something the way we left. There's a void that you have to fill up, or else the empty space calls for you to fill it up with the same damn thing. Photography does that for me. What do you fill yours with?"

Dale didn't hesitate in his answer. "Nina. My woman. She filled that void for me."

"Dangerous business, having women in that space. You have to have something of your own, and you never own a woman, at least not one worth keeping."

"You have someone?"

Charley laughed out loud and stomped his feet, once, on the floor. "Oh, women are one thing I have no shortage of, bro. I've got more than I need. But don't you think you need something besides your woman to give you purpose? It's putting a lot on her, that weight, whether she knows it or not."

"I never thought about it that way."

"Listen to the old gray dog here, Dale. I've been where you are before. I'm not saying that you have to get back in harness with the G. But men like us, we need to have something to do, and if training SWAT cops isn't giving you the juice, then you need to look around and find something that will. Something of your own."

"Something like this?"

"I don't know. It's what you want that's important. If you could do anything you wanted to do, and you didn't have to worry about money, what would you do? Where would you go?"

Dale raised his eyebrows in surprise and rocked back in his chair. "That's a good question."

"That's what determines the quality of our lives, man. The quality of the questions we ask ourselves."

"You surprise me."

"Didn't know I was such a philosopher, huh? Thought I was just another cock hound shooter?"

"Something like that."

"So what would you do?"

Dale drummed his fingers on the armrest of his chair and thought for a moment. "I think I'd be some kind of outdoor instructor, a counselor or something like that. Teach kids about camping and backpacking, spend a lot of time outdoors."

"Now see, I'd have never thought that for you. I thought maybe you'd be a cop, or maybe in the FBI, something like that."

"No," Dale said. "I don't think I'd be a good cop. I'd just want to shoot the bad guys."

Both men laughed, a clear sound in the night that surrounded them.

DOMINANCE RAIN HEADQUARTERS, FAIRFAX, VIRGINIA

Mike Callan lolled in the overstuffed armchair Ray Dalton kept for his visitors. A mug of expensive Jamaican Blue Mountain coffee steamed in his fist, and he cupped both hands around the mug to feel the warmth against his palms. Ray, in his orthopedic leather executive chair, rocked back and forth slightly behind his expansive desk.

"How far do you want them to go with this?" Callan said. "Are you giving them full license?"

"What does Dale say?"

Callan sipped his coffee, then said, "He's saying to warn them off. He says the Twins didn't know who they were going up against. They thought they just had private security hired by the family. He thinks telling them that the G's involved with Uday will back them off. The Twins are pros, they won't want to have a hassle with us."

"Damn right."

Callan narrowed his eyes and studied the other man intently. "Why do you want them dead?"

Ray stopped rocking in his chair. "They took out a source we were running in Venezuela. Joint project with the DEA, it was a money-laundering operation the narcos were running. Someone made our source and fingered him for the Twins. They took him out on a walk-up, their favorite modus operandi: one distracted him with a little skin, the other blew his brains out on the sidewalk in front of his house. His wife and kids were just inside the house, saw the whole thing, but the Twins let them be."

"The Twins don't hit families. They think it's unprofessional."

"Not much comfort to his wife and kids."

"Did they know he was a US asset?"

"Not as far as we know."

"Then clear your head, Ray. You're making it personal, not business. The Twins worked for us before. They stay away from our assets. They must have thought he was Venezuelan intelligence or narcotics, DISP or something."

"That's what it was."

"Let your field operator make the call, Ray. Dale knows what to do and Payne is top-shelf; you'd be hard-pressed to put together that good a crew. You always preach about keeping the personal out of operations. Who was this guy to you?"

"I met him . . . he was just a good young kid taking a lot of risks for not much payoff . . . You don't think we're better off having them both dead?"

"No, I don't. The Twins serve a purpose. We might need them again in the future. Put your feelings aside and let Dale and Charley warn off the Twins. Dale thinks he can persuade the Twins to let him know who they're working for, use the fact that the Twins were being run against the US without being told. He thinks they'll be pissed and willing, for a price, to finger who took out the contract on Uday. That would give us some insight into the mystery with this guy, and we need that."

"We do have some nasty pieces, don't we?"

"Smallpox is as nasty as it comes. You put together the pieces that Uday brought and it's starting to add up to a smallpox attack. You can bring in your medicos to Decatur and work on Uday, his rights and long-term treatment, well, you tell me how important they are in the face of that kind of threat. We've got great protection in place with good information security, we can launch Dale and Charley off to see what they can get out of the Twins. Give them a big checkbook and some favors from the favor bank and I believe Dale when he says he can bring something back."

"I hate letting those bitches go," Ray said.

"Save it for another time, that's my counsel," Callan said. "There's plenty of that to go around."

"Then let's make it so," Ray said. He cracked his knuckles absently. "It's killing time."

## AMSTERDAM, THE NETHERLANDS

The upper level of the converted river barge the Twins called home was split into two rooms: one great room that served as a bedroom/study for Marie and Isabelle, the other a smaller room that served as Ilse's bedroom, overflowing with stuffed toys, books, and games on neat rows of white shelves.

Isabelle stalked around her bedroom, tightening the already immaculate bed, brushing nonexistent lint from the covers, and then went into Ilse's room and straightened the already straight rows of books and toys. Downstairs, she heard Ilse laughing and Marie, between laughs, trying to read her a book in Dutch. They spoke both Dutch and English in the house and Ilse could go back and forth with ease, but lately they had been working on more Dutch to prepare her for preschool.

Isabelle went back to the study and the laptop set up on the desk there. She sat down and looked again at the e-mail she'd just received from the cutout on the Minnesota contract. He'd asked for another meeting. Isabelle decided to leave Marie with Ilse and take this meeting herself. She wanted to see the face of the cutout and get her own sense of him. She had a bad feeling about this whole affair. There were layers of deception here. She felt, faint and far off, the machinations of some puppet master running a larger operation that they were just a small part of. This was no clean hit of a group of Iraqi dissidents; this was something else. There was an intensity to the hunt that seemed out of scale for the target, which meant that they didn't have everything they needed to make a target assessment.

She was going to see to that herself.

She took care in dressing: black hose, a short black skirt and a white blouse, a loose leather jacket, heavy sensible shoes that could disable a man with one kick. She drew her hair back into her habitual working ponytail and decided to leave her features clean of makeup. From a small flat case taken from a locked cabinet in the study, she took out a folding fighting knife, the American Emerson CQC-7, and clipped it inside her thigh atop her stocking where it gathered into her garter belt. She took a few steps to make sure the knife didn't rub, then went downstairs where Marie and Ilse bustled in the kitchen, working together to make lunch.

"Will you want to eat?" Marie said.

"Save me something," Isabelle said. "I don't think I'll be gone long."

• • •

In a café across the street from the youth hostel her target was staying at, Isabelle lingered over coffee. After a short while, she saw the young Arab come out, his courier satchel slung across his shoulders, and watched him as he glanced around. Then he set off at a stroll toward the rendezvous point, a marijuana coffee shop a few blocks away. Isabelle followed him from across the street, taking her time and watching for any surveillance. There were no cars with extra mirrors and multiple antennas, no couples lingering overlong in storefronts, no solos suddenly changing direction to follow the young Arab. Satisfied that she alone was following the young man, she crossed the street and fell in behind him, studying his tradecraft. He stopped a few times to look in windows and watch for anyone following him; he looked across the street for anyone moving in tandem with him, and he hurried across the street when the light changed to see if anyone hurried to catch him. He stopped in one shop and bought a bottle of water, then came out and stood in front and slowly drank the water, giving any watchers time to show themselves. She'd continued past him without another glance. He gave her the appreciative look that men normally gave her, but she ignored him and went on ahead. She knew where he was going, and that was her advantage.

Isabelle stopped in a shop and looked at some boots till she saw the Arab pass by. Then she came out and fell in behind him again. The weight of the knife bothered her, and she brushed her hands over her skirt to make sure that the knife wasn't sagging against the fabric. She studied the nape of bin Hassan's neck, and thought about taking the heavy bladed knife and sinking it into his spine. Her anger over the contract and the inadequacy of the client's intelligence effort might find some short-lived release in that.

She looked for telltale signs of tension in his body. She had once studied massage, and with it anatomy, and found the knowledge the training imparted invaluable in her profession as a killer. The cutout was nervous and tense. She saw that in his shoulders and back. Amsterdam had no shortage of massage practitioners and was famous for its sex workers; why hadn't he taken advantage of that? Of course, he was Muslim, but he was also young and male and the demands of covert operations required release. If he had been on her team she would have sent him for a massage and some sex to relax him.

He paused just short of the coffee shop to look in the window of a newsstand, his eyes roving over the racked magazines and the stacks of cigarettes and small cigars behind the cashier's counter. She stopped beside him and said, "Hello, Joe from the States."

The young man startled, his features for a moment registering surprise and more than a little fear, then he caught himself and turned to her.

"You must be Marta's friend," he said. "Is Marta with you?"

"Not today, Joe," Isabelle said. She took his arm and tucked both hands into the crook of it. The young Arab tensed under her touch, and part of her filed that information away, even as she went to soothe him.

"Relax," she said. "No one is following us, it's a beautiful day, and we have some business to discuss." She steered him back onto the sidewalk and into the flow of passersby. "Do you like coffee, Joe?"

"Yes," Youssef said. "I do."

"Then let us go then, you and I, to this café here, where we can get a good coffee and sit and watch people. I enjoy that, do you?"

Youssef paused. "Yes. I do."

Isabelle gently steered him, letting his arm rest against her side and the swell of her breast. She was aware of his awareness of her sex, and she subtly encouraged his discomfort by bumping her body against him and pressing her breast into his arm.

At the café, they took a seat near the street, at a table away from the others, where the background noise of the street was just enough to mask their quiet conversation from the other patrons.

They sat quietly till their espressos arrived.

"So, Joe," Isabelle said. "How do you find Amsterdam?"

Youssef sipped at his coffee with enthusiasm. "It is a beautiful city."

"Yes it is," Isabelle said. "Quite beautiful. The people are good, too, don't you think?"

Youssef set his cup down, turned it slightly with one finger. "Yes."

They sat together quietly for a few minutes, watching the people passing by, each hurrying on their way in the beautiful light of the summer day.

"So, Joe," Isabelle finally said. "What of our business?"

"It is wondered if you can complete the contract."

"No," Isabelle said.

"I should say, it is wondered if you can complete the contract with additional information."

Isabelle sighed. "Even with exact targeting information, information more specific than before, the target has become much harder. Our people there were unable to determine where the target is, and the level of protection, much higher than we were told, is sure to have risen. We don't think that it can be done."

Youssef let a distressed look slip across his face. "We are told that you are the best. If you think it can't be done . . ."

"Not by us. We have had too much exposure and there isn't enough information." She paused. "If you don't wish to be the bearer of bad tidings to your people, I would be glad to talk directly to them and explain why. I understand how difficult it must be for you to explain to them . . . why not let me help you?"

She watched the play of emotions across the young man's face, and her intuition spoke clearly to her and guided her as it always did.

"It must be so hard for you," she said. "Being alone in a city where you don't know anyone . . . and then to have this difficult tasking upon you. Since we're ending the contract anyway, I don't think your people will mind meeting with me—I can help them make a decision about where else to go with the project." She studied him, touched her pony-tail, then folded her hands together on the table in front of her.

"Are you hungry, Joe?" she said. "Would you like to take a meal together?"

"Yes," Youssef said. "I would like that."

• • •

Over lunch they talked of inconsequential things. Youssef talked about his family, his friends from the camps, his loneliness; he poured it out to the sympathetic ear of the woman who told him to call her Isabelle.

"And what of the man who controls you?" Isabelle said. "Does he not spend time with you to help you with your tasks?"

Youssef shrugged. "He is a busy man, and there are many demands upon his time . . . he does the best he can."

"When do you meet him again?"

"He'll be coming here, in a few days. He'll contact me and let me know when."

"Then it's perfect for us," Isabelle said, stressing the *us*. "When he arrives we can meet and speak about the impossibility of continuing this contract. I can give him the bad news himself, to his face, and you need not concern yourself anymore with that."

Relief and worry alternated on the young Arab's face. "It's not good tradecraft. He will be angry . . ."

"There's no need for tradecraft between friends, and the contract is concluded. We are only a few people talking about past business, and we are very safe in this city. Let me worry about his anger, will you, my friend?"

"That would be good," Youssef said. "If you could help . . ."

"Of course," Isabelle said warmly. "What are friends for?"

She touched the top of her thigh where the fighting knife was sheathed, and studied the young man's neck.

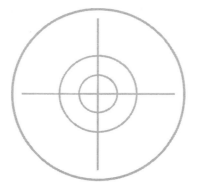

Ray Dalton sat at his desk, his isolation reinforced by the closed door and his instructions to his secretary to hold all calls and keep all visitors from his door.

He had a lot to think about.

On the desk in front of him were the latest reports, the ones he received as soon as each therapy session was completed, from the doctor working with Rhaman Uday. The frightening bits and pieces were coming together. Also on his desk was a report from the National Security Agency that pieced together intercepted communications with an old debrief from an Iraqi defector. The NSA report told of an Iraqi project to genetically engineer the smallpox virus. One of the project's goals was to make the incubation period longer, and to enhance communicability during incubation. Another goal was to increase the lethality of the virus from its normal 30 percent fatality rate. Like all of the Iraqi biological projects, the program had been swathed in secrecy, but the defector debriefing indicated that the engineering had been successful. The virus had been tested on live humans, prisoners, in a secret Iraqi test facility. Saddam Hussein had been so interested in the outcome of the program that he personally visited the facility and made sure that his high-level administration saw the effects of the virus. One of those people had been the administrator Rhaman Uday.

The name of the project, in English, was Sad Holiday.

ENROUTE TO AMSTERDAM/AMSTERDAM,
THE NETHERLANDS

During the three-and-a-half-hour drive to O'Hare airport in Chicago, Charley and Dale hashed out their game plan.

"What about weapons?" Charley said. "I'm not going light against the Twins."

"We'll be met at the airport once we clear customs," Dale said. "The contact will take care of that for us. I ordered you a Glock."

"I hate going naked."

"We won't be. The contact will provide us with transportation and a surveillance crew."

"That will save us a lot of time, if the crew's good."

"According to Callan they are."

"We're onboard the same boat when it comes to what we want to do here, right?"

Dale nodded, his hands steady on the wheel of the rented Jeep Cherokee. "You're right. Killing them isn't the right solution. They've got too many powerful friends and they've done too much work for the powers that be—including our people."

"Does that surprise you?"

"No," Dale said. "I lost my capacity for surprise about that kind of thing."

"You and me both, brother," Charley said. "Did it seem to you that Callan is moving pretty fast?"

"He is moving fast. There's somebody pushing him."

"You think?"

"I know. Callan and me, we've got history going back to Delta. He was a troop sergeant and I was the youngest kid on the block. He's a master of circumlocution when he wants to tell you something without being blunt about it."

"Circumlocution? I love it when you talk like that."

"He's running us for somebody else."

"We figured that. Agency?"

"That or my old outfit."

"That's a high-speed operation," Charley said. "We didn't know much about what you guys did, but we heard bits and pieces. It's too small a community for that not to come out. And you're right . . . this has a different flavor than a straight-up Agency gig. If there is such a thing."

"He was clear with me," Dale said. "We're just supposed to back them off, let them know they've been played against us by someone who didn't give them the whole picture, maybe even wanted them to get whacked in the process. And see how they take that, see if we can't leverage their anger into them letting us know who's paying for the hit. Then we track it back to the source."

"Are they getting good take out of Uday? Maybe that will fill in the picture some more."

"Filling in the picture is what this is all about," Dale said.

• • •

They parked the car in the long-term parking lot, then went to the ticket counter separately to pick up their tickets. They went through the security screening process without speaking to each other. Once onboard, they sat apart, and passed the long flight to Schiopol airport in Amsterdam as though they didn't know one another. In Amsterdam, they walked the long concourses, again separately, to customs and went through easily without being stopped or their carry-on bags searched. Outside of the customs area, they walked along until they saw a man holding a sign that said MILLER on it.

Dale walked up to the man, nodded, and started walking with him. Charley lagged behind, looking for surveillance. He saw nothing, so once they were outside, he lengthened his stride to catch up to the two men. The man who'd come to greet them was a short, chubby Dutchman with bright red cheeks and brilliant blue eyes.

"I'm Hans," the Dutchman said.

He led them to his car, a full-size navy blue Mercedes, and put their bags in the trunk. They got in and he drove away, carefully maneuvering the car through the busy traffic exiting the airport. He eased onto the highway and drove toward Amsterdam.

"I was thinking of taking the train," Hans said. "But we will be more comfortable in my car. You have reservations in your names at the hotel Artos, near the Central Train Station. It will be very convenient for you." He took a thick, oversized manila envelope from beneath the seat and handed it to Dale. "This is information you will find useful. You can get a VCR player in your room if you request it, here's some tape." He handed over a videocassette.

"Do you have some tools for us?" Charley said.

"Yes, in the trunk. I'll give them to you when we arrive at the hotel," Hans said. "Two Glock nineteens, one spare magazine for each, with Winchester Silvertip ammunition. You didn't ask for holsters."

"That's fine," Charley said. They didn't want holsters. If they needed to ditch the weapons, they wanted to be able to do so without having to strip off holsters that might give them away.

It was a longish drive in the heavy traffic to downtown Amsterdam.

"I needn't tell you that these women are very dangerous," Hans said. "I don't mean you any disrespect when I warn you not to take them lightly because they are beautiful women. They have killed many men and they are highly skilled at using that beauty against us."

"Have you run up against them before?" Charley said.

"I have seen their handiwork firsthand," Hans said. "They are total professionals, and they kill without hesitation, especially if they feel they are threatened. Someday I would like to talk to them. One can only admire their work."

Charley laughed. "You're a braver man than me, Hans. I'd rather shoot them from one hundred yards away with a scoped rifle. We've seen what they can do at close quarters."

"You have?" Hans said. "I would like to hear about that."

"Some other time," Dale said. "Let's get on with what we're here to do."

"Of course," Hans said. He pulled up in the crowded parking lot of the Central Train Station. He pointed across the canal at a towering hotel just across the bridge.

"There is where you will find your rooms," he said. "If you need anything, feel free to call at any time on my mobile phone . . . I will keep it clear for you."

The short Dutchman engaged the parking brake, then got out of the car and opened the trunk. He handed each man their carry-on bags, then took out an aluminum camera case.

"You'll find what we discussed in this case," he said. "Everything else you might need is in the envelope. The information is all current, and I have my team in place right now. Once you are ready, I can put you with them and you will see for yourself."

"That sounds good," Dale said. "Thanks for everything, Hans. We'll be in touch."

"Yes, please do," Hans said. "And I look forward to hearing the tale."

The Dutchman got back into his car and drove away, waving a hand out the window.

"Nice guy," Charley said.

"Remember need to know, Charley?" Dale said.

"He probably knows more than we do about what we're supposed to be doing," Charley said. "He's an operator and on our side."

"Let's get to the hotel."

Dale checked in first. Once he had his room assignment, he told Charley, who then checked in and requested a room on the same floor. They got rooms across the hall from each other. They met in Dale's room, where Charley took a large bottle of Heineken from the minibar and cracked it open.

"You can't get this good stuff in the States," he said. "This is stronger and has a better flavor."

Dale nodded and cleared the table of its menus and brochures on the sights of Amsterdam. He opened the oversized manila envelope and carefully laid its contents out on the tabletop. There were stacks of photographs, including aerial shots, detailed street maps with annotations, plastic overlays for the maps and photographs, and a surveillance log. He plucked out a photograph of the two women and a child.

"I didn't know they had a kid," Dale said.

"Is it theirs?" Charley said.

"Looks like it." Dale took a sheet of single-spaced printed material from the stack. "They live on a converted canal barge, a kind of houseboat."

"How far from here?"

"We'll be able to walk it."

The two men pored over the documents, pulled the maps out, and looked at aerial photographs that covered the houseboat and the neighborhood around it. They studied the urban terrain with the intensity of doctors looking at X rays of a critical patient. They wanted to know every inch of the ground for the confrontation they had coming. The Twins would have good information security; they would be living a low-key, low-profile life, fully integrated into their neighborhood, with a plausible cover story for their neighbors.

The dossier worked up by Hans's surveillance team confirmed that. The Twins' cover was that they were flight attendants for KLM; they took it to the point where they left for assignments clad in KLM flight-attendant uniforms. Their child, Ilse, was popular in the neighborhood with other children, and stayed with Marie Garvais's mother when the two went operational. They were quiet and stayed to themselves, interacting mostly with other parents of preschool-aged children, and their lesbian lifestyle attracted no attention in tolerant Amsterdam.

Dale and Charley studied the photographs with interest.

"Isabelle never smiles except when she's with their kid, you see that?" Charley said. He flipped through the sheaf of surveillance photographs. "Every single one of these, she's either frowning or neutral. Marie, she's a cheery little thing, smiles a lot."

"What's that tell you?"

"Don't know, Ranger," Charley said. "But I remember her face when she was tracking me with that Skorpion. Stone-cold serious, that one."

"That's both of them," Dale said.

They studied the maps of Amsterdam and tracked out the various routes that would take them by the Twins' houseboat. They ordered up a VCR player from the front desk, and studied the video tape Hans's surveillance team had made, showing the Twins at home in their houseboat.

"They know how to live a cover," Dale said. "They've been here for ten years in the same spot, same address."

"It's a wonder they've never had anybody track them back."

"Anybody who did probably didn't survive the meeting," Dale said. "They're cautious and professional in their business dealings— they don't meet people at their home and they've never worked an operation in this city."

"Stone pros," Charley said with real admiration. "Every step of the way."

"They've got the advantage, being women," Dale said. "Most operators would stop looking for a threat once they got a shot of their legs. They've used that to their advantage time and again. Most men will hesitate before shooting a woman, but these two won't blink an eye before dropping you."

Charley nodded. "Do we need to think about the approach?"

"We go with the plan. We brace them directly on a staged walk-up right outside their home, or in the immediate neighborhood. We make it clear who we are and who we're working for and we tell them in no uncertain terms that they've been played against us. Then we see which way it goes. I'm betting that they won't have a problem giving up their paymaster once they get the full story."

"I'll believe that when I see it," Charley said.

"Pretty soon," Dale said. "Shall we do a walk-through?"

"You think they'd remember us from Minneapolis?"

"Doubtful. They only got a glimpse of the two of us, and we were all shooting."

"Then let's go."

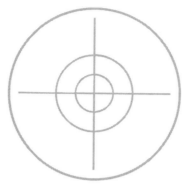

DAMASCUS, SYRIA

Ahmad bin Faisal turned away from the computer atop his desk, and stood. He walked slowly around the room and considered Youssef's request for a face-to-face meeting in Amsterdam. Such a meeting would serve two good purposes: he could verify Youssef's preparation and hand over the vials of the genetically engineered smallpox; and he could meet with the Twins and see to the conclusion of their contract. Youssef's thinly disguised plea for help in dealing with the Twins didn't disturb him. The younger Arab was only a mouthpiece and could not be expected to make such adjustments on his own. In truth, the Twins' argument that the contract was no longer feasible was a good one; the Al-Bashir network, despite its resources, had not been able to discover the whereabouts of either Rhaman Uday or his wife since the attempt at the Torture Center. All the support cells had discovered was that the targets were gone, and that the wife had gone before the husband. The husband had disappeared in such a fashion to lead the operational planners in Al-Bashir to believe that the US government had taken him up.

That would be problematic. But there was nothing to be done about it. While Uday might divulge some details of the operation to the US authorities, bin Faisal and his peers believed that the Iraqi's fragile mental condition would mask the precious information long enough for them to launch the operation against the US.

They were counting on that.

As they counted on the One.

Bin Faisal pursed his lips and thought about the fragility of the one operator the project hinged on. An older, more seasoned operative might have been a better choice, but Youssef's excellent, near-native English, his experience abroad, and the exposure to various lifestyles through his wealthy upbringing gave him a profile that a seasoned mujaheddin would have a hard time matching. And Youssef had displayed an exceptional operational mind while in training in the Sudanese camps. He had done a credible job on his shakedown runs in Amsterdam. Even his failed attempt to get the Twins to take up the contract was handled well.

So his fragility, while a factor, was outweighed by his operational strengths.

Bin Faisal picked up his telephone and spoke to his private secretary and had him book a flight to Amsterdam.

It was time to see Youssef for the last time.

## AMSTERDAM, THE NETHERLANDS

Isabelle and Marie sat out on the deck of their houseboat and lazed in the afternoon sun. Ilse was inside, taking her midday nap.

"He's just a lonely boy," Isabelle said. "He doesn't seem suited for this world of work."

"So when does his handler come in?" Marie said.

"Soon. I'll keep checking our e-mail."

Isabelle kicked her feet up on a rope line and leaned back in her folding patio chair. She sipped contemplatively from her coffee cup, then looked over at her lover.

"If they force the issue, I'm thinking of killing them both," she said.

Marie looked at her with surprise. "Why would you do that? It serves no purpose."

"It would send a message about trying to force us."

"Better to just let them go away. They can bring no leverage to bear on us; we've already refused second payment."

"I won't allow us to be pressured."

"Isabelle, Isabelle," Marie said soothingly. She reached out and took the taller woman's hand in hers. She smoothed the hand and eased the fingers of Isabelle's fist open. "We're not being pressured. You've seen to that. There's nothing to endanger us here. We'll meet with the boy and his handler and we'll see to them. All it requires us to do is to say no."

"I am suspicious," Isabelle said. "There's more to this than meets the eye. They are not telling us everything we need to know, and I don't mean just the target information. Whoever was guarding the item was very professional. It feels of government and that wasn't the deal."

"It wasn't the deal," Marie conceded. "But we walked away with only bruises and we banked that money."

"I would like to send them the heads of the boy and his controller in a sack."

Marie laughed. "You are so bloodthirsty! Come," she said, standing and taking Isabelle by the hand. "Let's go in the bedroom for a while."

• • •

In a café just off the Dam, Youssef bin Hassan closed his laptop, put it back into his courier bag, and slung it over his shoulder. He finished the last of his coffee, then threw a few loose coins down on the tabletop and got up. He joined the steady flow of foot traffic and let it carry him toward the Central Train Station. The latest e-mail from his controller informed him that Ahmad bin Faisal would be joining him in Amsterdam in two days.

That gave him time to refine his practice.

He strolled along, the atomizer palmed in one hand, the other hand in his pocket. Every so often, as he brushed against someone, he sprayed water on their pants leg, their pocket, sometimes their hands. It was best to get it on the hand, which so often made a trip to the face and the open mucus membranes there. It was too intrusive to spray directly in someone's face. You could spray behind their head, or on their neck, but sometimes a person would feel the mist and turn to look for the source.

In the train station, he studied the flow of foot traffic. He went to one of the stairways that led down, and then up to the train tracks. With the atomizer in hand, he let a stream of water go all the way on the central banister, the one most people touched. Then he paused beside one of the ventilation ducts with its massive fans. He reached into his courier bag and took out a small metal box, one inch by three inches, with a magnetic back. He looked around, then put his hand quickly into the hood of the ventilation duct, just short of the fan, and placed the small box. He pressed the switch on the side, and the box was fixed in place. Youssef stood back and studied the ventilation duct. The tiny box just inside the hood was invisible unless you were up close and looking directly into it. He made a note of the time, and then slowly walked through the station to the bicycle rental stand, where he rented a bicycle for a few hours and took a leisurely bike ride round the city. Though he didn't know it, he passed the Twins' houseboat once, admiring the neatly kept boathouse painted in bright blues and yellows.

After his bike ride and a stop at an Internet café to check his e-mail once more, he returned his bicycle to the rental stand and went back to the ventilation duct. No one paid any attention as he slipped his hand in and plucked free the small box, now covered with grime and dust from the steady intake of air that had passed through it for three hours. He put the box in his pocket and went into a public restroom, then into a toilet stall. He took out the small box, and using a ballpoint pen, popped open the top and examined the tiny vial inside and the atomizer equipment that crammed the innards of the box. The vial of water was empty, having been vaporized into a fine mist that had been sucked into the ventilation system and dispersed over the train station by the ventilation duct and fan system.

Perfect.

The equipment he had been given all worked well under field conditions. He wiped the outside of the dispersal box down and replaced it in his courier bag. He'd clean it and the atomizer later on, back at his tiny single room at the youth hostel.

Youssef went back outside. It was a beautiful day in Amsterdam. The sun was shining and the air was warm. He felt comfortable in his blue jeans and a short-sleeved shirt, with the afternoon breeze plucking at his sleeves. He thought about the woman from the Twins, the one he'd had lunch with. She was attracted to him, he thought, or perhaps she felt sorry for him in his obvious loneliness.

Perhaps she wanted him, or perhaps not. Western women confused him; in truth, all women confused him. He had little experience to base his observations and feelings on, after all. His college days had been spent in a horny haze when it came to women and he'd had little success with them. And in the camps, there were no women.

So he didn't know how to take the woman's measure. Perhaps when they met again he would know better. He stopped near the Anne Frank house and looked at the line to get in. He had never taken the tour. He studied the crowds and thought about practicing again, but decided he'd had enough.

He himself had only seen pictures of what the disease could do, but it was something he wouldn't experience; he'd been inoculated against the disease he bore. And the operational plan was spartan in its simplicity. Simple was good when it came to plans. Once he had made sure the dissipation mechanisms worked, and he had refined his own technique when it came to dispersing the virus, he'd be provided with the real virus to load into his equipment. Then he would make his own arrangements to enter America. He had already decided to go via Canada to take advantage of the soft routes into the US. Once there, he'd begin his operation.

It would be two weeks or so, give or take a few days, before the blooming began, the brilliant red of the rash and pustules that began at the extremities and covered the entire body. By then, with the engineered smallpox, the person would have been contagious with the symptoms of a cold for approximately seven days. Seven days to incubate, seven days of mild symptoms with maximum contagiousness, and then the blooming of the pox, and then three to seven days before death or the painfully slow recovery.

As a tourist, he had quite an itinerary: Washington, DC. New York City. Miami. Philadelphia. Boston. Chicago. St. Louis. Atlanta, Georgia. San Francisco. Los Angeles. Las Vegas.

He would travel between cities on a variety of transportation: bus lines, airlines, rental cars. He had plenty of time to cover all his targets, though it was a lot of ground for one man to cover.

The One.

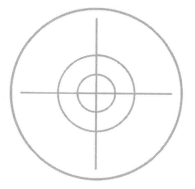

AMSTERDAM, THE NETHERLANDS

The surveillance operation mounted by Hans's people had complete coverage of the Twins' houseboat twenty-four hours a day. They'd had great luck, one of the many variables in covert operations, and were able to rent a weekly apartment directly overlooking the houseboat. Miniature cameras with expensive long lenses went into position overlooking the boat. A parabolic microphone went into place to pick up conversations on the street. They stayed away from trying to insert cameras or microphones into the houseboat; Hans believed in erring on the side of caution when dealing with professionals of the Twins' caliber.

The streetwalkers, the surveillance operators who worked the pavement following the Twins, exercised extreme caution. Though it was expensive and difficult to do, they rotated operators so that the same faces didn't show up repeatedly on the street. The streetwalkers kept their distance from the surveillance-conscious assassins—Hans had made sure that each operator knew the Twins bloody past. Fortunately for the watchers, the Twins were homebodies. When they went out, they didn't go far, doing their grocery shopping and their activities with their child in the immediate neighborhood.

Inside the apartment, Hans, Charley, and Dale sat behind the operator monitoring the camera that was trained on the houseboat.

"My people, they like these two," Hans said. "They dote on their child and they are good to their neighbors. Nothing to make you think anything other than what you see. They are very good at living their cover."

"Are you going to feed this to the Dutchies?" Dale asked.

"I'm sure they'd want it if they knew we were here," Hans said, with a broad wink.

They all laughed. The equipment operator, a thin man dressed in a black T-shirt and black jeans with heavy boots, and with both ears pierced, grinned and said, "Here they come now."

He moved a small control toggle and panned the camera to catch Marie and Isabelle coming out of their houseboat, Ilse between them clinging to their hands.

"Such a nice family," said the equipment operator.

"Where are they going?" Charley asked.

Hans picked up a radio handset and said, "Zero, Zero-Alpha. Package in progress."

"Roger, package in progress, Zero out."

Hans said, "We've got our people in two static street posts; they'll pick them up whichever way they go. Do you want to work the street or stay here?"

"We'll stay here unless you've got a vehicle," Dale said.

"We do, but they don't go far enough where it's useful," Hans said. "They like to walk and they do a lot of it. There's really no need for a car. They own an old Audi, but they keep it garaged. It only comes out for trips out of town."

"You can do that in this city," Charley observed. "I like that about Amsterdam. Never need to drive, you can walk most places . . . it's civilized."

"I'm glad you think that way about my home," Hans said. "Perhaps we'll get a chance for me to show you Amsterdam."

"I'd like that," Charley said.

The radio began to sound off with the transmissions of the streetwalkers working below.

"Zero, One, I have the package visual."

"One, Zero, you have the eye."

Charley and Dale watched as the camera tracked the couple and their child, one of the streetwalkers coming up behind them slowly. Ahead of them a man and a woman strolled arm in arm.

"Good coverage," Dale said. "Your people are good."

"Thank you," Hans said. "I think they are the best."

Without taking his eyes away from the screen, the black-clad equipment operator said, "That's right."

"So how do you want to do it?" Hans said.

"I'm thinking during one of their walks," Dale said. "The only problem is the child."

"There is that," Hans said. "They rarely leave the boat together without the child."

"It would serve to temper the confrontation," Charley said. "We can talk around it with the child there."

"I don't like it," Dale said.

"The only other option is to approach them when they're on the boat, and I think that's too dangerous," Charley said. "We want to confront them in a public space, give them room to move . . . and give us room to retreat while we're covered by Hans's people."

Dale gnawed at one cheek and stared at the monitor. The telephoto lens caught the couple and their child going into the local grocery.

"Have you seen them going out together without the child, using a sitter or anything like that?" he asked Hans.

"They don't use sitters," Hans said. "They do go out individually, to meet with friends, but it is rare. Their days are mostly about their child. The other day Isabelle went out and met with a friend and had lunch with him."

"Do we know who he is?" Dale asked.

"No," Hans said. "We have good footage of him, but his face isn't in our database as a known operator. It seemed innocent. Marie has gone out and had coffee with people in the neighborhood as has Isabelle. They are well liked, and while they keep to themselves, they are still social and civil to their neighbors."

"There's a possibility," Charley said. "We could just go up to the boat while they're there, and invite them to coffee."

"That's not going to work," Dale said.

"I think you will have to meet them on the street," Hans said.

Dale drummed his fingers repeatedly on the tabletop that held the monitors and laptop computers.

"What is it, dude?" Charley said.

"I don't like having a child in the mix," Dale said.

Charley nodded. "Nobody does. But the Twins aren't going to get hostile if they have their kid there. They won't do anything to endanger their child. They'll listen. There's a lesson in there for them. A hard one, but it's one they're up to. Remember, they're pros, not just women and mothers with a child. Remember Minneapolis? Keep that in mind."

"I've got it in mind," Dale said. "I just don't like having the kid in there. But I don't see any way around it."

"So let's work it out," Charley said. "Let's do this thing."

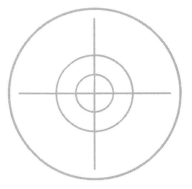

AMSTERDAM, THE NETHERLANDS, SEVERAL DAYS LATER

Warm afternoon sunlight poured through the porthole windows and splashed across the bed where Marie and Isabelle lay tangled together. Comfortable as dozing cats, they stared up at the ceiling fan that ticked slowly, sending a cooling breeze over their sweaty skin.

"It's fine, isn't it?" Marie said. "This life we've made."

"Yes," Isabelle said.

From across the hall came the sound of stirring, and then the loud sound of small feet on the decking outside their door, followed by a tentative tap.

"Mamas, Mamas? Can I come in?" their daughter Ilse called.

"Of course, my sweet," Isabelle said. "Thank you for knocking."

The door opened and Ilse came in, barefoot and dressed in a jumper rumpled by her nap. She flew to the bed and wormed her way between the two naked women, nuzzling first one, then the other. Marie and Isabelle stretched out their arms and hugged their child, then snuggled her between the two of them.

"So what shall we do today?" Marie said. "Lay in bed all day and listen to the water? That is Ilse's favorite thing, I think."

"No, Mama," Ilse said. "Ilse's favorite thing is a peach ice!"

"Peach ice? That sounds good," Isabelle said. "What do you

think, Mama Marie? Would an ice be good on this warm afternoon?"

"I would prefer a mango ice," Marie said. "Would you like to try one, Ilse?"

"No, Mama!" Ilse said, laughing. "I would like a peach ice."

"Then ice it is," Isabelle said. "Let's get dressed and go get some."

The two women dressed and then dressed their child for the street. They went upstairs to the main deck of the barge, and holding hands, the three of them crossed the gangway that connected the barge to the small dock that led up to the street. Swinging Ilse, laughing with joy between them, two of the most dangerous assassins in the world walked their daughter to the ice cream store.

• • •

"Here's your chance," Hans said. "They are out and moving and they are talking about going to the gelateria two blocks up. They go there often in the afternoon with Ilse."

Charley and Dale looked at each other. Charley spoke first.

"It's your call, Dale. Go for it now or not?"

Dale looked at the monitor and pressed his elbow against his side where a Glock 19 was tucked inside his pants.

"I call it now," he said. "Let's do this thing."

• • •

The two men inserted like a hunter killer team. The streetwalkers of the surveillance team formed a very loose cordon around the Twins and their child; they made the boundary of the moving target. Then Charley and Dale inserted within that boundary and followed a block behind the Twins. There were streetwalkers in front of, alongside, and behind the Twins, a full-force show with every operator Hans had out to keep the dancing cordon invisible to the Twins, who weren't looking for surveillance but concentrated instead on delighting their child.

Charley felt the familiar pang of adrenaline as he spotted the two women ahead. They stopped for a moment outside the Italian ice cream shop, then went inside. He and Dale slowed their pace, took their time on the approach. They walked slowly past the ice cream shop and saw the two women and their child inside ordering their cones. Charley and Dale paused in front of a tobacco shop and watched the front of the gelateria. The Twins came out, their daughter between them, all three occupied with their cones. They stood outside the shop for a moment, and then began to stroll back toward their houseboat.

"Okay," Dale said. "We follow, and we'll take them after they cross the street on the block where their boat is."

"Roger that," Charley said. "After they cross the street it is."

• • •

Isabelle saw the surveillance first. When she came out, she saw a man and a woman on the other side of the canal and recognized them from before, when they had been walking. They were lingering outside a clothing store that was closed for inventory, looking in the window. To the casual looker, there was nothing amiss. But it seemed to Isabelle that they were looking too intently at nothing, and the paned glass of the store provided an excellent reflecting surface to watch the front of the gelato shop while keeping their backs to it.

But the tip off was when the couple began to walk back toward the barge with them. Then a single man in a jogging suit came walking up quickly behind them, passing them, and when he did, the couple slowed, and then turned off on a side street. The woman looked back over her shoulder and then quickly forward and continued on, tucking her hands into her companion's arm.

It looked like a surveillance handoff. All of Isabelle's situational awareness antenna went up. She and Marie had not survived many long years in the field without having a finely tuned sense of what was going on around them, and they built on the woman's intuitive sense with the foundations of situational awareness and training. She looked casually around her. There were two athletic men a half block behind them, walking in tandem but not speaking to each other. Closer on the same side, a woman strolled along, looking in shop windows but not lingering, moving at the same pace as Isabelle and Marie. In front of them, another couple, walking hand-in-hand, stopped to look in shop windows, but only those at such an angle that they could see the sidewalk behind them.

They were in the box.

Isabelle fought down the sudden stab of fear in her belly, and quickly thought through her options. If they were the subject of a surveillance, and it appeared that they were, there wouldn't be any violence without more indicators. It was important not to let the surveillance team know they'd been made, or else the countermeasures they'd take would make the surveillance harder to spot the next time around.

If there was a next time.

And then there was the question of who? Who would be mounting such a large-scale surveillance operation against them? Comeback from a past operation? That was most likely. She thought immediately of the young Arab and the controller she had yet to meet. Anger came out of her fear and she fed it with images of what she would do to the Arab if it turned out to be the case. She scanned the area ahead to the houseboat. There was a bench they often stopped at in their afternoon strolls, where the two women could sit with Ilse between them and watch the passersby, their backs to the water.

That would be a good vantage spot.

● ● ●

"You notice how Isabelle is looking around?" Charley said.

"Yeah. You think she made us?" Dale said.

"I don't know. Hans's people on the other side of the canal made a clumsy handoff just now, and I think Isabelle might have spotted it."

"Damn it."

"She's playing it cool if she did. Check her out. She's doing a three-hundred-sixty-degree scan and disguising every move," Charley said with admiration. "This woman is a total pro."

"What do you think they're going to do?" Dale said.

"I'm betting she stops short of the houseboat and looks for signs of the team settling in around her. That'll be her cue. She won't let on that she's seen anything, but look at her shoulders: she's getting pissed."

"Then we'll brace her there."

• • •

"Isabelle?" Marie said. "What is wrong?"

Ilse looked up first at Marie, then at Isabelle. Isabelle reached down and stroked her child's jaw and said, "Eat your ice, darling, before it melts."

Then she looked at Marie and said calmly, "We're in a box. Three to our rear, one across the canal, two in front of us."

Marie stopped. "Where do we move?"

"We'll stop here," Isabelle said. She gently nudged their daughter between them and sat down on the weathered bench. "This is a good spot, eh, Ilse?"

"Yes, Mama," Ilse said. She sat, with their help, between them, her gleaming patent shoes winking in the bright sunlight as she kicked them back and forth, back and forth.

Isabelle saw the two men behind them and recognized them for what they were. They had all the signs: athletic build, hair cut short but not too short, comfortable clothes, shirttails out to conceal weapons. But what gave them away was their own intensity. Now she had to decide what that meant. She and Marie were unarmed. They kept a few weapons concealed in the houseboat for emergencies, but went out unarmed when they were home. She felt her shoulders tensing and deliberately drew in a deep breath to calm herself.

"If anything happens, take her and go," Isabelle said softly.

"Take who and go, Mama?" Ilse said.

"Nothing, little one. Mama is just babbling," Isabelle said.

Marie nodded and shifted her feet under her so that she could get up quickly.

The two men came on and there was no doubt who they were looking at.

• • •

"She's made us for sure," Charley said.

"We'll play it cool," Dale said.

"I hope she sees it that way. Do you think she's armed?"

"I don't think so."

Dale drew himself up and then took a deep breath, deliberately letting his shoulders droop and his posture slump. He made sure to keep his hands well clear of his waist and his hands open. Charley followed his example as Dale smiled and stopped well short, seven yards, from the two women who studied him intently, all pretense of not seeing him gone.

"Hello, Marie. Hello, Isabelle. And hello to you, too, Ilse," Dale said.

"Hello," Ilse said. "Who are you?"

Isabelle got to her feet, her weight forward over the balls of her feet, her hands relaxed and open at her side.

"Oh, these are some old friends of Mama's, darling. Marie, take Ilse on home while I visit with our friends," she said.

"No need for Marie to run off, Isabelle. We don't want to take up too much of your beautiful afternoon," Dale said. "We just want to speak to you about Minneapolis."

153

"I'm afraid I don't understand," Isabelle said, crossing her arms across her chest and letting one hand rise to the corner of her mouth. Marie placed one hand on Ilse's shoulder.

"Your daughter is beautiful," Charley said. "But how could she not be with two such beautiful mothers?"

"Thank you," Ilse said.

Marie's mouth was drawn thin. Ilse looked at her, puzzled.

"What's wrong, Mama?" she said.

Isabelle moved slightly and placed herself in front of Marie and Ilse. "This is not a good time to talk. This is our family time."

"Like I said, Isabelle, it won't take much time. It's just talk. That's all we're here for today," Dale said.

"Talk about what?" Isabelle said.

"Your last project. You were put onto something protected by people you don't want any trouble with. We represent those people," Dale said.

Isabelle was silent, her hands still bladed into a covert ready-position for unarmed combat. "And?" she challenged.

"And no one means you any harm," Dale said. "But we want you to walk away and leave the project alone. That's all."

Isabelle stood still. A slight tremble in the outer muscle of her thigh came and went. She looked at Marie, then back at Dale and Charley who stood well back, their hands in the open.

"Your friends," Isabelle said. "They're American, too?"

"Yes," Dale said.

"I see. That wasn't known at the time of the project. In fact, we were told otherwise."

"We're aware of that," said Dale, who had been unaware of that until she told him. "The people who put you onto that project were not fully forthcoming. They didn't tell you all they knew."

"I can see that now," Isabelle said. "What about our investment in the operation so far? Surely the people you represent understand the nature of our business."

"We are authorized to discuss a payment for your full under-standing of our position and to compensate you for expenditures you've had. We understand the nature of your business," Dale said.

Isabelle looked around and carefully noted the position of the surveillance team that had her and her family boxed in.

"I can see that," she said lightly. "Perhaps Marie and Ilse should go home now, and we can continue this conversation?"

"That will work," Dale said. "Nice seeing you again, Marie, and meeting you, Ilse."

" 'Bye, Ilse," Charley said. He smiled and waved at the little girl.

"I'll be along shortly, Marie," Isabelle said. "I'll just stay and chat with our friends. You take Ilse home now."

"Of course," Marie said. Her tone was flat. There was fear in her but it was changing into anger. She took Ilse by the hand and walked quickly away. It wasn't lost on her that the surveillance team stayed put in a loose ring around her lover. She had been let go, and she walked quickly to the houseboat.

Isabelle watched her family go, then said, "What shall I call you?"

"We don't need names, Isabelle," Dale said. "I hope that we won't need to meet again after this."

"Yes," she said evenly. "I hope so, too."

"How much for you to walk away?" Dale said.

"One hundred fifty thousand in US dollars. Cash," Isabelle said.

"That's a lot of money," Dale countered.

"We have put a lot of effort into this project. And surely the US government considers that small change?"

Charley grinned. He liked this woman.

"You realize what the people who brought you this intended?" Dale said. "They were hoping that you would be killed during the project. It would save them money."

"The thought has crossed my mind," Isabelle said.

"We have an interest in those parties," Dale said. "If you could provide us the contact information, I could get you your hundred and fifty K."

"That's not viable," Isabelle said. "It's not the nature of our business to give up our employers . . . no matter how careless they may be."

"It may be difficult to get that much money without something more to sweeten the pot," Dale said.

"It would be difficult for us to continue to work, for people including the people you report to, if it became known that we gave up such information, no matter what the price tag."

Dale watched the woman's face. She was deadpan and intent, carefully focused on watching him and he felt her sharp awareness probing for weakness in him.

"Perhaps you'd like to consider it further?" he offered. "Think on it overnight? You don't want to keep Marie and Ilse waiting. Maybe Marie would think differently."

"I'll do that," Isabelle said. She uncrossed her arms and deliberately put her hands into the deep pockets of her slacks. "Tomorrow, same place, same time?"

"Yes," Dale said. "Same place, same time."

"You should try the gelato," Isabelle said. "It's quite good."

• • •

"We have no other choice, Isabelle," Marie said, trying to soothe her enraged lover. "Give them the Arab and let it fall where it will."

Isabelle stalked from one side of their narrow living room to the other. Ilse was quietly playing in her room, and the sound of her came to them over the lapping of water against the side of the houseboat.

"They came to us in our home," Isabelle said through teeth clenched to bite back her rage. She fought to keep her voice low so as not to upset Ilse. "In our home. They have us any time they want us. This is comeback from the Arab and his handler. I told you there was more to this than meets the eye."

She took a deep breath and calmed herself as best she could. She looked at Marie, drawn up into a ball, hugging her knees, pressed tight in the corner of their couch, and she felt a pang.

"How are you? Are you all right?" she said.

Marie shrugged and said, "As well as can be expected. I'm worried for Ilse. She knows something is wrong."

"We must keep it from her."

"As best we can. We need closure."

"I should just give them the Arab," Isabelle said. "They offered to pay a hundred fifty thousand dollars. It's not much . . . I told them it was for our out-of-pocket expenses on the Minneapolis contract."

"That goes some way," Marie said. "But what we need is for this to be over. And the Americans gone."

"But we still have to work," Isabelle said. "If we give them the Arab, they can put us out of business . . . they can spread the word that we sold them the Arab."

"We can counter that. We don't know that they will. They need it to be over as well, and they've warned us instead of killing us. They could have had us killed, and where would Ilse be?"

"Americans wouldn't kill Ilse."

"Where would she be, Isabelle, without us? With my mother? We need to think about that. We have a chance to walk away with some money to see us there."

Marie paused and hugged herself tightly as though fighting a chill. "The Arab will be contacting us for the meeting with his controller soon," she said. "How about this: we don't give them the Arab, we lead them to the Arab and let matters fall where they will. They have us on a close surveillance now and they'll be watching us. We can give them the Arab that way and no one will know the difference."

Isabelle stroked her jaw and crossed her arms across her chest. "That would work. I won't use the computer here, I'll go to the cyber café and check the e-mail. I'll make sure they're following me."

She crossed the room and sat next to Marie, gently pried her hands from around her raised knees, and pulled her close.

"It will be all right, my love," she said softly. "Soon it will be like it was before."

157

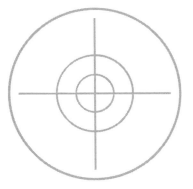

## AMSTERDAM, THE NETHERLANDS

Unlike Youssef, Ahmad bin Faisal enjoyed his trips to Amsterdam.
He sampled the fleshy pleasures in a house of prostitution that spe-
cialized in discretion, and so was popular with visiting politicians and
other celebrities. On one occasion he'd found himself sharing the sitting room with a famous senator from the United States and an aging
rock star, each preoccupied with the woman of his choice. In this
instance, he'd arrived two days before his meeting with Youssef to
give himself a chance to enjoy some of the pleasures that went with
his rank. He took full advantage of the leeway afforded by the operation. He strolled the narrow streets, enjoyed the sunshine, took coffee
in a sidewalk café, bought a book in a bookstore, and lingered in yet
another café for a long while before he went to an Internet café and
paid for the use of a computer. He drafted an e-mail to Youssef detail-
ing the particulars for their meeting. Since the weather was good, he
decided to meet outside, and set their rendezvous at the tourist information center just outside the Central Train Station. They could walk
and talk in relative security, as the open plaza and the surrounding
area made countersurveillance easy. He sent the message, then went
back out into the sun and found a place to read his book and enjoy his
day.

• • •

Youssef bin Hassan and Ahmad bin Faisal, brothers in arms in the struggle against the Great Satan, rambled along the pathway that paralleled the canal closest to the train station. They enjoyed a companionable silence for a time, and then the older Arab said, "How have you filled your days?"

Youssef shrugged and was silent for a time. Then he said, "I keep my days full with prayer and rehearsals. I walk and I have coffee. Sometimes I read. It is enough."

"You're young," bin Faisal said. "You should enjoy yourself more."

Youssef shrugged again, and bin Faisal thought how very young he looked in his baggy denim pants and T-shirt with the logo of an American music group, the Dave Mathews Band, on it, his courier bag hanging off one thin shoulder. The older Arab was struck by how harmless the most dangerous of men could appear.

It was time to launch him on his way.

"So have you contacted the Twins?" bin Faisal said.

"Yes," Youssef said. "I checked my e-mail before I came here. They want a meeting right away."

"What is their hurry?"

"I believe they wish to be done with us so they can move onto other projects."

"What is your assessment of their position?"

Youssef stroked his jaw with one hand, and scratched at the day's worth of beard stubble there. "I think they are right. They had their chance and it proved to be too difficult. We didn't have enough information, and it was hastily done. I think the target has been hidden elsewhere. It's possible that our people could find it eventually, but we don't know that. It will take time in any instance. I would say let them go and if in the future we developed better information we could go to them, or to someone else. Surely there are others just as skilled?"

Bin Faisal nodded in appreciation. The young man had thought it through.

"So our meeting, then, is it necessary?" bin Faisal said.

"They want to meet you. I believe they want to make sure

that their position is clearly stated, and not merely passed on."

"Where shall we meet them?"

Youssef noticed the compliment hidden in the remark; the senior man was deferring to the younger for operational details.

"I suggest a walking contact along one of the canals. It's difficult to mount surveillance there. I haven't seen any, and I believe we're secure. But it pays to be careful."

"How will you contact them?"

"They'll be checking their e-mail every half hour. I'll set up a meet for later today."

"Yes, that will be good," said bin Faisal. He thought of the woman he'd enjoyed last night, and wondered if he'd have enough time for another liaison tonight.

• • •

Isabelle dressed carefully for her meeting with the Arabs. Bare legs and clogs, a short black skirt with a white blouse worn out, and a black vest open over the blouse. That served to conceal the Sig-Sauer P-230 lightweight aluminum .380 pistol with a AWC suppressor mounted on the barrel. The suppressor effectively doubled the length of the weapon, making its balance awkward, but it holstered well enough in a thin sheath in the small of her back, the suppressor following the line of her spine into the swell of her buttocks. In the lining of her panties she clipped a Spyderco Co-Pilot, a folding knife with a two-inch razor-sharp blade.

She studied herself in the bathroom mirror, licked a finger, and brushed a stray eyelash out of the way. Her hair was pulled back in a businesslike ponytail and her face, as usual, was bare of makeup. She considered for a moment, then took the time to put mascara on her long lashes, and added a light coat of color to her full lips.

Now she was ready.

She went back out into the front room. The long shadows of late afternoon fell across the canal, cool where the sun was blocked by the tall row houses on both sides of the canal. Marie and Ilse sat at a table and toyed with a teapot and the remains of an afternoon tea.

"Where are you going, Mama?" Ilse said.

"I have to go out for a while, darling," Isabelle said. "Would you like me to bring you something?"

"Sweets?" Ilse said hopefully.

Marie and Isabelle both laughed.

"I don't know why we bother to ask," Marie said. "You always say the same thing."

"But it's what I like," Ilse protested.

"Of course," Isabelle said. "I'll bring you some sweets."

Marie stood and came to Isabelle and hugged her, let her hands roam over her back and tap on the concealed weapon.

"Do you really need that?" Marie said.

"I may . . ."

"Please, Isabelle. Not that. Let the Americans have them. If we start with violence here, where will it end? We have no choice."

Isabelle shrugged her shoulders stubbornly.

"I don't like being forced," she said. "And I don't know what will happen. But I won't be the one to start any violence."

"Promise me you'll be careful, Isabelle. Remember all the things we have to live for."

"I know, my sweet," Isabelle said. She kissed Marie gently on the lips. "I'll be back later."

• • •

"Isabelle is moving," said the equipment operator. Dale, Charley, and Hans were sitting at a kitchen table littered with the remains of a crusty loaf of bread and cold cuts.

The radio crackled.

"Zero, Four, I have the eye on Isabelle."

"Four, Zero, you have the eye."

The streetwalkers stirred from their static posts and began to form up the box around Isabelle, who walked away from the houseboat, and let herself be carried along in the after-work rush of foot traffic.

"Marie and the kid are still in the boat?" Charley asked.

"Yes," the cameraman said. "We've got a few extra people in case they go out."

"I wonder where she's going," Dale mused. "She knows she's under surveillance."

"She's not doing any overt countersurveillance," said the equipment operator. "If anything, she seems to be going slow enough to give us time."

"What is she up to?" Dale said.

"She could just be going out shopping," Charley said.

"They normally do everything together," Hans said. "All their daily activities, shopping, all that . . . they do it all together. The only time we've seen them go out alone, they meet someone."

"She's staying in the box," Charley said. "Let's get down there and work a little. I'm going crazy in here."

"We have camera coverage from two of the streetwalkers, using the wireless transmitters and a repeater," Hans said. "You could watch from here."

"She knows she's being watched, but she doesn't give any indication of it," Dale said. "Let's go. Let's work a little bit."

● ● ●

Isabelle strolled and thought of her child. She'd borne Ilse, though Marie was as close to the girl as Isabelle was herself. They wanted so much for her, like all parents do for their children. The money they made went first into a special fund for Ilse, an insurance policy against a day like today, when something might come back at them, then into another fund to pay for her schooling. Only then did they provide for themselves, but it was enough. They did well on their jobs, and their reputation, carefully built over the years, sustained them in the lean times.

She stopped for a moment outside a tobacco shop, then went inside and bought a pack of American Marlboros. It had been years since she'd had a cigarette, but she had a sudden craving, and it gave her time to watch the surveillance box form up around her. The team was good, there was no doubt of that. She was reasonably sure that she had made at least four operators, but there would be others. She hoped they were as good as they looked, in case the Arab was running countersurveillance. She asked for a lighter from the man at the counter, then stood outside and lit a cigarette and drew it gratefully in. She blew out a cloud of smoke and stood there, one arm hugging herself, and smoked her cigarette. Halfway through she dropped the cigarette and ground it out beneath her clogs and tucked the cigarettes into the pocket of her vest. Then she started out again.

It was a beautiful time of the day, when night and day were evenly balanced in the sky, and the air took on a certain crispness that was particular to the light; she loved the twilight. She walked along, her clogs loud on the pavement, the barrel of the suppressed pistol pressing against her back and buttocks with each step.

• • •

"Hans, move your gunfighters forward," Dale said.

The gunfighters were the armed streetwalkers whose job it was to fight if the unit was compromised. They were thin and hard and competent and heavily armed, and they moved up in the formation. Ringing Isabelle was the loose cordon of surveillance walkers; inside the cordon were two gunfighters and Dale and Charley, who made four armed men inside the surveillance box.

"What are you seeing?" Hans said, his voice tinny in the tiny earpiece Dale wore.

"Nothing yet," Dale said. "It's just the way she's acting. She's leading us somewhere."

• • •

Youssef bin Hassan and Ahmad bin Faisal sat at an outside table at a café beside a bridge that crossed over the canal. Their seating arrangements gave them a good view of the canalside walkway below, as well as the street in both directions.

Youssef saw Isabelle first. He recognized the particular insouciance of her walk, a strange combination of a stroll and a glide, as she came down the street toward the café.

"That's her," he said to bin Faisal. "The one in the vest and skirt coming this way."

"Finish your coffee," bin Faisal said. He tipped up his own cup, enjoying the last little bit of fine espresso.

• • •

Isabelle saw them now, sitting at a table with a good vantage point. Youssef was dressed much as she'd seen him before, in T-shirt and jeans with his courier satchel; he wore a sleeveless sweater-vest over his T-shirt against the cool of evening. She stopped and took out another cigarette and took her time lighting it before she came on. She walked past their table without stopping, slowing only to make eye contact with Youssef, who showed no indication that he knew her. Then she walked on down the stairway to the paved walkway that followed the canal.

• • •

Youssef and bin Faisal stood up, their coffees already paid for, and bin Faisal dropped a few bills on the tabletop. They took their time getting up, and then followed Isabelle down the concrete stairway to the canal walkway below.

• • •

"Hold up," Dale said to Charley. "Did you see those two men get up from the café?"

"Yeah," Charley said.

"Let's give them a little room. They're going down the stairwell to the walkway and we don't want a crowd there. We'll take the eye."

• • •

Isabelle walked for a while, then looked over her shoulder and saw Youssef and the man who would be his controller behind her. She came to the bench that was the designated contact point and sat down, still smoking her cigarette. Youssef and his companion came abreast of her, paused, and then Youssef said, "You are Marta's friend, are you not?"

"Yes, Joe," she said. "Have you forgotten already?"

• • •

"Put the cameras on those two," Dale said. "I want full coverage of those two men. Can you get a mike on them?"

"We can try," Hans said. "Perhaps it would be better for you two to withdraw."

"No," Dale said. "We'll walk by and then come up. I want to see those faces for myself."

• • •

"Who is your friend, Joe?" Isabelle said, blowing a perfect ring of smoke.

"This is my friend Arnold," Youssef said.

"And you are?" bin Faisal said.

"As I think you may already know, my name is Isabelle."

"I expected to meet your partner as well."

"She is otherwise occupied this evening."

"I see."

"Shall we walk?" Youssef said.

"Yes," Isabelle said. She stood up and ground the cigarette beneath her clog. She touched a finger to her lip and removed a grain of tobacco.

The three of them, Isabelle in the middle, walked along the canal.

• • •

"This is unusual," Dale said softly.

All around Isabelle and the two Arabs, micro–video cameras recorded their every move. Back in the command center, video shots of the two men's faces were run through a computer link with the mainframes in the US that maintained the huge database of people of interest to the intelligence community.

"Let them get ahead a bit," Charley said.

"I want a close look at their faces," Dale said.

"We've got good video coverage," Charley said. "Wait so that we can stay with them."

"I've explained our position to Joe," Isabelle said. "We can no longer go forward. The lack of reliable information is why. It nearly got us killed in Minneapolis. You gave us no indication that there was a protection detail of that size and competence on the target. That is why there was a failure. You don't have any better intelligence now on the whereabouts of the target, and you have little prospect of developing any. We've made more than a good-faith effort and we have exposed ourselves more than we are comfortable with. The contract is not doable. You can retain the portion remaining of the fee; we'll accept that loss as a cost of doing business. But we will not go forward with the operation."

"I understand your position," bin Faisal said. "And we're aware of your circumstances. If in the near future we were to develop better intelligence and targeting information, would you consider completing the contract?"

Isabelle was quiet for a moment, then said, "Of course we are open to discussing the matter, but our inclination would be to say no. We've been exposed and the quality of the protection on the target precludes us going against them again."

"I see," bin Faisal said.

• • •

"We have a hit," Hans's voice was tinny in the earpiece Dale wore. "The older Arab is Ahmad bin Faisal . . . he's a top lieutenant in the Al-Bashir organization. He's a planner and organizer, not normally in the field."

"Does he have any specialty?" Dale whispered, the microphone concealed beneath his shirt picking up his every word.

"He's one of the top planners for their operations . . . if you're looking for a connection, it doesn't get any better than this." Hans's voice was keen with the edge of the hunter in it. "The attack on the Dhofar barracks in Saudi Arabia, the shooting of an adviser in Yemen . . . those were all attributed to him."

"Download his info and we'll look at it later," Dale said. "Let's see what he's doing here. Hans, can you put a tail onto him from here?"

"Yes," Hans said. "What about the younger one?"

"Is there anything on him?"

"Nothing, not in the files, not in the databases. We have him in there now as an associate of bin Faisal's and as a suspected terrorist."

"Put some people on him, too," Dale said. "Let's take a look at them while we have them."

"Roger that," Hans said.

• • •

"The quality of the intelligence was unfortunate," bin Faisal said. "But perhaps in the future we can improve on it."

"Improve or not, as I said, we would be inclined to say no. The target's protection knows our profiles and it would be too difficult to launch against them again." Isabelle let a shade of impatience into her voice. "We've done all that we can do, and that will just have to be enough."

"Well then, we have nothing else to discuss," bin Faisal said courteously. He held his hand out to Isabelle, who paused a moment before taking it. "Thank you for your efforts. May we feel free to contact you in the future if we have business other than this contract?"

"Of course," Isabelle said. "We would be happy to work with you again on other projects."

She stood up and glanced around her. "Then we're through. Good-bye, and I hope you enjoy your stay in Amsterdam." She shook Youssef's hand. "Good-bye, Joe."

"Good-bye, Isabelle," Youssef said.

• • •

"The men are leaving," Dale said.

"I have an eye on each," Hans said. "You two stay back, let my people work."

"I want to see their faces," Dale said. "We're going to do a walk-by and then drop out."

"Wait until Isabelle is clear."

"We'll follow above, on the street, and see where they come up," Dale said.

"It would be better for you to stay clear," Hans insisted. "We don't want them to make anyone. We have sufficient video for you to look at their faces all you want."

"He's right," Charley said. "Let's hang back, let the streetwalkers do their thing."

Impatience and frustration crossed Dale's face.

"All right," he said. "We'll stay back."

• • •

Isabelle watched the backs of the two Arabs as they walked away, following the canal walkway. She sensed and felt, rather than saw, how the surveillance box had split. They were onto the two men now, and it was up to them with their high level of expertise to prevent the two men from spotting them. She was sure that the two would practice basic tradecraft and run a countersurveillance route back to wherever they were staying, but this team might be good enough to avoid detection. They surely seemed so.

She took out another cigarette, lit it, and drew hungrily at it. It tasted good and took some of the edge off the feeling in her belly. What was it she felt? Justified, she thought after a moment. After all, it was likely that she'd just signed a death warrant for those two men. She turned and went back the way she'd come, took the stairway up to street level, and began her walk home. There was a sweet shop along the way where she could pick something up for Ilse.

• • •

"Isabelle is on the move . . . she's still not running any countersurveillance. What are you going to do?" Hans asked over the radio.

"We're back to you," Dale said. "We have lots to talk about."

He tucked the earpiece of his radio in place more firmly, then began to walk back along the street above the canal.

"What did we just see?" Charley asked.

"It's the link we've been looking for," Dale said. "Al-Bashir is a Saudi-and-Sudanese-dominated operation . . ."

"I mean with Isabelle," Charley said. "This is one of the top street hitters in the world, and she just walks to a meeting with a top planner from Al-Bashir? She didn't even look over her shoulder. No countersurveillance at all."

"We know they rarely do business in Amsterdam . . ."

"C'mon, Dale. She knows she's under surveillance, and she knows it's American operators which tend to indicate the heavy hand of the Agency, and yet she doesn't make any effort at losing the crew? It's a message plain and simple: here's her answer to what we wanted. She's just given us what we wanted without having to do it our way."

Dale thought for a moment, then said, "That's right. So how do we deal with her now?"

"My vote is to give her the money," Charley said. "She's done what we wanted and she knows it, and she knows we know it now. Give her a package tomorrow at the meeting and say thank you very much, I hope never to see you again."

"What if we don't let on?"

"Dale, how can she not know? She knows, that's the whole point of this exercise tonight. She's handed over to us the people behind the contract on Uday, and it's up to us to figure out the rest. This is all she's got, and she's not going to play games with us. You saw how they were out there on the street with their kid—they won't do anything to endanger themselves and their daughter here on their home turf. She's smart, that Isabelle. This gives them the out they need—they can say they didn't actually give the Arab up, it was a surveillance operation. Not that anybody would know, or is going to find out about this transaction."

Charley rubbed his jaw and the day's collection of stubble there.

"That's my call," he said.

"You may be right," Dale said. "Let's see how good Hans's people are at tracking those two."

The two men hurried along the canal pathway and climbed the staircase back to the street.

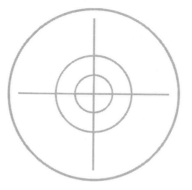

Callan and Dalton shared an early morning breakfast in the cafeteria of Ray's building. They sat well away from the other occupied tables as they discussed the activities in Amsterdam.

"It's Al-Bashir," Callan said. "I have all the video here." He tapped one finger on a compact disk on the table. "We're on both operators right now. One of them is Ahmad bin Faisal. The other one is a young guy, we don't know who yet."

"The Twins gave them up?" Dalton said with surprise.

"Not in so many words," Callan said. "But Isabelle led our crew right to the meet with the Al-Bashir people. So there're your paymasters."

"How do we know they're the paymasters?"

"Because Isabelle gave them up that way. There's no other reason a top-shelf pro like her would operate like she did, except for the talk she had with Dale and Charley. It's her way of giving them up without giving in to us."

"So what does she want now?"

"One hundred fifty thousand dollars, which I think is a bargain."

"Go ahead with that," Dalton said. "I think it's time I got on the dance card."

"Why piss off Dale now?" Callan said in a measured voice.

"He's doing a great job. You don't need to step in. You're getting all the take as soon as we get it."

"Sooner or later, Dale and I will have to come to an understanding."

"Concentrate on the big picture, Ray. You can worry about patching things up some other time. You and Dale, you're not the priority now."

Ray smiled coldly. "That's true." He took a pen from his pocket and twirled it in his fingers. "Ahmad bin Faisal. He would be a great catch."

"Yes, he would," Callan said. "But we want to see where he'll lead us first. You'll want a team of your door kickers ready to do a snatch on him."

"I can have a team on-site in eight hours."

"Do that, and have them stand off. There's no need to duplicate our efforts."

"Al-Bashir," Dalton said again. "Doing the hit as an Iraqi proxy or as a favor?"

"That remains to be seen. It would be good to squeeze bin Faisal for what he's got."

Dalton laughed. "Yes, it would, wouldn't it?" He grew serious. "And we'd get some answers about Sad Holiday."

"If you pick him up for the Dhofar bombing and the hit in Yemen or for any of the other operations you've got his signature on, he'll be in custody and you're going to have to deal with the legalities," Callan said. "If you let him run, let us work the surveillance, he may lead you to all the answers. Then you can pick him up and read him his rights."

"I like the way you think, Mike Callan," Dalton said lightly. "You sure you don't want a job?"

"I gots a job, Ray, and I make more than you do."

"But do you have as much fun?"

"Fewer headaches, that's for sure."

"Then let him run. Put your best people on him."

"They already are, Ray. They already are."

171

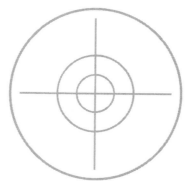

AMSTERDAM, THE NETHERLANDS,
NEAR THE TWINS' HOUSEBOAT

Charley and Dale stood outside the Italian gelato shop. Charley licked at a melting chocolate cone he held delicately between two fingers. He spotted Isabelle, walking alone, her hands clasped behind her back, before Dale did.

"Here she comes," Charley said. He took a quick bite out of the ice cream and discarded the unfinished cone into a trash bin, then watched Isabelle as she took her time walking up to the two men.

"I see you tried the gelato," Isabelle said. "Didn't you find it to your liking?"

"I enjoyed it," Charley said. "Just was making a mess."

"You Americans," Isabelle said. "The best things are sometimes messy."

"Yes," Dale said.

"Have you thought over our discussion?" Isabelle said.

"Yes," Dale said. He unslung the nylon bag he had over his shoulder and handed it to Isabelle. "The amount is what we discussed. Consider it reimbursement for your expenses and thanks for your consideration in this matter."

Isabelle weighed the bag in one hand, then slung it over her shoulder.

"Thank you," she said. "Do we have any other business?"

"No," Dale said. "We're done."

"Then enjoy your stay in Amsterdam," Isabelle said. She favored them with a slight smile, then left and walked away, back to her houseboat, her lover, and her child.

• • •

While Ilse slept in her room, Isabelle spilled the banded bundles of American hundred-dollar bills across her bed where Marie curled like an idle cat. Marie picked up a bundle and riffled through it.

"This makes it easy to count," she said.

Isabelle said nothing. She stood and looked down at the cash, her eyes calculating.

"What is it?" Marie said. "You've done well for us. What's wrong?"

Isabelle sat down on the bed. "I have a bad feeling about this. The whole thing. There is more than meets the eye here."

"Leave it alone, Isabelle," Marie pleaded. "Look at what we have! We walked away from this a winner on all counts. We don't need to concern ourselves with them anymore."

"I know where the boy is staying," Isabelle said.

"You said that he's no operator, you said that he was out of place."

"That's why I have this feeling about him. I mean to watch him."

"Isabelle . . ."

"There is something to him! I have an instinct about this."

Marie sighed, and dropped the bundle of money she held. "I should know better than to try and argue with you. You'll do as you see best. Let me get dressed, and we can take Ilse to my mother's."

"No," Isabelle said. "Ilse needs one of us. I will do this alone."

"Ah, Isabelle . . ."

"No, my love," Isabelle said, less forcefully than before. "I will see to this. I'll make sure that we are safe."

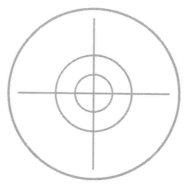

AMSTERDAM, THE NETHERLANDS, AHMAD BIN FAISAL'S
HOTEL ROOM

Youssef bin Hassan and Ahmad bin Faisal stood side by side and looked out the window at the night-lights of Amsterdam.

"It's beautiful, isn't it?" bin Faisal said.

"Yes," the younger man said. "It is."

"It's time to discuss the next phase of your operation," bin Faisal said.

"I'm ready."

"I've seen that you are. Your operational developments have been extraordinary; some of the techniques you've come up with will be added to the training curriculum."

"There will be others like me?"

"A few . . . this is a special tasking and requires special men, such as yourself. But there may be need for another special tasking . . ."

"Not if I do my job correctly. And I will."

"Of course, Youssef. Of course."

Bin Faisal took his suitcase out of the closet and spun the locks on the Delsey hard-sided plastic suitcase. He opened it up and took out a small Pelican waterproof case with a small lock on it. He selected a tiny key from his key chain and opened up the case. Inside, nestled in cutout foam, were five small vials, each the length of a medium-sized-man's little finger. He set the open container carefully down on the table, then took out two small plastic boxes and an atomizer the size of a small perfume spray.

"The devices you have will suffice for backup," he said. "These are brand new and have been tested. Of course, you will want to test them for yourself and see."

Youssef stood beside the table, and reached one hand, almost shyly, toward the Pelican case and the five vials in it.

"This is it?" he said softly.

"Yes," bin Faisal said. "This is Sad Holiday."

• • •

Later, Youssef walked alone in the dark. The Pelican case and the new devices barely made a bulge in his courier bag. It was a warm summer night, and the young people of Amsterdam were out in force. There were many couples walking hand in hand along the canalways and the narrow streets. Youssef eyed them with interest and more than a little envy. He thought of the two women he had slept with in his life. Not much to think about. He wondered if they ever thought of him, and decided it was unlikely.

He wondered whether he should feel sad about that or not. He didn't know.

He fell into the crowds and let them carry them where they would. He felt as though he were in an invisible capsule, riding along yet not part of the crowd. It seemed as though no one really saw him, and yet he was able to look at them with the avidity of the voyeur. There was much to see: two girls locked in an embrace, lips pressed together; a boy and a girl, their arms lazily draped around each other, sharing a marijuana cigarette outside a coffee shop; a tall prostitute dressed in a short leather dress under a full-length leather coat, striding along as though she were in command of the boulevard.

Youssef felt as though he were somehow connected and disconnected at the same time, and the slight weight of the deadly virus he carried in his courier bag couldn't dissuade him from the sense that something was tugging at him, clamoring for his attention. He fought down his uncertainty with the thought of his training, calmed himself and let a prayer rise up in him.

"Allah, let me do the right thing."

That was a peculiar thing to think about at this time.

"Hello, Youssef!" a woman said.

He jumped, startled out of his interior dialogue, and saw the blond woman from the homeless shelter looking at him.

"Remember me? Britta?" she said.

"Yes, hi," he said, confused.

"You look lost," she said. "Are you lost?"

He smiled uncertainly. "I don't think so."

"You were looking so sad . . . and you're alone again, aren't you?"

"Yes," he said. "I'm alone again."

"Would you like to get a coffee?" she said.

"Yes," Youssef said. "I'd like that very much."

• • •

She was short and plump and blond, and her hair was cut short with bangs across a forehead lightly dotted with acne, but she looked beautiful to Youssef bin Hassan.

"Why are you staring at me?" Britta said. "Has it been that long since you've had coffee with a girl?"

"Yes," Youssef said, thinking of his lunch with Isabelle. "Too long. I'm sorry, I don't wish to be rude."

"Are you Palestinian?"

"No, I'm from Saudi Arabia."

"How long have you been in Amsterdam?"

"Not long, a few weeks . . ."

"And you're still alone after all this time? You must enjoy it. Are you a writer? I see you carrying that laptop around with you. I think you must be. You are always looking around but you are never part of what you are watching . . . you just observe. I have a friend who is a writer and she is like that." She sipped at her coffee, enjoying his befuddlement. "You haven't told me yet."

Youssef smiled to hide his confusion. He'd lost practice in simple conversation. "I used to write poetry. But that was a long time ago."

"I think you were probably good at it."

"You are very kind. How long have you worked at the homeless shelter?"

"A few years. I enjoy the work, it feels good to help people."

"Yes," he said. "It would. But don't you get some hard people there? People who just want to take and aren't willing to help out in return?"

"Sometimes," Britta said. "But still I must help them. I can choose how I behave toward them, I can choose how to behave toward anyone. It's always a matter of choice, don't you think? Choice is what makes us human. We can choose to do something or not do something. We can choose to do good or we can choose to do evil. Don't you think so?"

Youssef's hand trembled as he took up his coffee cup and drank.

"Youssef? You look ill, is the coffee too strong?"

"No," Youssef said. "It's just that what you said is so interesting. About choice. Do you think that you could find yourself sometime wanting to do something that wasn't good, but you felt you had to do it? Maybe turn away someone who was rude, punish them for their behavior?"

"No," Britta said. "I don't feel as though it's my job to judge others. The world is full of judges. We don't know enough about people most of the time to judge what they do. I just measure it by whether they are doing harm or not. Whether they are hurting others or themselves. That makes for a pretty simple measure, don't you think?"

"Perhaps it is too simple a measure," Youssef said. "What if someone was doing evil or harm to others? Is it evil to do something to stop them from harming others, even if you have to use force?"

Britta mulled for a moment, ran her finger around the rim of her coffee cup.

"It's not evil to stop people from doing evil . . . but I wouldn't use force. I'd try to convince them of the error of their ways, talk to them. Most problems can be solved if you just talk to people, but we have a hard time getting past our own barriers to do that."

"What do you mean, our own barriers?"

Britta toyed with her coffee cup. "Preconceptions, prejudices, that sort of thing. The barriers in our mind we put up when we judge someone else without understanding them. We've all done it . . . haven't you?"

Youssef was quiet for a long time.

"Youssef? Are you all right? Did I offend you?" Britta said.

"No," Youssef said. "You didn't offend me. You just made me think about things that I've done, with those barriers."

"You see?" she said brightly. "That's the first step. Seeing what we do and taking responsibility for it."

Youssef pushed his coffee cup away. "Shall we walk? I feel like moving."

"Sure," Britta said. "Let's go."

They rambled in the narrow streets. Britta tucked her hands into Youssef's arm. He stiffened at first, then relaxed. He followed the slight tugs and urgings from Britta as they walked in silence and let her guide him. He felt as though he were afloat in a sea of people and Britta was his life jacket. Each time she nudged his arm, he clamped down for a moment, as though to hold her hands to him even more tightly. Finally, they came to a residential district. There were fewer pedestrians in this neighborhood.

"This is where I live," Britta said. "Would you like to come up?"

"Yes," Youssef said. "Very much."

She led him up the stairs to a tiny studio apartment dominated by a huge window that looked out on the street below.

"It's nice, isn't it?" she said. "I feel as though I can let the whole world in through that window, and I can close it anytime I want to. I can bring the world in or I can shut it out."

Youssef stood before the window and looked out. The view was mostly of the building across the street, but he could see across the rooftops as well, and there was a slice of canal to the left. There was a perfect view of the sidewalks below and a small café on the corner.

"It's very nice," Youssef said.

"I know you don't drink," Britta said. "Would you like tea, or some fruit juice?"

"I'd like fruit juice, please."

She brought him a glass of apple juice which he drank thirstily. She took the glass from his hand and set it down, then turned to him. For the first time that night, she seemed hesitant. Youssef sensed that and turned to her. He put the courier bag with its deadly baggage down on the floor beneath a small table, and took her in his arms.

● ● ●

In the street below, Isabelle stood and watched till the lights went out, then turned away and made her way home.

Dale stalked back and forth in the crowded operations room. The equipment operators gave him plenty of room, and Hans and Charley, both seated in folding chairs, exchanged worried looks.

"How did they lose him?" Dale demanded of Hans.

"We only had three people on him," Hans said defensively. "You should know how easy it is to lose track of someone in a crowd. He was running good CSR through the district. It was too much for the three of them. They lost sight of him and tried to reacquire, but couldn't find him."

"It happens with the best of crews, Dale," Charley said.

"What about bin Faisal?" Dale said.

"He's at his hotel and preparing to check out. He's got a flight back to Damascus midday," Hans said.

"Do we have that covered?" Dale said.

"Yes," Hans said. "We've got a crew ready to go, and we're setting up a reception team in Damascus."

"If it's any consolation, Dale," Charley said, "it's bin Faisal we want . . . the kid was just a cutout, a courier. We've got him in the system now. Bin Faisal is the mover and shaker and we've got him going home now. Don't worry about it."

"The 'kid' was high up enough to be privy to details of a sensitive operation," Dale countered.

"There's nothing more to be done," Charley said. "He's in the system now and that's it."

"Bin Faisal is in the lobby of his hotel," one of the equipment operators said. "He's going to the travel-agency counter."

"What's he doing?" Dale said.

"Give us a minute," Hans said irritably. "You want miracles and instant results."

Dale held one hand up, palm out. "I know you're doing the best you can, Hans. It's just . . . you know how important this is."

They all listened to the terse comments on the radio as the surveillance crew staked out in bin Faisal's hotel moved in.

"He's changing his ticket," the radio squawked. "He's changed his departure from today for Damascus to tomorrow for Athens. First-class ticket, oh-nine-hundred departure, KLM airlines."

"Athens?" Charley said. "I've got good connects in Athens."

"Why would he be going to Athens instead of heading home?" Dale said.

Hans shrugged. "Athens is a hotbed for Al-Bashir. They use it as a transit point and for staging operatives during long operations. They have many safe houses there, and they have a working alliance with the November Seventeenth organization."

"November Seventeenth?" Dale said. "They're bad news."

"For Americans, yes," Hans said.

The November Seventeenth terrorist organization was one of the most bloody-handed and efficient terrorist groups operating. They had assassinated the DEA attaché at the US embassy as well as the CIA station chief. They were believed to be a small and tightly disciplined organization focused on anti-American interests in Greece. They were known for their signature assassination technique, a walk-up shooting with a .45 automatic pistol. Recently, with the help of Al-Bashir, they had ventured into car bombings, being scrupulous about striking only American targets like the embassy, and an American Express office. They were careful not to injure

Greeks, only American businessmen and government officials.

"He could be meeting with them," Dale said. "What did you do there?"

Charley said, "I worked there with Special Activities, we ran a special operating group against November Seventeenth."

"Did you get anywhere?"

"Nope. There's no penetrating November Seventeenth. Tighter than turtle pussy, and that's waterproof. They're small and tight and—everybody believes—highly connected politically."

"We'll need to talk to Callan, see about getting some help on that end," Dale said.

"I've got it covered," Hans said. "We've worked many times in Athens. I can send a team today, to prepare for bin Faisal. Are you going to want to go, too?"

"Yes," Dale said, looking at Charley, who nodded his assent. "We'll be there, too."

• • •

Hans dispatched a special operating group to Athens. They would prepare a reception for bin Faisal at the airport: a few operators in the crowd outside customs waiting to spot him when he came out, and another team with vehicles waiting outside. The Amsterdam surveillance team on bin Faisal worked like smooth clockwork following him: they watched an expensive prostitute visit his hotel room and determined that he enjoyed oral sex, and that he had surprising stamina for a man of his age. The prostitute left at a little before ten that evening, and he ordered in room service, a small steak and a large salad and a bottle of chilled mineral water. Then he packed and went to bed.

In the morning he had a leisurely breakfast at the hotel restaurant downstairs, then took his garment bag and carry-on bag to the front, and took a taxi to Schiopol airport. Bin Faisal was relaxed, and practicing only minimal countersurveillance; he took a cab directly from the stand in front of the hotel after a slow check of the lobby. Hans and his people stood off, leaving only one man in the lobby.

182

The rest of the team covered all exits from the hotel with a vehicle crew standing off ready to follow the target vehicle. There were already operators out at the airport, ready to receive the surveillance subject when he showed up.

Charley and Dale sat in the backseat of a taxi parked on the street in front of the hotel. The driver was one of Hans's people.

"I'm glad Hans will be with us in Athens," Charley said. "This guy is golden."

"He knows his job," Dale said. "I wish he hadn't lost the other guy, though."

"They're still looking for him," Charley said. "And we got his image in the system, that's what counts."

"I'd feel better if we had him buttoned up someplace."

"He's probably already out of here and headed back home, wherever that might be."

"That's one of the questions we didn't get answered."

"Leave it alone, Dale. There's nothing to be done about it now that Hans and his people aren't already doing."

The driver looked at the two of them in the rearview mirror, then looked back at the front of the hotel.

"The subject is moving," he said. "He's in a cab and pulling out."

Their car followed at a safe distance the cab carrying bin Faisal. Two other surveillance vehicles rotated the eye between them, while another car paced ahead of the cab on the direct route to the airport. At the airport, bin Faisal got out, and the vehicle teams pulled off, one of them dropping an extra man to shadow bin Faisal into the airport and into the box prepared by the waiting operating group, who were positioned along the main entrance to the airport terminal building. They shadowed bin Faisal to the KLM counter, where he checked in, leaving his bags, and then went to the first-class lounge to wait for his flight.

Dale and Charley checked in. Both were traveling business–class, leaving Hans's people to insert one of their operators into first-class to be a close eye on bin Faisal.

"You want to go into the lounge?" Dale said.

"Not a good idea," Charley said. "Americans stick out, and he might remember you. This is a stalk, not a pounce."

"I want to see this guy's face," Dale said.

"Hey, your call," Charley said, irritated. "I don't think you should be exposed to him yet . . . we've got a good stretch of time ahead of us, and you can look at him on the plane. Don't give him a reason to remember you."

"I'll meet you at the gate," Dale said. "I'm going in to have a firsthand look at Mr. bin Faisal."

"Whatever," Charley said. He turned away, angry, and stalked off, leaving Dale watching him go. Dale went to the first-class lounge and showed his ticket to the woman at the front counter.

"Go right in, sir," she said courteously. "The departure times are listed on the monitor, and if you like, I'll call you for your flight."

"That's all right," Dale said. "The monitor's fine for me."

He went into the lounge. He looked the part of a business traveler. He was dressed in khaki trousers, a blue oxford shirt with no tie under a blue blazer matched with cordovan loafers. No one looked up when he came in. Bin Faisal was seated in a corner armchair in the lounge, reading the *International Herald Tribune*. Dale took a *Newsweek* magazine from the stand that held reading materials and took a chair where he could see bin Faisal in his peripheral vision. The Saudi was engrossed in his paper, and sipped from a steaming cup of tea on the end table beside him. Dale flipped through the news magazine without really reading, then went and got himself a sparkling water from the sideboard where the refreshments were laid. He went back to his seat and began to read the cover story, a lengthy piece about the new face of terrorism.

The Saudi was a handsome man, his face folded and soft at the edges with fine living. He was dressed in an immaculate business suit as though he were going to a business meeting. His cuffs were secured with expensive diamond links, and there was a motif of a repeated monogram on his silk tie. Dale wondered about his background. He knew what the databases had on him: the Saudi was the son of a wealthy family, who had spent much of his adult life without the inconvenience of a job thanks to his family money. That gave him the opportunity to delve into anti-American politics, always an undercurrent in the subtleties of Saudi Arabian government. His financial expertise was garnered from the finest business schools and his deft handling of his family's wealth had made him an ideal target for the Al-Bashir recruiters.

Dale thought of bin Faisal as one of the sheltered bureaucrats of the terrorist world; they enjoyed fine living while their operators and trigger pullers risked themselves on the operations planned and funded by the men like bin Faisal. As much as he loathed terrorism and terrorists, he sometimes felt grudging respect for the street-level operators; they were at least akin to him as an operator. They worked the same streets, underwent the same stresses. Even though one for one the Americans and their allies were better trained and equipped, the terrorists they faced were highly motivated and within the limits of their resources highly dangerous.

And they probably nursed the same loathing of the bureaucrats who sent them out on their missions as did Dale.

He felt his emotions across his face, and took a deep breath to center himself. Charley had been right; it was too soon to show himself to bin Faisal since the coming operation in Athens might call for him to play a role in close quarters to the Saudi. Dale chided himself for his impatience, and settled in to make himself the gray man, just part of the Arab's surroundings, as unnoticeable as the chair or the smartly dressed flight attendants. This was the hard part of the urban operator's job. This wasn't like the jungle or the mountains or the desert; the environment he had to fade into was often one that took him face to face with his opponent or his opponent's allies. His camouflage was his demeanor and bearing as well as the clothes he wore and the places he went.

He settled in and waited for his flight to be called.

185

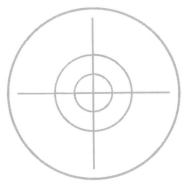

DOMINANCE RAIN HEADQUARTERS, FAIRFAX, VIRGINIA

"All they need to do is finger him," Ray Dalton said. "I've got a crew standing by in Italy. I can have them in place in hours. Once they've got him fixed, my boys can snatch him and we can have a leisurely debrief with Mr. Ahmad bin Faisal."

Callan grinned at Dalton's bloodthirsty eagerness. "They'll be able to do that."

"But we won't move too hastily," Dalton said, sitting back in his chair. "We'll see who bin Faisal hooks up with . . . I'd love a link to November Seventeenth . . . we owe those bastards a few."

"And then there's Sad Holiday," Callan said.

"Bin Faisal's the link we've been looking for. Al-Bashir provided the money for the hit on Uday."

Callan nodded, musing.

"We have the main paymaster in our sights," Dalton said. "There won't be any Sad Holiday as long as we keep bin Faisal right where we want him, which is out there running around on a very short rope, touching base with his operators and his support structure."

"Bin Faisal's a paymaster and finance expert for Al-Bashir; he's not linked directly to operational planning. He's not a fighter, he's a finance man. At least that's what he was at Dhofar and in Yemen."

"It looks as though he's doing more than that. He's out in the field getting face time with the Twins, who are as operational as they come, he's meeting with his cutout in Amsterdam, and now he's running to Athens instead of going home to Syria."

"There's more to this than meets the eye," Callan said with the sigh of an old field hand. "I don't think the story is going to end with bin Faisal."

"What do you think?" Ray said.

"I don't have enough to speculate and neither do you," Callan said mildly. "Al-Bashir has us in their sights as well, and a biological warfare operation, especially if Iraq provided them with the material, would be within their capability."

"Al-Bashir isn't one of the organizations we've linked to an active search for biological weapons."

"That doesn't mean it hasn't crossed their minds, Ray. As you well know. I know you're eager to take this boy, but let's not let this cloud the paucity of facts we have right now. You still don't have anything on Sad Holiday, other than the bin Faisal connection. There're still a lot of holes in the story we need to fill in."

"We'll fill them in when we have bin Faisal," Dalton said. "We'll take what we need right out of his head."

AMSTERDAM, THE NETHERLANDS, BRITTA'S APARTMENT

"May I stay here for a few days?" Youssef asked Britta, whose face was buried in his chest, her hand lingering and plucking at the smooth, hairless slope of his pectoral muscles.

"Of course," she said. "You're welcome to stay as long as you like."

"Only a few days," he said. "Then I must be on my way."

"Would you like coffee?" Britta said, rolling away from him.

"Yes."

"I'll make some, then."

Britta got out of bed and walked naked across the room to her tiny kitchenette, where she put water on to boil. Youssef enjoyed watching her heavy hips rolling easily with an unself-consciousness he found highly erotic. She took coffee grounds from the freezer of her small icebox and put them into a Melitta cone and filter, then put the cone onto a small carafe. She carefully poured the boiling water over the grounds and as the brew began to drip into the carafe, the powerful scent of coffee filled the studio apartment. Britta filled two big mugs from the carafe and said, "Tell me again what you like in your coffee?"

"Sugar and milk, please. Lots of both."

"You have a sweet tooth."

She took milk from the icebox and poured it into one mug and added two heaping spoonfuls of sugar. She returned to the bed and handed him both mugs to hold while she slid beneath the sheets again, then reclaimed her mug.

"There," she said with satisfaction. "That's better."

Youssef was quiet and drank his coffee in silence. It wasn't a heavy silence. It was the companionable quiet of two people who had no need to talk. Part of him was amazed at how comfortable he felt with this woman, only the third woman he had ever had sex with. Britta exuded comfort and warmth, and he felt himself opening to her like a flower to the sun. For a moment he considered telling her, unburdening himself about his mission, but that momentary madness passed and he found himself concentrating on staying in this moment, right now.

"This is very good," he said.

"Yes, it is, all of it, isn't it?" Britta said. "You, me, the coffee . . . what a wonderful time it is."

"How are you so happy all the time?" Youssef said in wonder. "Are you ever sad, or confused?"

"Of course," she said. She laughed. "All human beings are sad or confused sometimes. I think the key is not to hang onto it, to learn to let things go."

"Yes," Youssef said. "I believe you are right."

"It's important to pay attention to what is happening right now, instead of a week from now," Britta said. "So you can stay here. A week from now you'll leave, but I won't think about that. I have you here right now."

Youssef looked around the apartment. Despite its tiny size, it was full of homey touches: a colorful slipcover on the armchair; framed flowers on the walls; a board-and-brick bookcase overflowing with paperbacks, mostly novels, some in English; pillows stacked to overflowing on the bed, now all knocked in a colorful disarray on the carpeted floor.

"You have no boyfriend?" he asked.

"No one now," Britta said. She nudged him with her hip, causing her coffee to slop dangerously in the big mug. "Would you like to be my boyfriend? For the next week or until you must go?"

"Yes," Youssef said, seriously. "I would like that very much."

• • •

Later, Britta went to work at the homeless shelter, and Youssef stayed in the apartment. It was raining, and the sudden gloom in the middle of summer took him by surprise. But it was Amsterdam weather, and soon the gray skies began to part and let the blue of the summer sky back through again. He had placed the armchair directly in front of the window and sat there, bare-chested, and let the sun beat through the window onto his thin frame. He was confused by the turn of events; he had a plan that he needed to stick to, but for some reason he no longer felt as though he had a plan, but that he was part of someone else's plan. He took out his courier bag and opened it up. Beneath his few items of clothing were the Pelican case and its deadly vials of virus, and a small cloth bag that held the three dispersion devices and the two aerosol canisters. He opened the Pelican case and took out one of the vials, held it between his thumb and forefinger and held it up to the light streaming through the window. It looked so harmless, but it swarmed with enough pathogen to wipe out a city.

He felt a strange sensation in the pit of his stomach, as though he were on a roller-coaster and preparing for the sudden drop. He had a mission to do. He'd been entrusted with a great responsibility and the great honor to exact a killing blow against the foe. He needed to remember that, he reminded himself. What had happened last night and today was only coincidence, and useful to him operationally.

Youssef didn't want to think about using Britta operationally.

He replaced the vial in the case with its companions and gently closed it. He made sure the latches were in place and then replaced the Pelican case at the bottom of his satchel along with the dispersion devices, then put his clothing and his shaving kit in on top of it. The bag was bulky but sufficiently compressible so that he could still carry it slung over his shoulder. He took a change of underwear out and then closed the bag and went to the tiny bathroom and took a long, hot shower in the tub ringed with its curtain. Afterward he carefully shaved, then dressed and went out. There was a W. H. Smith bookstore they'd passed on the walk last night; he went there and then to the travel section. He bought a guidebook to Washington, DC and its environs. A detailed scale map was enclosed that showed the downtown area in great detail.

Youssef went to a coffee shop and ordered a small espresso and sweetened it with two spoonfuls of sugar and drank it while he looked over the guidebook.

There was a lot to do in Washington, DC.

ATHENS, GREECE

The final approach to the Athens airport is over the sea, and Dale Miller sat in his seat and watched the cerulean blue of the Mediterranean give way to the sandy brown of the shore and then the gray of the runway asphalt beneath him. The wheels of the 747 touched down once, then again with a slight bump, and then the plane began to slow. The aircraft taxied toward the terminal parking area, and stopped well short of the building where several passenger buses waited. Dale glanced over at Charley, who was boneless and relaxed in his seat, comfortable as a big cat. The tall man looked up and caught his eye and dropped a casual wink. Dale nodded and looked around the business-class section; no one had noticed the exchange. He leaned out into the aisle and looked forward in first-class but didn't see Ahmad bin Faisal.

Dale followed the other passengers out the door and down the ramp into the brilliant sun of a Grecian summer. He boarded the bus with the others, nodded to the armed soldier providing security on the bus, and rode a bumpy ride to the terminal, where those passengers who'd checked baggage picked it up and lined up in front of the customs counters. With only carry-on, Dale and Charley were the first through customs, where a bored inspector gave them a desultory look and stamped their passports. Charley and Dale slowed and waited till bin Faisal passed them on his way out of customs into the main terminal, where a small crowd waited to greet passengers from the flight. The two operators went to the small line in front of the currency exchange, and saw bin Faisal go out to the taxi stand and take the first cab in line. They watched him go, and then a slight, dark-skinned man came up to them and said, "You are Hans's friends, yes?"

"That's right," Dale said.

"I have a vehicle waiting," the man said. "My name is Peter."

"Hello, Peter," Charley said. "Is Hans already here?"

"Yes," Peter said. He led them out of the terminal to the parking lot, and then to a battered Fiat sedan. "Hans was with the first team, who will follow bin Faisal." He put their bags in the trunk and took out a portable Motorola radio with an earpiece. He put the earpiece in and turned on the radio as he got behind the wheel of the Fiat, gesturing for Charley and Dale to get in.

"This is Peter," Peter said to the radio. "We're up and monitoring."

He listened intently for a few minutes, then nodded, and started the car.

"Bin Faisal is checking in at the Athens Hilton Hotel," he said.  "A very nice and expensive hotel, and one we've worked in before. It's where the US embassy puts up its visiting personnel. We have people on-site right now, and once he has his room we'll work on a covert penetration for sound and video."

He pulled out into the traffic and accelerated sharply, pressing Charley and Dale back in their seats. The car was much faster than it looked.

"I forgot how you Greeks like to drive," Charley said.

Peter smiled. "You've been here before?"

"Yes," Charley said. "Many years ago. I enjoyed it very much."

Dale said, "Where are we staying?"

"We have a safe house prepared in the same district as the Athens Hilton," Peter said. "It will be cramped but sufficient for our needs. Hans and I, two equipment operators, and yourselves."

"Thank you," Dale said. He turned and looked out at the city whizzing past his window as Peter wove in and out of the busy traffic on the main street that led into downtown Athens. He kept a lookout for the first view of the Acropolis as he came in, and he remembered taking a walking tour there once when he had downtime between missions in Athens. A friend of his, a federal air marshal, had met him in Athens and they had done the tourist thing together. He wondered what Marcos was doing now. It had been many years since he'd seen him.

Charley said, "Will we be within walking distance to the Plaka? I'm trying to get oriented."

"A longish walk, but you can do it," Peter said. "We are very close to the American embassy, do you remember where that is?"

"Sure," Charley said.

Dale touched his hipbone with his elbow, then said, "Will Hans have pistols for us?"

"Yes," Peter said. "We have to be very careful and discreet with those. We have gunfighters, but we understand that you may feel more comfortable with your own pistols. We'll take care of that."

"That'll be fine," Charley said. "We may need them with November Seventeenth sniffing around."

Peter looked in the rearview mirror at Charley. "That is a true thing you just said."

• • •

Ahmad bin Faisal was satisfied with his room. He had a spectacular view of the city, and the room was well appointed and comfortable. The Arab unpacked his bags and hung his coat in the bathroom to let the wrinkles out. He studied the minibar for a time, then decided instead to go downstairs to the lobby bar for a light lunch.

The lobby was full of people coming and going; the Hilton was a popular meeting spot with the Athens wealthy and there were many other international businessmen going about their affairs. Bin Faisal was satisfied that he drew no attention from the tourism police, hulking in their plainclothes, who wandered the lobby looking for trouble.

The restaurant was serving full meals, but he had in mind something lighter; in the bar he ordered a Caesar salad and some bread. He settled back at his table and comfortable armchair and lit a Turkish cigarette, drawing with great satisfaction at the rich blend of tobacco while he waited for his meal. From his seat he could see the whole length of the bar into the lobby.

Ahmad bin Faisal believed in knowing his own weaknesses, and one of the things he freely admitted was that his tradecraft was not among the best. He was a financier and planner, a concept man who had never had to participate in the operations he planned with the other top lieutenants of the Al-Bashir network. His strength was in finding and moving money, putting in the financial infrastructure for the operations to come. His recent excursions into the field were prompted by the need to keep the One compartmented and yet busy while plans were finalized; the job had fallen to him to keep knowledge of the One to a bare operational minimum.

He practiced the tradecraft he remembered, but counted on more than anything the quality of his false passports and credit cards. He'd seen to that himself, making sure he had only the very best paper. With that, he was just another businessman shuttling around the continent in the interests of his company. He bore letterhead and a briefcase full of documents attesting to his business as a financial officer for an oil company, more than sufficient to put off any official interest in him.

195

But he had not grown to his age without being cautious. Even in Athens, where most members of Al-Bashir felt comfortable and moved about freely, it was good to be cautious. The one thing he remembered most from the intense man who had taught him rudimentary tradecraft was to pay attention to his intuition; quite often what we felt or intuited turned out to be the case.

And his intuition was bothering him.

He hadn't seen anything out of the ordinary in Amsterdam, and he was quite sure that Youssef hadn't either. Youssef had the discretion in the final phases of the operation to make his own arrangements to enter the United States; once in place, he could be contacted only by one-way messages encrypted and sent to certain Web sites. The messages were hidden in a piece of the code that made up a photographic image. Once the image was downloaded the information could be extracted. It was very nearly foolproof.

No, Youssef would be all right.

What he was worrying about was himself. Since he'd arrived at the hotel, he'd had a nagging sensation that he was being watched. He'd originally chalked it up to the plane trip; he didn't enjoy flying, the constant vibration and noise gave him a headache, and he disliked wearing earplugs. But now, seated where he was, it seemed as though there was a regular rotation of people coming in and out of the bar, people who didn't stay for very long. It might be just his imagination, since it was lunch hour, but he felt as though several of the people who had come in had looked him over carefully, more carefully than a casual diner at the same location would do.

His meal came, and he turned his attention to it. He asked for a newspaper, and took the *International Herald Tribune* when the waitress brought it. He folded it open, and held it with one hand while he ate with the other. The meal went quickly, and he decided against a drink. The day outside looked splendid, and he decided to go for a walk. It would give him an opportunity to test himself and see if his budding paranoia was in fact justified.

He went outside, and stood for a moment and looked at the flagpoles with their flags of many nations that stretched alongside the curved driveway that came to the front of the hotel. He lit another cigarette and drew on it nervously, then began to stroll slowly away from the hotel. In the lectures he'd endured, the instructors had stressed the need not to tip off the surveillance teams that they'd been noticed. That made it all the more harder if they knew and took steps to hide themselves. Better that they be careless and cocky and confident that their subject was unaware of their attentions. So he didn't look around or over his shoulder, instead he relaxed and let his eyes expand and widen his peripheral vision, and began paying attention to the surfaces around him that reflected and gave him some idea of what or who was behind him. Parked cars, shop windows, other people. He put on his sunglasses against the glare and to hide his own eyes.

The main boulevard outside the hotel was busy with streaming traffic in both directions. He walked down a quiet side street to a smaller street lined with shops and began walking his route. First he crossed the street so that the vehicle traffic on his side was coming toward him, then he slowed down and took his time, window-shopping, checking in the reflections if there was anyone staring at him or stopping to look. He went into a clothing store and admired the suits, then went out and crossed the street to a grocery shop and bought a small bottle of mineral water. He stood on the street and drank thirstily. Then he continued on, past a BMW dealership where he lingered for a moment and looked at the latest sedans, then continued on past the Holiday Inn and a series of bars and clubs. At street crossings, he found a reason to hold back, and then crossed just as the lights began to change, and made it a point to look and see if anyone was hurrying across to keep up with him.

Still, the feeling stuck with him. There were a few instances of people hurrying across the light at the same time as he, but they either passed him at his dawdling pace or turned off and went in another direction. There were so many vehicles that he had a hard time keeping track of them, but as far as he could tell no vehicle had come by and slowed to watch him, or appeared more than once in the endless parade of vehicles that clogged the streets of downtown Athens.

But perhaps it was just his imagination after all. He had done nothing to come to the attention of the Greek authorities, and the Israelis and the Americans would be hard put to mount a full-scale surveillance of him on such short notice. There were other people, including Greek Intelligence, who would be interested in his activities, but he was confident in the quality of his forged documents and his cover as a businessman. No, he decided. Today was not the day he was being followed. His mind made up, he continued strolling toward his final destination, a small family-run restaurant that served the finest roast lamb in Athens. It was time for a meal.

• • •

"Did he make anybody?" Dale asked Hans.

"I don't think so," Hans said. "But this is the first time we've seen him do more than cursory countersurveillance. We must be careful now."

Charley nodded. "Old boy doesn't have great moves, but he's got moves. Your guys are good, Hans."

"Thank you," Hans said.

"Let's stay on him tight," Dale said. "We don't want him to slip away."

"That's not going to happen," Hans said. "We have the ball."

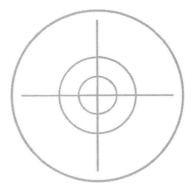

AMSTERDAM, THE NETHERLANDS, BRITTA'S APARTMENT

Youssef bin Hassan studied the maps of Washington, DC. He paid particularly close attention to the schematic that showed the routes and stops of the Washington Metro, the subway and light-rail network that linked downtown Washington, DC with the suburbs of Virginia and Maryland. From his previous briefings, he knew that many of the stations were underground, and the rapid movement of the trains passing through the station would be ideal for dispersing the weaponized smallpox across a large number of people. Placement of a dispersion device on the platform level of a Metro station during rush hours would ensure the maximum amount of exposure to the mass of commuters traveling then. That would cause outbreaks scattered throughout the larger metropolitan area and not just in downtown Washington, DC.

He touched with a grease pencil the Smithsonian stop; the world-famous museum had record numbers of visitors all year round. He planned to treat doorknobs and banister rails there, and then would investigate the interior of the building for likely spots for an additional dispersion device. The Metro would bear the brunt of the attack; he also planned to see about getting on a White House tour to see what he could do there. According to his briefers, the security was stringent on the people attending a White House tour, but it was possible to take a small atomizer—disguised as a breath spray as one of the devices was—in through security. Once inside, he'd have to be extremely discreet, as video cameras covered the tourists every step of the way. The Federal Bureau of Investigation building was another place to visit; they too had tours and opened their building to the public.

He had plenty of time. The original plan called for a rapid movement across the country from major metropolitan area to major metropolitan area. But the first and most thorough targeting was to be Washington, DC. Then New York City, then the systematic visits of the other cities on his target list. It would take about two weeks for the first cases to show up in Washington, DC, but by then he should be most of the way through the major cities on his target list. The subsequent focus would be on mass travel, for the American society was a mobile one; he could count on that.

Then his mission would be accomplished.

He planned to exfiltrate out of the country from the West Coast, leaving Seattle to the end, where he could take a fast boat to Vancouver, British Columbia in Canada, and from there a plane back to Europe. Then it was on to Syria and the Al-Bashir logistic headquarters for a lengthy debriefing and a great many congratulations. From there they would watch as the epidemic raged across the United States, safe and secure in their country, all of the operators inoculated against the virulent custom-engineered strain, and with sufficient vaccine to defeat any infection that crossed over to their host country.

Youssef wouldn't allow himself to think about what might happen to Britta if the smallpox made it from the United States to Amsterdam. After all, Amsterdam was a hub for several major US airlines. He mulled on that for a time and then, with the effort of training, put the thought out of his head. He tapped on the plastic-sheathed map of Washington, DC and let the image of success come up in his head. The first signs would be massive numbers of people getting ill with what appeared to be the flu, after a long incubation period. Then the rapid progress of the engineered virus would lead to the blooming, the outbreak of the pox on the skin that would make it recognizable to the health authorities. There would be widespread panic once the word got out that smallpox was loose in the United States, decades after it had been declared extinct and the vaccination program had ceased.

And then people would die, first by the dozens, then the hundreds, then the thousands.

Smallpox in its natural form killed three out of every ten people infected; the virulence of the engineered variety took that kill ratio up to seven out of ten. It had been fully tested on Kurdish prisoners in a secret underground laboratory on the outskirts of Baghdad and the course of the disease was fully and thoroughly mapped. His briefers had told him that the laboratory had often been visited by high members of the Iraqi government, especially the associates of Hussein Kamel, some of whom had enjoyed a small party with the scientists who had created the engineered virus. They had also perfected a vaccine, custom engineered just like the virus, and that had been cause for celebration as well.

That vaccine coursed through Youssef's veins. He would not be allowed to martyr himself, because he was the one and only operative sent to accomplish the mission. The planners had discussed and discarded a plan to send suicide vectors in large numbers because it left too plain a trail leading back to the source. They preferred instead to rely on one specially trained and highly motivated volunteer who was immune to the disease, someone who would not be hampered by disease or symptoms while carrying out his mission.

He was the One.

The thought of that filled him with great satisfaction tempered with fear. Much rode on his thin shoulders, and the aloneness of being the One had already set in. It was difficult to work alone on a mission of such magnitude. Despite the lecture and briefings, Youssef still keenly felt his enforced solitude. He justified his dalliance with Britta with operational reasoning; it was a good idea to change the place he slept, and staying with a woman gave him many resources as well as made him harder to spot; couples attracted less attention than a single man on his own.

He thought of that, and doodled aimlessly on the edges of his map. There was a youth hostel right in the heart of Washington, DC, a large one where his comings and goings would not stick out. What if he took Britta with him? He dismissed the thought almost as quickly as he thought of it; she would be quickly exposed to the disease and there would be no doubt about that. No, Britta would stay where she was.

The One traveled alone.

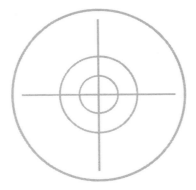

ATHENS, GREECE

Ahmad bin Faisal lingered over his meal. He'd had a simple country salad with big chunks of cucumber, feta cheese, and tomatoes drenched in olive oil and balsamic vinegar along with a crusty bread, then a platter of roast lamb, rich with the scent of garlic and wine and olive oil. He drank only orange juice with his meal, as the sense of being watched nagged at him, and many of his associates would look askance at a man of his rank enjoying a bottle of Demestika red wine with his meal. When he'd eaten his fill, he pushed away the plate and enjoyed a rich cup of coffee and a slice of baklava pastry. After the bill came, he called to the waiter and said, "Does Christou still work here?"

The waiter laughed. "He doesn't work here, he owns this place."

"Is he in?"

"Yes, I'll get him for you."

The waiter disappeared into the back of the taverna and after a few moments came back accompanied by a short man, so fat that he looked like a ball with legs. His stringy hair was combed over a huge bald spot.

"Hello, Christou," bin Faisal said.

"Many greetings to you, my old friend," Christou said. His

voice was surprisingly deep and melodic; he sounded as though he could sing.

"It's been a long time since our business has allowed us to visit," bin Faisal said.

"Why didn't you let me know you were here?" Christou said. "Give me your bill."

He took the paper ticket and tucked it in his pocket. "Your money is no good tonight, my friend. Will you join me for some retsina?"

"My religion doesn't permit me the retsina, friend, but I would gladly drink coffee."

"Coffee it is."

The fat man gestured to the waiter for another cup, then poured himself a glass of the fiery retsina liquor and sat down at bin Faisal's table.

"Is your trip pleasure or business, or a little of both?" he asked bin Faisal.

"I try to take pleasure in my business, old friend. But business is the principal reason. I may have a problem that you could help me with."

"I don't know what a simple restaurant owner could do for you," Christou said coyly.

"Perhaps the friends of a simple restaurant owner could help me," bin Faisal said.

"There is always that possibility."

"Perhaps your friends would watch over me for a short time . . . I need to ensure that no one follows me."

Christou's face grew hard. "You think you are being watched and you come here?"

"I took precautions," bin Faisal said, a faint tone of defensive-ness in his normally calm and cultured voice. "We are merely two people enjoying a drink together."

"Yes," Christou said. He looked around the tiny taverna at the few people there. Nothing looked out of place. He looked at Bin Faisal and let his eyes narrow, the folds of fat in his face making his eyes look like the twin barrels of a gun. "Let us hope your precautions were sufficient. Mine will be. Such a task, that involves expenses. Some of my friends cannot afford to work for free."

"I wouldn't ask them to work for free," bin Faisal said. "Of course I have considered expenses and whatever your friends would charge I would pay. I realize that such a favor is an expensive undertaking."

The fat man nodded his head affirmatively. "Yes," he said. "Things are much more difficult; the authorities never let up their pressure."

"It seems that they never grow closer. You are fortunate in your choice of friends."

"It is because all parties involved are very careful. It would be good for you to remember that, my friend."

"I will. How long will it take to put into place?"

"When can you pay?"

"I can arrange wire transfer, or I can pay you cash now."

"I trust you, my friend," the Greek said. "Stay and enjoy your coffee. When you leave here, you'll be watched. Give us some time, say an hour. You have no need to rush home to your empty hotel room, do you?"

"Thank you, Christou," bin Faisal said. "I enjoy your company."

"Excuse me then," the fat man said. He got up out of his seat and nimbly nudged it beneath the table, then said, "Let me make a phone call and then I'll return."

Bin Faisal watched him go, then looked carefully around the tiny taverna. There were only Greeks except for one table where three American women and one American man sat. From their loud and careless conversation he took them to be flight attendants from an American airline. They didn't have the look he was familiar with, and they paid him no attention, intent instead on their own conversation, so he ruled them out.

Leaving here would be a different story. He still wasn't sure, but when he left, he'd have the finest streetwalkers the efficient organization of November Seventeenth could provide.

• • •

All around the little taverna, the surveillance team and special operating group mounted by Hans the Dutchman stirred. There were streetwalkers and vehicle teams, camera teams and gunfighters, and spare bodies and vehicles standing off away from the taverna, ready to roll at a moment's notice. They watched as patrons came and went from the taverna, but bin Faisal didn't come out. They had eyes on the rear exit and the side alley, but except for a cook who stood out there and urinated, no one came out that way, either.

"He's still in there?" Dale said.

"Yes," Hans said.

"Are you going to put somebody inside?"

"It's a very small restaurant," Hans said. "If I put someone in there, I lose them for the street afterward. Bin Faisal would remember them."

Charley nodded in agreement. "Hans is doing fine, Dale. Let them run with it . . . it won't do to spook the game right now."

"Right," Dale said. "Let's just hope there isn't another way out of there."

• • •

A countersurveillance security team has a specific function: its job is to identify any surveillance on a given subject and, depending on the mission, either neutralize them or merely watch them watch the subject. It's one of the more difficult and demanding of the black arts, requiring a level of expertise on the street at least as high as the people they're going up against, and the ability to read the players' minds and read their moves as though they were playing a mobile and three-dimensional game of chess. November Seventeenth had some of the very best surveillance people in the business; their highly professional and high-profile assassinations took place only after long and extensive surveillance provided them with the information to pick a time and place for the killing. The five-person team, three men and two women, who approached the taverna were among the best the terrorist organization could field.

And they saw things that other people would not.

They noticed vehicles parked along the street with two men sitting in them, not talking to each other. They noticed people lingering in the street as though they were waiting for someone. They noticed how every route out of the taverna seemed to have vehicles and people that were out of place.

And that told them what they had come to see. They had a hasty conversation, and decided to lay back along a route they would have their subject walk. Forming a series of static posts, they would be able to identify the mobile surveillance as it followed their quarry past the static posts, giving the terrorists the opportunity to identify each vehicle and individual.

Then it would be time for further action.

• • •

"I have bad news for you, my friend," Christou said. "You were followed here." The fat man looked around the nearly deserted restaurant. Only a single couple occupied a table near the door, far from bin Faisal's table. "They are waiting for you outside."

"Who are they?"

"We don't know that yet," Christou said. "They are very good, though. You can be forgiven for not seeing them."

"I'm sorry for bringing this trouble to your door."

"It's not a problem," Christou said. "As you said, we are merely two people enjoying a drink together. But it will be different when you leave here. You will want to walk straight down the hill to the main street, turn left, and follow that back to your hotel. Don't do any countersurveillance, don't look around, just stroll back to your hotel. Have a cigarette on the way, take your time. Our people will be watching you and watching the others."

"I understand. I thank you, my old friend."

"We now have an interest in this," Christou said. "It may be that this is an opportunity for an action on our part. But that decision is not mine. You have a part to play tonight, though. Play it well."

Bin Faisal took his napkin and touched his lips, then his forehead. "I will do my best," he said.

"Then it's time for you to go," Christou said.

He walked the Arab to the front door and slapped his shoulder in a friendly fashion, then opened the door and stood there for a moment with bin Faisal.

"Thank you for coming," he said in his melodic voice. "Please come again."

Bin Faisal smiled at him and said, "I will. Thank you for such a delicious dinner."

The two men parted ways, Christou back in his restaurant and bin Faisal alone on the sidewalk. He took out a cigarette and lit it with his silver lighter, and took a good moment to draw on it. Bin Faisal was extremely nervous; this was not the sort of thing he was used to. He noticed that his hand was trembling and that there was sweat on the metal of his lighter. He had to force himself not to look around, and felt as though he looked hunted. Throwing back his shoulders and taking a deep breath, he started walking down the uneven pavement of the hill to the main street below.

• • •

"Subject is moving," came a tinny voice over the earpiece the operators in Hans group all wore.

Dale shifted on his tiny seat in the back of the delivery van parked a block away and craned to look over the shoulder of the camera operator who operated a camera hidden in a ventilator hood in the top of the van.

"Where is he?" Dale said.

"Right there," the operator said. He twisted his toggle slightly so as to better capture the image of Ahmad bin Faisal on the small monitor in front of him. "We've got him cold coming and going."

All around bin Faisal there were subtle movements. Cars started, and began to slowly pull out. People who had been lingering for a long while began to move, some with him, some along side streets not visible to him, prompted and guided by the small voices in their earpieces.

• • •

"They are very professional," one of the female terrorists said to her male partner as they lingered in a doorway, kissing. "It is a large team . . . I count two vehicles for sure with two men each in them, and four streetwalkers. That's on the street, not counting what they may have standing off."

"I wonder if they are Americans," the man said. "If so, their command and control element will be farther out. Let's go and see how they work."

He pulled himself off the body of his partner, and took her hand. They strolled out, a block and a half behind bin Faisal, apparently just another Greek couple enjoying the summer night air, on their way to a club or disco.

• • •

Hans's surveillance team was focused on their quarry. Surveillance is so difficult that it takes all the resources available to a team just to keep up with their subject, and so limits the amount of energy they can put toward watching their own backs. That's why they have gunfighters and security for the surveillance team. But those hardworking and conscientious operators have to be able to keep up with the surveillance operation and they can't lag behind.

So two of the gunfighters on the tail end of the moving box around bin Faisal took brief notice of the young Greek couple walking hand in hand behind them, evaluated them, and dismissed them.

• • •

Bin Faisal felt as though someone very large and very heavy was standing on his chest. He forced himself to relax, taking deep breaths, and once choking on the cigarette smoke he inhaled too deeply. He kept one hand in his pocket and the other one held his cigarette, which he drew on greedily. His stomach churned, and for a moment he was angry that his wonderful meal was spoiled. That was the least of his worries, he reminded himself, and got his mind back on what was happening. Right now, it seemed as though nothing was. There were a few cars that passed him coming down the hill, and there were people out walking, but people walked every night in Athens and its traffic was famously dense and thick and impatient.

He could see nothing, and he fought down the urge to look around for signs of the surveillance he knew surrounded him. The skin on the back of his neck seemed to tingle as the fine hairs there stood up in an atavistic response to being the hunted one, and for a moment the terrorist administrator had the sense of what it must be like for one of his operators out in the field, alone. Fear like this was new to Ahmad bin Faisal, and seemed so far away from his meetings in paneled rooms. This was the fear the street operator knew, and bin Faisal had a flash of self-awareness that comes at times like this and he knew that he could never do what he sent others out to do; this was not something his constitution could manage.

It was enough for him to keep putting one foot in front of the other. At the bottom of the hill, he paused and ground out his ciga-rette butt beneath one loafer-shod foot. He took out another and was grimly satisfied that his hand seemed to stop trembling. Maybe it was because he was on a busy thoroughfare now, dense with traffic and pedestrians, brightly lit, and well away from the dark street he had just walked down, alone but not, consumed with his own thoughts.

• • •

"That old boy is shaking like a dog shitting peach pits," Charley said. "Look at him . . . he's made the surveillance."

"He is nervous," Hans said. "That doesn't mean he's made us."

"What's he got to be so nervous about?" Dale said.

"He is not a street operator," Hans said. "He hasn't made us. He may think he has, but he hasn't. He's just not used to the street."

"Let's hope that's the case," Dale said. "Let's see how he does out here."

• • •

"They would have their command and control in that van," the woman said, turning and smiling brightly at her companion as though she was delighted with his company.

"Yes. That makes four vehicles counting the van, and seven streetwalkers."

"Those last two in the formation, I think they are fighters."

"Yes, or reserve walkers."

Across the street, a man with the paper folded up was reading the sports results beneath a street lamp. He cursed loudly, then crumpled up the paper and tossed it into the trash bin outside the closed storefront he stood outside of. He took out a pack of cigarettes, lit the last one, and tossed the crumpled pack underhanded to the trash bin, then began to stroll along, seemingly concentrated on his cigarette. He walked a little more quickly, coming up behind the two young and muscular men in dark leather jackets who walked in front of them.

"Hey!" he called in Greek. "What time do you have?"

The two men looked over their shoulder at him and said nothing.

"Hey!" the man said. "Didn't you hear me? What time do you have?"

One of the men shrugged and held his hands up. The smoking man switched to English and said in a thick accent, "Sorry, do you have time?"

The other man glanced at a thick watch on his wrist and held it out so the smoking man could see it.

"Thank you," the smoking man said, studying the watch. "You are American?"

"Yes," the younger of the two men said.

"Welcome to my country!" the Greek man said.

"Thank you," the younger man said. "Good night."

"Why hurry?" the Greek man said.

"We have to meet someone," the other man said.

The two younger men picked up their pace, leaving the Greek

behind. He watched them go, slowed his own pace, and noticed how the leather jackets they wore bulged just behind each one's right hip slightly when they walked.

They were gunfighters and the bulge was their hidden pistol.

The Greek recognized a fighter when he saw one. After all, he was one himself, and he had killed Americans before.

• • •

"He's not running any counter moves at all," Hans said. "He appears nervous, but he's not taking any action to counter it. Why?"

"Why is right," Charley said. "If he thought he was under surveillance, he might try some countersurveillance moves. Or maybe he's just playing it as cool as he can right now to see what happens."

"There's something not right about this," Dale said. "He's no operator, but first he's trying some moves and now he's not. What does he know that we don't?"

Hans said, "It may be that he's convinced himself there's no surveillance. Or he's nervous about something entirely unrelated. Maybe his dinner didn't agree with him, or there's something else on his mind. We don't know. Right now we have him where we want him and that should be enough. Let's stop second-guessing ourselves and take advantage of the fact that we have him."

"Hans is right," Charley said. "Let's just chill, Dale."

"I want this guy," Dale said. "I want to sweat him till his brains run."

"We all do," Charley said. "Cultivate patience."

• • •

Ahmad bin Faisal was settling into an easy rhythm. The fact that he hadn't seen anyone following him and that there were other people on the street gave him comfort. His stride began to lengthen, and he lit another cigarette, pausing for a good long moment to give people time to fix on him. He began to nod a simple greeting to the people who passed him on the street, each hurrying to enjoy the nightlife that Greeks lived for. For a moment he thought about going to a club, but his instructions from Christou had been clear: go back on the direct route to his hotel and stay there for the night and wait to be contacted by Christou's people.

So he stayed on the street, didn't look over his shoulder or around nervously anymore.

• • •

"He's settling down," the woman said to her partner.

"He's not used to this sort of thing."

"Who is he?"

"Al-Bashir."

"And he's not used to this?"

"He's higher up. Finance and support."

"Ah. That makes sense. That's why the pay is so good."

"He's bringing us a gift in more than one way," her partner said. Her hands were tucked into the crook of his arm and they continued strolling along, chatting like any of the other couple on the street. "This is an opportunity to strike."

"It may be. Costas closed in on their streetfighters just a while ago. They may be Americans, CIA. If so, it will be a good opportunity."

"They are very good. We'll have to be careful."

The two of them looked around and laughed.

• • •

"He's almost to the hotel," Dale said. "No brush passes, no contacts, no countersurveillance . . . he's been squeaky clean."

"Yes," Hans said. "But that makes sense. He's not a street operator; if he's going to meet with someone they will give him directions and a place and a route to walk; they'd be providing security for the meet. The logical place would be some sort of contact at his hotel giving him further instructions."

"You got a crew in there already, right?" Charley said.

"Of course," Hans said. "We have a room there adjoining his and we have a penetration for video and sound. The hardest part is keeping a presence in the lobby; the tourist police are everywhere down there."

"Do you have a connection with the police department?" Charley asked.

"Yes, but we're staying at arm's length due to the nature of this job."

"Makes sense," Charley said.

• • •

The terrorist couple followed slowly behind and watched bin Faisal go into the hotel via the front main entrance. They strolled along and went into the hotel, going directly to the lobby bar where they sat at the end of the bar and ordered aperitifs. The woman crossed her legs and dangled one foot impudently while she toyed with her drink. From her vantage point she could see into the lobby. Two tourist police, in plainclothes uniforms of leather bomber jackets, sweatshirts, and American Levis and combat boots, stood hulking near the entrance of the bar, looking out into the lobby. She paid close attention to the other people in the bar and outside in the lobby, lingering in the comfortable lounge chairs and sofas set tastefully among end tables in the lobby.

"How is your drink?" she asked her partner.

"Fine."

"I saw two in the lobby," she said.

"Yes, I saw them."

"There are more. When there's two, there's more."

"We have enough to proceed. Finish your drink."

The woman downed her drink, then set the empty glass down and stood. "Shall we go?" she said.

Her male partner finished his own drink and set the glass down on the bar and signaled for his bill. He paid it from a roll of bills in his pocket, then set the change down on the bar and led his partner out, holding her arm. The two of them went out the front main entrance and took a cab from the taxi stand in front of the hotel. The man gave directions to the driver, who accelerated off into the traffic quickly. After a few blocks, the man said to the driver, "Here, this will be fine," and the driver pulled over.

"For your trouble," the man said, adding a few bills to the small fare.

"Thank you," said the driver. He pulled away, hitting his fare light as he did.

The couple stood beneath a streetlight and looked around them. No surveillance on them, and they would have been very surprised if there was. After all, they were street operators working an active operation, and they were sure that they hadn't been made by the surveillance team working Ahmad bin Faisal. They walked a short distance down the block and then crossed the street where a sedan idled beneath a street lamp. The woman tapped on the rear trunk lid as they came abreast of the vehicle and the three occupants looked round at them. The man and the woman squeezed in beside the woman in the backseat.

"Do we have a count?" said the driver.

"Yes."

"Americans?"

"We couldn't tell," the second woman said.

"I could," said the older Greek named Costas. "They are definitely American. Very professional, better than the local CIA, who are very good. They are running an operation against an Al-Bashir financier. That's who they were following tonight."

"Do we have enough for our report?" the driver said.

"Oh, yes," Costas said. "I think we have an opportunity too good to miss here."

• • •

"They've put him to bed," Hans said. "He's in his room now, getting ready for bed. He won't be going anyplace. We've got a vehicle team and a set of streetwalkers standing by in case he does move tonight, but we'll have plenty of advance warning. Time for sleep."

"I could use some shut-eye," Charley said.

"I'm too wound up to sleep," Dale said.

"You should try to rest," Hans said. "You are very tense."

"We've got a lot riding here, Hans," Dale said.

"I know this," the Dutchman said. "So do I. You have to learn to trust us, Dale. Have we done anything wrong yet?"

"No," Dale said. "And I don't mean anything by it, Hans. I'm just used to working this sort of thing myself."

"You didn't work alone when you did," Hans said reasonably. "Even you need to sleep, eat, and shit sometimes. Trust us. Let us do our job."

"Sorry," Dale said.

"Nothing's going to happen," Charley said. "Let's get some time toes-up."

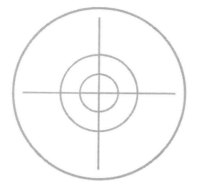

## AMSTERDAM, THE NETHERLANDS, BRITTA'S APARTMENT

Youssef and Britta lay in Britta's narrow bed, tangled in the sweaty embrace of lovers. Her breathing was deep and slow, and the rhythm of it stirred the skin on Youssef's chest where her head lay, heavy with sleep. He was still awake, strangely so, though drained of tension. It was as though there were thoughts he expected to hear, just on the threshold of his hearing, hovering nearby as he lay near sleep. Light from the street outside filtered through the big window and fell across the bed in slanting lines. There was a lone voice, distant, and then gone. It was late.

Youssef shifted slowly so as not to wake Britta. He stretched his legs, then relaxed back into the bed as Britta stirred slightly, then slipped back into deep slumber. Youssef let himself slip back into the dreamy reverie that comes right before sleep, and let himself slide into sleep as gently as any child.

A dream full of images came to him: he was as tall as a giraffe, walking slowly with a pendulous gait, and picking his way down a crowded street, striding over cars. Everywhere there were heaps of sick and dying people, their faces covered with the pustules of smallpox, and he couldn't recognize anyone, so distorted and inhuman they looked. There was a strange light in the sky, not from the sun, and he walked toward it, ignoring the human detritus all around him. He was wearing a traditional Saudi robe and headdress, and his feet were shod in leather sandals, and he heard the *whish whish whish* of his clothing as he walked. Here was a sick child and the mother, but he turned his face away from their pleading. He couldn't understand the noises they made, but his mind made them into words, pleading for help, for water, for mercy. There was a young man and his girlfriend, curled together in the bonelessness of death, the boy with his arms curled protectively around his lover even in death.

Death, death, death, everywhere.

Up ahead was the light, like a reversed cone from the darkened sky above, which boiled with turbulent clouds like cold milk into hot tea. Youssef stepped forward and entered the cone of light where it hit the street at a place empty of bodies and abandoned cars. He felt the the warmth of the light on his traditional robes. In the cone of sunlight he threw back his head and let the light warm his face, strangely cold, his muscles tense around his eyes from the not-seeing that he'd been doing, the deliberate turning away from the pestilence and death that surrounded him. There in the light he felt a presence. He turned and looked and saw Britta there with him, his size, towering over the street. But while he looked up toward the source of the light, she looked down and back at the people dying below. Her hands went out to reach for them, but pressed up against the edge of the light as though she were pressing on glass. She turned to him and her lips moved as though speaking, but he heard nothing. He reached out his hand to touch her, but it was as if she were behind a clear glass barrier separating the two of them. His hands splayed wide on the invisible barrier, he watched as her skin became flushed, then spotted, then the spots broke open into the blooming of the pox, her eyes open wide in horror, her hands clutching at her face. Youssef tried to look away but he could not; he couldn't look away from her china-blue eyes, even now dulling and fading, and he reached for her as she fell . . .

. . . and he awoke with a start, shouting "Britta!" throwing her arms from him in his need to be untangled.

"What is it, Youssef?" Britta said, woken from her deep sleep with the clarity of someone waking to an emergency.

"A dream," he said. "A horrible dream."

She cradled him and pulled him against her soft breasts like a child. "There, there," she soothed. "It was only a dream. Only a bad dream."

## ATHENS, GREECE, NOVEMBER SEVENTEENTH SAFE HOUSE

While other people slept, the terrorist surveillance team from November Seventeenth sat around a table in a house in a residential suburb of Athens, studying maps of the area around the Athens Hilton, writing their plans on big sheets of paper they put up on the wall of the room around them, drinking coffee and smoking cigarettes. The unexpected appearance of a full-scale American intelligence operation in their territory provided them with an opportunity to strike hard at their old foe, in a fashion meant to not only hurt but to publicly embarrass the American operators.

"Do we take them when they are static or while they are moving?" a woman named Anna said. She was half of the couple that had followed Ahmad bin Faisal to the Hilton hours earlier.

"I think static," the older Greek gunfighter, whose name was Costas, said. "While they are moving, it is to our advantage for escape, but they have the advantage of being already mobile. So I think static. We take them while they are sitting there watching our friend."

The man who had been the other half of the couple that followed bin Faisal, whose name was Stavrous, said, "Can we get the police response we want?"

"Yes," Costas said. "The tourist police are right there, we must mind them. Our man in the police department will be monitoring the emergency dispatch center and arrange to be first on the scene, before they have an opportunity to clean up and get their equipment and the bodies out."

"What of their gunfighters?" one of the other men said.

"Don't worry about them, Anton," Costas said. "I have plans to deal with them. They only have two on the street and they will be the first to go."

"I like it," Anna said. "You think a walk-up is the way to go? Perhaps we should ambush them from a distance and not take the chance of exposure."

"Too difficult to set up on short notice," Costas said dismissively. "Mobile teams to strike a coordinated strike at stationary targets, that's what we need. We need not kill all of them, in fact it's better for the police response that we don't. They'll be running around trying to see to their people and find us and they'll end up in a shooting match or in custody with the police. Then our friends in the press will splash this across the world's headlines. American CIA Agents in Gunfight in Athens Streets. That's what the American president will be reading over his morning coffee."

They all laughed at that. Costas said, "He will be shitting himself while we'll be drinking coffee."

"We had best sleep for a time, then," Stavrous said. "We'll have a busy day."

"Yes," Costas said. "Time for sleep."

ATHENS, GREECE, HANS'S SURVEILLANCE TEAM SAFE HOUSE

Dale, Charley, and Hans sat on folding chairs around a worktable in the hastily put together operations room in the safe house. Charley sat calmly, his hands loose in his lap, while Hans sipped from a bottle of water. Dale stood up, then sat back down.

"What's he doing?" Dale said.

"He's sleeping," Hans said. "Which is what we should do. I have static posts all around and people right next door to him. He's not going anywhere and no one can get to him without us knowing."

"So what did Callan say?" Charley asked.

"There's a snatch team standing by, they're in the country now," Dale said. "We've got the eye, they'll slide in and take him."

"When?"

"Soon."

"How soon?" Charley said.

"As soon as tomorrow," Dale said. "Six-man team working out of a van with a cover car, as well as all of us for support, surveillance, and cover."

"Seems like a lot for one guy without protection," Charley said. "That's a lot of exposure."

"It's pretty minimal, all things considered," Dale said.

"Yes," Hans said. "It's not as many as I've seen."

"Guess I was used to working on a beer budget. You guys are on the champagne standard," Charley said.

"This guy warrants it," Dale said. He toyed with a pack of cigarettes on the table. "They'll sweat him to fill out what Uday had to say, and we'll find out if this Sad Holiday thing is for real or just a pipe dream for the planners."

"I don't know about all of you, but I need some sleep," Charley said. "Time for this old dog to get toes-up. Anybody else?"

"Yes," Hans said. "We'll have a busy day tomorrow."

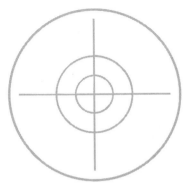

AMSTERDAM, THE NETHERLANDS, BRITTA'S APARTMENT

"Your sleep is very troubled," Britta said in the bright light of morning. The two of them lay together in bed, the sheets bunched up around their chests, mugs of steaming coffee in their hands. "What do you dream of?"

Youssef shrugged, embarrassed. "I've always had bad dreams," he said. "Ever since I was a young boy."

Britta reached out and stroked his hands. "You're fine now."

Youssef pulled his hand away and drank a long hot swallow from his cup.

"What's wrong?" Britta said. "Youssef, what's wrong?"

"I need to be out today," he said. "I need some air, some exercise."

Britta studied him, her hands cupped around her mug. "Of course we can do that," she said. "It's a beautiful day already. We can walk through the Jordaan today, it is a very lovely area, we can take coffee at a café, have a meal . . ."

"I need to be alone for a while."

Britta moved so that she could see his profile, his lips turned down, the furrowed brow.

"Of course you can be alone," she said. "But I don't think you want to be alone. I think you are used to being alone and that is why you don't know how to be with someone when you are troubled. You've been alone so much that you don't know what a relief it is to be able to unburden yourself to someone who will listen to you. Like I can listen to you, Youssef. Like I want to listen to you."

She watched the play of emotions across the young Arab's fine features: longing, wonder, anger, and then a mask of stillness.

"What is it that you think about?" she said, softly insistent. "What is it that you can't tell me? There's something, I can see that. Tell me."

"I had a friend," Youssef said. "Palestinian. We were good friends, went to university together. But when we graduated, he went back to the West Bank to participate in the armed struggle against the Jews. He was captured by the Israelis, and they tortured him. He was a fine musician, he played the piano. They put his fingers in a drawer and a soldier kicked it shut. He never played piano again . . . he died in their custody, like so many others. He will never have a day in the sunshine in Amsterdam, he won't have coffee in a café or take a light meal. There's nothing for him except the memories in the minds of his friends, and the actions that we would take in his name."

Britta sighed. "Oh, Youssef, are you political? Is that what this is?"

"If political means to be willing to take action, then I am political."

"What sort of actions can one man do? You are so alone, it seems that all you have is hatred. This is the first time I've seen that in you, Youssef. You're so much more than that. There's so much that is fine in you. Let your anger go. You're right, your friend can't enjoy those things . . . but why can't you enjoy them for him? Why should you deny yourself a life worth living because of past sadnesses? Your friend is gone . . . let us go and lift a glass in his memory today. Let yourself feel some good things, enjoy people and the day, Youssef . . . maybe then your anger will ease."

Youssef stared stubbornly at the foot of the bed, refusing to meet Britta's pleading look.

225

"It's easy for you to say that," he said. "Your life is so open and easy . . . it would be different if you had lost someone close to you to the Americans and the Jews. Perhaps you wouldn't be so happy, so carefree."

"I'm getting angry," Britta said. "You know very little about me, Youssef, but you're quick to judge me. Maybe I have lost people, not in the same way, but lost all the same. How we feel about things is a choice. We can choose to find the bad in it, or we can choose to find the good in it and go on with our lives. I will always take that path. I will always look to find the good and the good is always in there. It's up to us to find it and let it guide us on a good path. You've been wandering alone here in my city and you were guided to me. I believe that. And maybe you should take it as a sign that there is some sweetness for you instead of all the bitterness you carry around. Hasn't this been good?"

She gestured at the bed and the room and the open window.

"Hasn't it?" she said. "I know you've enjoyed yourself and I've enjoyed you. Let a little light in, Youssef, and enjoy life. Your friend would want you to do that."

Youssef threw back the covers, spilling coffee from the mug clenched in his hand. He stood up and set the coffee mug down on the floor. His shoulders were hunched and his hands came up as though to ward something off.

"You don't understand what I must do," he said. "I need to be alone today, do you understand?"

"Then be alone!" Britta snapped. She threw back the covers and got out of bed, snatching up her silken bathrobe and throwing it around herself. She went into the bathroom, slamming the door behind her.

Youssef watched her go with something akin to relief. Her anger gave him a sense of justification. He took his underwear from the floor and slipped it on, then put on his pants and shirt and looked around for his shoes. After he slipped on his low-rise hiking shoes, he picked up his courier bag and slung it over his shoulder. Then he went to the door and went out, shutting the door quietly behind himself.

From the bathroom he heard the sound of weeping, and he steeled himself against that sad sound as he went down the narrow stairs to the street. It was early yet, and there were only a few people out on the street. He wandered away, aimlessly at first, standing on a canal bridge and staring at the murky water beneath, then wandering along, letting his feet take him where they would. He passed Dam Square, and realized he was close to the Central Train Station.

Along the pedestrian walkway and alleys that paralleled the main street that led from Dam Square to the station were numerous small travel agencies specializing in discount airfares. Youssef wandered along, looking at the prices, and found himself standing outside one agency that posted a cheap fare from Amsterdam to Toronto. He thought about it for a time, and thought out a possible itinerary. He could fly into Toronto, go through the relaxed Canadian customs, then take a bus from Toronto into the US on his forged US passport. Then he could fly or stay on the bus to get to Washington, DC, where he could blend into the faceless crowds that filled the Washington, DC youth hostel during the summer. He could be one more traveler, seeing the sights of Washington, DC, enjoying the nightlife, just another face in the crowd.

He hadn't received his activation signal yet, but with Internet access he could get it anywhere.

Even in Washington, DC.

227

ATHENS, GREECE, HANS'S SURVEILLANCE
TEAM SAFE HOUSE

Charley tapped Dale on the shoulder and handed him a steaming mug of coffee.

"Here you go," he said. "They really know how to make good coffee here. They understand the subtleties."

"Thanks," Dale said, taking the cup.

"*Hoka hey*," Charley said.

"What does that mean?" Hans said from the sofa where he watched Dale and Charley hunched over the small monitors and computers set out on a battered folding table.

"It means it's a good day to die," Charley said.

Hans laughed. "You have a dark sense of humor, Charley."

"Well, it is, isn't it?" Charley said. "We've got the early part of what promises to be a simply stunning day. The sun is shining, and the girls are out in their short skirts and summer dresses, we've got the perfect box on the perfect quarry, and we've got the serious shooters coming in to bag and tag him. Then we can party. Damn right it's a good day."

Hans laughed and the equipment operator, a bone-thin pale-faced Dutchman dressed all in black, joined him.

"You know how to enjoy life, my friend," Hans said.

"It's all a matter of priorities, friend," Charley said. "A long time ago I learned the difference between being serious about what I did and taking myself seriously while doing it. The first is essential, the second is disastrous."

"That's wise," Hans said.

"That's because I'm an old gray-haired dog and I've reached the age of wisdom," Charley said. "Isn't that right, Dale?"

Dale mumbled something from his seat at the equipment operator's shoulder and drank his coffee.

"Now that," Charley said in a voice pitched for Hans's ear alone, "is a way too serious guy."

Hans bit back a smile and winked.

"Hans, run it down for me, will you?" Dale said.

"Sure, my friend," Hans said. "We have four people in the room next door, two equipment operators and two walkers, one of them armed. In the lobby we have four walkers, and standing off two minutes away I have three cars. We have radio contact with everyone and everyone is fresh. Bin Faisal is awake and has taken a shower. He had a pot of coffee and some rolls and a newspaper brought to his room; so far he hasn't gone out, which is not unlike him. He's taking his time reading and drinking his coffee and appears to be in no hurry to go anywhere. Callan is on the ground and on his way here. He will coordinate the snatch team to take bin Faisal on the street once we get him out and moving."

"Where's the snatch team?" Dale asked.

"They're in a safe house of their own choosing. Callan is keeping it compartmented right now. They will have a liaison man with us when Callan arrives, and he'll coordinate everything with us."

"So what about us?" Charley said.

"I assumed that you would want to be on the street when the snatch goes down," Hans said.

"That's right where I intend to be," Charley said. "Come too far to miss out on that. Dale?"

"Yeah," Dale said. He set his coffee cup down and got up and stretched his back and arms. "I intend to be in on the kill. All of us deserve that."

"Well, then, Mr. Ahmad bin Faisal," Charley said. "Get your ass up and moving. We're just about ready to take your terrorist ass."

NOVEMBER SEVENTEENTH HIT TEAM, NEAR THE ATHENS
HILTON HOTEL, ATHENS, GREECE

Costas, the leader for the operation, sat in a Fiat with stolen license plates down the street from the Athens Hilton. He could see one of Hans's vehicles, a watcher car. What gave them away were the small stick-on mirrors placed on each of the side mirrors which gave a true 360-degree view around the vehicle when you counted the inside rearview mirror. With a prepaid cell phone and a digital messaging pager he could communicate with the members of his hit team assembled loosely in a box that surrounded the surveillance team setting up around the Athens Hilton.

His pager beeped, and he looked down at the display which showed a line of numbers. This sequence meant that the lobby team had identified the surveillance-team members in the lobby, the ones that would be the first responders to any movement by Ahmad bin Faisal. While they couldn't be sure, it was a good bet that a team of this size and expertise had rooms in the Hilton, and penetration of bin Faisal's room. Costas's last instructions to bin Faisal had been to remain in his room till noon, then, if he hadn't been contacted, to go about his business and wait for them to find a way to get to him.

Costas entered in the numbers that sent the message MESSAGE RECEIVED and sent it to his lobby crew. With their pagers set to vibrate and a number code worked out in advance, they had a nearly untraceable and low-key method of real-time communications. Cell phones, ubiquitous in the crowded streets of Athens, were for real-time and urgent communications.

Anna, her long hair bound into a neat, tight bun at the top of her head, shifted in the seat beside him. Beneath a newspaper beside her was an Israeli mini-Uzi, the one without the collapsible stock. It was nearly useless for anything beyond pistol range, but at close range—say next to a car or a few feet away from a target—it would put eight hundred rounds a minute of 9mm into a human being. It was an excellent assassination weapon, and Anna was highly skilled with it. Costas, as one of November Seventeenth's premier assassins, carried a US government-issue Colt .45 Model 1911 semi-automatic pistol, one that had been pilfered from the stocks of weapons the US had hidden in Greece during the 1950s, when Greece had been a staging area for operations into communist Yugoslavia. The big .45 had been used in a number of assassinations of US diplomatic and military personnel.

The two of them planned to add to their body count today, although their primary job was command and control. All told, there were five teams of two shooters each, deployed loosely in and around the surveillance box of the Americans. The shooters blended into their surroundings, as it was their territory—a message they meant to bring home to the American intelligence agents working bin Faisal. They planned a straightforward killing of as many of the surveillance team as possible, leaving the bodies with their incriminating weapons and surveillance equipment, and enough people left alive to add to the confusion when the police and the press arrived to take note of an American intelligence operation blown in violence on Greek soil.

It would be a killing blow against the Americans and a clear message about operating on Greek soil. It would be a great embarrassment to the American president and his anti-terrorist campaign and a severe blow against US–Greek relations. And November Seventeenth would fade into the background once again, their signature of the .45 in several killings and a message taking credit for it in the press.

Anna and Costas found it exciting to the point of sexuality. They'd had sex three times last night, and the older man found himself rising like a young stallion to the younger woman. But now they were focused on the job ahead of them, and they were both cool and calm and collected like the professionals they were.

There was killing to be done.

## ATHENS, GREECE, HANS'S SURVEILLANCE TEAM SAFE HOUSE

Mike Callan rode in the back of a panel delivery van with big side-sliding doors. Crouched in the back, dressed in leather jackets, work boots, and Levis, with balaclavas rolled up like hats on their heads, were six operators from DOMINANCE RAIN. Following closely behind the van was a Chevy Suburban with blacked-out windows that contained six more men, all heavily armed, the cover car.

"Let me out at the corner," Callan said to the driver. He stepped over the men crouched in the back and slid into the empty front passenger seat. The van slowed to a stop, and Callan, touching his ear where he wore a radio earpiece, got out without another word. He strode away, down a few doors in the residential neighborhood, then bounded up the stairs to the lower doorway entrance to the safe house where Hans had set up operations. He pushed the button beside the door and waited for the door to buzz open, then went up where he was greeted by one of Hans's gunfighters, his hand on a weapon hidden beneath the front of his jacket.

"Where's Hans?" Callan said.

"Right here," Hans said from the door behind his man. "We're in here."

Callan came into the small operations room and looked over the folding tables burdened with laptops, monitors, cameras, and radio equipment. Dale and Charley stood to greet him.

"Right on time," Dale said.

"That's my definition of right on time—ten minutes early," Callan said. "You ready to go to work?"

"We've been working, Massah Callan," Charley said. "We's been working hard."

Callan grinned and helped himself to a cup of coffee from the pot warming on a corner of a folding table. "I know that. Good work, too. We're just about ready to wrap this guy up."

"Are you going to run coordination for your team?" Dale said.

"Yeah, I'm going to sit right here and watch the deal go down. You guys working the street or are you going to stay here with me?"

"Working the street," Dale said. "I want to see this guy go down."

"Likewise," Charley said.

"I will be here," Hans said. "I don't have the bloodlust of these two."

"I'll enjoy the company," Callan said. "It's been a long while since we talked, Hans."

"Run down what your crew is going to do, will you, Mike?" Dale said.

"Sure," Callan said. "Straightforward and simple, just the way I like it. They're standing off in a van with a cover car two blocks away from the hotel. When Hans's people put bin Faisal on the street, they'll box him in and we'll know where he is. There're a number of places along all the routes out of the hotel where we can pull the van in; we pull the van alongside, door opens, my boys go out, grab him, and throw him in the back of the van. He gets hooded and shot up with tranquilizer while the van evacs with the cover car sweeping up behind if necessary. Then they move to a staging area, a warehouse a few miles from here, and we dope him up some more. Then he goes on a military transport out of the airport as diplomatic cargo. He'll come to his senses in a safe house in northern Virginia, where we will begin the process of straining his brains dry."

"Sounds good to me," Charley said.

"Have your guys done a snatch before?" Dale said.

"They swept up that Serbian prison commander in Belgrade and a narco in downtown Bogotá, right out of the middle of his security detail," Callan said. "They know what they're doing."

"Not your usual private sector–type action," Dale observed dryly.

"We're a long way past that," Callan said. "You knew that going in."

"I like it where I'm at," Dale said.

"Bin Faisal is leaving his room," the equipment operator said. "He's getting ready to go."

"Let's hit the street," Dale said.

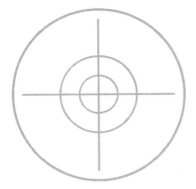

## ATHENS HILTON HOTEL, ATHENS, GREECE

In the lobby, busy with guests coming and going from the front desk and the restaurant, Hans's four streetwalkers prepared themselves. An unshaven young man, casual in a rumpled polo shirt and khaki pants, eased himself out of an overstuffed armchair directly across from the concierge desk. He walked out the tall glass doors and lingered by the taxi stand directly in front of the hotel entrance. His three partners stayed in the lobby, positioned to watch every entrance, exit, and elevator. Their slow movements were unnoticed by everyone except the two middle-aged Greek men parked behind newspapers in adjoining armchairs nudged in a corner. One of them took out his digital pager and tapped out a short message.

Out on the street, slouched behind the wheel of his car, Costas looked down at his pager display.

Subjects moving.

"It's time to work," Costas said, looking at his partner Anna, who patted the paper bag that concealed her weapon.

Back at the Hilton, Ahmad bin Faisal entered the lobby from the central elevator. He looked cool and aquiline in a short-sleeved light blue silk shirt and linen trousers. The Arab paused, looked round the lobby as though he expected to see someone, then took out a cigarette from his silver case and lit it with his gold lighter. His head wreathed in aromatic smoke, bin Faisal went out the hotel entrance doors to the taxi stand outside.

"May I call you a cab, sir?" the doorman asked.

Bin Faisal regarded him for a moment, then said, "No. It's such a beautiful day, I think I will walk."

He turned away from the doorman and gazed up at the flags of many countries on the long row of flagpoles that followed the curved driveway out from the front of the hotel to the car-choked Vasileos Konstantinou Boulevard. The flags snapped and fluttered in the morning breeze. Bin Faisal drew deep on his Turkish cigarette, and let the smoke eddy and whirl around him. Then he walked to the crossing in front of the hotel, crossed the street, and turned left onto Vasilissis Sofias, a quiet side street. He had in mind an easy stroll that would take him to the Plaka for some light shopping, and then a late lunch at the Hotel Bretagna in Syntagma Square. As he had been instructed, he took no cautionary countersurveillance measures, and was careful to look the part of the tourist. He suspected he was being watched, though; the hair on the back of his neck stirred.

All around him, careful and discreet action took place.

Two of Hans's streetwalkers from the lobby followed him out. A woman in a tan pantsuit that was a size too small passed him quickly and paced ahead of him; a tired-looking man crossed to the other side of the street and stayed abreast of the Arab. Fifty yards behind him, two other members of Hans's team got out of a battered Fiat and followed.

Bin Faisal was in the box.

And Hans's operators were in Costas's box.

Close behind the two trailing Dutch streetwalkers were two of Costas's shooters, heavy-set middle-aged men with the look of grocers or butchers, each armed with a Skorpion machine pistol ideal for close work. As Hans's surveillance vehicles began to stir along bin Faisal's route, Costas's crew moved, too. Costas's plan took advantage of the surveillance team's focus on their moving target, which left them vulnerable to the unseen foe stalking them from behind. The streetwise November Seventeenth terrorists had identified all of Hans's lurking cars, and waited till the movement of the suspect vehicles paralleled bin Faisal's. That simultaneous motion cemented the target identification and marked the vehicle occupants for death.

Costas craned his head out his open window and inched his car into the traffic. His target vehicle, a battered mud-brown Audi that moved faster than it looked, was six cars ahead of him.

"Send the message," he said to Anna.

She reached out and plucked his pager from his belt, then entered the numbers 666 into the message body and hit broadcast, which sent the message simultaneously to all the network pagers.

It was the release code for his shooters.

Once they had that message, they were free to kill their identified targets and any targets of opportunity. The shooters on foot would fall back to predesignated rally points where other November Seventeenth operators in cars and vans would pick them up and take them away before the police could respond. The nearest police station was the thinly manned tourist police post in the Athens Hilton, and their first responsibility was to the hotel guests.

Killing time was here and now.

• • •

In the back of the delivery van parked two blocks from the hotel, the DOMINANCE RAIN kidnap team checked their equipment and made sure it was handy. One man examined a slap syringe, designed to inject a powerful tranquilizer on contact. Another operator set into his belt already-looped plastic flexicuffs for the subject's hands and feet, then tossed underhand to the man across from him a black hood for bin Faisal's head.

Hans's voice crackled over the radio net, tinny in each man's earpiece. "Subject is moving. All call signs, this is Zero, Bravo-Two has the eye."

"Zero, Bravo-Two, roger I have the eye," came the response from a streetwalker.

A DOMINANCE RAIN operator, a hulking man with the battered cheekbones of a boxer and a wad of tobacco in his cheek, spat into a sawed-off pop can and said, "Are we up?"

The senior man looked back from his seat behind the driver. "We're all up."

The driver nodded and nosed the van out into the street. He pulled into the turn lane that would take him onto Vasilissis Sofias, glancing into his rearview mirror to make sure that the heavy Chevy Suburban with the blacked-out windows was right behind him. When there was a break in the traffic, he goosed the van across and onto the side street where Ahmad bin Faisal strolled, cigarette in hand.

"This is Charley-One," the driver said, his words picked up by the microphone mounted on his visor. "We're on Route Blue, in position."

"Charley-One, Zero." Hans's voice was calm and clear on the radio. "Roger you on Blue, in position."

The voice of the driver in the Suburban came over the net. "Zero, Charley-Two, Blue, in position."

"Roger Charley-Two," Hans said.

Just ahead of them, idling at the curb in a shiny blue Volvo, was Bravo-Two, one of Hans's teams of one driver and one spotter. The

Volvo pulled out and closed on bin Faisal, who ambled along, looking in the shop windows through their grated gates, still closed at this time of the morning. The four streetwalkers, two in front and two behind, who boxed bin Faisal began to close on him as well, the leading surveillance operators slowing to let the man come to them, the training ones stepping up their pace. The Volvo driver looked and saw the van grow in his rearview mirror. He nodded and said into his radio, "Charley-One, I have you visual."

The van driver looked back at the team leader, who nodded. The driver gripped the wheel more firmly, then said, "Charley-One has the eye, Charley-One has the ball. All call signs, stand by, stand by, stand by."

In the back of the van, the men positioned themselves: two rows of two men each directly behind the door, their hands free; one man braced beside the sliding door, his hand on the handle, the security man off to the other side, a H&K MP5SD silenced submachine gun held in his hands, ready to return fire if there was trouble. The driver eased a H&K MP5K, the machine-pistol variation with a four-inch barrel, into his lap. Like a cruising shark on final approach to its prey, the van pulled close to the sidewalk and idled along, a half block behind Ahmad bin Faisal.

"C'mon, c'mon," one man muttered, bracing himself with one hand on the van's roof.

The driver said, "Stand by."

• • •

Dale and Charley stood on the corner across the street from where bin Faisal approached on foot. They watched with anticipation as the van began to slow down behind the unsuspecting terrorist leader.

"You ever seen this before?" Charley said.

"Not from this perspective," Dale said. "Done it a couple of times."

"Not me," Charley said.

"It'll be over before anyone knows what's going on. Four guys, one for each arm and leg, throw him in the van, shut the door, and move out. They're only a couple of seconds out of the van. They bag him, tag him with some tranquilizer, and move to the rally point while the cover vehicle blocks behind them. Clean and sweet."

241

Charley looked up and down the street. "Couple of pedestrians, light traffic . . . should be a go."

Dale pressed his elbow against the pistol concealed beneath his light windbreaker. "Let's do this thing," he said, touching his teeth to his lip. "We're good to go."

• • •

The two November Seventeenth assassins following Hans's street-walkers split up. One jogged across the street, nimbly dodging traffic; the other continued on his side of the street. The two men exchanged glances, then moved in quickly on their prey. They fell into step, closing in behind their chosen targets, then drew their Skorpion machine pistols, lengthened with a dull silver silencer, from beneath their baggy windbreakers.

They fired just as Hans's operators looked back over their shoulders.

The only sound was the clatter of the bolt and the tinkle of spent casings striking the sidewalk. At short range, the machine pistols poured 750 rounds per minute into the surveillance streetwalkers. Both of them dropped instantly, their backs mottled with holes that spouted blood across the sidewalk. After pausing for a moment to put a short burst into the downed operator's head, the November Seventeenth shooter jogged back across the street to meet his partner. They both began running down the block in the same direction as Ahmad bin Faisal.

A short distance behind them, Costas and Anna pulled up beside the four-door Fiat sedan they were following. Just as the driver looked over, Anna leaned out the window, the mini-Uzi in her fist, and fired a long burst into his head and shoulders. The Fiat veered to the right and crashed to a stop against a parked Audi. Costas stomped on his brakes, and Anna jumped out, changing magazines as she went. The surveillance man in the passenger-side front seat threw up his hands as though he could block the bullets that came through the windshield. Anna fired from almost contact distance through the glass, putting a long burst into the face and skull of the surveillance operator. She turned and coolly reloaded as she hurried back to the car and got in beside Costas, who rested his hand on the .45 tucked in his waistband.

"They're done," she said.

Costas scanned the road ahead, the cars slowing to see what had happened, and saw in the rearview mirror his two shooters running from their killing.

"Here is Stavrous and Dimitri," he said.

The two men threw themselves into the backseat, their weapons out.

"Go! Go!" the first one shouted.

"Calm yourself," Costas said, jerking the wheel sharply and

accelerating into the street. "We'll pull ahead of the Arab and see if there are any others left."

He pulled wide around a Chevy Suburban with blacked-out windows and a slow-moving delivery van.

• • •

The DOMINANCE RAIN operator behind the wheel of the van saw the whole thing. "Who the fuck is that? They hit somebody right back there!"

He tilted his head and snapped into the hands-free microphone. "Charley-Two, this is Charley-One, we have unknown shooters engaging targets in the street, Zero, do you copy?"

• • •

From a block away, slightly uphill, which gave them a good vantage point, Charley and Dale watched the shooting unfold. Dale leaned forward, his weight on the balls of his feet, and reached beneath his coat for his pistol.

"They're coming this way," he said. "Get the cover car to block them, we can take them on the street."

Charley reached out and took Dale by the arm. "Don't go out there!"

Dale shrugged off his hand, drew his pistol, and, holding it under the open front of his jacket, crossed the street, dodging cars like a football receiver dodged blockers.

"Shit!" Charley said. He drew his own pistol and began to pick his way across the street, following in Dale's wake.

• • •

In the back of the delivery van, the DOMINANCE RAIN team leader, his words terse but carefully controlled, said, "Where's the target?"

The driver said, "He's stopped on the sidewalk."

"We take him now," the team leader said.

The driver nodded in assent, then said, "Stand by!"

He slammed on his brakes and the van shuddered to a stop. In the back, the door man yanked the door open and the four-man snatch team exploded out, two of them scrambling across the hood of a parked car to get at the Arab, frozen with fear on the sidewalk. Bin Faisal barely had time to turn his head away before a beefy forearm struck the nerve plexus in the side of his neck and hard hands grabbed at his arms and legs.

• • •

In the November Seventeenth car, Anna gripped the dashboard with one hand to steady herself and said, "They are taking him now!"

Costas cut the wheel sharply to the right and pulled in front of the van at a forty-five-degree angle.

"Take them!" he said.

The back doors opened and the two shooters in the rear sprang out. Anna opened her door and followed them. Costas set his foot on the brake, then drew his pistol, keeping his free hand steady on the steering wheel.

• • •

The DOMINANCE RAIN operator behind the wheel of the delivery van barely had time to raise his weapon before Anna fired a long burst into his face. That stopped the van for the time being. She circled around the front of the van while her two partners went around to the rear. On the sidewalk four men struggled with bin Faisal. She closed on them, her weapon steady in her hands, coming to nearly contact distance so as to be sure not to hit her fellow terrorists. The nearest man to her saw her and turned suddenly, letting go his grip on bin Faisal's leg, rushing her and grabbing her weapon. He forced the muzzle away from his chest and into the air. Her short burst went into the sky. Anna gripped the mini-Uzi fiercely and drove her knee into the man's groin. She pulled one hand from his iron grip and raked at his eyes while she drove her knee again and again into his groin. He was big and strong and she was losing the tug-of-war for her weapon, but still she hung on, determined not to let go. She clawed harder at his eyes, and his grip loosened for just a moment, just long enough for Anna to lever the muzzle back on-line with the man's thick chest and squeeze the trigger. The five-round burst tore into his chest. The mortally wounded operator fell back a step, stumbled, then went to one knee. Anna put her weapon to his head and squeezed off a short burst into his skull.

• • •

The DOMINANCE RAIN security man leaped out the van door, his MP5SD held at the ready. He pressed the muzzle of his submachine gun against the baggy windbreaker of the November Seventeenth terrorist at the rear of the van and pressed his trigger, blowing the terrorist back against his partner. The remaining terrorist grabbed the muzzle of the MP5SD and shoved it to one side, then brought his Skorpion up and thrust it in the security man's face, then fired a short burst that opened the other man's skull, dropping him cross-legged in the gutter.

The three DOMINANCE RAIN operators struggled with bin Faisal, whose fear made him strong. Dimitri, the remaining terrorist, emptied his magazine across the back of the operator closest to him. Anna stepped around the front of the man with her reloaded mini-Uzi in her fists, arms extended and locked, and closed in on the two remaining DOMINANCE RAIN operators. Suddenly her face blossomed red, like a gruesome flower, and she fell backward onto the sidewalk streaked with blood. A cover shooter from the Suburban had fired his M-4 at her from the backseat, the muzzle blast from the unsuppressed weapon stunning his partner in front.

• • •

Dale sprinted down the sidewalk, his boots slapping the concrete as he came. He saw the flurry of action, heard the shots, and saw people going down. The Glock was warm in his hands as he closed to be sure of his shots. The muddle of men struggling on the sidewalk made that necessary. He forced himself to control his breathing—a deep breath, hold, a deep breath, hold—and eased the pounding behind his eyes so that he could fight. The female terrorist went down, and a shot cracked close by his head, from the other terrorist or from one of his own, he couldn't tell. The remaining male terrorist, fumbling to reload his machine pistol, suddenly jumped and twitched as though pulled by marionette strings as a cover shooter from the Suburban, his M-4 tucked tight in his shoulder, put a three-round burst into him. Dale's attention was tunneled in on the terrorist going down; he had his Glock covering the man going down and missed the motion in the front seat of the car blocking the van.

Charley was behind him, moving up fast, and he saw the man in the front seat of the terrorist-blocking car duck low.

• • •

Costas watched Anna fall, and his rage rose as a fierce fighting force in him. He ducked low as he threw open the door, moving surprisingly fast for a man of his age and bulk. The battered old government-model .45 automatic was clenched in his fist. He saw the man running down the sidewalk toward them stop short of the car and point his pistol at someone behind the van; that gave him the opening he needed. He slipped around the open door and braced himself low across the hood and aimed.

• • •

Charley shouted, "Dale! The car, behind the car!"

His words were lost in the clatter of gunfire. Still running, he threw his Glock up and snapped a quick shot at the man leaning over the hood of the car. The older man was fast; he turned and fired two quick shots at Charley.

• • •

Dale saw the movement at the hood of the car, saw the flash of the pistol going off, saw the old man aiming at someone behind him. For a moment his attention was split. He looked over his shoulder and saw Charley crouched as though hit.

"Hey!" Dale shouted, to draw the shooter's attention away from Charley. "Right here!"

He snapped fast shots that ricocheted off the hood of the car, leaving grey streaks that appeared as though by magic. The old man behind the pistol swiveled like a tank turret and Dale saw, in slow motion, the gaping muzzle of the .45 suddenly flaring bright and rising off the hood of the car. There was a sudden punch in his chest and he staggered back a step, still trying to acquire the target and then he heard a snapping sound in his skull that brought bright light to his eyes, a bright light that blotted out everything else, and in his last moment of consciousness he felt the concrete unfold beneath him like a quilted blanket across a bed.

• • •

Charley saw Dale's head jerk sharply to the right and the sudden bloom of blood spout from his head. Even as his friend crumpled to the sidewalk, Charley fixed his front sight on the terrorist behind the hood of the car and walked forward, every step a shot that splintered his opponent's face. He ran forward to the downed terrorist, kicking the .45 free from the man's limp hands, then quick-scanned 360 degrees. All the shooters from the cover car were out; some of them covered the others, who were throwing their dead and wounded into the van. One operator was already behind the wheel of the van.

Charley went to Dale and knelt beside him. "Help! I need help here!"

Dale was still breathing, but a wound in his upper chest and an entry wound in his skull spouted blood. Charley pressed his hands against the wounds. Two of the operators pushed him out of the way and grabbed Dale up by his arms and legs and ran with him into the back of the van.

"Mount up!" one shouted. "We're out of here!"

Charley ran to the closing van door. A hard hand grabbed his jacket and yanked him in while someone else slammed shut the door. The van floor was awash in blood. Charley sat on one body, still warm—there was nowhere else to sit. Pressed into the rear corner, Ahmad bin Faisal, his hands cuffed behind him and a black bag over his head, whimpered with fear.

MARCUS WYNNE

"Motherfucker, motherfucker . . ." a DOMINANCE RAIN operator chanted as he worked on Dale, tying pressure bandages in place.

"We're gone!" the driver shouted. Everyone grabbed for a hold as the van tore away from the curb, followed by the Suburban, leaving the limp bodies and bullet-riddled car of the November Seventeenth terrorists behind.

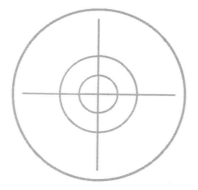

ATHENS, GREECE, HANS'S SURVEILLANCE SAFE HOUSE

The Dutchman gripped the edge of his worktable as though it might fly away. All of the speakers carefully ranged around the battered table crackled with panicky voices and the sounds of gunfire.

"Zero, Bravo-Four, we've been fired on . . ." came from one speaker.

"Zero, Alpha-Two, man down, we need medical and extraction . . ." came from another.

Hans looked from speaker to speaker in confusion. "What the fuck is happening? What the fuck is happening?"

Mike Callan bulled him aside and grabbed the microphone from his limp grip. "Charley-One, Charley-Two, this is Charley-Actual, abort, abort, abort, get the hell out of there now . . ."

A tense voice replied, "Actual, this is Charley-Two. We have the package and all our people. We need immediate medical attention and evacuation, we have critical injured on board . . ."

Callan slammed his fist into the table, jarring the monitors and speakers. "Two, this is Actual, move to designated rally point, medical is standing by." He turned to Hans and said, "Can the medic on-site deal with trauma?"

Hans stared, frozen, at the camera monitors. The wireless video in his cars transmitted scenes of carnage from the street.

"My people," he said. "My people."

# PART 3

## DOMINANCE RAIN HEADQUARTERS, FAIRFAX, VIRGINIA

Alone in his office, Ray Dalton hunched over his desk, the handset of his secure telephone held to his bowed head. All his attention was on the voice, tinny with encryption, that came over the line.

Mike Callan's voice was thick. "I lost four of your shooters, Ray. And Dale Miller is critical . . . he's got a forty-five slug lodged in his head. The doc is working on him, but there's not much we can do till we get him to a hospital . . . they're doing the best they can. Hans has eight dead, and three wounded. They were all picked up. The Athens police and Greek Intelligence are all over this. His gunfighters were armed, and the rest of the team had surveillance equipment . . . it's a huge flap."

"Bin Faisal?"

"The secondary safe house. We can't move him or the team. The whole country is on a terrorist alert and the Greeks are in a full uproar."

Ray rubbed his eyes again and again. "The Greek prime minister has been on the phone to the president. The US ambassador has been on the carpet all day. Hans's operators were sterile, but the wounded . . . we'll have to straighten that out." He forced himself up out of his defeated posture, straightened his back, and rested against the cushioned contours of his executive chair. "If we can't get bin

Faisal out right now, we'll bring the mountain to Mohammed. I'll send an interrogation team in."

"Charley Payne's started to tune him up."

"Tell him to leave it alone. I'll have a crew out of Frankfurt Station in six hours or less, and a backup crew from the States by tomorrow. Maybe by then we'll figure a way to get them all out."

"There's no talking to Payne. He and Dale were close. And he is the only one here that's up to speed on bin Faisal's priors."

"Do what you can to keep him off. I want him fresh for the interrogators."

"I'll try. The whole crew is strung tight . . . they need to be left be for now."

"No time for that," Ray said. "They need their acts together for exfiltration."

"Hans's people are on their own till you come up with something. I'll take what's left of his command and control out with me. I've got a line on a military transport we can rig up with support equipment for Dale. What about Payne? Do you want me to send him home with your people?"

"He's still your employee."

"I'll take care of it, then. Jesus, Ray . . . I'm sorry for all this."

Ray pursed his lips and nodded. "We didn't know that November Seventeenth had us in their sights. And we didn't know bin Faisal was connected to them. Now we know. We owe November Seventeenth payback. We'll add this to accounts receivable. My boys will be back to visit in the very near future."

"I want in on that play," Callan said.

"Take care of business first, Mike."

"All right. Out here."

Ray set the handset down into its cradle, then interlocked his fingers and rested his elbows on his desk. In front of him was a battered leather organizer, open to the day's page, with scribbled notations and Dale Miller's name circled in red. He touched a finger to Dale's name, then flipped the page over and began to write.

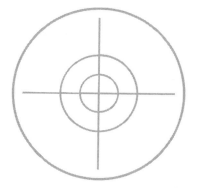

ATHENS, GREECE, DOMINANCE RAIN
SECONDARY SAFE HOUSE

Charley sat, his chair backed into the only corner of the room that wasn't occupied with medical equipment, and watched the doctor and a male physician's assistant hovering over the pale, still body of Dale Miller. Multiple IVs ran into Dale's hand, his chest was bare and streaked with blood and Betadine around the wadded bandaging that surrounded his upper torso, and his head was swathed in more bandages.

"What else can you do?" Charley asked.

"That's it," the doctor said, an athletic man with the freshly scrubbed face of a teenager. "All we can do is stabilize him right now. The round's not in deep, but I don't want to touch it without a neurosurgeon. He's in a coma, and we need him in a hospital right now."

Charley shifted in his seat, nodded, and said, "The plane we'll be going out on, they've got an operating theater set up in it. It's military, good equipment. They're bringing a neurosurgeon in."

"We need to image the damage . . ." the doctor began.

"We can only do what we can do," Charley said.

"Yes," the doctor said. "That's right."

"Why don't you get something to eat or drink?" Charley said. "We can watch him. We need you fresh."

The doctor wiped at his face. He had a thin sheen of perspiration across his smooth brow. "That's a good idea."

He left the room. The physician's assistant took Dale's pulse, checked the rate against his wristwatch. "He's got a strong heart," he said.

"That's a true thing you said there, Doc," Charley said. "You need a break? I can watch him."

"I've got to take a leak."

"Go ahead."

"Thanks."

The PA hurried from the room, quietly shutting the door behind him. Charley picked up his chair and moved it right beside the bed where Dale lay.

"Oh man, what a mess you are, bro," Charley said. "Those forty-fives will fuck you up, now, won't they?"

He watched the rise and fall of Dale's chest, the slow pulse at his neck.

"You're going to be all right, though. Just hang in a little longer, we've got help on the way. You're going to have a hell of a headache for a while, but you've lived through worse. I'll take care of our business, don't you worry about that. Me and our good friend Mr. Ahmad bin Faisal, we're going to take care of business. No Sad Holidays on your watch, bro. I promise you that."

He looked up as the door opened and the PA came back in.

"Everything all right?" the PA asked.

"Never better," Charley said. "You got things here?"

"Yes."

"Good. I've got a few things to tend to."

Charley got up and left the room. He paused by the open door of the bedroom beside the one that had been converted to a makeshift aid station. This room had been converted to a morgue. Still forms, swathed in plastic, were neatly stacked beside each other. Charley wondered at the thinking that planned ahead to put body bags in a safe house. But whoever it was had planned right.

In the front room, the remaining members of DOMINANCE

RAIN sat in flimsy chairs or slumped on the floor. No one spoke to each other; most of the men stared into space or toyed aimlessly with their personal weapons. One man looked up when Charley came in, nodded to him, then looked back down at the floor beneath his feet. Charley stood there for a moment, then slowly edged his way through the room, careful not to jostle or bump anyone. He went to the last bedroom, where one man sat outside the closed door in a wooden chair with a loose leg that squeaked when he shifted his weight.

"Is he awake?" Charley said.

"He was," the guard said.

"I think it's my turn in the barrel."

"Knock yourself out." The guard pushed his chair back so Charley could get to the door. Quietly and slowly, Charley opened the door and slipped through into a darkened room with no windows. The room was close and small, empty except for two chairs facing each other in the center of the scuffed wooden floor. Ahmad bin Faisal, his head hidden by a black hood, his hands cuffed behind him, was seated in one chair, secured by swaths of duct tape around his chest and legs. Charley stood for a moment and watched the man in the chair, saw how his hooded head tilted at the slight sound of the door opening and closing. Then he went to the empty chair and sat down.

Charley studied the man, looking for the signs in his body that would lead him to what was happening in his brain. The Arab was silent. Tremors came and went in the big muscles of his thighs and shoulders. He was deathly afraid, as was to be expected. He was soft meat in the hands of predators he couldn't see, predators who padded quietly around him, waiting. Charley figured he had three or four hours before the interrogation team arrived and took his prize away, leaving him with no closure to the day's events.

That wasn't going to happen.

He had to figure out how to proceed.

Bin Faisal was no field man. They'd established that early on. He'd never been through the terrorist training camps; few of the upper hierarchy had. They preferred to let their money and organizational expertise insulate them from that rough and dirty business. So he would have minimal, if any, experience in resisting interrogation. Why would he? Men like bin Faisal never dreamed of being caught, much less interrogated. Pain would buy a certain amount of information, but the threat of pain and violence was a better tool against a man like bin Faisal. An operator, a seasoned field hand, would have thought out in advance several layers of information, true and false, to slowly give up to the interrogator at each step of the process. Someone like bin Faisal would try to hold out everything, not knowing any better, and when he went, he would go all at once, giving everything up. If the interrogator played his hand right.

So he had to capitalize on the man's fear, and his imagination of what might happen.

"You don't know much about this end of the business, do you?" Charley said, in a soft conversational tone. "You're not the type to get your hands dirty. That's what you pay others for. I know your type, you see. There's someone like you in every organization. You're the guy who signs the checks and gives the orders, but you stay nice and clean in your office or your fancy hotel room. It's the man out on the sharp end of the stick that gets bloody. But you sure got your hands dirty today. That was good work, setting us up like that."

Charley slid his chair closer, so that he sat knee to knee across from bin Faisal. The Arab's chest rose and fell as though he were running a race.

"What is your name?" Charley said.

The Arab's voice was high. It quavered as he said, "What do you want with me? Who are you? Is it money?"

Bin Faisal was going to put up a fight.

Charley let a hint of menace into his voice. "Don't think me a fool. You know what we want, you know who we are, and you know it has nothing to do with money. You want us to think that. You want to be seen as just another Arab businessman from Syria. A good try, but foolish. Don't you think so?"

He slapped the Arab sharply, boxing his ear, raising dust from the dark hood.

"Can you hear me clearly now?" Charley said. He kept his tone level. "I want you to think before you speak. I am not a fool. I am not willing to suffer your foolishness. You are an intelligent man. You realize what has happened. There is no escape for you. Your comrades aren't coming to kick these doors down and rescue you. Maybe they will try something dramatic to demand your release. But any such attempt is a long time away. So that's useless thinking for you. Do you hear me?"

The hooded man's shoulders were slumped, his head bowed forward and canted to one side, the hood beginning to darken in spots with either sweat or tears.

"Yes," the Arab said. "I hear you."

"That's good," Charley said. "What is your name?"

The Arab twisted uncomfortably in the chair. His linen trousers, dirtied and torn in the struggle to get him into the van, were bunched tightly beneath the duct tape that held him in place. The hood rose and fell over the open O of his mouth, where he struggled to get a full breath of air.

"My name is . . ."

"Yes?"

"My name is Ahmad bin Faisal . . ."

Charley nodded. He pulled a small tape recorder out of his shirt pocket, looked to be sure that a tape was in place, then switched it on.

"What is your position with the Al-Bashir terrorist organization?"

The mind sends clear signals to the body, which in turn sends a clear signal in the language of posture and muscular tension to the trained eye. Charley saw resistance begin in the stiffening of bin Faisal's shoulders, the turning in and tensing.

"I don't know what you're talking about . . ." bin Faisal began.

Charley reached out and took the hooded head between both his hands. Bin Faisal twisted, turning against his duct-tape bonds, trying to pull free from Charley's iron grip. Charley held bin Faisal's head steady as though in a vise, then let his thumbs slip over the

Arab's eyes, fluttering beneath the hood, to where the nostrils meet the upper lip. Then he dug his thumbs hard into the nerve plexus there. The Arab arched backward, stretching the duct tape to near-popping, thrashing his head from side to side, crying out in pain. Charley let go his grip, sat back in the chair, and watched submission return to the Arab's body. The terrorist organizer shifted his whole body away from Charley, his shoulders slumped, and his head drooped.

"It hurts, doesn't it?" Charley said, the conversational tone once again in his voice. "And it leaves no mark. It's very crude when you consider the many ways we have to make you talk. You don't have the experience or the training to fight me on this, Ahmad. You're not a man of the street."

The Arab began to cry silently. His shoulders shook, and the black fabric of his hood darkened around his eyes.

"It's nothing to be ashamed of," Charley said. "There is nothing you can do to resist us. We have too many ways: pain, sleep deprivation, chemicals. But you don't need to go that way. Cooperate with me now. You can avoid all that. You are an intelligent man, you prize the functioning of your brain . . . have you ever seen a man who has been tortured? They are broken in a way that can never be fixed. Think about that, Ahmad bin Faisal."

Charley eased his chair back and stood. He walked slowly, deliberately, weighting each foot, till he stood behind the hooded man, whose shoulders shook as they rose in an attempt at self-protection. Charley rested his hands on the Arab's shoulders and felt how he trembled, like a guitar string pulled to the point of breaking.

He was almost there.

"We can protect you," Charley said. "Your colleagues in Al-Bashir, they don't want you to talk to us. We know that. But they are forever out of reach now. There's only you. And us. We can make things very good for you . . . once you help us. Give me a little something now, something I can give the people I work for, something to show that you mean to help us."

Bin Faisal's voice quavered. "What do you want?"

"Tell me who your contact with November Seventeenth is. Tell me who you contacted to set up the hit."

The man's lips moved soundlessly, twisting beneath the hood. Then he said, ". . . The only contact I have is a man named Christou. If I needed to make contact, I was to go there and have dinner and ask for him, tell him what I needed."

"Go where, Ahmad?"

"To his restaurant, Christou's it's called, after him."

"I know this place. That's good, Ahmad. You went there last night?"

"Yes."

"And what did you tell him?"

A convulsive twitch ran through the man's whole body. Charley reached down and touched his chest and felt the runaway pounding of his heart.

"Easy, Ahmad," Charley said. "Take a deep breath, that's right, now hold it, then let it out slowly. That's right. Once more. Good. Now tell me what you told Christou."

"I told him that I thought I was being followed. That I would pay for someone to watch my back."

"Did you tell him to kill the watchers?"

"No! I didn't," bin Faisal said. "I had nothing to do with that. I had no idea that was going to happen."

Charley checked the tape in his recorder.

"I believe you, Ahmad," he said. "Tell me something else, now. Tell me about Sad Holiday."

The sudden twitch and dip of the Arab's shoulders were eloquent.

Charley lifted his hands as though he were a pianist at the end of a recital. He walked around the bound man and sat back in his chair facing his prisoner.

"Careful, Ahmad," Charley said, watching the other man's chest rise as he prepared to speak. "Be careful here. Remember what I said."

"What do you want me to tell you?"

"Tell me about Sad Holiday, Ahmad. You know what I'm talking about. It's your project. You can be proud of what you've done so far. But it's over, and I want to know more about it."

Charley let the man be silent for a long time. Then he said, "Would you like a cigarette, Ahmad? I know that you smoke. Perhaps a cigarette would help you remember."

Bin Faisal remained silent.

Charley reached out and delicately unbuttoned bin Faisal's shirt pocket and took out his silver cigarette case and gold lighter.

"Very nice," he said. "When I traveled in the Middle East, I used to smoke these."

He took a Turkish cigarette out of the case, snapped the case closed, then tapped the cigarette lightly to settle the tobacco. He lit the cigarette in the bright blue flame of the gold lighter and took a long, appreciative draw of the smoke before he got up and loosened the hood ties around bin Faisal's neck. He lifted the hood, keeping the Arab's eyes and head covered, then held the cigarette for the man to suck. There were tear tracks on bin Faisal's face; fresh moisture glistened beside his nose and on his upper lip.

"There, there," Charley said. "It's all right. Just enjoy your cigarette. Don't think about anything else; you'll have plenty of time to think about those other things. Just enjoy this moment for what it is. Taste your cigarette. Enjoy."

The skin of bin Faisal's lips clung to the moist paper of the cigarette. The cigarette trembled in his mouth.

"That's right," Charley said. "Think about that."

He plucked the cigarette from the Arab's lips, then ground it out on the floor beneath his boot.

"Did you think I was going to burn you?" Charley said. "That's old fashioned and, frankly, beneath us. You and I, we're reasonable men. My colleagues, though . . . you are responsible for the death of their men. You may not completely understand just how close men can be to one another when they have worked together and suffered together and been afraid together. It creates a bond, you see. A bond like no other. And losing someone from that bond, it's like losing a child or a loved one. So think carefully before you answer me, Ahmad. What is Sad Holiday?"

Ahmad bin Faisal bowed his head as though to the executioner's axe.

"It is a program . . ." he said, ". . . to spread smallpox through the United States . . ."

• • •

Ahmad bin Faisal talked and Charley Payne listened. Tape cassette after tape cassette went in and out of Charley's small tape recorder. Finally, Charley said, "You've done well, Ahmad. This is all good. But now I want to know something you haven't said. Who is the One, Ahmad? Tell me about him. Who is he? Where is he? How will he know to begin his mission?"

The Arab's voice was low and hoarse. "He is a young man. His name is Youssef bin Hassan. He is an Arab. He lived in Saudi Arabia and went to school in England. He was last in Amsterdam . . . and he has already begun his mission."

Charley leaned forward, his face only inches from bin Faisal's. "What do you mean he's already begun his mission?"

Bin Faisal flinched and turned his face away even as he spoke.  "He was given the go-ahead. He will go to the United States by a means and at a time of his choosing. He is to have no further contact with us . . . so as not to betray his mission. The only means of communication we have with him is one-way. He checks every day a pornographic Web site and looks for certain photos with names known to him. He downloads those photos and then runs a program on his computer that will take a tiny piece of code out of the picture and translate it. That's how we communicate with him."

Charley forced himself to remain calm. "He was in Amsterdam with you? The young man you met there?"

"If you saw us there, then you saw him. He is the One."

"What about the smallpox agent?"

"I brought it to him in Amsterdam. It requires minimal care to keep it active. It's fully weaponized that way."

"What's his fallback? If he can't get the agent into the States, how do you get him more?"

"There is a diplomat in the Egyptian mission who is one of us. He's used the diplomatic pouch to convey material for us before. He also has the agent. If there was a problem, the One was to proceed to Washington, DC and leave a signal, a chalk slash on the side of a mailbox near the Egyptian embassy on a Tuesday or a Thursday before nine A.M. That is the signal to meet the next day at a certain bench on the National Mall near the Smithsonian Museum. That is where the handover would take place."

"What is the Egyptian's name?"

"Ramzi Abdullah. He is a vice-consul."

"You must have a signal to stop the operation in the event of compromise, Ahmad. How do you stop him?"

"There is no stopping him. Once launched, he is expected to accomplish his mission. That was the intent. Once he was launched, he would be unstoppable."

"Think carefully. There is no way to stop him?"

"Only if you can find him in time. We have no way to stop him." The Arab paused and licked his cracked lips. "May I have water?"

Charley stood and left the room. On his way to the kitchen, he passed the table where the DOMINANCE RAIN survivors huddled around a camera monitor tuned to bin Faisal's chamber. A tape recorder, plugged into the monitor, turned slowly. The men looked up at Charley and gave him a thumbs-up as he filled a glass of water and returned to the room. He closed the door quietly behind him, then came forward and held the glass for the bound man, who sipped eagerly, as a child would, at the glass.

"Take it easy," Charley said. "Don't choke."

Bin Faisal drank the entire glass, then held his head higher. "I don't know how you can stop him. He has been instructed to ignore any message telling him to stop once he's released. The communication channel was set up to be one-way to pass on additional target information or warn him of any threat against him. It is because he is alone that he is expected to succeed."

"We're not going to let that happen," Charley said. "You're going to help us stop him, aren't you, Ahmad?"

The Arab lowered his head once more, as though staring through his hood at the scuffed toes of his expensive loafers.

"Yes," he said. "I will help you."

• • •

Afterward, Charley shook off the congratulations of the DOMINANCE RAIN survivors and the newly arrived interrogation crew. He went by himself, first into the room where the body bags lay, and he stood and looked at them and breathed in the foul odor of drying blood. Then he went into the makeshift medical room, where the trauma team that had ridden in with the interrogators worked over the limp body of Dale Miller. He sat once again in the corner of the room, pressing himself back, making himself small and out of the way, and watched the electronic monitors that captured the steady beat, beat, beat of Dale's heart.

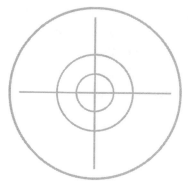

AMSTERDAM, THE NETHERLANDS

Youssef bin Hassan left the Golden Tulip travel agency and lingered a moment, looking back through the window plastered with cheap bills advertising cut-rate fares for destinations all over the world. His image was distorted by the faded and peeling paper on the other side of the glass. A one-way ticket to Toronto, Canada was in his courier bag. There was a well-beaten clandestine route from Toronto to New York state; the immigration authorities along the northern border were less stringent than elsewhere. He'd considered a direct flight to Washington, DC; his documents were good enough. But he'd decided for caution and the circuitous route to his target.

There were new lines in his face, he decided, and he didn't know if they were from lack of sleep or from worry. He turned away from his reflection in the glass and let the crowd take him down to the canal, and he walked along there, letting the gentle curve of the sidewalk following the canal take him where it would. Thoughts of Britta fought for his attention, and he tried to put away the memory of her face, coloring as she orgasmed beneath him, her plump white body straining up against him again and again. He tried not to think of her gentle ways, and the look on her face when he had left her, angry and hurt and disappointed.

She made him question what he was doing.

But he had the tenets of his training to cling to. He had a mission to perform, and he was out doing his work, preparing the logistics of his insertion, just as he should be.

Then why did he feel so wrong?

He wasn't wrong. He had to remind himself of that. What he was doing was vital and important. Powerful men had handpicked him to be the One, the One who brought the crippling blow to the Great Satan. That was what he needed to remember, not Britta beneath him in her narrow bed and the way it felt, after, to lay there together and not speak.

What would she say, what would she think, if she knew he was the One?

He stopped, and leaned on the metal railing and looked down into the murky waters of the canal. His reflection was muddled by swirls of oil and scum. The discipline he'd learned in the classrooms in Sudan asserted itself and he used it to clear his mind of the conflicting thoughts and let the needs of his mission rise up. He had to put her out of his mind and make himself ready to move. He had everything necessary now: his computer, the viral agent, papers, and a plane ticket. Clothing, toiletries, and other incidentals he could buy along the way. He would need to, so he could check a bag. To do otherwise would draw too much attention to him when he traveled by air. He needed nothing else.

Except a clear mind.

It would be easy if he could only stay angry at her, rage at her naiveté and inexperience, hate her for her childish view of the world. But a part of him wondered if she wasn't right, and questioned the drive that had kept him going all these long months. Hatred and anger had fueled him, but his time with her had washed much of that from him.

And he hated being alone. With her in his life it had been so easy. He had justified it as living his cover, but it was so much more than that.

His wanderings had taken him past the Dam and toward the Central Station. He saw the gabled gilt façade of the station through

267

the narrow streets lined with tall row houses. There was no need to hurry for a train; one left every ten minutes for the airport. He stopped outside a small café, where a single empty table seemed particularly forlorn in the busy stream of pedestrians walking briskly past. Inside, he paid for a coffee, then took it outside and sat down at the table. The sun was bright overhead, and fought to filter down through the tall narrow houses to the canal's side street. But Youssef sat in shadow.

He would drink his coffee. And then he would decide.

• • •

Across the canal, in front of a dress store with a large plate glass window that provided a mirror image of the coffee shop on the far side, Isabelle Andouille studied the reflection of Youssef bin Hassan. She had followed him since his stormy departure from Britta's tiny apartment, and tracked him through the streets to the Golden Tulip travel agency. It was the work of a moment and a mild subterfuge to find his destination.

"My friend Joseph?" she said breathlessly to the heavy Dutchman at his desk. "He just left? Did he buy a ticket for America?"

"Your friend?" the Dutchman said, smiling at the beautiful woman. "No, he's going to Toronto. Maybe he'll drive to America. Are you going with him? Would you like a ticket?"

"Oh, no," she said. "If I go, he'll pay! Thank you!"

Then she was out on the street and behind Youssef, so preoccupied that he practiced no countersurveillance or tradecraft. He just ambled aimlessly along, oblivious to everything but his own thoughts. Twice she thought of closing with him, bumping him with her shoulder and going for his neck with the razor-edged knife she kept palmed in one hand, but something cautioned her—she needed to know more.

Toronto. He would be going the soft route into the United States, crossing into New York. From there he could disappear into the teeming masses and end up anywhere. She remembered the books she'd seen him buy. Washington, DC. That would be easy enough from New York. There was a train as well as regular short flights.

She touched the tip of her tongue to her lips.

Kill him now, or kill him later? Serve him up to the Americans or simply make him disappear?

She had things to decide.

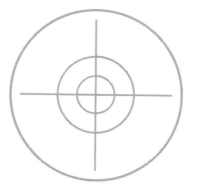

## ENROUTE TO VIRGINIA/DOMINANCE RAIN
## HEADQUARTERS, FAIRFAX, VIRGINIA

The open cargo bay of a C-141 is a noisy, vibrating place while in flight. Charley Payne sat in a netted seat hung from one bulkhead, where he rocked in time to the bumps and jolts of the jet aircraft as it climbed to its cruising altitude. Across from him, a full medical team was clustered around the raised table where Dale Miller was firmly strapped. The IV bags on the tree beside him bent in the direction of the aircraft's climb. The tubes that ran from his nose and mouth shook with the noise of the jet turbines. They had done the best they could, but the best was only enough to stabilize him till they could get him to a fully equipped surgical theater adequate for delicate neurosurgery. The bullet lodged in his brain had done enough damage on its entry, but the bleeding and swelling of the delicate brain tissue around it promised to do more. Dale stayed in his coma, a serene look on his face beneath the tubes and surgical tape, and the lead doctor on the team had told Charley that Dale might remain in that coma forever.

In the center of the aircraft cargo bay were several wooden pallets that supported large wooden crates with US diplomatic seals on them. Those boxes contained stainless-steel coffins, one for each of the fallen US operators from Athens. Even through the sealed coffins and wooden crates, there was a faint odor of decay and blood. Or so Charley thought.

He stretched out his feet and braced them on the metal floor. The seat's constant swaying annoyed him. After a minute of fumbling for purchase, he gave up and got out of the seat. He went down the length of the aircraft to the small window beside the rear ramp and looked out. The blue of ocean was small beneath him. They were over the Mediterranean and would soon be out over the Atlantic, bound for Andrews Air Force Base in Maryland. He'd leave Dale to the doctors, and the bodies to the cargo handlers, and go to a safe house in Fairfax, Virginia for his debriefing, where he would meet Callan's boss, Ray Dalton.

"Ray's the man behind all this," Callan had said. "He runs the shooters, he writes the checks."

"Outfit?" Charley said.

"Yep. Stand-alone special project, that's him."

"Dale used to work for him."

" 'Used to' is the operative phrase. Dale wouldn't have had anything to do with this if he'd known Dalton was behind it."

"I don't have that same history."

"That's why I'm telling you this. If you want to play, and get some payback, you're going to have to make nice with the big boss."

"You all need me."

"That's true," Callan said. "But that doesn't necessarily add up to a ringside seat when it's killing time."

"I want that."

"I know you do. So make nice when necessary. It probably won't be . . . he knows he needs you, and you're well equipped to see this through. Just don't let your well-known temper fuck things up for you."

Charley laughed and shook his head at the memory of that conversation. He craned his head to look up through the porthole at the sky and the scattered clouds they flew through. He wondered what Dale would have made of all this. Dale. Charley thought of the younger man kicked back in a chair in Sebastian Joe's outdoor courtyard, sipping

271

a latte and watching the women go by. It was strange how the two of them had been in the same neighborhood, traveling in the same tiny circle of mutual acquaintances and neighbors, and yet had never bumped into each other before the shooting at the art store. Fate was strange.

He worked his way back to his hanging seat, and situated himself. He stared at Dale and the medical team that labored over him, and wondered if Dale would ever again sit in his favorite spot in Sebastian Joe's courtyard.

• • •

Ray Dalton hunched over his desk like a predatory bird and studied Charley Payne with interest. He'd read Payne's file thoroughly; the two-inch-thick folder still sat on his desk. After reading it and before Payne had arrived, he'd called Payne's last supervisor in the Special Activities Staff.

"Charging Charley?" said the supervisor, a weary veteran of years on the sharp edge of clandestine operations. "One of the very best guys I ever had. And one of the worst. Top-shelf out on the street or in the field—hard-working, never complained, immaculate tradecraft, top-notch skills, a vital member of the team. But he's stubborn as all hell, hard to handle when things don't go his way, a bit of a prima donna. He's emotional, he's an artist. I was glad he had his photography to give vent for that. But he just took things too personally. You know how it goes . . . orders come down, ours not to question why, ours just to do or die. Charley never saw it that way. He chafes under supervision, and he hates managers, especially upper managers. He's got no patience with the way things have to be done in an organization. So he went his way. That's all I've got on Charley Payne. He's not in any trouble, is he?"

"No trouble," Ray said. "We're looking at him for something."

"He won't come back," the supervisor said. "Not enough money in the bank to bring him back. And if you try to leverage him, he'll find a way to screw you, believe me."

"I'll keep that in mind," Ray said. "Thanks for your insights. They're useful."

"No problem. Call again if you need to."

The memory of that phone call was fresh in his mind. Payne looked tired and drawn, the lines in his face especially deep. But he didn't seem impatient. He slouched in one of the easy chairs, his long legs kicked out in front of him and crossed at the ankles, relaxed as a cat lazing in the sun. No, Payne looked as though he'd been thinking through what might come from this meeting, and he'd made up his mind to be patient.

That was a good sign.

And since he was best in the field, Ray had every intention of leaving him there.

"We have his picture and his name on the border with Customs and Immigration," Ray said. "He's flagged as a known terrorist, and there are special instructions to seize and handle all his baggage and personal belongings as suspect. But we've been directed not to bring up the smallpox angle."

Payne shifted forward in his seat, and Ray lifted one hand to ward off the protest he saw coming.

"That comes from the president, Payne. The position is that spreading that information would cause a nationwide panic and a run on medical resources we're not prepared to handle—at least not yet. The Center for Disease Control and select regional public health officials have been told to heighten their surveillance for any suspicious outbreaks, but smallpox is just one of the list they watch for. The official position is that there's a heightened threat of biological warfare—but that's been there for a while."

Ray leaned back in his chair and interlaced his fingers across the belly of his starched oxford shirt. "So my specific tasking is to find Youssef bin Hassan and stop him before he launches his agent in the United States. I want you to lead the operation."

Payne was doing a good job of hiding the eagerness in his face. Ray knew about that eagerness; it was the desire of a hunter to be in on the kill, to run his prey to ground and finish him. And Payne would feel that he had a score to settle.

"How does that sound to you, Charley?" Ray said.

Payne was deliberate in his answer. "What do you want me to do?"

"You've seen all of the major players in this: Rhaman Uday, Ahmad bin Faisal, and Youssef bin Hassan. You can eyeball-ID the One. I want you to run this down, follow up aggressively on the leads we get. And you get to take him down. I'll give you a team."

"I'd rather work alone."

"Not going to happen. You'll need support and backup."

"With good communications, you can get all that to me. I'm not ready or willing to be running an unknown team right now. Your best use of me will come from letting me run after the One when we have something fresh, and to field-coordinate with whatever team you put out."

After a moment's consideration, Ray decided it was a good idea. It would take too long for Payne to get up to speed with team considerations; there were other people who could do that.

"All right," Ray said. "You act as the focal point for the info coming in, work with our analysts till we have something credible. Then you're adviser to the shooters. And you're still in at the kill."

"That makes sense."

"You seem surprised."

"No, just relieved."

The two men laughed.

"You'll work out of here till we have something," Ray said. "I'll set you up in a secure conference room down the hall. You have walk-in access to me twenty-four/seven. We've got aircraft standing by to take us wherever we need to go, whenever we need to."

"That'll work."

"Then it's settled."

Payne drummed the fingers of his right hand on the plush leather arm of his easy chair. "What about Dale?"

Of course he'd want to know about Dale.

"He's being worked on at Johns Hopkins in Baltimore, by one of the finest neurosurgeons in the world," Ray said. "We're sparing no expense to get him taken care of."

"The surgeon on the plane said he doubted Dale would make it. Too much time had passed with the bullet lodged . . ."

"We're hoping for better than that. That's why we've got the best on it right now."

Payne nodded slowly. "I wonder how he'd feel if he knew you were footing the bill."

"There's some history there, as you seem to know already."

"What happens after the surgery?"

"No matter what he thought, Dale was always one of us. We take care of our own. If he doesn't come out, then he goes to a skilled critical-care facility we own outright, where he gets the best attention possible for as long as he lives. If he does come out of it, he'll be given rehab and everything he needs will be provided. We'll see to it."

"I don't have the history you two have," Charley said. "All that sounds good to me. I'd hate to see him dumped in a VA facility for life."

"Never happen. Not to one of mine. Dale was like the prodigal child. It was just a matter of time before he came back."

"As long as he's tended to. I'd like to be able to see him, if we have time."

"I don't know that you'll have the time. But it's not far, and you'll have a driver. But you need to get your mind around what's in front of you."

"Done."

"Then let's go to work."

• • •

Things happened. The conference room down the hall from Ray's office became crowded with extra tables laden with computer monitors, fax machines, and telephones. Every inch of spare space on the tables and chairs became littered with computer printouts, fax sheets, stale cups of coffee, and the remains of sandwiches. Charley sat in an orthopedic executive chair at the head of the largest table, carefully leafing through the reports that poured in from border crossings all around the US. The Immigration Service and Customs were busy looking for the face of Youssef bin Hassan and scanning passports for the false names Charley had pulled from Ahmed bin Faisal, and they updated the task force constantly.

But there was nothing. Yet.

• • •

Satisfied with how things were working, Ray slipped out of the building and met his driver in front. During the drive to Johns Hopkins, made lengthy by the maddening Beltway traffic, Ray stared out the window and thought through all the things that needed to be done yet in this operation.

At the hospital, he spoke briefly to the attending physician, then went into Intensive Care, where he stood at the foot of Dale Miller's bed. The young operator's head was swathed in bandages, and his eyes were closed. Both hands lay at his side, his left hand pierced by multiple IVs that hung from a stainless-steel tree beside the bed. Monitor leads ran from his chest and head to the panel above the bed, and a tube was inserted into one nostril.

"You look like hell, Dale," Ray said.

He reached out and gently patted the comatose man on his foot.

## TORONTO, CANADA

In a hotel in the Red Light District that catered primarily to prostitutes and their customers, where renting a room by the hour was common, Youssef had carefully prepared his equipment. The atomizers were already labeled as breath freshener, and he made sure the vials contained only scented water. The small vials of actual smallpox agent were carefully placed into a condom, then placed inside another for additional padding before he lubricated the bundle with K-Y Jelly and inserted it into his rectum. He grimaced at the unpleasant feeling in his bowels. He stuffed himself with prescription-strength Lomotil, available over the counter in Amsterdam, ensuring that his bowels would remain frozen for the flight across the Atlantic. Youssef checked himself in the mirror, satisfied with everything except for his slightly stiff walk. He'd have to work on that.

The boarding and flight were uneventful. The security people hadn't given him a second look, dressed as he was now in a dark gray summer-weight business suit, concentrating instead on the scruffy young backpackers, many of whom still reeked of marijuana. The next hurdle was Canadian Customs. The passport he presented was one of several he'd obtained while in Amsterdam; it was an American passport in the name of Roy Hunter, a name his controllers wouldn't know. It was an additional measure he'd taken to ensure his security.

The Canadian Customs inspector, a surly looking gray-haired man whose belly bulged beneath his too-small uniform shirt, looked at the passport and then at Youssef. Roy Hunter wasn't a name he was looking for, and he had only his intuition and experience to guide him.

"Purpose of your visit?"

"Vacation," Youssef said.

"How long are you staying?"

"Just two weeks."

"You're coming from Amsterdam?"

"Yes."

"Where do you go from here?"

"Home to New York," Youssef said. "Then it's back to work."

The customs inspector gave Youssef a lingering look, then nodded curtly. He stamped the passport and handed it back. "Have a nice visit, sir."

"Thank you," Youssef said, putting the passport in his inside coat pocket.

In a rest room near car-rental kiosks, he removed the bundle of smallpox vials and relieved himself. The bundle of vials went into a spare plastic bag he'd reserved for just that purpose. Then he picked up the rental car he'd reserved over the Internet, and drove south and east, crossing the border into Buffalo. The Border Patrol officer at the crossing made a cursory examination of his passport, glanced at his face, and made a notation of his license plate. Youssef left the car in the long-term parking at Buffalo's small airport, and from the terminal caught a public bus downtown, where he found the Greyhound bus station and paid cash for a one-way ticket to New York City. He got directions to a nearby Motel 6, where he checked in, paying cash once again. He took out the vials of smallpox he'd carried, then carefully replaced the canisters of scented water with live agent. The atomizers seemed heavier in his hands.

The next day he rode the bus into downtown New York. It was

a long ride, and Youssef enjoyed looking out the window, watching the rolling countryside of rural New York slowly morph into the built-up city. From the bus station it was a short cab ride to Penn Station, where he bought an express-train ticket for Washington, DC's Union Station. The train arrived after midnight, but he had a reservation at a small business hotel near Union Station. One night there was enough. Tomorrow he would disappear into the anonymous world of the youth hostel.

• • •

Across town, at the International Youth Hostel, the tired girl at the front desk looked up as someone came through the front double doors. A woman, her jet-black hair cut in sharp bangs across her forehead and the rest falling straight to her shoulder, came in lugging a single overstuffed duffel bag.

"Hi," the dark-haired woman said. "Can I still get a single room or is it too late?"

"No, we've got plenty," the girl said. "Are you an IYH member?"

"Yes, but I've lost my card."

"That's all right. Cash or charge?"

"Cash." The dark-haired woman pulled a handful of bills from her jeans pocket and held it out. "Take what you need, I'm still learning the money."

"Where are you from?" the girl asked, plucking eighteen dollars from the sizeable wad.

"Amsterdam," Isabelle Andouille said, flipping the ends of her black wig away from her face. "My flight just got in. I'm looking forward to my visit."

WASHINGTON, DC

Charley grew restless in the confined conference room. The smell of stale coffee and hot office equipment oppressed him, so he called for a driver to pick him up at the front of the building.

"I'm on the radio with a cell phone backup," he said to the severe-looking assistant Ray had lent him, a bone-thin youngster in his early twenties. "I should be back in an hour or so."

"Yes, sir," the assistant said, looking up from the sheaf of computer printouts he was poring over. "I'll tell Mr. Dalton when he returns."

A driver, casual in a leather bomber jacket and khakis, sat inside a black Lincoln Town Car outside the front entrance to the nondescript office building that housed the operation. Charley tapped on the glass, and climbed in front beside the driver.

"Where would you like to go, Mr. Payne?" the driver said. He had a faint Bostonian accent.

"Let's go down Sixty-six to downtown . . . I want to go down Constitution and then over to the Air and Space Museum."

"Roger that. Sixty-six to downtown it is."

Interstate 66 was busy, but not the bumper-to-bumper crawl it would be later in the day. They crossed the Potomac on the Theodore Roosevelt Bridge into the District and turned off onto Constitution

Avenue. Charley got a little thrill when he saw the Washington Monument standing bright and clear in the sun. The patriot in him was just under the skin, and he relished the sight of the monuments to his country as they drove slowly along Constitution Avenue.

"Let me out here," he said, when they came to Seventh Street. "I want to walk a little. Meet me in front of the Air and Space Museum."

"You've got a radio?" the driver said.

"Sure do. I'm on Tactical One."

"Tactical One it is," the driver said. He picked up his handset and keyed the microphone. "Car to Payne, Car to Payne."

His voice was tinny in the speaker of Charley's handheld.

"We're five by five," Charley said.

He watched the car idle away slowly in the traffic, then stretched his arms above his head and leaned back to ease his spine. Too much time in a chair indoors was dulling his thinking. He set out at a brisk walk down the National Mall, the grass soft beneath his booted feet. It only took a few minutes for him to cut across the grassy expanse to the park benches on the far side of Jefferson Avenue, directly across from the National Air and Space Museum. The third bench from Charley's right was, according to Ahmed bin Faisal, the designated meeting point for the Egyptian vice-consul and the young Arab they all referred to as the One. Charley went and stood beside the bench for a moment, then sat down.

Though he couldn't see them, he knew that there was a surveillance team nearby with cameras focused on the bench, with one crew on the roof of the Air and Space Museum, and another in a disguised panel-truck parked in front, both equipped with the latest optical equipment and the computers necessary to run a scan of a subject's face through the database of known terrorist operators. A sizable team of shooters lurked in a small room borrowed from Smithsonian security, directly beside the main entrance to the Air and Space Museum, ready to respond at a moment's notice should the One be spotted.

Charley stretched his legs out and ran his arms outstretched along the back of the bench. It was hot and humid, and the weight of the sun on his shoulders, while pleasant now, would soon become a burden. He couldn't take off his windbreaker as that would expose the Glock holstered at his hip. But now the warmth felt good, and he turned his face up to the sun and closed his eyes.

He'd spent many mornings like this in Minnesota, sitting in front of the Linden Hills Café and soaking up sun while he sipped his morning coffee. Dale preferred the courtyard at Sebastian Joe's, but he too had dragged his chair out to the sidewalk to catch the early morning sun while he nursed the tall lattes he was partial to. He wondered how Dale was, now. Ray kept him informed; there was no change. Dale still lingered in his coma, in the twilight between consciousness and sleep. There was some brain activity, but no one, not even the top experts, could say how he was going to be when he woke, if he woke. Charley had found easy excuses to keep him from visiting Dale. He'd not wanted to see his friend in that state. A part of him chided himself for his cowardice; another part said that if he really was a friend, he'd put a bullet in Dale and finish the job. Charley, like so many active men, harbored a dread of a physical disability that would keep him bed-bound—the thought of being in a coma or paralyzed was his deepest fear. While he would, if he were in Dale's position, wish for death, he didn't think he had it in him to put a friend down out of mercy. He'd like to think he did, but when it came down to shooting time, he thought he would hesitate to pull that trigger.

Strange thoughts, and not useful right now. Charley stood up and looked around him, knowing that the One wasn't there, yet hoping he would see him and take this operation to its conclusion. There was full-time surveillance here and at the Egyptian embassy, where the signal location for the clandestine meeting was, as well as on the vice-consul himself. There were plenty of trip wires, and their prey hadn't tripped one yet.

Yet.

Charley keyed his handset and murmured into the speaker, "Car, this is Payne. I'm ready for pickup in front of the museum, on the Jefferson side."

"Roger that," the driver responded. "Be right there."

Charley walked to the curb and saw the gleaming black length of the Town Car inching its way toward him. He walked to meet the car and got in.

"Let's head back," he said.

"Okay."

In the slow traffic, Charley had plenty of time to study the faces of the people walking on the Mall and crowding in and out of the Smithsonian Museum buildings. So many faces from so many different places. On any given day you could hear the accents of dozens of countries and every regional accent of the United States. It truly was America's Mall and everyone came here when they visited Washington, DC.

Sooner or later, Youssef bin Hassan would come here.

He'd come here on an operational reconnaissance, to make sure he knew which bench to go to, to make sure there was no construction or other changes that might impact on his meeting. It would be part of his training to be sure, and Charley was counting on that. They'd catch him on camera and then the immediate response team would take him. The computerized face-scanner made the job much easier. The program wasn't foolproof, though; it could be mistaken, especially if the subject took rudimentary disguise precautions. But his facial geometry remained the same, and that would give the target away.

Charley hoped that bin Hassan would do as they expected him to do. Bin Faisal insisted that the plan called for him to start in Washington, DC and then spread out by public transportation, hitting key cities along the way. If the One stuck to his plan and his training, they had a good chance of catching him in DC, which was as well prepared to deal with the bio-terrorist threat as any city.

Charley turned and looked back at the city as they drove west to Fairfax. Everything seemed so clear in the light of day.

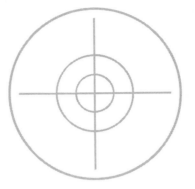

INTERNATIONAL YOUTH HOSTEL, WASHINGTON, DC

Youssef bin Hassan shifted his overstuffed courier bag, his only luggage, around his thin frame and said to the blond girl with her knotted dreadlocks at the front desk, "Hi. I'm Youssef Ameer, I have an Internet reservation for a single room?"

"Hi, Youssef," the girl said. She checked the printout list on the desk before her. "I see you here. We've got your room." She took a key attached to a golf-sized ball, and handed it to him, along with a flyer.

"Those will tell you about the rules and the activities we have scheduled."

"Thank you," he said.

She smiled brightly, one crooked tooth attracting Youssef's attention. "Is this your first visit to the United States?"

"Yes."

She looked down at the printout. "You're from Amsterdam?"

"Yes."

"We've got a lot of people in from Amsterdam. Maybe you'll know some of them. I love Amsterdam, it's a fun city."

"Yes, it is."

"You'll enjoy DC. You'll want to check out Dupont Circle and Adams Morgan for the clubs. We take a group bus down there on the weekends. There's some great dance clubs . . ."

Youssef cut in and said, "I look forward to it. But now I just want to rest. I need to wash up and get some sleep."

The girl, her hurt look morphing into one of disdain, looked up at the clock and said, "You can get in your room now, if you want."

Youssef nodded and turned away from the counter, oblivious to the look the girl gave him. He was past caring what she thought of his rudeness. He took the elevator up to the floor where the private rooms were clustered, and followed the numbered doors down the curving hallway till he came to his room. As he'd requested, he was right beside the emergency exit stairwell. He could get in and out of the building without having to go through the elevators and the main lobby. The key stuck in the lock, and he had to wiggle it to get the door to open.

It was a tiny room, like the rooms in the other hostels where he'd spent so much time in the last few months. There was a narrow bed, already made up, a small desk and chair, a closet, and a stand for a suitcase. That was it for furniture. The drapes were drawn back from the single window that looked out on the city. The white obelisk of the Washington Monument dominated the view. That helped him get oriented. Despite his intense study of the city maps in the guidebooks he'd read, there was no substitute for being on the ground. He would take time, later, to get familiar with the city. There was much to prepare for.

He was in the heart of enemy territory now. He had to be careful. Reconnaissance and rehearsals would be kept to a minimum. The major tourist sites were well-known and well-trafficked; he'd be just another face in the crowd, there and on the Metro subway system.

Just another face in the crowd.

He went into the tiny bathroom adjoining his room and turned on the water in the narrow shower. After the water heated, he stripped off his clothes and then stood beneath the streaming water. He turned the water as hot as he could stand it and let the heat work its way into his bones. Despite the sleep he'd had last night and this morning, he felt old and tired. The tension of being in the enemy's camp wore on him. Memories of Britta nagged at him. He'd left without saying good-bye, without returning to the small apartment with the big window looking out over the canal, and the bed where they had made love for hours. His last memory was of her telling him to get out and be alone. He wondered what she was doing now; whether she was crying in sadness or laughing in relief, whether she was still at the homeless shelter doling out sympathy with blankets, whether she was thinking of him and wondering what he was doing.

He turned his face to the showerhead and let the water beat on his face. There was a heat in the corner of his eyes that didn't come from the shower. After a while, he let his head hang down and the hot water streamed hard on his neck and shoulders. Soon the water began to cool, and he turned off the shower. The bathroom was filled with steam. He had to wipe the condensation off the mirror to shave. He was conscious of a tremor in his hand as he scraped the razor across his face, and carefully avoided looking at his eyes in the mirror. He knew what he would see there: sadness, weakness, a patent misery that came from being alone on a lonely path.

He reminded himself that it was his path by choice. The most important thing remaining to him was accomplishing his mission. There was no room for weakness and hesitation now, even though he felt them like a cancer inside him. He was ashamed of the trembling in his hands and the burning in his eyes.

The best thing he could do, he decided, was to rest for a while and then go out and do a run-through of his operation. That would settle his mind, keep him on track.

He spread out his few belongings on the bed, sorted out the clothing, and hung them in the small closet. The busywork helped his mind. Sitting alone on the blankets were the black Pelican case that held the vials of weaponized agent, the three dissipation devices, and the two aerosol canisters. He dragged the chair beside the bed and sat down heavily, his elbows on his knees, his face in his hands. So much destruction in such small things. He had the death of thousands, perhaps millions, resting on his bed. In America's capital, in a crowded youth hostel, here he sat, the One, the One who carried death with him, and he was afraid of what a young girl in Amsterdam would think of him were she to find out what his true purpose was.

He shook his head in disgust, even as he reminded himself that he could check his e-mail here in the hostel. There was a roomful of computers for just that purpose. There might be an e-mail from Britta.

Youssef replaced the Pelican case and the devices in his courier bag and slung it over the foot of his bed, then went out into the hall, locking his door behind him. He went down the stairwell, relishing the small exercise of descending stairs, and came out in a hallway near the lobby.

A black girl in a tie-dyed dress smiled as she slipped by him.

"Where is the computer room?" he asked her.

"Just there," she said, pointing down the hall. "Near the Coke machines."

"Thank you."

He went down the hall and into the computer room. Six Apple I-Macs were set up in individual cubicles on one big table. Two of the machines were taken, so he sat at the farthest one and logged onto the Internet, then called up his Hotmail account and checked his messages. There was no message from Britta, but there was a message from someone named FriendInAthens. He clicked on the message.

"The product that was delivered to you has been recalled for a manufacturing defect. Please check our Web site for directions on return and replacement."

That was the entire message. The product was flawed? It was possible. He'd taken no special measures to safeguard it, as he'd been told that wasn't necessary. The virus had been engineered as though it were to be launched in a missile, and was supposed to be easily sustained for the period of time he needed. He stared at the message. He didn't need to check the Web site for further instructions; going to the pornographic Web site that was the operational communications channel would attract too much attention here. He'd have to do that later, with his laptop. But he'd memorized the instructions and contact procedures for replacement of the product if necessary. That, too, had been planned for. Today was Wednesday, and the designated days for communicating with his contact at the Egyptian embassy were Tuesday or Thursday. But perhaps he'd be able to do a reconnaissance today.

He deleted the message and logged off the computer, then went back upstairs to his room. From the outside pocket of his courier bag he took out a street map of Washington, DC and studied the area around the Air and Space Museum, and then the streets around the Egyptian embassy. He traced the distance between the two sites with his forefinger, thought for a moment, then folded his map and tucked it back in his courier bag. Then he put the dispersion devices into his toilet kit, and he tucked that and the Pelican case beneath his bed, out of sight from a casual looker.

Now he was ready to go out.

Downstairs in the lobby, there was a crowd of hostel tenants around the front desk. They were all in their twenties, like Youssef, wearing backpacks festooned with odd bits of gear, dressed in a variety of baggy and bright-colored clothing, their bodies decorated with tattoos and piercings and dyed hair. Youssef felt quite plain in his baggy jeans and beige T-shirt. He felt as though there was a wall between him and their bright chatter with the accents of many countries; even though he walked out the door with them he was apart. A girl he recognized from the hallway outside the computer room smiled brightly at him, the smile of someone hoping to make a connection, but he didn't smile back; he kept his eyes down and only glanced up to make sure he was headed in the right direction. A white shuttle bus, a whirring air-conditioner mounted above its rear window dripping condensation, was parked at the curb, its door open. There was a group of bicyclists geared up on mountain bikes beside the bus. One of the bicyclists, a muscular woman with long straight black hair beneath her helmet and her eyes hidden behind mirrored sunglasses, looked at Youssef and then away. He paid her no mind, pausing for a moment to consider. It was hot, and a long walk from the hostel to the Smithsonian. He decided to take the shuttle bus. He followed the herd of young tourists aboard the bus, then took a seat in the rear, away from everyone else, and stared out the window as the bus pulled away from the curb and made its way through the slow traffic toward the National Mall. A couple of the bicyclists paced alongside the bus; in the busy traffic they made better time than the shuttle.

The bus's first stop was outside the National Archives Building, where a long line of people waited patiently for entrance. Youssef stood on the corner and looked up at the granite expanse of the building with its ornate lettering beneath the cornice. The sun cast sharp-edged shadows from the building. He turned his back on the Archives and crossed the street to a tree-shaded enclosure that was labeled the National Sculpture Garden. He continued up Seventh Street, the weight of the sun heavy on his head and shoulders. The oppressive humidity brought out a thick sweat beneath his thin T-shirt. After months of temperate weather in Amsterdam, the heat and humidity was sweltering. A fat black man, his shirt hanging like a flag on him, sat on a stool beside a pushcart with bottles of water, hats, T-shirts, and postcards.

Youssef stopped and reached into his pocket for his roll of bills. "Two bottles of water, please."

"Two bottles of water, yes, sir," the black man said, galvanized into sudden movement. He reached into the tub of ice and water and plucked out two cold one-liter bottles. "Big ones? Better buy."

"Yes, big ones," Youssef said. He handed the man several bills and took the bottles, placing one in his courier bag for later, and cracking open the other one and taking a long, satisfying drink from it.

"Too hot out here to play around, no, sir," the vendor said. "You'll want to cover your head. You got a hat? I got hats cheap, you need one to cover your head, this heat."

He picked up a baseball hat with the letters FBI on the front. "Try this one."

Youssef shook his head no, and wiped the sweat from his forehead with the back of his hand.

"All right then, how about this one?" the vendor said. He replaced the baseball cap and took out a plain straw panama-style.

"Give you a good price since you already a customer. Five dollars take it away. Man needs a hat on a day like this."

"All right," Youssef said. He handed a bill to the man and took the hat, placed it on his head.

"Where you from?" the vendor asked.

"I'm from Amsterdam."

"You don't look Dutch."

"There are many different kinds of Dutch."

"I guess that be so. How do you like America?"

Youssef settled the hat on his head and took another pull on the water bottle he had nearly emptied.

"It is very busy," he said. "Very crowded. And it seems very rich."

The black man laughed. "Oh, it's busy all right, and crowded, too. But don't let the look of things fool you, there ain't a lot of rich out here. Oh, you gots some that are, but most of us are just struggling to get by."

Youssef nodded. He finished the bottle of water and handed the empty back to the vendor.

"You were thirsty, weren't you?" the vendor said. "Want to watch that, easy to get dehydrated on days like this. Don't want our Dutch visitor to faint on the street, no we don't. You sure you don't want another bottle?"

"No, thank you," Youssef said. "Where is the Air and Space Museum?"

"You're looking at it," the vendor said, pointing across the block-wide lawn at a glass-fronted building on the other side. "That over there, on this side, that's the National Gallery of Art."

"Thank you," Youssef said.

He walked away slowly, letting himself be carried by the crowds of tourists in shorts and with cameras hung around their necks. A tour bus disgorged a horde of Japanese tourists, and the guide began her spiel, punctuated with waves of the flag she carried.

"And this is the National Gallery of Art . . ."

Youssef followed the crowd up the bank of stairs, then paused and sat down on the stairs. There were a few others on the stairs, sun worshipers mostly, soaking up the heat. From his vantage point he had an excellent view of the benches in front of the Air and Space Museum, though he was over a hundred yards away. He watched the steady stream of people back and forth across the Mall and from the steps of the Air and Space Museum. The uniformed security people who stood outside the Air and Space Museum seemed to pay no particular attention to the benches; instead they spoke to each other and to the occasional tourist. They rotated back into the building at fifteen-minute intervals. He could see the cameras mounted on the side of the museum, but they all seemed oriented to cover the approaches to the building and there were none that were directed outward toward the benches. No signs of surveillance, though there were some panel trucks and vans parked in the delivery zone in front of the museum.

Everything seemed clear.

There was a group of bicyclists riding on the gravel path that bordered the grassy expanse of the Mall; he recognized them as the group from the youth hostel. One rider split off from the others and rode over to the benches in front of the museum and stopped, resting one foot on a bench, a neighbor to Youssef's target for tomorrow. The rider took off her helmet and shook out long black tresses, then took a bandana from the pocket of her shorts and wiped her face and neck, then took her water bottle from the bike frame and tilted it up for a long drink. Even from where he sat, Youssef could tell that she was beautiful. It made him think of Britta.

He got up then, and brushed the seat of his pants, damp with perspiration. He walked down to the street level where a yellow taxicab let out a group of four tourists.

"Wait!" Youssef called to the driver, who nodded to him. Youssef ducked his head and climbed into the air-conditioned comfort of the cab, slammed the door, and said, "Would you take me by the Egyptian embassy, please?"

The driver nodded, and pulled away from the curb.

● ● ●

Isabelle had watched Youssef for some time. It had been easy to follow the bus; the bicycles made better time than any car in the traffic,
and the trip was a short one. The heat made it onerous, but she was an
athlete and inured to hardship. While the bike–tour guide had made
an attempt to keep her with the group, Isabelle had ignored him and
gone ahead to where she could stop and watch the young Arab on the
Mall. There had to be a reason, other than simple sight-seeing, that he
chose to sit in the blazing heat on the steps of the Gallery of Art. He
seemed interested in the Air and Space Museum, and had paid no
attention to any of the goings-on around him. It would be hard to
spot surveillance here, she thought, with the crowds and vehicles constantly coming and going. But then that would make a surveillance
team work all the harder, which would make this a good spot for a
clandestine meeting. He had come directly here, instead of working a
route, as if he'd been going to a meeting, or wandering the way a true
tourist would.

She cursed under her breath when she saw him get into the cab.
She didn't even try to hurry to get herself back together and ride after
them; the cab bolted to the busy traffic of Seventh Street and disappeared around the corner. She'd have to reacquire him at the hostel, a
risky business as she didn't want to get too close to him. The black
wig she wore seemed to magnify the heat on her head. She took off
her sunglasses and wiped the sweat from them on her bandana, then
arched her back to relieve a kink while she looked around and studied the entrance to the Air and Space Museum. The crowds went in
and out, and she wondered what attracted Youssef to this place. It
was possible that she wouldn't be able to determine what he was
looking for through surveillance.

She might have to take him and force the information from
him.

• • •

In the back of the panel van parked across the street from Isabelle,
where two surveillance men sweated, a laptop chimed and a video
frame captured from the hidden lens appeared beside another pic-

ture, one of her face from the shooting in Minneapolis. The pop-up alert said, POSITIVE MATCH.

• • •

The cab driver worked his way through the slow traffic tangling the streets around the Egyptian embassy. Youssef had plenty of time to study the streets and the surrounding neighborhood; it was a pleasant area, with many old row homes lovingly restored, and the old Colonial mansions turned into office space or embassies. The driver slowed as he approached the embassy.

"I just want to see it," Youssef said. "You don't have to stop."

"Where are you going?" the cab driver asked, a thin black man with a goatee, sweating even in the air-conditioning of the cab.

"I want to go to the International Youth Hostel."

"Should have said that earlier."

"Sorry, I just wanted to see the embassy."

"You Egyptian?"

"My father was."

"Guess that makes you, then."

"Yes, I suppose so."

The cabbie snorted, and bulled his way back into the traffic stream. Youssef studied the walled mansion, and the two guards on duty in front. They passed a street with many shops on it, and Youssef saw a sign for an Internet café. That was useful. And there, right where he had been told it would be, was the mailbox he was to mark tomorrow.

His reconnaissance was done. Now it was time for a meal and some sleep. Tomorrow would be a busy day.

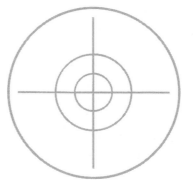

DOMINANCE RAIN HEADQUARTERS, FAIRFAX, VIRGINIA

Ray Dalton turned a folding chair around and settled into it, crossing his long arms along the back of the chair. The conference room was, for once, still. The assistants and operators were busy at work elsewhere, leaving Ray and Charley alone. Charley leaned back in his chair and rubbed his eyes, then said, "Well?"

"What sign?"

"Nothing," Charley said. "Lots of nothing. So we wait. The only thing that's happened is that he's read the e-mail message. Today."

"So he's here."

"He's here."

"What about his directions on the Web site?"

"The hackers have been through there with a fine-toothed comb. They inserted our message right where it should be."

"Do you think that will work?"

"It's the best shot we've got. He was told to ignore any messages telling him to stop once he got his final go-ahead. Total fail-safe. This is the best we can come up with to get him into our ambush."

Ray nodded. "You've talked to the shooters?"

"Yes. They're good. They're talking with the CDC team now."

"We've got people from Fort Detrick as well."

"The more the merrier," Charley said. "But we'll stay lean and mean with our team till we roll this boy up. Then you can cut loose as many of the bug boys as you want."

"What else do you need from me?"

"Just keep signing the checks, Ray. Really. We're good to go."

They both looked up as an assistant, a blond woman with a pinched face, came in and went directly to a computer monitor. She tapped quickly on the keyboard, then said, "You'll both want to see this. We have a hit."

Charley and Ray went around the table to the monitor. The image of Isabelle Andouille on the National Mall filled the screen, with a smaller photo of her inset into the image.

"She's one of them, isn't she?" the assistant said. "The Twins."

"What the hell is she doing here?" Ray said.

Charley sat down beside the assistant. Several other assistants and operators came into the room and clustered around the terminal, but he ignored them. "Take me through it," he said. "Tell me the story."

The woman's face became less pinched as she worked the keyboard. "Here it is. She came up on the face scanner five minutes ago. She was part of a group of bicyclists, but she split off and went to the benches, not the target bench, but right next to it. Then she took off her helmet and sunglasses, had a drink, geared up again, and rode off."

"What did she do while she was there?" Charley said.

"That's it. She looked around at the Air and Space Museum, but not like she was doing a survey."

"Do we know what she was doing before she went to the bench?" Charley said.

"Just riding with a group of bicyclists. Then she broke away and went midway across the lawn, then the rest of the way to the bench. That's it."

"What was she looking for?" Ray said.

Charley patted the assistant on the shoulder. "Thanks. Good work."

He stared at the screen and the familiar face of Isabelle. What was she doing here? What would bring her here to the States except some connection with the One?

"She wants to lead us to him," Charley said.

Ray looked puzzled. "What?"

"Like she did in Amsterdam. Somehow she's onto his tail, she wants to find him and finger him. Either to take him out or to turn him over to us. She knows about Sad Holiday."

"That's a stretch. How would she know?"

"Why else right here, right now? What else would she be doing? She and Marie wouldn't mount another operation in the States after we warned them off. It has to be Sad Holiday."

Charley turned to the assistant and said, "Any idea of where she went?"

She shook her head no. "The teams stayed put. By the time we got it sorted out, she was away on her bike. We've told them not to move till we have a positive ID on the One—that's what they did, they stayed in place. We could put an additional team in, have them patrol the area and see if they spot her."

"Do that," Charley said. "And tell the teams in the field to stand by. The One is in the area."

Ray said, "Is that your call?"

"That's my call," Charley said. The timbre of the hunter was in his voice. "He's here. And Isabelle is going to lead us right to him."

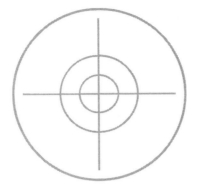

## WASHINGTON, DC, NEAR THE EGYPTIAN EMBASSY

After a fitful night filled with uncomfortable and half-remembered dreams, Youssef woke and prepared himself for his operation. He made his way near to the Egyptian embassy, and stopped at the Internet café he had seen the day before during his reconnaissance. Cyber Joe's, it was called, and a wooden sign with a steaming cup of coffee and a laptop carved in it hung over the door. The smell of fresh coffee thickened the air inside the café. The tables were mostly occupied with early morning customers reading the *Washington Post* over their cups of coffee. Long rows of Apple I-Macs lined the walls, and there was a separate section of small desks enclosed in cubicles.

"Can I help you?" said the man at the front counter. He was dressed in a black T-shirt and black jeans, and his gestures and expression had a languid femininity about them. He made Youssef nervous.

"Are those laptop cubicles there?" Youssef said.

"That's what they are. Would you like to use one?"

"Yes."

"Well step right up here, and I'll take care of you."

The man seemed amused by Youssef. He took Youssef's cash and handed him back his change, letting his fingers linger in the palm of Youssef's hand.

"There you go," he said. "Would you like some coffee?"

"No," Youssef said. He pulled his hand away and dropped the coins into his front pocket, wiping his hand on his pants leg, a motion that didn't go unnoticed by the other man.

"Suit yourself, big boy. Have fun on the Net."

Youssef went to the cubicle farthest from the counter and closest to the window. He plugged the T-1 line into the Ethernet port on his laptop and logged on. He looked around; the gay man at the front counter looked at him, then away. Youssef typed in the URL of a pornographic pay site. On the site, he clicked MEMBERS, then entered his password. He ran the cursor down a long row of buttons till he found one that said TEEN SEX. A pageful of thumbnail images came up. He scrolled through them till he found one titled SAMANTHA. When he clicked on the image, it expanded into the picture of a young brunette girl with a shaved pubic area inserting a massive black dildo into herself. He downloaded the image, then exited the Web site and logged off the Internet. He clicked on the image icon and the picture expanded to fill his screen again. A few keystrokes activated a separate program, one that rendered the photograph into bits and bytes and then extracted a particular line of code that was  buried in the image of the young girl's thigh. That line of code went to his desktop, and then he ran another program that decrypted the ones and zeros and turned it into text: PRODUCT YOU RECEIVED IN AMSTERDAM IS FLAWED, EXCHANGE FOR NEW PRODUCT FROM LOCAL CONTACT.

Youssef studied the words for a moment, then carefully deleted the text, the encrypted line of code, and the pornographic image. He unplugged his laptop and left the cubicle and went to the front counter. The gay man took his time looking up from the newspaper he was reading.

"Yes?"

"There is an art store near here. Which way is it?"

The gay man looked Youssef up and down. "You don't look like the art type."

"The store," Youssef said. "Which way?"

"Out the door, turn right, and walk. You can't miss it. Don't let the door hit you in the ass, sweetheart."

Youssef's hands shook as he slid his laptop back into his courier bag. He almost dropped the computer while fumbling with the door, the low laughter of the gay man ringing in his ears. Outside, he stood for a moment and turned his face up to the sun as though bathing in the shower of light. He took off the straw hat he wore and let the sun beat down on his head through his close-cropped hair, then he replaced his hat and slung his courier bag. The sign for the art store he'd seen was clear even from a block away; it too was a wooden sign, with an artist's easel and the words ART SUPPLIES carved on it.

Inside the store he stood and studied the long rows of shelves. He asked a passing clerk, "Where do you have chalk?"

"Aisle four, halfway down on your right."

Youssef took a box of plain white chalk from the shelf and went to the cash register and paid for his purchase. Once he was outside, he opened the box and took a stick and put it in his front pants pocket where his hand could rest on it. The open box of chalk went into his courier bag.

From here, it was only a short walk to the mailbox near the Egyptian embassy.

• • •

On the far side of the street, Isabelle strolled along, staying behind Youssef. All her senses were on alert; something was not right with the young Arab. At the hostel he kept himself apart from the other guests; on the street he didn't practice even minimal countersurveillance. It was as if he didn't care, or else he was so sure of his cover that he had become careless. She wasn't sure which was the case, but in any instance he was far too careless for an operator working in the very heart of the enemy. He seemed preoccupied with his thoughts instead of tuning up his situational awareness; something seemed to weigh on his mind while he went through the motions of an operator preparing. Isabelle felt frustrated. The young Arab's actions gave her little clue to what his intention might be. He had probably received instructions via e-mail at the Internet café; he had done that in Amsterdam. But she didn't dare get close enough to him to tell. Her disguise would serve to protect her at a distance, but up close . . . Youssef would remember her from their lengthy lunch and meetings in Amsterdam.

Isabelle put her frustration away and concentrated instead on watching the street ahead. While the Arab seemed oblivious to his surroundings, she could not afford to be. Here in Washington, DC there were many different agencies to worry about, intelligence both foreign and domestic, as well as law enforcement. She'd worked here often and was confident in her ability to operate, but she had no idea what Youssef might lead her into. It was especially dangerous in this quiet neighborhood with its tree-lined streets and row houses. There were many foreign embassies here, and subsequently a larger law-enforcement and security presence. She looked the part of a tourist, in a loose-fitting denim dress that fell to her knees and a large straw hat and black sunglasses hiding her face, with a guidebook and map sticking out of the oversized shoulder bag she carried. So she walked slowly, pacing her quarry across the street, wondering why his head was bowed and his shoulders bent as though beneath a heavy load.

• • •

Marcus Williams and Robert Sanders huddled in the back of a dusty white panel truck parked around the corner from the Egyptian embassy, directly across the street from the mailbox where the One was to make his clandestine signal to his contact. Battery-powered fans moved the air around, and a big bucket of dry ice in front of one fan served as an air conditioner. Despite those efforts, both men dripped sweat.

One monitor ran from a small camera mounted flush against the inside wall, its lens pressed against a pinhole hidden outside by the paint job. The camera was focused on the mailbox and provided a clear view of anyone near it. Another camera was mounted in the false ventilation hood on top of the truck; with pan and tilt capability, it zoomed in on anyone of interest in the general area. Leads from the monitors ran into a small server powered by batteries; the results of the constant scanning of faces came up on the monitor beside it. There had been a flurry of activity earlier, when the early morning work rush was on, and people stopped at the mailbox to drop letters while walking to the bus stop around the corner or on their way to work. The computer program had turned up no hits on those faces, and since then there had been only a few individuals mailing letters.

Williams checked the power-cable connection on the back of the small server, and looked at the gauge on the battery pack. Plenty of juice left for the day stretching out before them. He fished a plastic bottle of spring water out of a bucket filled with melting ice.

"Water?" he said, holding a dripping bottle out to Sanders.

"Yeah," Sanders said. "Thanks."

He twisted the cap off and drained the quart bottle in a long series of gulps. Williams watched him, then gestured at a gallon plastic water jug half-full of urine.

"You'll have to piss again, drinking like that."

"Yeah, yeah," Sanders said. "I don't need borderline dehydration. Too damn hot to play around."

Williams shrugged and sipped from his own bottle, slowing, rinsing his mouth before swallowing. "Want to switch?"

"Sure."

Sanders edged from his folding stool and squeezed past his partner and slid into the undersized lawn chair Williams favored.

"I don't know how you get your ass into this thing," Sanders grumbled.

"Got to be lean and mean."

The radio crackled. "OP, this is Zero, radio check."

Sanders picked up his microphone and said, "Zero, this is OP, I have you five by five."

"Zero, out."

"Payne working the radio himself again?" Williams said.

"Sounds like it. He likes hands-on."

"Probably sick of the boss breathing down his neck."

The radio crackled again. "OP, this is Gun, radio check."

Sanders said, "Gun, this is OP, I have you five by five."

"Roger, Gun out."

Sanders replaced the microphone in its cradle. "I feel sorry for the shooters," he said. "It's hot as hell out there and they can't run the AC."

"They'll get over it," Williams said. He adjusted one of the fans to blow directly into his face. "Surveillance turns out to be a pretty good gig, huh? You could be out there sweating with the gunfighters."

"Yeah," Sanders said. "Instead I'm in here sweating with you. Some good gig."

On the camera monitor, a dark-skinned young man in a straw hat with a courier bag slung across his back, walked toward the mailbox.

• • •

Youssef had stood off for a time, lingering in the shade of a tree, leaning against the concrete planter box and sipping from his bottle of water. He looked like just another pedestrian desperate for a moment's relief from the oppressive heat. While he waited, watching the mailbox, he scanned the streets for signs of surveillance: people lingering for too long, parked cars with passengers, delivery vans or trucks that seemed out of place. The problem was that there were all of those things on these streets, and they seemed to be the norm. There is a rhythm to a street during the workday, a flow of pedestrians and cars that has its own beat. Youssef struggled to find that beat, to look for the watchers who would be still notes in the rhythm of the street. After a few minutes, driven by the sense of impatience that had been growing in him, he decided the best course was to just get on with it.

The longer he waited, the less likely he was to do it.

That thought surprised him. He hadn't consciously considered not making his meeting until this moment. What would he do? Walk away from the mission, abandon the job of the One? The thought nagged at him, but he put it aside, as he put aside his thoughts of Britta, and instead concentrated on what needed to be done.

He took a deep breath, as though diving into a pool, and crossed the street at the crosswalk when the light changed. He turned to his left, momentarily alone as the other pedestrians went their way, and slipped his hand into his pocket and palmed the long piece of chalk. His heart pounded, and he stopped for a brief moment, as though he were admiring the architecture of the old Colonials on the street. Then he walked to the mailbox, paused again, then took his hand out of his pocket and dragged his hand and the chalk down the side of the blue mailbox.

The chalk broke in his hand, and the piece that remained skittered across the heavily painted surface without leaving a mark. Youssef tried again. The chalk squeaked on the slick surface and left only a few pieces in the pits and bubbles of thick paint. His breath caught in his chest; he had a moment of panic. He was spending too much time on the target. He drew the shortened chalk stick across the concrete planter beside the mailbox, leaving a long horizontal streak. Then he slipped the chalk back into his pocket and walked away.

Surely they would not tell him to leave a chalk mark on something that couldn't be marked on. They must have meant the concrete planter, which took the chalk well. He hoped he was right. A sudden foreboding came over him, and he hurried away, glancing once over his shoulder. A bus pulled into the bus stop just past the mailbox, and heeding a sudden urge, Youssef boarded.

"How much?" he asked, extending a handful of change to the driver. "I'm a visitor here."

The driver, a thin Hispanic man with a patina of sweat on his face and a light-blue uniform shirt darkened in the armpits and back, plucked out a few coins and dropped them into the fare box, then tore off a paper transfer slip and handed it to Youssef.

"Thank you," Youssef said, as the bus pulled from the curb. He walked all the way to the back of the bus and sat sideways on the rearmost seat, where he could look out the rear window and watch the mailbox as the bus rumbled through traffic. There was nothing there that hadn't been there before, but something, perhaps the sixth sense of the hunted, told him to get away. He watched till he couldn't see the mailbox anymore, then turned front, then back once more.

• • •

"Did you get that? Did you get that?" Williams hissed. "The one in the hat."

Sanders frantically worked the control toggle for the camera mounted beneath the false ventilation hood.

"I lost him! Damn it!" Sanders said. "He's walking away."

"Did you get his face?"

"Yeah . . . the hat breaks up the image, puts too many shadows on the face . . ." Sanders muttered, punching keys on the keyboard. "Put the shooters on him."

Williams grabbed the radio microphone and said, "All stations, this is OP, we have a possible, dark-skinned male approximately five feet ten inches, baggy blue jeans and beige T-shirt, straw hat and a black satchel slung across his back. Subject is moving south away from the mailbox. Looked like he was trying to make a mark on the mailbox."

The two closest streetwalker units went into action. Each car let out one man who hurried to the mailbox. One of them went to the corner and looked after the bus pulling away; one stopped beside the mailbox and saw the chalk mark on the concrete planter and a shard of broken chalk on the ground. He picked up the chalk and said into his lapel mounted microphone, "Zero, this is Gun-One. There's chalk here. Somebody tried to make a mark on the planter next to the mailbox."

"Gun-One, Zero. Where is he?"

"He's not on the street, I think he got on the bus that just pulled out of here."

"All street stations, on the bus." Payne's voice was clipped.

The streetwalker on the corner saw the bus two blocks ahead pulling away from another stop. He whispered into his coat lapel, ignoring the curious looks of the passing pedestrians, then stepped into the street and waved down his partner in the car.

• • •

Sanders ran a program to enhance the image captured by the camera. "It's not perfect, but it's seventy-six percent. The hat and the shadows broke up the face."

"The guy made a chalk mark there. That's the tradecraft we're looking for," Williams said. "What are we calling it?"

Sanders said, "I call it as the target."

Williams picked up the handset and said, "Zero, this is OP, we call it as Target-One, say again, Target-One."

"Roger OP, this is Zero, we confirm Target-One. All stations, all stations, Target-One is in the area."

• • •

After the confirmation, Charley got up out of his chair so quickly it spun like a top. With Ray in his wake, he hurried down the hallway to the express elevator that took them down to the basement garage. The two men climbed into the back of a black Chevy Suburban with blacked-out windows. On the bench behind them two leather-jacket-clad shooters checked their MP-5 submachine guns.

"How fast can we get there?" Charley asked the driver.

"The traffic now? Half hour, forty minutes."

"Can you run the light bar?"

"That's not going to get the cars off the road."

"We've got people on it," Ray said. "You're just going to have to trust them to do the right thing."

"I should have been down there," Charley said.

"Let them do their job," Ray said. He turned up the volume on the radio crackling with traffic from the streetwalkers. "Let's go."

• • •

In the back of the panel truck that served as the observation post, Sanders and Williams looked at each other, then exchanged high-fives.

"Now it's down to the streetwalkers and the gunfighters," Williams said.

"I'd like to be out there," Sanders said. He wiped his hands on his pants and picked up his bottle of water. "Wouldn't you?"

Williams adjusted his fan slightly. "I did my time running and gunning. I like this just fine. Let the young men run."

Sanders snorted and wiped a lank lock of hair off his forehead. "You're letting your age dictate what you do."

"See what you think when you're in your forties, young blood."

The monitor chimed and both men looked over at it. The image of a young woman in a denim sundress, a wide straw hat, and large sunglasses she had just taken off to wipe with a bandanna plucked from her shoulder bag filled the screen along with the message: POSITIVE MATCH. Another image, of the same woman straddling a moped, with a machine pistol in her hand, popped up within the larger image.

"Jesus Christ, it's Target-Two," Williams said. He picked up the microphone and said, "Zero, all stations, Target-Two is at Location Alpha, positive identification of Target-Two at Location Alpha."

Sanders zoomed the camera in on the woman. "It's her," he said. "Isabelle."

• • •

In the back of the Chevy Suburban, Charley picked up his radio handset and said, "Gun-Actual, this is Zero."

The cool, laconic voice of the gunfighter leader on the ground said, "Go ahead, Zero."

"Move on Target-Two. Pick her up."

"Let me be clear on this, Zero. I'll have to pull units from Target-One."

Charley hunched over the radio, thinking it through. If he pulled a team off the One, he might lose him; on the other hand, Isabelle obviously had a line on the One and the information she carried might bring the operation to a close that much faster.

"Do it," he said, ignoring the look he got from Ray. "Take her."

"Roger, Zero. Understand and will comply. Gun-Actual out."

• • •

Isabelle stood before a wrought-iron fence surrounding a particularly handsomely restored row house. She'd seen Youssef do his clumsy marking, and watched the sudden appearance of two men, obviously watchers of some kind. Taking her time, she took off her sunglasses and wiped them carefully with a scarf she plucked from her bag. She turned casually, looking in all directions for the surveillance vehicles that would be there. A black Chevy Suburban turned the corner sharply, its wheels squealing, the truck shifting ponderously on its springs. Isabelle tucked her scarf back into her bag and replaced her sunglasses, then lowered her hands, careful to keep them in plain sight.

The Suburban screeched to a halt. The rear doors flung open and three men burst out, all of them holding MP-5 submachine guns.

"Don't move!" one shouted as they ran at her.

Isabelle stood calmly and waited.

• • •

Gun-One and Gun-Two were the team to get behind the bus first. They were in a tan four-door Ford Taurus five blocks behind the bus. Gun-One pulled a pair of binoculars from the gear bag at his feet and tried to focus on the bus ahead. His view was blocked by the gentle curve of the road and long lines of traffic.

"I can't see," he said. "I can't tell if he's gotten off or not."

His partner called in the location of the bus and alerted the other responding vehicles that the One might be on foot again.

"Can you see?" he said.

"Just hurry. Get another team in front of the bus."

• • •

Youssef remained sideways in his seat and kept a cautious eye to his rear. The traffic was so heavy that the bus inched along, and then burst into a sudden rush when there was a gap between cars. The driver bullied his way to the curb, forcing cars out of the way, and so made good time from stop to stop. Passengers crowded on, leaving standing-room only and forcing Youssef to face front. An obese black woman in a pink taffeta dress squeezed onto the bench seat beside him.

"Oh my," she said. "It's so hot."

Youssef nodded and turned away to avoid conversation. The big woman sensed that and settled into her seat, her hands folded primly in her lap, quiet as a child. Youssef took a deep breath to calm himself, and the thick scent of the woman beside him filled his nostrils.

"Excuse me," he said. "I have to get out."

She shifted over so he could stand. He pushed his way forward to the exit door. After five stops, he saw a sign for a Metro stop. He took his hat off and held it to his chest, and got off behind several other passengers and blended into the stream of people going down the escalator into the depths of the subway station. It was cool in the station, a welcome respite from the heat above. He replaced his hat and went to the fare machine, where he inserted a five-dollar bill for an all-day excursion card. Then he went through the electronic gates and down to the platform.

The morning rush hour was almost over, so there was a longer interval between trains. Youssef stood away from the other passengers waiting on the platform. There were ventilation ducts on the walls at the end of the platform, beside the dark and gaping maw of the tunnel the train ran through. He walked slowly toward them, then looked up and saw the video cameras covering the track and platform. Careful to appear as though he was ignoring the cameras, he walked to the edge of the platform and spit out onto the track, then went back, working his way into the crowd of passengers waiting. It would be difficult to plant a dispersion device here with the cameras. He felt a sudden rush of air coming through the tunnel, pushed ahead by the oncoming train. The air brushed hard against his face, and he turned away, as did the man beside him.

"Feels like it would blow you away, doesn't it?" said the man, dressed in the tourist uniform of shorts, T-shirt, hat, and camera.

Youssef nodded and thought of how far the contents of a single spray from his atomizer would carry if he stood on the upwind side of the track.

That would work.

The white train eased into the station and stopped. The doors hissed open and a handful of passengers got out, the passengers on the platform patiently waiting to one side till the doors were clear, then boarding. Youssef got on and sat near the door beside a window. Mounted on the bulkhead beside the door was a map of the Metro system. He was only two stops from the Smithsonian. The train lurched into motion, and the train operator announced over the loud-speaker the next station. It took only moments before he reached the Smithsonian stop. He got off the train and let the flow of people carry him up the stairs and through the turnstile to the escalator that rose up out of the underground station. For a moment, as he rose smoothly into the light, he was reminded of the nightmare he'd had in Britta's bed.

In the bright heat of the day, he put thoughts of Britta out of his mind. He was sure no one had followed him. He looked over at the green expanse of the National Mall. A sudden lassitude came over him, and he longed for the comfort of her bed. His bed, he cor-rected himself, a sour look on his face. He turned away from the Mall to the busy street, and flagged down a passing taxi.

"Youth hostel, please," he said to the driver.

He had time to rest. All the time in the world. Or at least till tomorrow.

## GOVERNMENT SAFE HOUSE, GEORGETOWN, WASHINGTON, DC

Isabelle sat in a wooden chair with no armrests, her hands held together by a plastic flexi-cuff in her lap, her long legs crossed and relaxed. Her gaze was cool and faintly challenging as she looked at Charley. They were in a secure room in a Georgetown safe house where the command and control group had relocated, at Charley's insistence, after the morning's fiasco. Surveillance and apprehension teams prowled and crisscrossed the streets around the Egyptian embassy, sniffing at the sign the One had left behind. They traced him as far as the Metro, where an examination of the video-surveillance tapes showed him on the platform and boarding a train. A small army of federal agents fanned out to Metro stations to look at videotape of passengers leaving the station, but it was as if the One had disappeared into thin air.

Charley waved the two gunfighters who stood guard away.

"Want us to leave the door cracked, boss?" said the senior gun-fighter, a thin man with wispy blond hair receding from his gleam-ing forehead, who shifted his MP-5 to his other hand as he went to leave the room.

"I'm good, Daryl," Charley said. "Isabelle and I know each other."

Isabelle turned her head and smiled up at Daryl. "I promise not to hurt him."

Daryl stopped, his submachine gun dangling from his hand. "Okay," he said. "And I promise not to kill you . . . for now." He stood there for a moment, then went out the door, shutting it quietly behind him.

"Oh," Isabelle said, facing Charley again. "Did I say something to upset him?"

"We don't share your sense of humor, Isabelle," Charley said. He reached back and adjusted the butt of his Glock in its holster, then leaned back in his chair and crossed his arms over his chest. "Where is he, Isabelle?"

"Where is who?" Isabelle said. "You have me at a disadvantage. I don't know your name." She held up her cuffed hands. "Are these necessary?"

Charley reached for his belt and took his Leatherman tool out of its sheath. He opened the pliers, then got out of his seat and used the wire cutters in the pliers to snip neatly through the plastic flexi-cuffs around each of Isabelle's thin, muscular wrists. He stood over her for a moment while she rubbed the red impressions the cuffs had left.

"How's that?" he said.

"Thank you."

"My name is Charley."

"Charley. Short for Charles, yes?"

"That's right."

"Where is who, Charley?"

Charley snapped the Leatherman tool shut, replaced it in its sheath, and sat back down. He took his time answering.

"You and I both know who we're talking about. Let's cut to the chase. We want Youssef bin Hassan. You followed him here from Amsterdam. You know where he is or where he's staying. We want that. We don't have the time to play with you."

Isabelle's seeming calm irritated Charley. She seemed so unruffled and unconcerned, her breathing slow and regular, her gaze level and direct.

"We want him," he said.

"This I can see," Isabelle said. "For what do you want him?"

"That doesn't concern you."

"What concerns me is what you intend for me and my family."

Charley tilted his head in confusion. "You and your family?"

"Yes."

"What about you and your family?"

Isabelle laughed, but there was no humor in her face. "You Americans. You think everyone else is so dense. You think I don't know what you plan for Marie and me?"

"We made a deal, Isabelle. You took the cash and you walked away. And you handed over the two Arabs. We got what we wanted, you got what you wanted."

"As though you would leave it like that! I am not a fool."

Charley chewed his upper lip, then leaned forward, his elbows on his knees. "Listen to me, Isabelle. There was no further action planned against you. We got what we needed and we left you alone. We held up our end of the deal. But you? You're here, right now. Why?"

"I want certain guarantees," Isabelle said. "For my family. And me."

"This isn't the time for bargaining."

"Then find him yourself."

"We will, eventually."

"Why are we talking?"

"Do you know what he's here to do, Isabelle? Do you? I don't think so. You're a mother. You have a beautiful child. What he's here to do endangers your child."

"We are very far from Amsterdam."

Charley leaned back in his chair and crossed his arms on his chest. It would create new problems to tell Isabelle the particulars of the case. But the pressing problem was locating the One before he could act on his plan, and Isabelle was the key to that.

"Do you know where he is?" he said.

"Probably. I know where he's been staying."

"What do you want?"

"A guarantee that you will leave me and my family alone. A guarantee that there will be no comeback from either Amsterdam or here."

"Isabelle, what kind of guarantee can we give you that we haven't already? We let you go in Amsterdam, we paid you what you wanted. Wasn't that guarantee enough?"

She was silent, and even with her stone-faced expression, Charley's intuition told him that she hadn't thought that far ahead.

"No matter what you think, we don't make war on families," Charley said. "Your daughter was never in any danger from us."

"What do you want with the boy?" she said. "He's not much."

"He's more than he appears."

"If he is so important, then it is easy for you to make an agreement."

The door opened and they both looked up. Ray Dalton leaned into the room and signaled to Charley. "I need to speak to you."

Charley watched fear and curiosity play across the woman's face.

"We don't have much time," he said to her. "And it's running out."

He got up and followed Ray into the hallway.

"Offer her whatever she wants," Ray said with no preamble. "We'll sort it out later. If she insists on stalling, then we're going to rip it out of her head with drugs. I've got a medical interrogation team on its way right now."

"She doesn't even know what she wants," Charley said. "What kind of guarantee can you offer a paranoid?"

Ray seemed struck by the question. "What do you think?"

"I think we tell her the truth about the One. She's smart enough to see the risk to her family if bioengineered smallpox starts spreading across the country. It's only a short jump to the Continent. I say just tell her and get her to work with us. That's proof enough that we're not going to job her and be done with it. Then send her on her way with money and a promise."

"Will that work?"

"We don't have time for anything else."

"Then do it."

Charley nodded, then went back into the room. Isabelle looked over her shoulder at him, crossed and recrossed her legs, and watched him till he sat down across from her again.

"Well?" she said.

There was a slight tic in the corner of her left eye, the only indication that she felt any nervousness at all. Charley admired her self-control; for a fleeting moment, he fantasized about what he might do if they had met as man and woman someplace. But then, men weren't really her thing, were they? He smiled, and she smiled back, a cold and controlled smile, one that showed long practice.

"Isabelle, what do you know about smallpox?"

A flurry of emotions flickered beneath the smooth mask of her face: surprise, curiosity, puzzlement, and then a carefully concealed comprehension.

"Yes," she said. "That would command your attention, would it not?"

"You understand why, now."

"Is he infected?"

"No. But he has the agent with him."

Now it was worry that furrowed her brow, her composure slipping away. "Has he been spreading it? In Amsterdam?"

"No, Isabelle," Charley said patiently. "Ilse and Marie are safe, for now. It's here that he's to spread the agent. But Amsterdam doesn't seem so far now, does it?"

"They wouldn't dare," she said. "They know what you Americans would do to anyone who did."

"They're doing it as we speak. They being your old paymasters at Al-Bashir. Now we've talked enough, Isabelle. That's why we want him. And we're willing to pay you, provide you with whatever assurances you need, whatever you want. But you will tell us where he is."

Isabelle licked delicately at her lips. For the first time, Charley noticed how her lips were chapped, and the lower lip looked as though she'd chewed on it. How had he missed that?

"May I have water?" she said.

Charley went to the door, and one of the technicians who was monitoring the room from the communications center brought him a bottle of spring water.

"Thanks," Charley said.

He went back in and sat down, the seat hard against his back, and handed the bottle to Isabelle.

"Thank you," she said. She cracked the seal on the bottle, tipped it up, and drank off half its contents in one long swallow.

"That's better," she said. She toyed with the cap in one hand, flipping it between her fingers like a magician working a coin. "I should have killed him in Amsterdam."

"Did you mean to?"

"I knew you wanted the elder. I thought of killing them both, but I didn't know what you wanted. I regret being involved with them . . . it is not like us to be used this way."

"This is your chance for payback. And a bigger payday than you got the first time around."

"Yes," she said. "I will want that. Do you want me to kill him for you?"

"We want him alive, if possible. With his product. And we mean to see to that ourselves."

"Of course. I will tell you what I know. He is staying at the International Youth Hostel in downtown Washington, under the name Youssef Ameer. He is in a single room on the third floor, beside the fire-exit stairwell. Today he left very early and went to a cyber café near where you took me. Then he made his signal near the mailbox. And got away. Yesterday he went to the National Mall and sat on the steps of the National Art Gallery, then took a taxi somewhere. I lost him there. He stays by himself for the most part, alone in his room, only coming down for meals and to use the computers at the hostel."

Charley looked at the door, then back at Isabelle. "What else?"

"That's it. I planned to follow him, to see what he was doing, and then either kidnap or kill him. Whichever would get me the guarantees from your people."

"You have our guarantees. And as of now, you're working for us."

Isabelle laughed. "Such is the way of our world, is it not, Charley?"

## INTERNATIONAL YOUTH HOSTEL, WASHINGTON, DC

Things happened. Federal agents and DC police set up vehicle surveillance posts on the streets around the hostel. Armed men in plainclothes loitered near the hostel exits. Two DOMINANCE RAIN operators and a DC vice officer, all in plainclothes, went to the front desk and asked about their friend Youssef Ameer. A blond girl with dreadlocks was on duty.

"He's in his room," she said. "Room three-fourteen, on the third floor. He came in a couple of hours ago, said he was tired and was going back to bed. I told him he shouldn't be out too late."

"Thanks," said the vice cop, a blade-thin black man dressed in a leather car-coat too heavy for the heat, and black dungarees. "He was probably out partying. I'll go look him up."

"If he's not there, check the computer room. He spends a lot of time on-line."

"I'll do that."

The two special operators signaled for the vice cop to wait. They went down the hallway where the computer room was and walked slowly by, looking in. There was one heavy Germanic-looking youngster, his ears elaborately pierced, and a black woman in her thirties typing busily at the terminals. No sign of the One.

"What do you want to do?" said the vice cop, whose name was

Earl Long. "We can go up, knock on his door, eyeball him, make sure he's there before the team comes to get him."

"No," said the senior operator, a muscular Filipino man with graying hair. "We're not going to approach him. We'll recon the floor, check the room and the stairwell, but we don't want to wake him if he's sleeping. We'll leave the wake-up call to the team."

"If this guy some kind of bad-ass terrorist, why he staying in a youth hostel?" Long said.

"Who's going to look for him here?" the Filipino operator said.

"Word," Long said. "Let's get it done, then."

They split up, the junior operator going up the fire-exit stairwell to the third floor, the vice cop and the quiet Filipino taking the elevator. The elevator went slowly, and the floor numbers ticked off on a LED screen greasy with fingerprints. On the third floor they got out, squeezing by two long-haired travelers dressed almost identically in baggy hooded sweatshirts and cargo pants drooping off their thin hips. Then they were alone in the curving hallway lined with doors. There was a constant hum of sound: voices in discussion, a television from a communal room tuned to a talk show, the distinctive voice of Dave Mathews playing on a stereo turned up loud, the rattle of air conditioners at their highest setting.

Earl Long pursed his lips in a soundless whistle and tapped his fingers against the body mike he wore beneath his heavy jacket. He wiped sweat off his brow with one forefinger and said, "I wonder where my room be?"

The Filipino operator, whose name was Eddie Aledo, brushed his fingers along the open front of his photographer's vest, which served to conceal his holstered pistol. He looked both ways down the curving hall, then inclined his head to the right. "This way."

He walked down the center of the corridor, his hands loose and ready by his side, Earl Long following behind him, occasionally glancing over his shoulder. Room 314 was at the end of the hallway on the right-hand side as they came directly beside the fire-exit door that led to the stairwell. Aledo's partner stood there waiting for them.

Aledo gestured for silence and he walked up to the door and

listened for a moment. Any noise from the room was drowned out by the sound of the air conditioner going full blast. Then he checked the fire-exit door, trying the handle on the stairway side. Even though it turned freely, he took a small roll of duct tape from his vest and plastered a piece across the bolt, so that the door couldn't be locked. He leaned close to his partner's ear and whispered, "Anything?"

The younger man shook his head no. Aledo nodded, then touched Long on the shoulder and indicated that he should stand on the landing behind the fire door. There was a small vertical glass-insert in the door that enabled the man standing on the landing to see down the hallway and the door to room 314. Long nodded, dabbed at his sweaty forehead with the back of his hand, and took a position where he could see the door through the glass.

"We'll be back," Aledo whispered in Long's ear.

"Damn right," Long hissed. "Better hurry your ass up."

The two DOMINANCE RAIN operators went quickly down the stairs and through the hall on the lobby floor to a side exit, where they were met by two plainclothes FBI agents, who nodded at them as they passed. There was a large panel delivery truck with the logo of a plumbing company parked in the no-parking zone beside the side exit. The two operators went to the cab and Aledo leaned in the window and spoke to the man in the plumber's overalls sitting there.

"We've got a live eye on the door and stairwell," Aledo said. "It all looks like the diagram. Are you all set?"

The relaxed man in the overalls nodded. "Got the CDC back there. They're not used to shooters. Four of them and my six. Ready to go on the word."

"Then let's do this now."

The man in the cab picked up a radio and said into the handset, "All stations, all stations, stand by, stand by, stand by." He paused for a moment, then said, "Entry, go, go, go."

The sliding door at the back of the van slid up and six men jumped nimbly from the back. They were clad in black overalls with heavy body armor covering their chests and backs and padded protectors on their knees and elbows. Black helmets covered their heads, and throat mikes and earpieces wrapped around their necks. They all carried silenced MP5SD submachine guns. A strange note was the dark surgical masks they wore across their mouths and noses. Behind them came four men clad in white overalls wearing respirators.

They formed a line as they jogged to the side door that the two federal agents held open, and they slipped quickly into the building, brushing past an astonished hostel resident, who gawked at them as one might gawk at aliens landing on the street. Once through the door, they turned sharply and went up the exit stairwell, taking each turn quickly up to the third floor, where Earl Long stood beside the blocked door.

"Anything?" the assault-team leader, first in the stack, whispered.

Long shook his head no. The four-man containment unit from the CDC stood on the landing beside Long, who was visibly nervous at their sight.

"What the fuck you got them suits on for?" he said.

The assault team eased into the hallway and lined up along the wall beside the door. One man came forward with a fiber-optic camera equipped with a flexible lens that would fit under the door, but the team leader shook his head no. The team leader waved forward the third man in the stack, who came up and quietly set into place a small explosive charge, a lock cutter, between the door handle and the jamb. He took his place in line and waited while the team leader counted off 1, 2, 3 with his fingers. On the count of three the charge went off, and the team leader aided the acceleration of the door with a violent kick that sent it flying back into the room. The assault team rushed forward into the tiny room, two men in with one standing back by the door, the other three covering the hallway.

In the room, the rumpled bed was empty. As was the bathroom.

"Where the fuck did he go?" the team leader snarled.

In a Suburban parked on the side street, Charley Payne threw his radio to the floor and smacked his fist into the seat.

A rapid search of the hostel turned up only bewildered and in some cases defiant hostelers. The curious were told that they were looking for a drug dealer, and the CDC crew was kept hidden away from view in the back of the panel plumbing truck.

Ray and Charley stood on the street, to the casual eye just two men watching the police activity in and around the hostel.

"What now?" Ray said.

"We wait," Charley said. "He's got to make his meet tomorrow, and we'll have everything in the world set up on him."

"Do you think he made the surveillance crew?"

"Maybe," Charley said. "Or maybe he's just changing where he sleeps."

Isabelle joined them, her dress spotted with perspiration across the back.

"What's the word?" she said.

Charley said, "Do you have any idea where he might have gone?"

"None," she said. "None at all."

BETHESDA, MARYLAND

On the fourth floor of the Residence Inn in Bethesda, Maryland, Youssef bin Hassan lay on his king-size bed, his hands interlaced behind his head, and stared up at the ceiling fan which slowly stirred the air crisp with air conditioning. He glanced over at the clock radio on the nightstand beside the bed and saw that it was after five o'clock in the afternoon. He'd slept most of the day away after he had returned to the hostel to pick up his few belongings and slip out the side door. He'd walked to the Metro and taken the Red Line to Bethesda, and after exiting the station crossed the street to the Residence Inn. He wondered if he would attract too much attention, checking in with only an overstuffed courier bag for luggage, but his story of waiting for his lost bags to catch up with him elicited sympathy rather than suspicion from the desk clerk.

"The airlines these days, it's a wonder more people don't lose their bags," said the plump white woman, tucked into a red-and-white dress a size too small.

"Thank you," Youssef said as he took his room key. "Would you call me as soon as the bags get here?"

"I'll do that, but don't hold your breath. They may be a while."

"Thank you for your kindness."

"Oh, it's nothing, dear. You go on and get some rest, you must be tired after your flight."

The slow revolutions of the fan lulled him, and he lingered in that dreamy state between slumber and waking. His mind, for once, was clear of conflicted thoughts and images. The good rest had done wonders for his thinking. He remembered an instructor at the camp telling them that they should always eat and sleep whenever they could, because both those things would be in short supply once they went into action. He'd learned that was true.

He ran the details of the meeting through his mind once more. Between twelve and twelve thirty, he would be on the designated bench with the day's copy of the *Washington Post* opened to the style section. The smallpox agent would be in a plain brown paper lunch bag. His contact would come and sit beside him and ask him about the lead article in the style pages. Youssef would hand him the newspaper and tell him he was free to keep it. The contact would also have a plain brown paper lunch bag containing the new agent. Youssef would switch the bags and walk away. Simple and foolproof.

He crossed his feet at the ankles. The whirring blur of the fan above him was hypnotic. He closed his eyes and let his thoughts wander. Britta's face rose in his mind, and instead of forcing it down, he toyed with it. Would she still be in Amsterdam when he left America? He'd first go to Syria, for his debriefing at a hidden camp there, but afterward he imagined he might be free. He would be the One who had struck the Americans a mighty blow, and there would be rewards for him.

Perhaps he could see Britta again.

Just outside his door, he heard women's voices.

"Where do you want to go eat?" one said.

"There's a cute little sandwich shop, Booeymonger's, just around the corner."

"What kind of name is Booeymonger?"

"I don't know. They have good salads and sandwiches, though."

The sound of their voices dwindled as they went down the hall toward the elevators. The mention of food brought a rumbling to his stomach, a reminder that he hadn't eaten since morning. He sat up on the side of the bed, then reached beneath the bed for his courier bag and pulled it out. He removed the small Pelican hard case. He opened it up and studied the small glass vials with the liquid agent inside. He took one vial and held it up to the room light, then replaced it carefully with the other vials and shut the Pelican case. The hard case went into his courier bag and then back beneath the bed. He put his shoes on, then picked up the remote control and turned the television set on with the sound up high. He went to the door and opened it and looked out into the hallway, then set the DO NOT DISTURB sign on the outside handle as he went out the door, shutting it behind him, and trying the door once to ensure it was locked. In the elevator, he hummed a tune as the floors ticked off on the indicator. He went directly to the front desk where the woman clerk smiled at him.

"Did you get some rest?" she said.

"Yes, thank you, I did. I'm hungry now. There is a place called Booeymonger's?"

She laughed. "Isn't that the funniest name for a sandwich shop? It's out the door and to your right, right on the corner. You can't miss it. They have excellent soups."

"Out the door and to the right. Thank you."

"Oh, you're welcome."

Youssef stood outside the hotel entrance for a moment and watched the rush of traffic. It was still hot and humid, maybe even more so than when he'd checked in. There was a steady flow of commuters coming up the escalators from the Metro station across the street, and the traffic seemed as congested as ever. He wondered if there was ever a time when the traffic slowed. It always seemed the same, no matter what time of day.

He wondered how it would look once the disease began to spread. Would there be as many people on the streets? As many cars? He doubted it.

He went to the corner and saw the sign for the sandwich shop. There were a few people sitting at the metal latticework tables outside, and a few more inside. There was no one else in line when he ordered a tuna-salad sandwich, a fruit cup, and a glass of orange juice from the teenaged boy behind the counter. He took his tray with his meal to a window table inside and sat down where he could watch people going by. The sandwich was good, heaped high with tuna speckled with green onions on chewy wheat bread. There was a television set mounted on the wall tuned to a news station with the sound off; Youssef ignored it while he ate his meal. When he was finished, he took his tray to the trash bin and emptied it into the bin, then placed his tray on the rack atop the bin. He glanced up at the television set as he went to the door and stopped. The screen showed the International Youth Hostel ringed by police cars. Youssef's stomach churned suddenly, and he felt nausea rise like a wave in him. The image changed to an Asian newswoman soundlessly mouthing commentary. Youssef hurried out the door and stood in the steamy air to catch his breath.

He calmed himself with the disciplined breathing he'd been taught, a deep breath in, hold, release, repeat. There had been no picture of him, and it may have been that there was some other reason for the police to have been at the youth hostel. He hurried back to the hotel, rushing past the smiling desk clerk who looked curiously after him as he entered the elevator, mashing the third-floor button with his thumb. In his room, he sat on the bed facing the television set and flipped through the local channels with the remote. He caught a station with the same image and the newscaster's voice saying, "Police and federal authorities raided the International Youth Hostel today in search of a major drug dealer reported to be staying at the downtown Washington, DC facility . . ."

The report was short and to the point. There was no description of the drug dealer, nor any picture. Youssef stared at the television screen, his thoughts racing. Was this true? Could there have been such a coincidence? Or was it just the coverup that the authorities would use if they were looking for him? He toyed with the idea of going back to the hostel, but that of course would be poor tradecraft and defeat the purpose of moving in the first place. A part of him wanted to go, though; wanted to see if he'd be picked up, his mission compromised and exposed. That would be one way out.

The thought had come from nowhere, and he was angry with himself again. The weakness and indecision he thought he'd put aside had returned. Would there be no end to this? He had to think. What if the mission was compromised? What if the Americans were turning all their formidable resources to bear on him? How could they know? And even if they did, what could they do to stop him?

That was of some comfort. There was no way to stop him—once he had the live agent, and he'd have that tomorrow. Tomorrow. He turned off the television and sat hunched in thought on the bed, one hand stroking the remote, the other drumming on the wrinkled bed-spread. The events of the day unrolled in his mind as though on a movie screen, and he ran his memory of the signal he'd left over and over again. He'd felt as though he'd been watched, even though he hadn't seen any overt surveillance; some of that could have been nerves. But if he'd been spotted and followed successfully to the hostel, why hadn't they taken him then? He felt confident that no one had followed him on the bus and the Metro, and his final evasion in the taxi had ensured that no one was on his tail.

So would the meeting be safe?

There was only one way to tell.

He took his courier bag from beneath the bed and removed the Pelican case. Then he took a vial of the agent and inserted it into the atomizer, careful not to discharge any of the contents. The process comforted him almost as much as if he'd been able to prepare a handgun to defend himself. The atomizer felt heavy in his hand, a live weight to it. Or dead weight, if one chose to think about it that way. There were more voices outside his door as people passed on their way to the elevator. Should he go out, test the product? It would be days before he'd know whether it was live or not, and by then he'd be long gone.

Youssef stood and slipped the atomizer into his pocket, curling the fingers of his hand around it. He went to the window and, using both hands, threw it open and looked down on the street below. The sense of being up high and looking down brought back the memory of his nightmare in Amsterdam. This was the second time he'd thought of that, remembering the vision he'd had earlier today on the Metro escalator. He wondered if that was an omen. His mother was a dreamer of that sort: she wrote down what she dreamed, and insisted that there were messages in her dreams. He wondered what his mother and father would think if they knew he was the One. He wondered if they would be proud or appalled. He struggled to put that thought and the others away in a place in his head that felt crowded with such thoughts.

Too much thinking was bad for an operator; too much imagination led to the musings he now had and that was a weakness. He remembered an instructor at the camp in Sudan, a former Russian KGB officer who taught about the demands of undercover work, and the tricks the mind could and would play, if you gave it free rein. It was up to the operator to discipline his thinking and prevent the insidious doubts from rising and interfering with his mission.

So it was up to him now to do as he'd been trained. He could use more rest. He'd already run through what needed to be done tomorrow. He would sleep in, eat a good breakfast, then make his way to his appointment.

Youssef left the window open. The street sounds rose, slightly muted, to his room. He lay back on the bed, fully dressed. He took out the atomizer and held it lightly in one fist, as though he were holding a bird in his hand, feeling its heart pulse against his fist.

And then he slept.

GEORGETOWN SAFE HOUSE

Charley opened his eyes and blinked twice, deliberately, before he rolled onto his back and looked up at the ceiling of the room he slept in. All around him, other members of the special operating group breathed the deep sounds of slumber from their folding cots. His mouth was sticky and foul from sleep. He took out the bottle of water he kept beneath his cot and drained it, then got up, careful not to disturb the other men crowded into the room, and went to the bathroom down the hall, where he had a long and satisfying piss. He washed his face slowly and thoroughly in the sink, then shaved carefully. He studied himself in the mirror. The gray in his hairline seemed pronounced today, as were the lines in his face. The three deep furrows that crossed his brow seemed deep as valleys. Bluish bags beneath his eyes made him look more tired than he felt. He stroked his cheeks to feel for any rough spots he'd missed shaving, then took a stick of anti-perspirant from his shaving kit and applied it to his armpits. He stowed his gear back in the nylon bag he kept it in and went back in the hall, where one of the equipment operators stood patiently waiting.

"Morning," Charley said.

The man nodded curtly as he went in. "Boss."

Back in the sleeping room, the other members of the command

and control group stirred. Charley took out a Cordura duffel bag from beneath his cot and checked his gear as he donned it. The radio was good, the batteries fresh, and the mike he'd conceal beneath his photographer's vest was brand new. He holstered a Glock 30, the .45-caliber compact pistol, with three spare magazines on his belt, two in a double pouch and the first one in a competition pouch set up for a fast reload. He touched his two knives, the personal totems he wore whenever he operated: a Perrin neck knife as done by Ernest Emerson and an Emerson CQC-7 clipped in his right front pocket. He wore loose blue jeans with wide belt loops to accommodate his gun belt, and a baggy beige polo shirt worn tucked in. A photographer's vest went over all that to conceal his weapons and radio. Plainclothes and a photographer's vest were the uniform of the special operator in an urban environment; he knew that. It was also the uniform of a photographer at work, and it amused him how his past and present occupations merged. Was he a photographer playing at being a special operator, or a special operator playing at being a photographer? All he knew was that he was a shooter, whether of guns or cameras, and the trappings of both professions crossed over. His second profession would provide cover for his first, today. He'd borrowed a camera with a long zoom lens from the surveillance team, and it  would hang around his neck like any other avid photographer. But the body held no film. The lens would provide him an easy way to keep tabs on the situation without drawing attention to himself, and it rounded out the cover his clothing established.

He was ready.

He went down the hallway to the room where around-the-clock equipment operators perched in front of computer monitors, fax machines, telephones, and radios.

"Anything?" he asked the two men on duty in the room.

They both shook their heads no. One said, "Nothing yet, Charley."

They were responsible for monitoring the massive surveillance set up around the park bench where Youssef bin Hassan was to meet his contact from the Egyptian embassy. There were panel vans equipped with cameras and computers, busily screening the faces of anyone who walked near the bench, and whose lenses covered all approaches to it. The bench itself had a tiny but powerful listening device affixed to the bottom of the seat slats. Since sunup, burly men with shirttails worn outside to conceal their weapons lingered in the area. Parked nearby were vehicles containing more armed men.

There was a cordon tight as a bell jar wrapped around the bench. Charley had artfully crafted a precarious balance of resources, trembling between a presence so heavy it would tip off their target and a presence adequate to respond to any threat. To deal with the biological weapon the One would be carrying was a team from the Center for Disease Control, completely outfitted with their space suits and decontamination equipment, sitting in a room borrowed from Smithsonian security. Crouched on top of the Smithsonian museum buildings were snipers armed with rifles capable of penetrating any body armor the One might wear; the marksmen were capable of a wounding shot as well. The overriding goal was to take the One alive with his deadly package. If that meant a rifle shot to the leg, then so be it. They had medics equipped with a full range of combat trauma equipment, and they were only a short helicopter flight away from a major trauma unit. Two helicopters made a slow circle around the Mall, carefully picking their way through the restricted airspace that blankets Washington, DC. Each helicopter held a sniper team and spotters, for surveillance or interdiction.

Charley listened to the crackle of radio checks coming across the command and control frequency. Everyone was up and on the ball; there would be no communication foul-ups.

"Thanks, you guys," Charley said. "You need any coffee or anything?"

"No, boss. Thanks."

Charley went into the kitchen. Ray Dalton and Isabelle sat together at the table, Ray eating a cinnamon roll and Isabelle sipping delicately from an oversized mug. Charley poured himself a big mug of coffee from one of the three pots set up on the sideboard, then put plenty of cream and sugar into his cup. He sipped slowly from it, then turned and leaned back against the sideboard and considered the two at the table.

"The couple from hell," Charley said.

Isabelle made a moue and set her cup in her lap, both hands wrapped round it. Ray snorted and said, "Want a roll? They're in that box over there."

"Not yet," Charley said. "I need to wake my stomach up first."

"How was your sleep?" Isabelle said.

Charley smiled at her and waved his mug in salute. "You're so polite for such a killer, Isabelle. I find that charming."

She lifted one eyebrow. "One must do what one can do to get along. Things are difficult enough."

"That's true," Charley said. "To answer your question, not very well. And you?"

"The same. I am eager to get on with things."

"That's three of us, then," Ray said. "How are things out on the street?"

"Everything is in place," Charley said. "It's as tight as it can be."

"When are you going down there?" Ray said.

"Once my driver's up and got some coffee in him."

"And what of me?" Isabelle asked.

"Yes, what of you?" Charley said, looking at Ray.

"Your call," Ray said.

Charley considered the woman for a long moment, then said, "You can come with me, Isabelle. You don't have a part to play, but I think you deserve to see it all come down."

"Yes," she said. "I deserve that. Will you give me a weapon?"

"I don't think so," Charley said. "We've got shooters. I want you for an extra set of eyes, you know bin Hassan."

She shrugged, a gesture eloquent in its European fashion. "As you like. Of course you will protect me."

Charley laughed and was pleased to see a hint of a smile on Isabelle's face. "You're the least likely person to need protecting I've ever meet."

"I suppose that is a compliment," she said.

Ray watched the interplay with a sour look on his face. He didn't seem pleased with the ease between Charley and Isabelle.

"Are you ready to go?" Ray said.

Charley's driver came into the kitchen then and poured coffee into a plastic to-go mug.

"Perfect timing," Charley said. "Did you eat?"

The driver shook his head no. "If you don't mind, boss, there's a bagel place on the way. I'd just as soon get something I can eat in the car."

"Bagels sound good," Charley said. "Let's go. Isabelle?"

"I need only a moment," she said. "Excuse me."

She left the kitchen after setting her mug in the sink. Ray watched her go, then turned to Charley and said, "I hope you know what you're doing, Payne."

"We've got our deal," Charley said. "Her only motivation is to protect her family. As long as she has that, she's perfectly fine to do what we want."

"I'll pull the car around front, boss," the driver said, hastening out of the room.

"I'll be right there," Charley called after him. "You're scaring the help, Ray."

"Get on with it," Ray said.

"I will," Charley said.

Ray ran his finger around the rim of his coffee cup and studied Charley for a long minute. "Bring him in alive, Charley."

"I'll do what I can. How it goes down depends on him."

Ray nodded. "Good hunting."

RESIDENCE INN, BETHESDA, MARYLAND

Youssef bin Hassan rose with the sun, rested after a surprisingly peaceful night of sleep. He'd dreamed peaceful dreams for once, dreams that lingered at the edge of consciousness and slipped away when he tried to grasp them. That was well enough. The light of day filtered through the gap between the heavy curtains across his window, and when he stood and opened them, the light washed across him like a warm shower.

It was a good morning.

He took a long, hot shower, then carefully shaved his face. In the mirror, his face was calm and unlined, in repose. He wondered at his ease; there was no sign of the tension that had ridden him for so long.

He took it as a sign that he was at last truly ready.

The sun fell in a long sheet through the windows and across the pale blue carpet. He stood at the window and looked down at the street below, already busy with the morning rush of commuters on their way to work. He laid his palm against the window, and even with the coolness of the glass against his hand felt the heat of the day building outside. It would be hot today, and he considered that as he selected an oversized white T-shirt to go with his loose-fitting blue jeans. He opened the small Pelican case and checked the vials of smallpox agent, then took the charged atomizer from his pocket. Shouldn't he replace the atomizer cartridge in the box? Something told him to wait. He shrugged, happy to go with the flow of his thoughts on this day, easy as they were, and put the charged atomizer in his pocket and the Pelican case into his courier bag.

Youssef slung the bag over his shoulder and went out of the room and downstairs in the elevator, where he nodded good morning to the other guests as he made his way to the breakfast room. There was a serving line set up with a variety of breakfast foods and an eggs-to-order station; he ordered a spinach and cheese omelet, then loaded his plate with extra potatoes and a smaller plate with some pastries. The coffee was especially good, so much so that he had three cups, enjoying the slight rush the caffeine gave him as he worked his way through his big meal. There were free copies of the *Washington Post* and *USA Today* for guests; he plucked one from the pile at the end of the breakfast counter and sat back down to his coffee, flipping to the style section. The lead article was a profile of the actress Susan Saran-don, someone Youssef knew little about. He glanced through it, then carefully folded the paper so that the style section was foremost, then slid it into the outside pocket of his courier bag where it could be easily reached.

The clock behind the serving line read seven thirty. Youssef weighed his options; he could linger here and relax till it was time to catch the Metro to his meeting, or he could go early and kill time on the street. He left his table with the dishes neatly arrayed for the bus-boy and went into the lobby and out the front door. The heat and humidity was oppressive even this early in the morning. Across the street long lines of people streamed in and out of the Metro station, and cars honked and hurried to beat the lights. He pursed his lips, then went back inside. The young girl on-duty at the front desk smiled brightly at him.

"It's going to be a hot one today," she said.

"Yes," Youssef said. "I think I'll wait a while before I go out."

"Are you here on vacation or business?"

"A little of both."

"It'll be hotter later on. Supposed to be over a hundred today. Might be a good day to go to the Smithsonian—they have great air-conditioning there."

"That's a good idea," Youssef said. "How long is the Metro ride there?"

"Not more than twenty, thirty minutes at the most."

"Thank you."

There was an assortment of magazines on the coffee table in the lobby seating area. Youssef took a handful and went to the elevator. Back in his room, he set the courier bag in a chair by the window and lay down on the bed and began to flip through the magazines. From time to time he glanced at his watch. Even though he felt rested, he set the magazines aside and closed his eyes as though to nap. It was good to rest.

Soon he would be very busy.

NATIONAL MALL, WASHINGTON, DC

The black Chevy Suburban rumbled as the driver eased the big truck through the traffic in front of the National Gallery of Art, separated from the Air and Space Museum by the grassy expanse of the Mall.

"Drop us here," Charley said. "Then park over by the Air and Space Museum, the space they saved for us."

"Roger that, boss," the driver said. He slowed to a stop directly in front of the sun-washed steps that led up to the entrance of the National Gallery. "Right here?"

"Fine," Charley said. He opened the passenger door and got out, then opened the rear door for Isabelle. "I'm on the radio."

The driver nodded as Charley shut the rear door. The Suburban drove away to circle the block and make its way over to the Air and Space Museum.

"It's quite warm," Isabelle said, brushing the long black locks from her wig back from her face.

Charley stood and surveyed his killing zone. Not a killing zone, a capture zone. But in his mind it was the killing zone of a massive ambush. He went up the long flight of steps in front of the National Gallery, and at the top the scene spread out before him. Overhead, his two helicopters made a wide circuit of the Mall; they attracted no special attention, as helicopter traffic was common in downtown

Washington. Across the Mall, at the Air and Space Museum, there was construction on the Seventh Street side of the building. The many trucks coming and going provided an excellent cover for his surveillance vans parked there. He looked carefully at the roof of the museum for the snipers he knew were there, but there was no sign of them, which was as it should be. Lingering on the sidewalk on this side, spread out in small groups across the lawn and on the steps of the Air and Space Museum were twenty-four men and women, all armed and equipped with covert radios. They looked like college students, tourists, office workers on a break, but they were all specialists in unarmed apprehension, ready to bag the One once he appeared. Several of them, dressed in baggy skate-rat clothes, tossed a Frisbee back and forth while others sat on the patchy lawn and watched.

Isabelle took Charley's arm and rested her head on his shoulder, to all appearances a loving girlfriend, and said softly, "The ones playing Frisbee? They need to be more careful, some of them, their pistols are printing against their shirts as they play."

"You're a star, Isabelle," Charley said. He led her to a stretch of stairs empty of tourists, and whispered into his microphone. The effect of his communication was immediate; the Frisbee players immediately slowed down, and a couple of them walked off the lawn to parked cars, and then returned.

"What of the Egyptian?" she said.

Charley looked around to make sure no one was within earshot. "We're going to keep it simple. If he shows up, we take him. He'll be PNG'd and deported."

Isabelle smiled brightly up at him, as though he'd told a witty joke, and said, "You Americans. You are so sentimental. You should kill him to provide a lesson."

Charley laughed and patted Isabelle on the hand as he led her across the street to the lawn. "Let's walk the ground, darling. You're starting to scare me."

RESIDENCE INN, BETHESDA, MARYLAND/NATIONAL MALL,
WASHINGTON, DC

Youssef woke from a light dream with a start. He looked at the glowing red LED of the bedside clock radio and saw that it was nearly ten thirty. He'd dropped into sleep for almost three hours. Where had the time gone? And why was he so tired after such a good night's sleep? He went into the bathroom and splashed cold water on his face, drying it with the rough towel hung beside the sink, then studied his face in the mirror.

He was afraid. There was naked fear in his face, and he'd slept to hide from it.

Youssef could acknowledge that now. As the time grew nearer for his total commitment to the mission, his doubts and fears grew. He knew that. And he knew he had to overcome that and move forward.

Movement and action were what he needed.

He brushed at the redness of his eyes, then washed his face again, slowly and thoroughly with warm water, then dried himself again. He folded the towel neatly and set it beside the sink, then went into the other room and began to gather up his odd bits of clothing. They made a pitifully small pile on his bed next to the courier bag that held the smallpox vials. He picked up the pile of clothing and set it on the dresser; he'd return for that. The hotel would be his base for the time he needed to take in Washington.

He sat down on the bed, and felt the weight and bulge of the loaded atomizer in his pocket. He took it out, and weighed it in his hand, then carefully withdrew the loaded vial and replaced it in the Pelican case with the others. The Pelican case rested on his lap, and he hunched over it like a schoolboy over a book, studying the black plastic as though it held a secret he could not decipher. He thought of Britta, and he put the thought away; he longed for his mother, and he put the thought away; he thought of Ahmad, twisting in the hands of the Israelis, and even that couldn't move him—the thought had become thin and pale, like a faded photograph.

What finally moved him was the sudden need to urinate. His hands trembled as he undid his fly in the bathroom, and he was ashamed of how fear had taken hold of his body. He turned away from his reflection and hurried to the bed, and slung the courier bag across his shoulder, the only weight that of the Pelican case and the newspaper and his cheap straw hat.

No more time for thinking.

He forced himself to shut the door quietly, though he felt like slamming it again and again. The DO NOT DISTURB sign was in place,  and he left it swinging slightly as he went to the elevator and waited, his head bowed. Eventually the elevator chimed, and he got in. He had the elevator to himself as he rode it to the lobby. At the front desk, the matronly woman who had been on-duty when he first checked in looked up as he came through the lobby.

"Hello there, dear!" she called out. "Did your bags ever arrive?"

Youssef made a smile, and mumbled, "No, I'm still waiting . . ."

"Are you all right, honey?" she said. "You don't look well."

"I think I am just tired."

"You want to take it easy, then. You don't want to get sick on your holiday. Don't try to do too much today."

Youssef felt a sudden urge to cry. His eyes began to well, and his throat constricted. He hurried out the door, leaving the desk clerk looking after him, puzzled.

The heat and humidity struck him like a blow after the air-conditioning of the hotel. Even at a quarter to eleven, the streets were busy, though the pedestrians all seemed slowed by the weight of the sun. Youssef jogged across the street, not waiting for the light, and hurried to the down escalator that descended into the cool depths of the Bethesda Metro station. He had the sense of flying as he rode the escalator down; he wiped his eyes on the back of his hand, embarrassed by the sudden and unwelcome surge of emotions he couldn't control.

What was wrong with him?

He felt like screaming. He felt like dashing his courier bag against the concrete walls of the station, spilling out the useless agent like urine against the wall. Why had he taken this upon himself? What was he doing? He stopped at the bottom of the escalator, ignoring the people who brushed past him impatiently. As though it had a mind of its own, his hand went to his pocket and came up with a fistful of crumpled bills. He sorted through them mechanically till he found a five-dollar bill, then inserted it into the slot of the ticket-selling machine and bought an all-day excursion card. That was good. That was something concrete, something real.

He went through the electronic gate and down to the track and waited for an inbound train. It was only a few minutes before the lights on the platform began to flash and the characteristic rush of air announced the arrival of a train. The few other passengers on the platform moved toward the doors as the train slowed to a stop. Youssef hung back, watching, then waited till everyone had gotten on board before he hurried and skipped through the door just as it began to close. The synthesized voice of a woman announced over the loudspeaker in the car, "Doors closing." Youssef sat down in a window seat, clutching his courier bag to his chest, and watched the gray walls of the subterranean tunnels whir past as the train accelerated to the next station. It seemed like only moments, though more time had passed, when the conductor announced, "Metro Center."

Youssef stood and let himself be carried along off the train, and then to the other platform where he caught an Orange-line train bound toward the Smithsonian stop. He stood for the short ride, and in his confused state stared at the other passengers. Two teenage girls, both wearing T-shirts with a picture of a boy and the name JUSTIN TIMBER-LAKE on the front, giggled together as they looked at Youssef; a black man in an expensive business suit read the *Wall Street Journal*, a tired-looking woman in a gray pantsuit flipped through the pages of a *Cosmopolitan* magazine. They all seemed separate from Youssef, as though they rode in a car within the car, cut off by an invisible membrane that only Youssef could sense.

The train stopped at the Smithsonian station.

Youssef swayed where he stood, as though buffeted by an invisible wind. He turned to the doors and went out when they opened, then followed the other passengers up and out of the station. He took the stairs, looking down at his feet for each step, and rose slowly into the heat and the killing sun on the National Mall. Behind him was the white pillar of the Washington Monument, in front of him the long expanse of grass that led to the US Capitol Building. To his right were the Smithsonian museum administrative offices, on the far side of Jefferson Drive, and farther down the Mall, about the distance of four city blocks, were the imposing edifices of the National Gallery of Art and the National Air and Space Museum.

He walked north and slightly east, toward the multi-storied and sprawling Museum of National History, across the Mall. Despite the heat and the sun beating down, there were people out playing a pickup game of soccer, bicycling, walking, and jogging. There was one group of joggers, military men by the look of them, who ran in a loose formation past Youssef and continued on along Madison Drive toward the Capitol. He came to Madison Drive and continued to the right, staying on the grass, looking down at his feet, carrying his burden as though he were weighted down with a massive pack. The sun beat down on him mercilessly, and he remembered his hat in his bag. He stopped and fished out the straw hat and placed it on his head. He squinted against the glare as he did so. Across the street in front of the Museum of Natural History were several cart vendors. Youssef crossed the street and stopped at the first one with sunglasses. He plucked a pair at random, not caring how they looked, and put them on, then fished out his wad of bills and extended it at the Asian man tending the cart. The vendor looked surprised, then took a five and a one and said, "You want your change?"

"No," Youssef said.

"You have a nice day."

The cheap glasses cut the glare and, more important to Youssef, hid his eyes. He felt as though everyone who walked by him could read his gaze, see through his eyes to his soul, see all the secrets he held bottled up inside. He thought of returning to the hotel, climbing into the bed and pulling the covers over himself until the world came to knock on his door.

But he still kept walking toward his rendezvous.

At the corner of Madison and Ninth Street, he crossed back over to the lawn of the Mall. Despite the heat, there were many people out: federal employees on their lunch break, tourists and students and a smattering of the homeless. Youssef slowed as he passed a tree, where on a blanket spread in the thin shade a young man and woman were entwined in each other, deep in a kiss. He looked at them avidly; for a moment he imagined the girl looked like Britta. But no, this girl, while blond, was thin and brown, while Britta was as pale as milk under moonlight.

He came to the crossing at Madison and Seventh Street, and waited for the light to change. A tourist family waited there, an overweight father burdened with a day-pack and a camera bag, and a mother holding the hands of the eager children straining to go ahead.

"These lights take a long time to change," the father said, looking at Youssef, who ignored him. The father looked at his wife and shrugged. The light changed and Youssef crossed the street, looking straight ahead, as though he were marching to a tune only he could hear. He lengthened his stride and left the tourist family behind him, the children's voices fading in his ear. There would be no children for him, and a wave of sadness welled up in him again.

It was time to put that away, too.

The National Gallery of Art loomed on his left; to his right, across the expanse of lawn, was the gleaming, glassy structure of the

Air and Space Museum. People streamed in and out of both buildings, but for now he walked slowly across the street, toward the steps of the National Gallery, already thronged with tourists disgorged from the waiting tour buses. He made no pretense of countersurveillance; it was as though part of him knew he was invisible in the crowd—or just didn't care anymore. He thought back to what the surveillance lecturer in the Sudanese camp had taught them. You were to look for the people who paid too much attention to what was going on around them; most people paid little attention to anything other than what was right in front of them. Out here, with so many people lingering and people-watching, it was impossible for him to pick anyone as standing out.

He slipped between two big tour buses, their engines idling, the air conditioners going full bore, and stepped onto the sidewalk. The first bus had let out a load of Japanese tourists, all of them huddled in one great mass, each one waving a camera, and following like obedient ducks after the tiny tour leader, who held onto a stick above her head—a yellow pennant with the words YOSHITUNO TOURS. Youssef went along with them, and followed them up the stairs to the entrance doors of the National Gallery. There he stopped, and let the Japanese tour group flow past him through the open doors. Then he turned and looked out across the Mall at the bench where he was to meet his Egyptian contact.

The bench was empty. The benches on either side, separated by a good distance, were occupied. There was a group of young people playing Frisbee near the bench, and a scattering of people under the trees that provided the only shade. Below him, on the steps of the National Gallery, were dozens of tourists sweating in the sun. A couple of dedicated sun worshippers were laid out full-length along the bottom steps.

Youssef stepped forward, out of the shaded doorway, into the bitter light of the sun.

Targets, all of them.

He hefted his courier bag and felt the weight of the Pelican case within, then glanced at his wristwatch. Eleven forty-five.

He was ready.

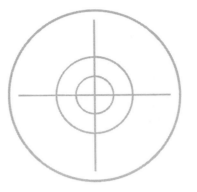

NATIONAL MALL, WASHINGTON, DC

Charley Payne and Isabelle Andouille sat side by side on the hot cement steps on the Mall side of the Air and Space Museum. They looked like a long-married couple, at ease with the silence between them, sweating in the beating sun. Charley held his long-lensed camera loose in his hands, and Isabelle had her hands folded in her lap, pressing the denim fabric of her dress together for modesty's sake.

Isabelle looked around, her eyes hidden by round oversized sunglasses, and said, "Is he here yet?"

Charley tilted his head, listening carefully to the occasional message that came through the tiny earpiece he wore, then shook his head no.

"I think he is here," Isabelle said. "I feel him."

Charley regarded her for a moment, then lowered his head and whispered into the microphone concealed in his vest. "All stations, stand by. Check again."

The earpiece buzzed with acknowledgments.

"Shall we walk?" Isabelle said.

"No," Charley said. "No need. We've got the best seats in the house right here."

"As you wish. I would have them check the steps of the National Gallery again. He stood off there before to survey the area."

Charley's earpiece crackled. "Zero, this is Big-Gun-Actual."

Big-Gun-Actual was the sniper team leader atop the National Air and Space Museum, hidden behind the raised wall on the roof, with a powerful spotting scope to augment the telescopic sight on his .308 rifle. Charley whispered into his microphone, "Big-Gun, Zero, go ahead."

"We have a possible subject on the top steps of the National Gallery, just before the entry doors, dark-skinned male wearing a straw hat, white T-shirt, blue jeans, and carrying a black shoulder bag."

Charley's face grew taut. As his face changed, Isabelle responded by looking more intently across the killing zone.

"Roger, Big-Gun," Charley said. "Break, Eye-One and Two, do you have a make?"

The surveillance vans, one of them with a boom camera mounted beneath an elevated cherry picker, were running the computer face-matching program on any and all suspect faces in the vicinity of the bench. They were silent for a long moment, and then Charley's earpiece filled with their response.

"Zero, this is Eye-One. We have a make, say again, we have a make. Suspect is positively identified as the same individual we spotted yesterday."

"All stations stand by," Charley said. "Subject has been identified."

Isabelle stood and brushed at her dress, then plucked at the sweat-darkened fabric. "It's time," she said.

Like a dangerous animal drowsing in the sun, the apprehension teams stirred.

• • •

Youssef bin Hassan, the specially chosen operative of the Al-Bashir network, the One, stood in the shade cast by the ornamental stonework outside the doors of the National Gallery of Art and let his random thoughts rise. What if he were to miss this meeting? What if he were to forego the meeting completely? Would they even look for him? How would they find him? They couldn't. That was the whole point of Sad Holiday. The One was unstoppable because he couldn't be found. What if he just disappeared, made his way back to Amsterdam, found a job, and lived with Britta? Let all this death go?

He wondered why he couldn't let these thoughts go.

The only thing that emptied his mind was action. He looked at his wristwatch. Almost noon. Time to move. He adjusted his courier bag, then dipped into the outside pocket and took out the *Washington Post* opened to the style section, and held it in his left hand. Then he began his slow descent of the stairs, and a sense of déjà vu swept over him. He remembered the nightmare he'd had in Britta's bed, of his descent from a great height onto streets filled with the dead and dying, and he looked at the tourists and innocents that surrounded him and knew that they could all be dead in weeks. The words of the clerics and the instructors in the camps, and those of his controllers in Al-Bashir seemed so far away now. This family, the suntanned children laughing and grabbing at their parents' legs, what did they do to deserve to die? What did this couple lying together in the sun, enjoying their love, what did they do to deserve the horrible death that would soon come to them?

He would be the instrument of their death.

He would spread a horrible and lingering death to innocents, doing exactly what the Americans had done but on a larger scale than anything they had accomplished with their planes and their bombs. And then he allowed himself to acknowledge what he had known for some time: what he was doing was wrong, horribly wrong. He hesitated, stumbling on the bottom steps as the broken rhythm of his thoughts distracted him. What he needed to do was to concentrate on one thing at a time. To stay focused. First he needed to cross the lawn and go to the bench. Then he needed to make contact. Then he needed to exchange the product. Then he could make up his mind.

That would work.

• • •

Charley leaned forward, his weight on the balls of his feet, and watched his ambush come together. The lone figure of Youssef bin Hassan hesitated at the bottom of the stairs in front of the National Gallery, then disappeared for a moment behind a tour bus, then reemerged as he crossed Madison Drive to the Mall. The terrorist walked with his head down, as though deep in thought, not scanning his surroundings as you'd expect an operator making a clandestine contact would.

That bothered Charley. What did the One know that he didn't?

"He's not doing any countersurveillance," Charley said. "Why do you think that is?"

Isabelle licked at her upper lip. "Because he is a boy, and he is afraid."

"Afraid of what? Us?"

"He is afraid of what he is supposed to do. He is not suitable for what Al-Bashir wants him to do."

Charley raised his camera to his face and looked through the viewfinder, zooming the 28mm-300mm lens in on the head of bin Hassan. The tension in the young man's shoulders and head all told a story. Charley twisted the ring on the lens and opened it up to wide-angle, and stood as though framing a shot. One by one, his operators were delicately and discreetly positioning themselves around the terrorist operator. Two of his people, stationed on the National Gallery steps, fell in behind bin Hassan; as he continued across the lawn several others got casually to their feet and began to pace him.

From almost directly in front of him, a young family, a mother and father and their toddler, crossed the street from the steps of the Air and Space Museum and walked toward the target bench. Charley swore under his breath. The One was halfway across the lawn and already within the invisible net spread for him. They couldn't have a family in the middle of the takedown.

He whispered into his microphone. "All stations, Zero. Change of plan. We're going to take him as he's walking. Steer clear of the civilians near the bench. Alpha-Team makes initial contact on my command. Stand by, stand by, stand by."

Alpha-Team, the group of operators playing Frisbee, began to shorten the length of their throws, pulling them closer together. Youssef bin Hassan drew abreast of them, and angled around their play.

• • •

The close-cropped hairs on the back of Youssef's neck dripped sweat. He shrugged, irritated by the sensation, and wiped his hand across the back of his neck. All his senses seemed more acute. The hiss of grass scuffing beneath his shoes, the slow progress of a drop of sweat across his brow, the individual voices of the people around him calling to each other, all of it seemed so immediate, demanding what little remained of his attention.

A Frisbee disk skittered across the grass and landed at his feet.

Youssef looked up and saw the Frisbee players jogging toward him. "Little help?" one of them said, pointing at the disk.

Youssef looked over his shoulder then, and saw others closing on him, their eyes bright with the gleam of hunters, and he knew.

• • •

"He is going to run," Isabelle said. She leaned forward like a starter in the blocks.

Charley took her shoulder and held her as he said into his microphone, "All stations, go, go, go!"

• • •

Youssef spun to his left and ran toward Fourth Street, in the direction of the US Capitol building. He dropped the newspaper from his hand and pulled his courier bag across his chest as he deftly sidestepped one of the federal agents reaching for him and ran as though herding the ball down a crowded soccer field. The apprehension team, all pretense abandoned, raced after him. He fumbled with the straps on his courier bag as he ran, then pulled the Pelican case from within, then spun to face his pursuers. He held the case up as though it were a totem that might stop the rush of men and women at him, and then he felt a mighty blow against one leg as a big man kicked him right on his nerve plexus and another man snatched his hand and a woman plucked the Pelican case free. Then his legs flew out from beneath him and all he saw was a dizzying whirl of grass and buildings and sky. He was ringed by men and women while hard hands held him to the ground and he struggled until someone struck a hard blow against the nerves on the side of his neck and he felt a feathery lassitude come over him, and it was as if he floated on the finest of beds, lingering in the dreamy space that comes right before the endless sleep of night.

CIA PRIVATE MEDICAL FACILITY, FAIRFAX, VIRGINIA

The curtains on the one big window were thrown back, so that the room was washed in light. The walls were a cheery yellow highlighted by paintings of wildflowers, and the two richly upholstered armchairs were blue. Charley sat in one of the chairs and watched Dale Miller breathe. He watched for the rise of the chest, and the slow fall; his friend's breaths were deep and sure. Dale's face was pale, and the skin beneath his closed eyes appeared bruised. His head was swathed in bandages.

"So that's how it went down, partner," Charley said. "Young Mr. Hassan is singing and singing. Our girlfriend Isabelle was right . . . they had the wrong guy for the job. He was thinking of ditching the whole thing before we got to him. And Al-Bashir . . . well, your brothers in DOMINANCE RAIN and a couple of other outfits have been taking them apart, one cell at a time. Al-Bashir is dying, bro, in Sudan, Somalia, Yemen, everywhere they had an operation."

He laughed softly. "Oh, you'd get a kick out of how the bureaucrats scurried around this one, bro. They couldn't do enough for me. They're going to take good care of you. Only the best, I made sure of that. And I'll be back to check on you to make sure it stays that way. It may be a while before you're healed enough to know, but I'll be back to see you."

Charley stood, then went to Dale's bedside and watched his friend inhale and exhale. The sound of breathing was loud in the room.

"Good-bye, bro."

350

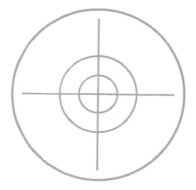

LINDEN HILLS NEIGHBORHOOD, MINNEAPOLIS, MINNESOTA

Charley Payne sat at his favorite outdoor table at the Linden Hills Diner and watched the traffic flow by. The day's *Star Tribune*, two dirty dishes and a half-full coffee cup cluttered his table. He lifted his cup and took a slow sip of the still-hot coffee, his eyes closed in a moment's satisfaction.

Life was good.

He opened his eyes and by habit scanned near, and then far, watching for . . . what? He laughed at himself and the force of habit. Then he glanced down at his shirt front.

A small red dot of laser light bounced on his sternum.

Charley's breath caught in his chest, and, keeping both hands on the table, he looked up and across the street. Isabelle Andouille leaned against a car parked on the far side of the street, a laser pointer in her hand. She smiled as she put the pointer into the pocket of her snug-fitting walking shorts, and waited for a break in the traffic before she crossed. Men looked at her and she ignored them; her eyes were for Charley.

"Hello, Charley," she said.

"You have an unusual way of announcing your presence," he said.

She laughed. "I like your neighborhood. It reminds me of home."

"Yes, it would. How are Marie and Ilse?"

"Very fine, thank you. They are quite happy. Your generosity has made our life very easy."

"Nothing you didn't earn, Isabelle."

She thrust both hands into her pocket and continued standing over Charley, who shielded his eyes to look up at her. She was silent for a long moment, as though considering something, then she took her left hand out of her pocket and set a slip of paper on the table before Charley.

"What's this?" he said.

"My phone number," Isabelle said. "We should work together sometime."